COURT OF THE
UNDYING SEASONS

ALSO BY
A.M. STRICKLAND

Beyond the Black Door

In the Ravenous Dark

COURT

OF THE

UNDYING

SEASONS

A.M. STRICKLAND

FEIWEL AND FRIENDS
NEW YORK

Some of the thematic material in *Court of the Undying Seasons* involves child neglect and abuse, issues of consent, violence, including blood drinking and murder, and substance use. For a more detailed description of sensitive content, please visit adriannestrickland.com/court-of-the-undying-seasons.

A Feiwel and Friends Book
An imprint of Macmillan Publishing Group, LLC
120 Broadway, New York, NY 10271 • fiercereads.com

Our books may be purchased in bulk for promotional, educational, or business use. Please contact your local bookseller or the Macmillan Corporate and Premium Sales Department at (800) 221–7945 ext. 5442 or by email at MacmillanSpecialMarkets@macmillan.com.

Library of Congress Cataloging-in-Publication Data is available.

First edition, 2023

Book design by Trisha Previte
Feiwel and Friends logo designed by Filomena Tuosto
Printed in the United States of America

ISBN 978-1-250-83262-7 (hardcover)

1   3   5   7   9   10   8   6   4   2

To my mama, Deanna, for showing me
the strength of a mother's love . . .
and for failing to notice when I read
Interview with the Vampire far too young.

———————⋆∾ᗤᗧ∽⋆———————

RIP, Anne Rice. Thank you for helping me
realize how delightfully weird I am.

THE
UNDYING HOUSES

THE BLUE COURT
aka the House of Winter Night

MOTTO: *Revel and Remember*
SPECIALTIES: revelry,
masking, shapeshifting

THE RED COURT
aka the House of Spring Dawn

MOTTO: *Blaze and Bleed*
SPECIALTIES: weapons,
seduction, the arts

THE GOLD COURT
aka the House of Summer Day

MOTTO: *Shine and Steward*
SPECIALTIES: governance,
mind reading, enthrallment

THE SILVER COURT
aka the House of Autumn Twilight

MOTTO: *Protect and Preserve*
SPECIALTIES: the sciences,
healing, preservation

THE BLACK COURT
aka the Nameless House

MOTTO:——
SPECIALTIES: hunting,
shadowstepping, mistwalking

I

BEGINNING

1

I wasn't born a monster.

As a child I had no bloodlust, no desire to manipulate or control. No dream of immortality. I wanted to survive the long winters. I wanted my mother back.

But now I must face *them* as my mother did. Now I feel as murderous as a monster, as cold as one of their walking corpses.

They arrive in our village like a funeral procession in an enclosed black carriage drawn by a matching set of four horses, with two more following, just as the first snow begins to fall.

It's risky for a carriage not to carry skis at this time of year in case of deep drifts, but the wheels and horses look to be in fine condition. Better than fine. The stallions in back have no leads and yet no one astride the polished leather saddles. Eerier yet, there's no one atop the driver's seat of the carriage.

The horses seem to halt on their own. The carriage rolls to a stop at the edge of our village square, a stretch of frozen dirt with a dry basin of rough-hewn stone in the center that the headman generously calls a fountain. The square still smells of fish, offal, and dung—the remnants of the market, packed away for the occasion. Now the space only serves to make the clomping hooves echo forlornly in the late autumn air.

The carriage sits, gleaming and malignant in the dying light, an ill omen made real. As we all wait in a line, shivering, I wonder without hope if it's empty.

Of course, it isn't.

Only when the snow-shrouded sun finally drops behind the mountains do *they* flow like water out of the carriage: one male, one female, and one seemingly neither, all clothed in finery. Long velvet cloaks, gowns, and robes in deep red, black, and silver. I'm wearing whatever scraps I could find, though the scarves and shawls wrapped around my neck and waist serve a dual purpose, hiding what I want hidden.

Showing your neck to them is bad luck. Showing what's at my waist would be a death wish.

They clearly have no such concerns. Their skin flashes everywhere despite the cold, their complexions and hair as varied as their clothes. The female has fair skin, perfect brown curls that fall to her waist, and full crimson lips to match the color of her eyes and her plunging gown. The male has light brown skin, black hair pulled back into a sleek ponytail, and a black silk shirt crisscrossed with knife belts over dark leather pants. The third is remarkably pale, with snow-white hair, silver eyes and robes, and no telltale signs of being male or female. I've heard they can be like that, among the many ways they can be—live however they want, at seemingly no cost to themselves.

The only similarities among these three are their unnatural eyes and flawless faces, not a wrinkle or pockmark in sight. They all look to be in their early twenties, late twenties at most, but I know they're not. The creatures' faces never reflect their true age. Despite their seeming youth, they're long dead. And despite their cold limbs, they move like stalking predators.

They *are* predators. Predators that glow like lanterns in the darkness, inviting their prey to be consumed like moths to flame.

I want to back away. Only Silvea standing next to me in line holds me steady. She's my only friend. And maybe more than that, if only on my end. I need to make sure she's safe, and a place at her side is more appealing than these creatures will ever be. Far more tempting than *becoming* one of them.

Even when I've been starving, lying awake at night getting gnawed at by a nameless longing for something, someone, someplace I don't know, I've never hungered for an endless existence sustained by the blood of others. Never for shadowy figures with gleaming eyes and red lips and mocking laughs to haunt my waking hours as well as my dreams. Never for luxurious, frozen courts that never sleep, cloaked in garments of scarlet and gold, silver and midnight.

I'm the child of a dead fisherman, and I lost my mother to *them*. They are the enemy: overtaking our lands, usurping our gods, terrorizing our nights.

Drinking our blood.

To want to be like them, to live a richer life despite being dead, to share their hideous craving, would be worse than a foolish dream. It would be deplorable.

But that's why they're here.

The male holds out a black bag, his lips quirked, while the female says in a musical, disinterested voice, "Is this all?"

It's quiet enough to hear the falling snow, no one brave enough to speak. But it is *all*, according to their terms: all the children I've grown up with and have mostly hated and occasionally tolerated, now on the cusp of adulthood, standing before them.

Silvea shifts in place, and her shoulder presses against mine, startling me. I immediately tilt away, assuming it was an accident, but she leans closer. I stay exactly where I am, hardly daring to breathe. She never usually touches me. I let myself lean back into her, just a little bit.

Even now, I wish she were somewhere else, but "wishes won't feed you," as my father used to say. This is our first Finding ritual, but the rules have been in place since before anyone can remember: Once per year, these creatures come to six different villages, and all youths aged seventeen to nineteen must gather for a drawing, like children at the Midwinter Festival lining up to receive a hotcake.

The only gift we'll receive here is our lives, if we're lucky. And if we're unlucky, death. If you choose the wrong lot, the creatures give you a new life that's no life at all—and you're supposed to thank them. To revere them.

I hate them.

They must not be too impressed with us, either. Or at least the female isn't. She glances at the male, her red eyes shining like wet blood. "Nothing to pique my interest here, Maudon, but let's get on with it."

The male—Maudon—drinks us in with his dark gaze before he moves to the head of the line. His eyes are completely black, I realize, the pupils indistinguishable from his irises. As he stands before each of us, holding up the bag, his stare could swallow me whole.

I suppress a shiver. I don't know why he seems so interested. The others who have come for past Findings usually seemed bored. Never mind that this seemingly mundane task determines our fates.

And yet, no one in our village would dare defy that fate by hiding or fighting. No one does anything but the role that's assigned to them. For me, it's all the same:

Listen to your father or be beaten.

Gut fish for pennies or starve to death.

Gather in the square when the creatures tell you to or be hunted.

Even their bag is luxuriant, its black silk gleaming like Maudon's clothes. They make all of us standing in the line seem dull and lifeless in comparison. And especially pungent, in my case. Odd, since they're the ones who are dead. Dead things usually sag and smell.

While I haven't dreamed of becoming one of them, I *have* fantasized about killing them when making precise slices into cold fish bellies with my fillet knife. It wouldn't be murder because the creatures aren't alive, or so I tell myself.

Maudon steps in front of me and Silvea. He spares me only a glance, taking in Silvea like he wants to eat her. She pulls away from me, straightening her shoulders to bravely meet his gaze. He pauses before her longer than he has any others, tipping his head as if listening to something. For some reason, the female is staring fixedly at Silvea, too. *Both* their gazes are alight with what looks like hunger. I know too well what they hunger for.

But then Maudon reaches out and brushes Silvea's cheek with one light finger, almost a caress. She shudders, and I want to smack his hand away.

Maybe they think Silvea's pretty, not just delicious. Under her patchy fur hat, her hair is a flowing blond, compared to my lank, dull locks that I keep hacked short. The better to keep clean—as clean as possible, given what I do. My hair always smells like fish. Silvea smells like herbs, her skin is washed and clear, and her blue eyes are bright and determined.

The creatures like pretty people. At least, they're more likely to steal pretty humans. I wonder why they even bother with a Finding when they can just snatch anyone they want in the night.

As Silvea reaches into the bag, I twitch, wishing I could stop her. It almost seems to swallow her hand.

A smile grows on Maudon's face.

This can't be good.

Before Silvea can withdraw, I glimpse a white feather between her fingers. I know what it means—it's the only white one among dozens of black. It signifies who they'll choose. The sacrifice. The foundling. The one they take to Castle Courtsheart, their horrible fortress. The one they take *everything* from.

Only I see the feather's color because of how close we stand. Silvea's the only one among the group who would let me draw so near with the stink of fish about me. For that alone, I would do anything for her.

But she saved my life once. I was seven, and I got a fever after cutting my palm on a fillet knife just after my father fell into the sea while fishing—probably drunk—and drowned. She took herbs from her mother, the healer, drew the poison from my wound, and brought down my fever. Like I was worth saving.

I've loved her ever since, desperately, hopelessly, and she let me stay close. She taught me how to read—as a healer-in-training, she had to learn to follow herbalists' and anatomists' journals—and she often shared what little food she could from her own meager plate. She's been one of the few people in the village to show me kindness. To not look away from me. To see me as more than a half-starved, walking pile of fish guts.

Perhaps now she sees me as someone worthy of standing beside her.

And for that, I would die for her.

I move faster than my sense of self-preservation can. I stuff my hand inside the bag, over Silvea's, nudging her aside before she can reveal the feather.

"Let me go first," I breathe in a rush. When everyone stares at me, I blurt, "I'm older."

It's true, even if I don't look it, standing shorter than Silvea and far scrawnier—and barely older, a fresh nineteen years to her eighteen.

"No, Fin——!" Silvea tries to pull away, but I wrench the feather from her fingers under cover of fabric, unseen by any of *them* standing in front us. "Stop!"

She must have glimpsed the white feather, too. She's trying to save me again. But it's my turn.

And even if it kills me, maybe I can make my dreams come true at the same time: A knife against cold flesh. Revenge against them, for taking my mother from me. I'm prepared. I have my fillet knife strapped to my waist, buried under the folds of my dirty shawl.

The smile vanishes from Maudon's lips. His pit-black eyes widen and his nostrils flare, giving me the barest glimpse of outrage lurking behind the smooth mask of his face. Even the female hisses like a cat.

Blood and piss, I curse in silent fear. Somehow they know what I've done.

They wanted Silvea. Not me.

And now they're going to kill me where I stand.

But then the pale, silver-clad one arches a brow as fine as frost. "Age is about the only thing we honor as you humans do. Don't you agree, Maudon? Claudia? It is the filthy one's right to go first."

I can't help but wonder what the creature means. Do they not respect wealth or social standing or husbands or fathers—what humans seem to honor most and all of which I lack? Does that mean I won't be less than nothing among them, like I am here?

Before I can help it, my chest clenches around something other than fear. I don't want to know what the feeling is.

"Are we going to let them *all* start doing that now, Revar?" Maudon asks with the suggestion of a sneer. "Next they'll be shouting over one another who is the oldest or the youngest instead of waiting in a nice line."

Revar shrugs. "In any case, the claim has been made. I will honor it, as you should."

The female, Claudia, watches Maudon until he grudgingly nods. After that, the anger in both seems to subside—clearer by the feeling in the air than their expressions, which haven't changed all that much.

Silvea withdraws her empty hand, but I don't yet reveal the feather. I stare back at *them* over the top of the bag, my heart pounding against the walls of my chest like a fist. As if I can fight this. But I can't fight. Not them.

Not *yet*.

A horse paws the frozen earth, breaking the silence. I still can't move, and yet those three perfect faces, too smooth and still, watch me patiently. Like they have all the time in the world. Or they're bored again, now that the moment of drama is over.

So be it.

Silvea's sob cuts the heavy gloom as I pull the white feather from the bag. It looks so clean next to my hand. Revar was right. Dizzily, all I can think is, *I am filthy.*

"You got the white feather!" the baker's son shouts in horror. As if he cares. As if he never threw rocks at me.

My eyes fill with tears, my throat too choked to respond. This was my choice. I knew what would happen. But Silvea's grief slices me like a knife I wasn't expecting.

All the more reason I go in her stead. Besides, she's the healer's daughter. I only gut fish. Even from a practical standpoint, it's better she stay and I go.

"Finally," says Claudia. "We have our chosen one. The wait was killing me." There's a spark of humor in her voice, but it dies as her red gaze passes over me.

Her look is murderous. She obviously resents me for taking Silvea's place.

Already two of the creatures hate me, and I haven't even left with them yet. An unfortunate beginning to my ending.

Their horses' breaths send great plumes of fog into the air. The beasts' eyes gleam with an eerie yellow light, like someone lit a candle behind them. Save for that glow, they'd only be dark, empty windows.

Enthralled, then. Forced to do the creatures' bidding. But still alive.

Still alive, I tell myself, swallowing my tears. *I'll still be alive.* Though I doubt I will be for long. I want to believe I can fight or flee later, but I know the truth. Soon, I'll be as cold as the creatures before me, whether I have strange eyes and flawless skin or empty sockets and worms riddling my flesh.

Or, maybe worst of all, I might be warm and alive but have

someone else's will shining behind my eyes. They need servants, after all. It makes me think having my blood drained might be the preferable end.

My only comfort in going with these creatures is in the possibility I might understand how they live—and see if I can end them forever. This is the best chance I'll ever have.

Sighs rise in the village square, likely only in relief. No sadness. Few will miss me, and none would even think to help me. We used to be a fighting people, great warriors and raiders. But that was before *they* came. Now, at most, there might be an embarrassingly quick scuffle and a river of blood splattered across the snow.

Not everyone would even want to resist. Some view being selected as the highest honor. An incredible chance to escape this life.

The creatures certainly see it as a gift. The *vampires*. I might as well let myself think the word, if not say it. I'm about to join them, after all.

Maudon smiles again, showing fangs of pure white. "Welcome to the start of your first undying season, young one."

"What a marvelous season it will be," says Revar. "Your name is Fin?"

I manage a jerky nod. I don't want to tell them the name started as a mocking insult when I began carrying buckets of cast-off fins and guts to the village cesspit as a tiny child. It ended up sticking, like a stench. Even my father was calling me that before he died. Now no one remembers my original name. I've gotten so used to Fin I don't mind it.

"Fin, as in the flattened appendage of a fish, which can be as thin as parchment, nigh translucent, and angular, as you are. Deceptively simple for something so well designed for its environment." Revar looks me up and down, but surprisingly, there's no cruelty in their silver eyes. Maybe calling me *filthy* was more a statement of fact than an insult.

11

I'm so flattered I can only blink in response.

"Well then, Fin." Revar gestures the way to the carriage, offering me their arm. "Let us hope you have hidden spines, because your environment is about to change."

I can barely catch a full breath. I look at Silvea, hoping to find comfort.

But the force of her glare hits me like a punch to the belly.

"You dirty, backstabbing bitch," she growls, pale cheeks flushed. Tears pool in her blue eyes, making them *burn*. "I should have let you die when I had the chance."

The bottom falls out of my stomach. My insides feel like they've dropped to the frozen ground.

She did have the chance. And she not only saved me, she seemed to *see* me.

Now there's only hatred in her eyes.

"What?" I let out in a pained gasp. "Silvea . . ."

And then it dawns on me. Silvea *wanted* the white feather. She *wanted* to be chosen. Perhaps she was shuddering with anticipation, not dread, when Maudon touched her. She's not even wearing a scarf around her neck, even though she's bundled up everywhere else. I was too nervous to notice.

"I hope you die," she says.

When she spits in my face, I understand that I never really knew her at all. Never truly saw *her*, blinded by my foolish love. Just as she never really saw me.

Her words wound me deeper than anything ever has before. They leave something hard and cold behind, and I seize it like a weapon.

"I will die," I reply, not bothering to wipe my face. "But you'd better hope I die all the way or else I'm coming for you."

I relish the fear in her eyes for a petty moment.

Revar holds out a silk handkerchief. It looks far too nice to be within an arm's length of me, never mind touching my skin. But they keep it raised until I take it and swipe at my cheeks, now hot with anger and betrayal.

"She's beneath you now, young one," Revar says, offering their arm again. "Forget her. Come."

I turn away from Silvea and follow the three vampires to the black carriage. Maudon and Claudia move to mount the two stallions behind; at least I won't have to ride with them. Revar opens the door for me. Aided by a too-cold hand, I step into the darkness. I'm leaving behind everything I've ever known, but any farewell turns to bitter ashes in my mouth.

I don't look back. It's surprisingly easy not to.

I wasn't born a monster.

But, if I live long enough, maybe I will become one.

2

At first, there's silence in the carriage. Revar sits across from me on the richly upholstered bench. They lean back, silver eyes glowing in the moonlight. The interior looks different from anything we would have in our village: rich black silk and velvet embroidered with curlicues of silver. I think the vampires brought such styles with them when they moved into—rather, *conquered*—our lands.

Revar looks too still against the swaying movement of the carriage, like some sort of ghostly apparition. I feel sick to my stomach and try to focus on the flicker of the moon through the bare trees outside. The approaching winter has left all of them skeletal.

I wrap my rags tighter around myself, unable to keep my teeth from chattering. The carriage is freezing—vampires don't need heat.

I've heard the stories of how they hunt, unbothered by rain or snow. How they can see in the dark. Track by scent. Run faster than any human on foot and bring you down, tearing into your neck quicker than any wolf or wildcat.

I've seen the bodies to prove it.

"*Running* is not really my specialty . . . but then that's not surprising in a vampire of the Silver Court," Revar says conversationally. "We prefer reading."

I stare at them for a moment, realizing with horror how they responded to something I never said aloud.

"You can hear my thoughts?" I say, before I can cover my mouth. *Blood and piss.* I should draw as little attention to myself as possible. Make myself as thin as parchment. Translucent. Until they don't notice my sharper edges at all.

I pointedly do *not* think of the fillet knife hidden under my shawl.

"Yes, I can hear them," Revar replies. "You'll learn the trick of it soon—in your second season—as well as gain some measure of protection against it."

That's how they knew that first Silvea, and then I, had the white feather. They must have read it in my mind as if I'd shouted it.

"Perhaps that is indeed how they knew," Revar says. "But who can say? The ability doesn't come equally to all—mine is particularly strong—and vampires can't read *one another's* minds."

Interesting.

"Maudon seemed to want Silvea," I say hesitantly.

"We can develop fixations on humans," the vampire says in a way that makes me think *this* one doesn't often. "But that is not what the Finding is supposed to be about. The Finding is about discovery."

"So even though I didn't exactly follow the rules, he didn't follow them first? That's why you let me use my age as an excuse to go before Silvea?"

"Exactly."

Not because you wanted to help me, I can't resist thinking. It's easier to keep my mouth shut than it is my thoughts silent. I'll have to learn quickly.

"I supported your claim because I was curious, too," Revar says, and then gestures at the dark landscape outside. "It's why I come on these Findings—humanity is a curiosity. A chance to discover something new." They turn back to me, pinning me with those bladelike eyes. "You, for example. Why would you put yourself in this situation when you hate vampires so?"

"For my *friend*," I say, folding my arms tighter. Luckily my bitterness is strong enough to drown out the rest of my thoughts—the part about knives against cold flesh. About *revenge*.

"Ah, you're learning how to mask your thoughts already." Revar sounds pleased, but then their voice drops. "That human wasn't your friend."

"I gathered that," I say through gritted teeth, tears threatening to spill. I dash my hand over my eyes. "I'd still rather be with my own kind."

Revar smiles, surprisingly gentle. "Do you know where we're going?"

"Courtsheart," I whisper.

"What do you know about it?"

"Not much," I admit. "It's a castle." *A prison.*

"It's more like one large castle and four smaller castles within a fortress," Revar clarifies. "And it's not a prison. For vampires, it's where the five courts debate and mingle. For you, it will be a school, where you have your first few undying seasons as a novice, and where you'll decide which court you wish to join as a newborn vampire."

"But I can't escape."

The vampire shakes their head slowly, their stark silver eyes almost sad. "No. You can't." They shrug. "You won't *want* to leave, soon enough."

"When will it happen? How?" I don't bother to hide my apprehension.

"You'll be given vampire blood to drink at a ceremony called your Beginning. This is what will allow your training to commence."

I once stole a pan of chicken blood from a yard where the bird had just been killed. I was so hungry I just drank it, already cooling and thickening. I nearly threw up.

I imagine vampire blood is more disgusting than a chicken's, since vampires are long dead. It would certainly be colder.

Revar ignores my horrified look. "You'll only take a little at first as you adjust, and more over time. It will grant you new abilities in a limited fashion at the start, which will increase in potency along with the blood in your system. You'll learn to hone these abilities before you become one of us fully." He pauses. "It's . . . safer, that way."

Nothing about this sounds safe at all. I can't resist clutching my stomach, folding over on the carriage bench, my head practically between my knees.

I almost made it, at nineteen. Next year, I wouldn't have had to attend the Finding, if the vampires had even come to our village at all. They only draw foundlings from six villages at a time, and ours wasn't selected every year. I can only remember two Findings before this one, and barely the first one when my mother was taken, it was so long ago. Even if our village had been unlucky enough to be chosen two years in a row, I would have been too old.

My mother didn't make it, either. She was nineteen, too.

I only remember fragments of her face. Even then, those fierce eyes and smiling lips, shaping the sound of my name—the nearly forgotten one—might be something I cobbled together from dreams. Even if I remembered her fully, it wouldn't help me find her. Whatever has happened to her, she's not the mother I knew and loved. I wouldn't recognize her, and she wouldn't remember me.

For all I know, she could be toiling away in some dark court, her hair gone gray and thin, her hands rough as she scrubs bloodstains off a floor, her ribs poking through dirty rags. Swollen bite marks on her scarred neck, eyes strangely lit, a vague smile on her face. A human thrall. *That* image of her has haunted my nightmares more than any other. Her fierce gaze lost and hopeless behind the glow, her lips cracked and bleeding as she grins.

I shudder. It's my worst nightmare—and not just for her, but for myself. Death would be better.

"Child, your thoughts are loud." Another gentle smile from Revar.

"I didn't know your mother was a foundling. That is likely something you'll wish to keep to yourself."

I jerk upright in my seat—too fast. I'm dizzy. Hungry, despite being nauseous. "Why?"

"Human bonds don't matter to vampires, for the most part, and you'll want to emulate us as quickly as possible." *For the most part.* An interesting qualification, but what they say next drowns out the thought: "Forget your mother. She has forgotten you."

I nearly choke, but not because the thought is new. I've heard those *exact* words before, from a half-forgotten visitor, long ago. I thought I'd maybe dreamed it, but now I remember . . .

A cat, sitting by my pallet late at night, while my father snored nearby. A cat with eyes that glowed like coals. A cat that seemed to speak without words . . .

I scramble to change the subject. Remembering is the opposite of what I'm supposed to be doing now, according to Revar. "Is that why you take us when we're young?" I ask, adjusting the ragged strips of cloth wrapping my hands. "So we forget quickly?"

"Indeed. And because you also *learn* quickly. We can make vampires out of older humans, but they take to the life less well. They have their own thoughts molded by years of human experience. That has led to strife among us in the past. This system of selection was designed to carefully increase our ranks with those most likely to thrive, in the most controlled and considerate fashion."

"Considerate?" I say. Much like *safe*, *considerate* doesn't seem to enter into this. "How? And for who?"

"*Whom*," Revar corrects absently. "For both humans and vampires. When humans feel they or one of their family have a chance of becoming one of us, it makes them less rebellious. Less resentful."

"Does it, now?" I say, a hot fist of anger gripping my chest.

The vampire smiles. "Maybe they appreciate the thought of gaining immortal life. Your lives are short and brutish, and ours shine like stars in comparison."

Vampires are supposed to be the new gods. The old worship has long been forbidden—which doesn't bother me, since I've never cared for the idea of the Father or his marauding sons and vicious daughters, a description that covers most of the old pantheon. But I'm not about to worship vampires, either.

Revar tips their head. "Or perhaps humans simply hate to imagine what it would feel like to kill a vampire wearing the face of a daughter or a brother—never mind that we can and often do change our faces. Either way, for better or worse, we want humanity to feel involved with us beyond . . ."

It's the first time the vampire has hesitated. "Beyond being your food?" I say, unflinching. "But why hold a Finding when vampires can just pick whoever they like most?"

"*Whomever*. We do that, too, but it's strictly controlled. A vampire needs to gain permission from their House to take on a novice—a still-human vampire-in-training," Revar clarifies. "And they mustn't already have a novice *or* an apprentice."

"Apprentice?" I brace myself as the carriage goes over a bump, but Revar barely sways.

"A newborn vampire who is still studying under their maker after joining their chosen House. It's what you will become in your fourth season at Courtsheart, after your noviceship."

Maker. The word makes me swallow. It doesn't seem much better than *Father* or *gods*.

"Think of it like a *patron* if that makes you feel better," Revar says. "Do you know what a patron is?"

Before I can shake my head, a thought suddenly comes to mind. Not a memory, exactly, but more an illustration of the word: a painter, leaning over her canvas, brush in hand, a richly dressed merchant-type standing over her shoulder. A supporter of both art and artist. I've never seen anything like it, certainly not in our village.

Revar doesn't seem to notice my confusion. "Except, in this case, the novice, and later the apprentice, are both the painter and painting in one, and their patron is the one who molds them." They sigh. "*Maker* is still more precise, but sometimes one must sacrifice precision of thought for another's comfort. Not very Silver Court of me, I must say."

Realizing what has happened, *how* I've understood what I have, I claw at my temple, scrambling away from Revar. "Don't do that!" I cry. "Don't get in my head!"

Revar arches a frosted brow at me. "You should grow accustomed to it. But for the duration of this trip . . . as you wish." The vampire settles back, folding their hands into their lap.

They pick up right where they left off. "Of course, one's favored human must also be of a proper age, as we've discussed. Beyond that, it's only up to the vampire, once they've gained permission from their House, to decide whom they wish to take as a novice. This could lead to accusations of favoritism with regard to whom we choose . . . or to a false sense of security. So, as you know, each year we randomly select six young humans to attend Courtsheart."

So I'm an *un*favored foundling, without a vampire . . . patron? The word is still strange.

Revar purses their lips. "Maybe *mentor* would be preferable?"

Either is better than *maker*. Whatever they're called, maybe I'll soon wish I had one. I only have vampire *enemies*, so far.

I slide back down the bench. "It's all very . . . considerate."

"Indeed," Revar says, perhaps failing to notice my sarcasm. "And, of course, our own purposes are served. We maintain a robust population, ensuring no House gains undue sway, and we're less likely to be ambushed by humans and left out in the sunlight with stakes in our hearts."

"Huge fortresses and vampire armies probably help with that, too," I say before I can help myself. Revar puts me at ease, despite everything they're saying. Perhaps too much at ease. There are no doubt many things I shouldn't say. But then the vampire could probably just hear my unspoken thoughts, anyway.

Revar nods in concession—either to my words or my silent musing, I don't know. "But are you not better off? We are able shepherds of the human flock, no? Our influence—and, at times, our more direct control—has often improved your lot in life."

I don't know much about geography or politics, but I know *my* lot, either back in my village or in the shape of a white feather, isn't better because of vampires.

But then I think of Silvea's hatred. Of my nearly starving to death. The smell of fish guts in my hair. Fists knocking stars across my vision. Maybe some would think this lot *is* better. But only because I have the chance to join them. For those who don't have that chance . . .

"Vampires are cruel," I insist.

A slight grimace mars the perfection of Revar's face. "Not all you've heard is the province of imagination, though perhaps more embellished than you might think. Human fear spreads like disease, and there are human rulers in the past who have been just as cruel, if not worse." They blink. "Do you even know which House you dwell under?"

I suddenly feel small in the shadow of that question. I begin to shake my head, and then jerk my hand up. "Don't do that thing again!"

"I assured you I wouldn't," Revar says calmly. "Anyway, it's the Red Court, but no matter. The stories you heard concerning vampiric reigns of terror likely started in the lands overseen by the House of Winter Night—the Blue Court. Life there can be . . . unpredictable."

I choke out a laugh. "That's one way to describe being hunted for sport."

"The Blue Court is one of the most traditional among us, holding to the old ways before we became the five courts we are today. Indeed, we still drink human blood for sustenance, but we do so with restraint. And yet, even as we are now, there are . . . disagreements regarding the treatment of humans. They are well governed but more likely to be enthralled into service in Gold Court lands, or forced to study our ways of thinking in Silver Court lands—though that is where the finest libraries are. There's always a trade. The Red Court looks most favorably upon humans, and yet are more likely to . . . mingle."

Aside from the occasional Finding or missing person in my village, we're mostly left alone—to starve, to prosper, it doesn't seem to matter to this Red Court. Maybe it's because our village is small and remote, but we seem to be nothing to them. "There are five courts?"

"Yes, identified by our colors for brevity. The true House names are longer and more accurate."

I don't care to hear them. "Red, Gold, Silver, Blue," I recite. They're not difficult to repeat, but the vampire looks pleased anyway. "That's only four."

"Ah, good, you can count," they say, their praise untainted by mockery. "One less thing to learn. I believe you can read, too?"

I clench my jaw, not wanting to think about Silvea teaching me. "Yes, passably. What's the fifth?"

"The Black Court. The Nameless House."

That *House* isn't terribly inviting, sounding more cursed without a name; I'm not sure I want to ask about it.

And I don't have to, because before I can, the carriage jolts violently. I nearly launch out of my seat. The cramped quarters are all that prevent me from falling to the narrow strip of floor as we jounce around.

Revar peers out the window steadily, seemingly undisturbed.

"We've met up with the first of the other five carriages that will join us on the road to Courtsheart. It almost collided with us."

"Do they not know how to drive?" I gasp, trying to brace myself as we lurch to a sudden stop.

"I believe they are under attack." Revar pauses as I gape. "Ah, correction—*we* are under attack."

Foot-long claws punch through the top of the carriage, stopping only a handbreadth from my upturned face. I shriek. Revar only looks on, calm as ever. I shrink away, cowering, but the claws drag toward me, tearing long gashes in the ceiling.

Before I know it, I've wrenched open the carriage door, and I'm stumbling out into the freezing night.

3

I don't make it far before nearly careening into two horrifying figures. The first is horrifying for its inhuman shape; the other, a
young man clutched in the creature's arms, for being covered in
blood. More figures surround the two carriages—one still perched
on top of my own—their features cloaked in shadow. But the moonlight is enough to make out enormous wings, towering horns, and
massive claws.

The young man's eyes are rolled back in his head, his lips pale and
bluish, and blood drips down his chest. The clawed hand in his hair
exposes his neck for the horned creature's mouth, which is clamped
on and sucking hungrily.

I scream. It's a foolish, preylike response I can't help.

It draws the attention of the blood drinker, who pulls away from
the young man's neck. The creature's eyes are the impossible blue
of glowing sapphires—and they stay fixed on me as everything else
around them starts to change. Horns and wings and claws begin to
retract, eventually melting into the shape of another young man:
beautiful, with warm brown skin, a cloud of curly brown hair halo-
ing his head, and those startling blue eyes that now crease charmingly
at the corners as he smiles at me. His full lips and straight teeth are
stained with blood, his canines long and sharp.

I knew vampires could change shape; I just didn't know how terrifying those shapes could be.

"Another treat for me?" he says, and then holds up a finger. A claw sinks into the tip, becoming a normal, manicured nail. "I'll be with you in just a moment." He bends his head back toward the young man's neck.

I'm tempted to scream again. Instead, my hand fumbles at the shawl tied around my waist, seeking the fillet knife hidden underneath.

But the vampire freezes, his jewel eyes widening slightly. Not because of me or *my* blade. A shadow has appeared over his shoulder, poised to strike him directly in the temple with a strange black dagger. Some of the surrounding, monstrous shapes crouch and hiss, even retreat, at the sight of the blade.

"Not a *dread blade*," the vampire gasps in mock horror. "How *dreadfully* serious. That might actually kill me. Are you sure you want that? It's so final. And I'm so beautiful."

A different, deep voice clucks in disapproval from the darkness. Shadows gather, and suddenly there's another vampire, this one man-shaped and holding the dagger, dressed all in black. His dark brown hair is straight and shoulder length, shaved on at least one side. Leather straps bind his clothing and multiple daggers to his pale, muscular form. He appears younger than Maudon, maybe twenty, though I know that doesn't mean anything. He's beautiful, too, of course. All these monsters look beautiful when they're wearing a human mask.

His irises are indistinguishable from his pupils. His eyes flick to me and away, discarding me as a threat. Or perhaps as *anything* worth his attention. "You know you're not supposed to be here, Kashire."

The blue-eyed vampire's lips spread once more into a bloody grin. "Hello, Gavron, my love. I thought that might be you. The others and I are just having a bit of harmless fun before the Beginning. You wouldn't want to interrupt, would you?"

"The Blue Court grows ever bolder," says the black-clad male— Gavron—both humor and scorn coating his voice.

"And the Black Court grows ever more boring." Kashire sighs. "Come now, we do this every year."

"Harass the carriages, yes, and cause a fright among the peasant-born foundlings by playing the monstrous, evil vampires," Gavron says, rolling his dark eyes. He almost sounds more dismissive of *us* than Kashire. "But you've never *killed* one of them before they've had the chance to arrive at Courtsheart."

Kashire blinks down at the now-limp body in his arms. "He is dead, isn't he?" He lets the body fall to the ground, and I can't help but leap back. "Alas, he might not be if you hadn't distracted me from my meal. But what's the start of an undying season without a little bit of death? Besides, the Black Court despairs of foundlings. What did you call them—peasant born? You should be thanking me." His sneer belies the words.

"Like them or not, it's the Black Court's duty to protect them as potential future members of the other Houses," Gavron says through clenched teeth. His canines are just as long and sharp as Kashire's. "You only did this to goad me, but it's too far. You've committed a crime."

"Against a *human?*" Kashire sniffs. "No such thing. They're not vampires yet, so no one cares. Certainly not the Black Court. See, I think *you* only came because you knew *I'd* be here. Admit it, you miss me."

"Don't be ridiculous," Gavron scoffs. "Of course the Black Court cares—"

Kashire raises his arms, forcing Gavron to step back. "Maudon practically gave me permission to put on this little show. Why else would your own commander be nowhere in sight, when he was part of their escort?"

Gavron only glares at Kashire, giving nothing away.

The other foundling's glazed, unblinking eyes stare at me from a pillow of dead leaves. I have to swallow repeatedly to not throw up.

Both vampires notice the movement of my throat. Kashire's bright blue eyes seem to light up even more at the sight.

"Don't, Kash," Gavron says, lifting a pale hand warningly, the black dagger held in the other. I wonder if it can truly kill vampires—a prospect that would consume my interest at any other time. "You've caused enough trouble."

"Ooh, so now it's Kash again, when you want me to listen. When you were busy breaking my heart it was all 'Kashire' this and 'arsehole' that."

"You don't have a heart to break and you *are* an arsehole, but I could just use knives instead of words, if you prefer," Gavron says with a hard smile.

"Oh, *Gav*, I thought you'd never ask. How I've longed for the touch of your blade once again." He tosses his head at me with a suggestive leer. "Just be sure to not accidentally poke *her* with it."

And then he charges me.

I run, my hand tangling in my shawl, but I don't have time to draw my fillet knife before Kashire is on me. He spins me around, cradling me against his chest, one strong arm across my shoulders, maybe so Gavron can see both our faces when he drinks my blood. Kashire's other hand reaches up to caress my cheek, slowly but firmly tipping my head sideways. And then he rips off my scarf, exposing my neck, sending a burst of cold panic through me.

Gavron suddenly appears less than an arm's length from us. I don't even see him move.

"Kashire, stop this," he says, sounding impatient.

He's not even looking at me. He doesn't actually care about me, of course. Never mind that Kashire just killed someone, and he's about to do it again. My captor's breath against my skin makes me shiver.

But my hand is still under my power.

When I feel the sharp points of Kashire's teeth brush my neck,

I *stab* behind me blindly. I don't actually expect the fillet knife to even find the vampire's skin, but it does. I drive it deep into his side, miraculously missing his ribs and hitting meat and organs.

"What's this?" To get a better look, Kashire shoves me forward, practically into Gavron, who sidesteps as if to avoid touching me. The Blue Court vampire's hand stays clamped around my neck, fingers digging into my throat, strangling me from behind. While I gasp for air, Gavron looks from Kashire to me in nearly pleasant surprise. A laugh bursts from him.

Amused, is he? I'd be happy to stab him, too, if I get the chance.

I twist around in Kashire's grip, straining for my knife still lodged between the vampire's ribs. But Kashire gets there first. He draws the blade slowly, casually from his side.

In the icy moonlight, his blood gleams a dark blue. Like his eyes, the color of his House runs in his veins. Kashire frowns down at the hole in his shirt, then at me still dangling at the end of his arm. "This was my favorite shirt."

"You can always mend it," Gavron suggests.

Kashire scoffs. "I don't mend things. I break things." He smiles at me, jewel eyes flashing. "Like you."

He drops my knife to the ground as five long, black claws spring from the tips of his fingers.

And then he spears me straight through the chest.

The claws reach up under my breast, and I feel them come out the back of me.

I guess I am parchment thin.

I can't make a sound. As my knees buckle, I slide slowly off his claws. *Those* make a horrible, wet noise as they come out of me. I smell the copper tang of blood, hot in the air. I don't feel as much pain as I imagined, only a horrible pressure in my lungs and a numb weight in the rest of my body. I think perhaps he severed my spine.

Gavron, surprisingly, catches me before I hit the ground. It seems more on reflex, because he looks surprised, too, as he eases me down. And then his black eyes narrow.

"*Kashire*," he says, as if Kashire is only a child who has made a mess.

I *am* a mess. Blood burbles in my mouth. Panic strangles me even more.

I'm dying.

Wings and horns now spring from Kashire along with his claws, and he takes flight. Gavron snarls and follows him, vanishing from above me. There's shouting, hissing, the sound of more wings on the air, the clashing of what must be blades and claws, and then silence.

Everything is getting darker. I'm drowning in my own thick, coppery blood, my shoulders convulsing, but I can't move. I'm helpless.

Gavron reappears above me. He tosses his dark hair back, tying it away from his face and revealing a fine jaw and high cheekbones. He'll probably be the last thing I ever see.

I wish he weren't so beautiful.

He sighs down at me, as if I'm most inconvenient. Then he drops into a crouch next to me, his expression deadly serious as he studies me. His long, pale fingers brush my hair off my cheek, trailing blood.

"Only tethered to this body by a delicate thread," he says. "Human death is so lovely compared to a vampire's." And then he mutters, "Alas, you're not to be lovely tonight."

I expect him to lunge, bite me like a predator over their injured prey. He bends closer. *Not* for my neck. His eyes swallow my vision as he hovers only a handbreadth above my face.

Before I can guess his true intentions, he presses his lips to mine, parting both of ours with a practiced motion. I feel his tongue dip into my mouth. Then again. It's like the deep kisses I've seen stolen behind barns between village youths. Except this is utterly passionless, I'm still choking, and he's lapping up my blood.

I want to cry out, scream, but I can't. I'm dying, and he's feeding on me? With a *kiss*, after calling me ugly? It's insult upon injury, to say the least.

I would laugh, if I could. Maybe I'm delirious.

"It's better than me biting you," I feel him murmur against my mouth, before he sips more of my blood. He straightens after a short time—I think it's short, though time is beginning to feel strange—and he licks the red from his lips. "You have enough holes as it is. And, *please*, I'm not preying on you. How pathetic would that be? I need your blood because—never mind. I'm helping you." His impatient expression twitches into a grimace. "Bloody Founders, you smell like fish."

I'm too far gone to try to spit on him. My body feels like it's sinking into the ground. Like I'm already dead and buried.

"Not yet," Gavron says, and then he lifts his wrist to his mouth. He rips away some of the thick leather with his teeth easily. And then he tears into his own skin.

The blood begins to flow immediately, black as midnight. It falls in viscous rivulets onto the wounds in my chest. Where it lands, heat blossoms.

Now I can feel everything. I scream as a sensation burns through me like a brush fire. And then, as suddenly as it began, the pain is gone and I'm sitting up and clawing at my chest.

There's a lot of blood—red and black, mine and his—but no wounds under my shredded clothes. I don't wonder at it for long. I scrabble around on my hands and knees until I find it: my fillet knife.

I raise the blade, glancing around frantically as I stagger to my feet.

I'm alone. My only company is the body of the other foundling. Gavron, Kashire, and all the rest are gone. The horses haven't even panicked. They look as peaceful as if we've stopped for lunch, not because a horde of monsters from the Blue Court attacked us. The faint light of someone else's will still gleams behind their placid eyes.

"Ah, are you ready?" says a calm voice behind me.

I yelp and spin, brandishing my knife. Revar only stands, looking more like an apparition than ever against the dark forest.

"I thought you might have hidden spines," they say, glancing down at my knife. "Good. I look forward to seeing what you will become." And with that, they turn and walk back to the carriage.

They leave the other foundling where he lies dead in the snowy leaves. Food for wolves is what *he'll* become.

Despite the risk of ending up like the boy, I want to kill vampires all the more.

I keep staring at the body, feeling that cold hunger grow, until Revar calls, "Let's carry on to Courtsheart, shall we?"

But as I shuffle numbly toward the carriage, I remember I've just seen something that *can* kill them.

A so-called dread blade. Which at least some of them possess.

Which means, even as I get closer to their stronghold, I'm also one step closer to a weapon to use against them.

———※☾☆※———

We arrive at Courtsheart shortly before dawn, our carriage traveling deep inland into the freezing mountains.

Once the thrill of near death fades, I'm utterly exhausted. And yet I can't sleep for fear of another attack. Revar doesn't have much to say to soothe my nerves. The vampire tries to tell me more about the courts, about what to expect, but it all swirls around in my head in a nightmarish jumble streaked with blood.

My blood. *His.*

I keep touching my chest, where claws entered and blood like tar healed me. My lips, where Gavron tasted me. I remember the feeling of his tongue almost more than the claws.

Revar doesn't seem surprised in the least that I nearly died, or that I was miraculously healed. Perhaps it's yet another thing I should get used to in my new home. As for my ulterior motive for wanting to arrive in one piece, the vampire doesn't seem to have noticed.

Being a foundling is a bad-enough start. If it becomes clear that I want to kill vampires . . . None of the outcomes I imagine are pleasant.

When our carriage crests a rise and we finally get a view of the fortress, it isn't pleasant, either.

The distant, pale glow of the sun behind snowy peaks is enough for me to make out the looming shape of a five-pointed star made of walls nearly as imposing as the mountains themselves. One of the star's points is separated from the rest by a moat, a single bridge connecting it to the main structure. A wide, winding path is leading us—Revar's and my carriage, along with the other five, one of them empty—up to tall, spike-covered gates, lined in arrow slits and topped with teethlike battlements. This point of the star is a gatehouse, then. One more frightening looking than any prison I could have ever imagined.

"The Black Gates," Revar says. "This is where the Black Court dwells within Courtsheart, guarding the other courts from intruders . . . and sometimes from one another."

Guarding the entrance . . . and the exit.

Beyond the Black Gates and across the moat, the rest looks just like Revar described it. The other four points of the star have soaring structures atop those already-staggering outer walls. And in the center is the main castle. It's like nothing I've ever seen before, all towers and arches made of razor-sharp spikes and delicate filigree, reminiscent of the patterns in a snowflake. My entire village could fit inside the main castle, several times over. My jaw drops. I don't care that I look like an ignorant peasant. This place makes me realize, in all truth, I am one.

The carriages stop at the foot of the Black Gates, our way forward uncertain. These gates look as if they could repel an oncoming longship. Even if they did open, I'm not sure why anyone would want to go inside. They don't look like the type of gates that will ever let you back out.

Fear seizes me. Dreams of killing dead things aside, I'm suddenly hoping the doors won't part, that the vampires have changed their minds about accepting foundlings. But I hear the deep groan of some mechanism. The gates split inward, the maw widening for our line of carriages.

And then I'm headed into Courtsheart. My new home.

As the gates close, I can't get a deep-enough breath. But then I think of my mother, of Silvea, of the dead boy left in the woods, and the fear turns cold and sharp in my chest. Whether it's a weapon I'm honing inside or a wound piercing me through, my pounding heart slows, and I can breathe again.

Because, whatever I become—monster or corpse—at least I have a purpose. Even if they end up discovering me, I intend to take a few of them down before they kill me.

It's the least I can do to repay them. For murdering the boy in the woods. For making Silvea want this life more than her own—and making her hate me for taking it from her. For stealing my mother from me.

For leaving me with no other dreams but those of blades, blood, and cold.

4

It's difficult to see much from the carriage as we head deeper into Courtsheart. I can only see walls of gray stone through the window. The cobbled path we travel seems empty.

"Members of the Black Court, the Nameless House, don't like to be heard or seen unless they want to be," Revar says. "But they're there."

I remember Gavron appearing from seemingly nowhere, from only shadow . . . and then stepping back into it, vanishing.

Before long, we're crossing the bridge over the moat. It has a complex system of thick ropes, heavy pulleys, and winding mechanisms. Revar tells me it's a drawbridge that can be dropped or raised at a moment's notice. After we cross, our carriages finally stop in a massive central courtyard, the clopping of hooves echoing all around. I crane my neck and still can't see the tops of the towers rising above, only arched colonnades like the bars of an elaborate stone cage enclosing us.

Revar gets out of the carriage. I emerge, my legs unsteady, to find other bedraggled youths stepping stiffly out into the pale predawn light. A couple of other vampires are with them, those who took enough pity on their foundling charges to stay, as Revar did for me. It appears I was one of the lucky few to have a guide the entire time.

None are as dirty or as bedraggled as I am. I wonder if their trips were as eventful as mine.

"Welcome to Courtsheart, the greatest endeavor in vampire history," Revar tells me, a hint of pride in their tone. "We came together like never before to build this for the protection of us all. Think of it as the crossroads between the mortal and immortal worlds." They turn a slow circle, arms spread. "Some, like the Red and Gold Courts, think of it as more of a diplomatic mission, a safe place for mingling. For others, like the Blue and Black Courts, it's the first line of defense—a place for recruitment and reconnaissance."

"And Silver?" I ask.

"Why, for us it is first and foremost a place of learning. And now your education begins. You will be staying within Castle Courtsheart proper—the main castle, here in the fortress's *heart*," Revar emphasizes, "until you complete your basic studies as a novice. Once you apprentice under a maker within your chosen House, you will move into whichever of the outer four halls belongs to their court." The vampire gestures at the spires rising from the four corners of the star-shaped fortress, topped with distant flags in the different court colors.

"What about the Black Court?" I ask.

"Few want to join them, and they take fewer than that." They shrug. "But yes, I suppose you could also move out to the Black Gates once you're an apprentice."

I shudder. That's the last place I want to end up—unless it's on my way out, escaping all of this.

"Shush, now, with all of that," Revar murmurs, stepping nearer to me. "Remember, guard your thoughts closely until your Beginning."

Choked with fresh fear, I ask, "When will that be?"

"Tonight. And now, I must follow the darkness *inside*."

Of course. The sun is about to come up. Most vampires don't remain in the sun for long. It burns older, stronger vampires, sapping their strength. Weaker ones, it incinerates outright. Or so I've heard.

"O-okay," I stammer. As strange and unsettling as the vampire has been, they've at least become a familiar face. Oddly, I don't want them to go. "Thank you," I add.

Revar gives me a half smile, and then in a swish of silver silk and white hair, they stride away toward the Autumn Hall, leaving me standing in the courtyard alone.

Not entirely alone. There are four strangers here, too, foundlings now abandoned by their vampire escorts and most looking as lost and uncertain as I feel. All *except* the girl who comes marching over to me. She has a halo of tight brown curls spreading around her head in the widest, densest mass I've ever seen, and dark brown skin. Her clothes are the finest looking of all of ours, a fur-lined leather tunic layered over a creamy wool dress embroidered with red flowers. Leather gloves cover her hands, and a pretty woven belt adorns her waist, a sturdy knife tied to it. She's tall and well-fed. She's a merchant's daughter, perhaps, or a village headman's.

"You are *covered* in blood," she states, amazed. "Were you with the other carriage?" Her voice drops. "You know, the *empty* one?"

I barely manage a nod before she demands, "What happened? What attacked you?"

I shake my head. I don't want to tell any tales, since I don't need any more vampire enemies than I already have. Maybe Kashire will consider us even since he stabbed and nearly killed me. Maybe Gavron will just forget about me. He already acted like he wanted to.

"Quiet, huh? That's fine. You're the only other one who thought to bring a weapon, and it looks like you can use it," she says, nodding at my fillet knife, now exposed on my hip. "I project enough for two, anyway, or so my singing tutor says." The young woman sticks out her hand. It's very clean. "My name is Marai."

I don't take her hand. She might not like me when she sees how truly filthy I am. Some of that could be attributed to the skirmish, but not when she smells the fish. "My name is Fin. Sorry, my hands are bloody."

Her smile takes on edges. "I have a feeling all of ours are about to be, one way or another, and I'd prefer to still be standing like you are."

I hold her brown eyes. Nod. "Me too."

Not that Marai will approve of how I want to go about it. Not everyone hates vampires, as strange as it seems to me.

"We're a team, then, Fin," she says, as if that is that.

It's not so simple, nor do I trust her so easily, but I'm not going to argue right now, not when I have no one else. She puts her hands on her wide hips, her fingers toying with the hilt of her dagger as she looks around, mostly ignoring the other three, who've formed a frightened huddle. I can't help but think of sheep.

Like Marai, I'd rather be a wolf.

She asks, "Now that the vampires are gone, who's going to show us around?"

As if her question summoned them, several servants dressed in black-and-white livery step out through the colonnade.

"Right this way," a woman says. "We'll show you to your rooms, and a warm bath." Her eyes glow softly from within, her smile vacant.

Human thralls, all of them. I want to recoil. I manage not to run, but it takes all the strength left within me. I follow the servants with the rest of the foundlings, but I hang back as much as possible. Marai shoots me a curious look, but she doesn't say anything, only slowing to walk with me.

Castle Courtsheart swallows us.

———— ·◦✠◦· ————

The warm soup I eat—spilling it down the front of me I drink it so fast—is the second-best thing I've ever had in my life. The bath turns out to be the best.

The bed doesn't look bad, either, and the room itself is smooth stone lined in plush rugs and tapestries. It, like the rest of the castle, is freezing. But a fire has been lit in a massive fireplace, far grander than the sooty pit I'm used to, and a shining copper tub has been filled with steaming water. Marai and the others were already taken to their rooms. All of this is for me and only me.

There are luxurious cakes of soap in various colors on a stand next to the tub, some even containing flower petals, alongside bottles in different shapes and sizes. Someone has already poured what smells like rose and cedar oil into the bath. Dawn light shines through narrow, stained-glass windows and turns the rising steam to gold. It looks and smells divine.

I don't hesitate, stripping off my bloodstained rags. It's only when I'm in, the water almost painfully hot and entirely blissful, that I spot the strange marks on my chest that aren't washing off. They're black and spidery, spreading like sickly veins across my breast. Right where Kashire's claws pierced me—and Gavron's blood healed me.

It must be his dead blood, somehow knitting me back together. I wish I could scrub myself clean of it, despite what it did for me.

I make good work of the rest of myself, trying a bit of everything in the bottles, and washing my hair no less than three times. Somewhere in the middle of the third washing there's a knock on the door. A servant enters with fabric in her arms, primarily in deep russets, blacks, and browns. I freeze as she begins to lay out several items of clothing on the bed, along with a pair of slippers.

"I tried to match your size, and to pick styles and colors similar to what you were wearing," she says, as if only half-present.

My *style* and *colors*? My style was "whatever scraps I could find" and my colors were "my blood," "Gavron's blood," and "dirt."

Russet, black, and brown, I suppose.

"A tailor will come tomorrow night to get your measurements and preferences." The servant then bundles up my rags on the floor without even wrinkling her nose. The thought of even trying to wash those would make me laugh if I didn't suddenly feel panicky.

"Wait!" I cry, as she turns to leave. "My knife."

As easy as it was to leave my village behind, something in me can't let go of this. My father gave it to me, and as much as I hated him and his drunken bouts of fury, *he* was all I had left of life with my mother. With him dead, that makes the knife something like my last physical tie to her. Besides, it's the only weapon I have to protect myself.

She pauses, and then sets the fillet knife on a stand near the door. I catch the strange glow in her eyes. "I suppose I can leave this, but I'm to burn the rest. Try to get some sleep. I'll wake you at sunset with breakfast."

She leaves before I can say anything else.

The servants, enthralled. My clothes, burned. Breakfast at dinner-time. I guess we're supposed to sever our human ties as quickly as possible. And if we don't, the vampires will do it for us.

Our Beginning is tonight. I wonder what it involves, with no little trepidation. My knife obviously won't provide enough protection. At least I have something to wear that isn't covered in dried blood and reeking of fish.

I get out of the bath, wrapping myself in a thick robe, and start poking at the clothing on the bed. One is a black silk nightgown, another a gown in rich russet with brown fur trim and black lacing, and the last a heavy velvet cloak, hooded and lined in more fur—warm, at least, and with more folds of material than I know what to do with. I'm about to try on the cloak when the door opens yet again, this time without a knock.

Marai comes striding in, curvaceous in her own black night-gown, her velvet and fur cloak around her shoulders, and a silk wrap around her head. She looks like a queen in the same clothes I now apparently have, but I can't imagine giving the same impression.

"You haven't tried them on yet?" she says. "Ooh, what did they give you? I think your gown is different from mine!"

"I—I haven't . . . ," I stammer. "I'm not sure. About any of this."

She blinks. "Aren't you at least a little excited?" When I don't answer, she says, "Come on, there must be something you're looking forward to here!"

"What is there to look forward to?"

She throws up her hands. "Anything and everything! Now that you've had a bath, you could use some more food, for one. But that's peasant stuff. Once we're vampires, we can do whatever we want. *Be* whomever we want."

I stare at her like she's mad. Maybe she is. Or maybe I'm still stung by *peasant stuff.* "Who would we be, if not us?"

"Anyone. Vampires wear faces like clothes. Turn into animals. They can look like men, like women, or like neither. They can be *with* men, women, or neither. In any case, we can be something new and amazing, too."

I shake my head. "Who cares who you can take a tumble with when you're dead and need to drink human blood?"

"*Who cares?*" Marai demands, folding her arms. "Maybe you've never had to care, but some of us aren't so lucky to fit in so perfectly."

I've never fit in. I wonder at the ways Marai's felt limited, with her fine clothes, full plates of food, and obvious education. She's given me a clue. Women loving women isn't forbidden, but it's considered odd since it doesn't lead to children—obviously something a vampire wouldn't care about, but that doesn't help many humans think it less strange. I'm wondering now if that was one reason I never told Silvea how much I loved her. I never really thought about her like that, much less about *doing* anything with her, but maybe because it was impossible like so many things in our village. I never thought about boys much, either, for the same reason. I only worshipped Silvea from afar, more than I ever worshipped the Father or any gods, because she seemed to deserve it. I just didn't realize how little I truly mattered to her. But I don't want to think about any of that.

"So . . . ," I say, trying to pick up the torn threads of the conversation. "Vampires don't much care what we do? Not even as novices? As *young ladies?*" I manage to not snort.

The excited gleam comes back into Marai's eyes, replacing the anger. "Not who you kiss *or* tumble with. That's lesser stuff. Fun. *Encouraged*, if you want it. A blood claim is the serious commitment."

My stomach does a little flip. "Blood claim?"

"Vampire society isn't built on marriage, man to woman. On children or heirs. This is their version of all that, rolled into one. Whatever you do, don't take it lightly."

I resist rolling my eyes. "I still don't know what *it* is, Marai."

She looks surprised. "It's when a vampire gives you their blood. Blood is potent, and drinking a vampire's blood gives them influence over you. But it's a gift, too. Even before their blood eventually turns you into a vampire, it lends you some of their strength while staking a claim over you. They're like your . . ."

"Maker," I say, my tongue feeling suddenly dry. I can't bother with a word like *patron*. If I can say *vampire*, I can say the rest. Call dung *dung*, as they say. "Which would make you their *thing* that they've created."

Marai pulls a face. "You don't have to see it like *that*. Or at least I don't want to." She sighs dreamily. "I think it could be romantic. Once you've been claimed by their blood, you belong to that vampire, for a time. Until you can stand on your own, in their world. And even then, you'll always have ties to them."

Marai must have more pleasant familial ties than I've had. "That's not romantic," I say. "That's disturbing."

She rolls her eyes at me. "Romantic, barbaric, disturbing, useful, whatever. We can see things how we want now. But it's serious. A blood claim only loses its power when it's over. When *they* decide they're done with you. And there's always an echo of what you once had. You're more open to their suggestions. You want to trust them. And in return, they're more protective of you, even if they're no longer honor bound to watch over you. Like . . . family, almost, such that vampires have it." She waggles her fingers like crawling things—spiders, I guess, when she says, "It creates complex webs among them, since they've probably claimed or been claimed by several others."

"How do you know all this?"

"I'm from Varrell, in Gold Court lands. Vampires are directly involved with human leadership there."

I don't recognize the place name, so I don't say anything.

Marai stares at me, cocking her head. "You really don't know about any of this, do you?" When I don't answer, she says, "I *know* you're not accustomed to thralls. I saw how you acted back in the courtyard. A ton of us get enthralled where I live." She shrugs. "It's not that bad."

"*You've* been enthralled?" I say, aghast. To lose control like that—no, to have your will *taken* from you like that . . . As little as I've ever had, that's *all* I've ever had. And yet, Marai is talking about my worst nightmare as if it were little more than a passing winter illness.

She looks defensive. "Yes. But I won't be enthralled anymore, not once I'm a vampire. It's impossible, after that." Her dramatic groan drowns out any response I could have mustered. "Come on, Fin! We're going to be something else. We're not bound by mortal rules anymore, or by mortal bodies, or by mortal lives. We can be our wildest dreams."

Our wildest dreams. What even *are* my wildest dreams? I only have the simple dreams of someone who isn't expecting to live for long.

"If we live that long," Marai adds, as if reading my mind. "Which is why I'm sticking with you, knife girl."

"'Sun calling the moon bright,'" I say, quoting the old saying. I can't help my smile, but it fades quickly. "Don't be so sure I'm lucky."

She grins back. "You're here, aren't you? You drew the white feather, you survived some sort of attack, and you look tough as a willow whip . . . if as thin as one." Before I can glare, she adds, "All the better, so there's plenty of room in your bed."

I'm about to debate her over what qualifies as luck, but then I blink. "What?"

"I don't know about you, but I don't want to sleep alone in this terrifying castle filled with vampires."

I bark a laugh. "I thought you were excited to be here."

"That doesn't mean I'm not frightened at the same time. Besides, if you hate thralls, you're going to need someone else to lace you into that dress, trust me." She hesitates. "I can help you, if you help me."

It's like she's asking me without asking me.

"All right," I relent, glancing toward my bed. It's cold, anyway.

With a squeal, Marai throws herself on top of the mattress, sinking deep into the down covers. "Good, because it's also *freezing*."

<hr />

I dream of my mother that night—day. I relive my one and only memory of her, assuming I didn't imagine it. She holds me on her lap near our firepit. Her intense gaze, sparking amber in the glow, would have better matched a grimace or a frown, but her lips form a smile as she mouths my old name. She smooths a hand over my hair, and it's one of the first and last times I remember feeling safe.

Because, what will be only days later, vampires will take her from me. As if to remind me of what will happen, my mother's smile keeps growing until it's unnaturally large, her toothy grin turning bloody, her eyes glowing and wild. Dream twisting to nightmare. I can't tell if she's a vampire or thrall. She usually turns to one or the other.

Before she has a chance to change further, rough, claw-tipped hands—much like Kashire's—pull me from her lap while I'm screaming, reaching for her.

"Forget me," she says through bloodied teeth, "I've forgotten you."

I jerk awake, sitting upright with a gasp. For a long moment, I have no idea where I am. Marai's sleeping form curled under the covers reminds me. Somehow, I haven't disturbed her.

The light looks to be fading outside the beautiful glass windows of my room. Twilight. Our Beginning will start soon.

My new life.

My nightmare mother's words repeat in my mind—a twisted echo of what Revar said, which in turn was a clear echo of that other strange, dreamlike memory of the cat with glowing eyes.

Forget your mother. She has forgotten you.

No matter what happens to me in the coming days, I won't let this place change me that much. Even if my mother has forgotten me, I'm not going to forget her.

I'm going to avenge her. Somehow.

5

The hall Marai and I enter together, following a procession of servants and initiates decked in finery, makes *all* of us humans look like peasants. My gown makes me feel like I'm drowning in velvet. It's not that the dress is shapeless; I am. Too many years without enough food has left me flat chested and without hips. But it's not myself I mind—I want to claw my way free of the fabric and throw it out a window.

Marai wears a white gown wreathed in red embroidery and bound by a tawny leather corset. She positively *glows*, like she's taking her first steps toward her wildest dreams.

I don't belong here. In this dress. In this hall. I'm out of my element, indeed. A fish out of water. I hope I have the spines to survive.

Despite the incredible number of candles burning in the chandeliers, the arched ceilings are so high I can barely make out the figures painted overhead. From what I can see, the painted figures are beautiful, entwined, and have inhumanly hued eyes. Or if they don't, they're draped in graceful poses that nonetheless suggest they are dead, red paint dripping from their necks or wrists.

Candelabras light the way forward through a forest of pillars supporting elegant balconies, with many perfectly smooth, gorgeous faces peering down upon us, brighter and far more real than the paintings. Though they have the same strange eyes that follow us as we enter.

"Welcome to your first undying season, initiates, both those already favored by a House and those who are foundlings," says a calm, familiar voice: Revar's. As we're led farther inside, I see the Silver Court vampire standing at the center of a wide semicircle of other vampires, the floor of the cavernous room before them as big as my village square.

I feel like we're sheep being brought in from pasture, where we'll at best be sheared and shaped into something different to suit the needs of our overseers. Or, worst, slaughtered for food.

"As the Silver Court's acting voice on the final eve of this autumn season, allow me to introduce you to the Houses that will soon be your new homes, to what will be your new way of life."

I feel like the laces of my gown are squeezing me too tight to breathe. Marai, however, shoots me an excited glance, dancing on the balls of her feet.

"Our formal House names come from the markers of time," the vampire continues. "They illustrate that, while we are different, we share boundaries and continuity, and all possess an equal measure in an everlasting cycle—the undying seasons. First I will introduce who we like to say is the most human among us: the Red Court, of the House of Spring Dawn."

Revar gestures to where a banner hangs from a balcony above, showing a bright sword crossing the stem of a red rose, blood dripping from both blade and blossom, with the words *Blaze and Bleed* woven artfully underneath. The House motto, then. Claudia is standing directly under it in another red gown, amid a sea of other red-clad, red-eyed vampires. She has a longsword strapped to her back, the tip nearly reaching the floor. I look quickly away as Revar continues, "They are the romantics among us: the artists, musicians, and poets, the fighters skilled with human weapons. They are those who are passionate and blood driven. The Red Court strives to be the sworn guardians, the troubadours, or simply the paramours—"

"There's nothing simple about *that*, Revar," someone says with a laugh from the Red Court crowd.

"—of those who sit upon the thrones of the world, whether human or vampire," Revar finishes.

"When you sit *upon* the person seated on the throne, I believe that makes you superior," says the same voice.

Revar ignores the comment and the ensuing titters, gesturing to a new banner depicting an open eye with lashes like golden sun rays resting atop an ornate scepter, with the words *Shine and Steward* underneath. "Next, we have the Gold Court, of the House of Summer Day. The charismatic advisers and leaders who possess unerring focus and control. The Gold Court strives to be those who are seated on the thrones of the world."

A different voice, belonging to a stunning golden-eyed woman, says, "Just *try* to sit on my lap, my Red Court dears. You'll find yourself groveling, instead."

Revar clears their throat. "My own home is the Silver Court, of the House of Autumn Twilight, where we strive to *Protect and Preserve*." On the next banner, those words rest underneath an image of an open book, its pages whipping up into a spray of loose leaves and skeletal trees. "We are the theorists, historians, and philosophers—"

"Obsessive, aloof, and terribly boring," adds another, all-too-familiar voice. *Kashire.* His dark blue silk vest gleams under his muscular and bare arms. His feet are bare, too, under swirling silk pants. He looks as wild and beautiful, and as terrifying, as when he stabbed me in the woods. Luckily, he hasn't seemed to notice me yet.

"—who are most interested in the undying, in preservation," Revar continues, undeterred, "before settling into winter. The Silver Court are the healers and scholars behind the thrones, with the necessary knowledge to keep those we deem worthy seated upon them."

Kashire snorts.

"Which brings us to the Blue Court, of the House of Winter

Night." Revar throws a careless hand to the banner hanging above Kashire. The words *Revel and Remember* scroll underneath a pair of spreading wings with feathers that somehow turn to grinning teeth, raking claws, and wickedly pointed horns—a beautiful, terrible tangle of images.

Kashire catches my eye and bows with a flourish.

So much for him not noticing me.

Our last encounter flashes in my mind. I practically feel the claws skewering my chest again, and for a moment, fear blinds me.

Don't panic.

"The Blue Court represents both the traditional and chaotic entwined," Revar continues, "embracing and celebrating our *inhu*man nature without attempting to adapt to the mortal world, often sowing chaos."

"Indeed, we prefer to *topple* thrones," Kashire says brightly.

"But don't be dissuaded from joining them," Revar adds, as if defending the Blue Court from their own claims. "I hear they are most lively and charming among one another."

"We throw the best parties, by far—don't let Red or Gold tell you otherwise," Kashire says. "But, Revar, you haven't yet gotten to the *best* court, the *least* boring, the *most* fun . . . Oh, wait, I have that backward."

Frowning, Revar gestures at the final banner. There are no words upon it, only a black tower with a jagged space like lightning striking through it. "The Black Court of the Nameless House. They are silent, invisible, and unnamed, outside the undying cycle. They keep the balance—the few who can stomach putting a stop to their own kind. But only when absolutely necessary, of course."

I catch a graceful nod in the crowd underneath the black banner—Maudon. "Of course," he says.

Is the Black Court for the vampire peacekeepers or vampire executioners, then? Perhaps both? I suddenly want to scrutinize them with new interest. Gavron, the only vampire I know to possess a dread blade—a weapon supposedly capable of killing vampires—is from the Black Court. Maybe they all wield them.

Revar continues, "In return for wearing this heavy mantle of power, the Black Court is unburdened by any other, unable to take a seat on the Council of Twelve. We have three Council members per House, and each court presides during their own undying season with one voice for each month. No House is heard above the rest." Revar gestures at the half circle of eleven other vampires.

So, Revar is not only a member of the Council of Twelve, but the voice of it this month. Perhaps that's also why Maudon and Claudia bowed to Revar's wishes regarding me at the Finding.

And yet, it's the end of the month. Winter is about to start. I'm going to begin my life among vampires at a time when the worst of them are presiding. I try not to shiver, let alone catch Kashire's eye again with errant thoughts.

"We on the Council reside here at Courtsheart during our tenure, as does a delegation from each House in our respective halls." Revar nods at the walls, as if taking in the four towers around the castle proper. "Otherwise, each court controls their territories from their own distant strongholds, except for the Black Court, of course, whose permanent dwelling is in the Black Gates. This place is our meeting ground—the court of courts, in a sense. The court of all the undying seasons."

My village is in Red Court lands, supposedly, and Marai's city in the Gold's. I've never seen any of their individual strongholds, and I hope I never have to. Especially not the Blue's.

"There is no true first season in the undying cycle," Revar says, reaching out their arms to include all the banners and vampires crowded around the hall, "but if we had one, it belongs to the Blue Court. Winter is both beginning *and* ending, the season holding the darkest day of all—just as the night is both the death and birth of light. Let us herald the start of a new winter, a new year, as well as honor the end of this one. And may the House of Winter Night guide us wisely."

Wonderful, I can't help but think.

Revar's eyes flick to me before sweeping over the others gathered nearby. Now that I can tear my eyes away from the vampires, I see more humans beyond the other four foundlings—those already favored by Houses.

"Tonight you will become novices under a maker who has chosen to take you under their wing. Think of yourself as nestlings, utterly dependent on your maker and welcome here in Courtsheart—but still partly human, not yet secure in a House. So listen to me carefully. While your new gifts will make you feel powerful, you can still die. Beware the peculiar dangers of the castle, and especially what lurks outside it."

More like who lurks inside *it*, I think.

"Hear me." Revar holds all our eyes, their words drawing us in. "If your heart stops beating before we fully replace your blood with ours, you die forever. And if you fail in your studies, or to otherwise assimilate, you will join the other humans of Courtsheart instead of our immortal ranks."

Meaning we'll become thralls.

"However, if you do well in your studies these first few seasons, you will apprentice in the final season, next autumn, under your chosen maker and their House. You will become one of us, a fledgling vampire learning to fly—or to hunt, fight, or enthrall, as you wish."

"Or to love," says the Red Court vampire.

"Or to *die*," mutters yet another familiar voice. Gavron.

I spot him standing in the shadows next to Maudon, leaning against a pillar. When he meets my eyes, I flinch and look quickly down at the floor.

I *was* looking for him, unlike Kashire. And yet, if he can detect

50

my thoughts, it might end even worse for me, since I was specifically trying to spot what might be a dread blade among the many daggers on his person.

Revar frowns slightly. "Death is possible as a newborn if you're not careful, but unlikely if your maker looks out for you properly and if you, of course, follow their guidance. If you survive your apprenticeship, you will then join your chosen House as a full member, a young blood on your own for the first time. In your time here at Courtsheart, cleave to those with experience. There's no rush. You'll have all the time in the world, and all the world to taste."

Kashire makes a lip-smacking noise that echoes among the columns, and several vampires laugh or grin, their long canines showing. Gavron, I can't help but notice, doesn't even glance his way.

"Before we proceed with your Beginning," Revar continues, "a word about your studies."

"Hurrah," Kashire says without feeling.

Revar eyes him. "As you'll be teaching on behalf of the Blue Court for the first time this year, I hope you're enthusiastic, Kashire. Initiates, you'll learn the fundamental lessons from each of the courts in your first season. Only after which, in your later seasons here at Courtsheart, will you proceed to the more advanced skills. Every court has a specialty. A vampire needs only to master one in their chosen House, but, to be well rounded, have proficiency in all four."

"Five," Maudon corrects. "To be the *best*."

"Ah, yes," Revar says with a gracious nod. "The Black Court's skills are notoriously difficult to hone, and they haven't always been the most generous in teaching them. You're more than likely to end up forever lost, horrifically maimed, or simply deceased. So studying under their House is optional, but novices are more than welcome to try."

To die, is what I hear. Gavron's bottomless dark eyes find me, and I curse myself for looking in his direction again.

"Otherwise," Revar continues, "I'll let your instructors—all of them young bloods eager to teach what they've learned—explain more about your studies on the morrow: Claudia from the Red Court; Pavella from the Gold; Jaen, my own pupil and one-time apprentice from the Silver; Kashire from the Blue; and Gavron from the Black."

"Thank the Founders for that," Kashire says, only somewhat stifling a yawn.

"Young bloods nearing their maturity are not only allowed to teach the basics," Revar says, ignoring him, "but they're permitted to claim the foundlings brought here tonight, as a trial of their abilities."

Because no one else wants us, I can't help but think, *and so we're disposable as practice.*

Kashire flashes a sharp grin at me.

"Although a young blood must cede claim to any mature vampire who wants that foundling," Revar adds. "But first, let us introduce our initiates who have already been claimed."

My thoughts and stomach are in knots as Revar goes through the names, twelve in total. These favored humans step out onto the gleaming floor to greet their future vampire makers. They're gorgeous or strong looking, all of them, and dressed in finery that makes us foundlings look ill-fitting and plain despite the efforts the servants went to. The vampires who meet them in the center of the room are even more stunning, touching them with a familiarity that would make me blush to see between couples in my village. They move around each other with graceful gestures and soft caresses. It's as if I'm at a court ball, but without dancing. The vampires soon guide their young charges away.

In not much time at all, it's the foundlings' turn.

Revar states our names, and then asks, "Anyone wish to lay claim to one chosen in the Finding?"

For a long, stretched moment, there is only silence.

If no one claims us, I wonder, *will we be made into thralls before we can even try to prove ourselves?*

Marai squeezes my hand so hard it might have been painful if I weren't squeezing hers back as tightly.

Then Claudia steps out into the center of the hall, red gown swaying around her, as poised as a dancer despite the longsword on her back. "I choose her," she declares, lifting her finger.

For a heart-stopping moment, I think she's pointing at me, until she says, "Marai," and my heart does another flip.

Marai lets out a tiny cry of relief, dropping my hand to move toward the Red Court.

I'm not relieved. Claudia is terrible. At least, she's a vampire who seems to hate me. And now she's taking Marai—the only human resembling a friend of mine here—like she couldn't take Silvea. Maybe that's exactly why Claudia is picking her.

"Are you sure you're ready, Claudia?" Maudon asks, frowning.

She smiles back at him, but her expression is blade sharp. "Do you doubt my abilities—you, who were my maker, once?"

The *once* seems even sharper. Claudia is part of the Red Court, Maudon of the Black. She must have chosen a different court from his, chosen a different maker, when she went from novice to apprentice—severed, at least partially, the strongest tie that vampires have.

"No, I don't," Maudon says. He shrugs and turns away as if he's lost interest, though I know enough about men—even vampire men—to see through it.

Marai doesn't look back at me. She practically floats over to Claudia, who takes her hand and leads her away. I haven't noticed where the other vampires have gone with their chosen ones, and now I'm both desperate and terrified to find out.

As if Claudia broke the ice, two other foundlings are claimed in no time, with what might pass as a warm welcome from one vampire and a hungry look from another. I'm next to last, alongside a boy even scrawnier than me. My face burns as the entire hall seems to fillet me with their eyes, seeing everything inside me and obviously finding me lacking.

When Kashire speaks, my heart kicks in panic. "Well, I'll just say it if no one else will . . ."

Please, no, I beg silently.

". . . I smell someone *else* on the girl, don't you?"

I blink. That isn't what I was expecting.

Kashire takes a step closer to me, lifting his nose and sniffing the air. "Why, is that . . . *Gavron*'s blood? Have you already claimed her, my love? No one will want to cross you if you have."

If Gavron's eyes were daggers, they'd be buried deep in Kashire's chest. His smile, however, comes easily, as if laughing at a joke. "Of course I haven't claimed her. I only healed her. Remember, after *you* attacked—"

"Well, then!" Kashire interrupts. "Maybe the Black Court should finish what they started and take a foundling as a novice for once." He cocks his head at Maudon.

When Revar nods their agreement, the other vampires of the Council all do, too.

Maudon shrugs again. "Perhaps we could."

Even his indifference is hard to believe, based on how he's treated me. I'm sure he'd rather throw me off a cliff.

Gavron's smile vanishes.

"But certainly not *you*, Maudon?" Kashire asks, raising a hand to his chest in mock concern. "Not after losing Claudia to the Red Court? Has that wound healed yet?"

Maudon's jaw grows harder. "I haven't thought about it in years, and as for taking on a novice, I have more important things to look after at the moment. Gavron can, as you've suggested, 'finish what he started.'"

Now Gavron looks like he's subtly choking to death. And like he wants to strangle Kashire, as well.

"Fabulous!" Kashire shouts, glee written all over his face. He waves me forward. "Come, then! Go with Gavron."

My feet are rooted to the ground. So, apparently, are Gavron's. But, at a look from Maudon, the young Black Court vampire shifts stiffly, and then with more fluid grace as he steps out onto the floor—as graceful as a mountain lion stalking their prey. He manages a charming smile as he stops in the center of the hall and holds out one pale hand. It, too, is elegant, but I know it would rather be holding a dagger.

"Fin, is it?" he says with admirable charm. "Delighted."

I certainly can't pretend as well as he can. I still can't move. My breath has frozen in my lungs.

His black eyes flash with impatience, and with his next step, he vanishes.

I nearly scream when he appears alongside me. The other foundling actually does. Gavron doesn't even look at the flailing boy, eyeing me critically. At a distance, he would look pleased to see me, when I know he's anything but.

"You *do* look like a fish out of water," he says under his breath. "At least you don't smell like one anymore." He takes up my arm with as much elegance as one would expect, but his grip is like iron. "Let's go."

"Be gentle!" Kashire calls, winking at us. "It's *both* your first times!"

My face turns to fire. "Where are we—" is all I have time to ask before the entire hall, all the vampires, vanish. Rather, *I* vanish from the hall with Gavron, and we appear somewhere else.

We're both suddenly standing in a long, dark corridor, lined in alcoves and mostly dead candelabras. A wave of dizziness slams into me. I nearly fold over, though Gavron's hand on my arm prevents it. It's all I can do not to vomit all over the gleaming marble floor.

"Founders, that's all I need to make this evening better—human vomit," Gavron mutters. "At least we don't have a bloody audience anymore."

"What——" I choke. "What was that? What did you do?"

"I shadowstepped."

I stare up at him in horrified outrage. "You mean the thing that can *kill me*?" At least, that's what Revar's less than encouraging words on the Black Court's skills seemed to imply.

"Please, I didn't even mist us. That's how you accidentally end up dispersed or becoming one with a stone wall for the rest of eternity, and I can do *that* without thinking. Although, taking another person is a different level entirely." He gives me a meaningful look—a *threatening* one. "Shall I continue practicing, or are you satisfied with my abilities?"

I nod, and then regret it when another spell of dizziness hits me. "Satisfied. Where are we?"

"A hallway nearby. It's unimportant. We just needed to be anywhere else." When I look at him blankly, he says, "This is supposed to be enjoyable, at least for appearance's sake. Either you or I would no doubt betray the lie, and that would be embarrassing. It's a sacred, time-honored tradition, so on and so forth. Everyone does like to go on about it."

Despite his apparent disregard, he almost sounds apprehensive.

"*What* is?" I can't keep the fear out of my voice.

His jaw hardens. "Remember what got me into this abysmal mess? I had to drink your blood, so my own blood would recognize you as part of me and heal you?"

I nod, hardly able to breathe.

"Well, now you have to drink *my* blood, so your body recognizes *me*." He pauses, inky eyes detailing my face. In a flash, I remember him looking at me like that as I was dying—almost as if seeing something I would never be able to. "As your maker," he finishes.

I knew this would happen, but I can't help recoiling at the sound of that word, all thoughts of learning their secrets forgotten. Gavron's hands clamp on my elbows like manacles.

"Maker?" I hiss, glaring down at his hold on me. "Like you're some sort of god?"

Without letting go, he manages a shrug as if it's inconsequential. "You get a taste of my power," he says, "but at the same time, you'll be *under* my power. You'll be mine." He smirks. "Unfortunately."

I don't know if he means unfortunately for me or for him.

He leans toward me, his voice dropping. "My novice." He leans closer, like he's about to kiss me, lips almost brushing mine. "My responsibility. My duty." Even *closer*, but he turns his head so his lips are alongside my cheek, near enough to whisper in my ear, "My enormous pain in the arse. Until I can get rid of you."

Before I can register *that*, he adds, his voice low and seductive, "I should have let you die."

I should have let you die. The exact same words that Silvea said to me, gutting me. The difference is, I loved her.

I hate Gavron.

This time, I'm the one to spit in someone's face. Or at least *at* it. Gavron dodges with a blurring flick of his head. I still hope it's enough to distract him as I try to rip away from him.

It's not. His hands only spin me in place, pinning me against his chest, like how Kashire held me in the woods. Except Gavron doesn't bring his teeth to my neck. He brings them to his own wrist once again. He rips open the skin there in one quick motion and presses the wound to my mouth before I can blink or scream. I try to turn away, but he tucks me against his shoulder, holding me tighter. There's no escaping him.

"Let's just get this over with, shall we?" he says, as if we're both hauling water or doing some other mundane chore.

That black blood starts filling my mouth, and it's cold, like I expected, and . . . sweet. Delicious. Not like I expected. And absolutely *not* like chicken blood. It's more like the most amazing chilled wine I never could have afforded, but thicker. It's better than anything I've ever tasted.

I know already that I'll always remember the flavor. Always *want* it.

But why does it have to be *his*?

I don't swallow, my thoughts screaming. At the edge of my vision, I see Gavron bring his black-smeared lips to my ear. He murmurs softly, almost singsong, "Drink, Little Fish, drink."

I jerk in his arms, but it's like fighting against bands of iron. I try to elbow him in the stomach, but he simply bends around the motion, like dipping me in a dance. I shriek, but I end up gurgling on his blood, sputtering some of the precious liquid against his wrist and smearing it on my face.

And yet, there's so much more where that came from, flooding my mouth. My breath rasps frantically through my nose, and my rabbit heart tries to pound out of my chest.

"Shh," he whispers, his lips brushing my neck. A thrill of terror streaks like lightning across my skin. He smells the veins along my throat, and I feel the hint of teeth there.

A threat?

"Not yet," he answers my unspoken question. "But soon."

A promise, then.

I feel him nod. "The more of my blood I give you, the more of your blood I'll take from you. But now you just get a sip. And *I'm* not hungry." I can hear his smirk. "For your blood, at least, Little Fish. I've already had some, and that was more than enough. Not to my taste, frankly."

His blood doesn't stop, and I can't spit it out. It fills my mouth too full, making me desperately need to swallow.

It doesn't help that part of me desperately *wants* to swallow.

Gavron makes a noise of amused frustration and tips my head farther back against his shoulder. I stare up into his black eyes, panicking like he's holding me underwater, begging him without words to free me. He only smiles down at me. And then, with a free hand, he pinches my nose shut. I convulse, and some of his blood trickles down my throat, despite myself. I make a strangled sound and cough in muffled wetness.

"There you go." He lets go of my nose to pat my head, brushing the hair out of my eyes. "It's over now. Stop fighting it, you fool," he says gently.

It's the gentleness that gets me more than anything. *Fool, indeed.* I choke, but I swallow. It's a relief, even though I'm screaming inside. Even though tears are leaking out of the corners of my eyes. I sag back into him, knees buckling, making a cushion of his chest as I drink.

It's downright blissful. A new best.

Gavron snorts, still petting my hair. "Dear Founders, you've gotten blood everywhere. We're going to have to work on that. Don't worry, we have time." He sighs. "Endless time. But maybe we'll have to dress you in black in the meanwhile." His voice suddenly sounds almost dreamy. Almost drunk.

Does he feel something, too? If it's even close to what I'm feeling, I don't know how we're both still standing. He's entirely holding me up.

"Yes, I feel something, curse them," he mutters resentfully. "I guess it's like they say it is. Founders, I hate this."

He *hates* this? How? Even *I* don't hate this, and I should be trying to stab him instead of clinging to him. All I want to do is drink and sink deeper into his embrace.

But then he leans down, resting his chin on top of my head. We're nested together such that I don't know where he begins and I end. He sighs in what could be pleasure, if I didn't know any better.

Maybe I don't. Because a moment later he drops a kiss on my crown, as if by accident. Then he does it again, this time pressing his lips to my hair as tightly as he holds his wrist to my mouth.

Even stranger, it feels like we *belong* like this. His kiss feels as right as everything else that should feel terribly wrong about this situation.

"Stop thinking. Drink," he repeats, his voice both commanding and melodic.

I stop thinking, and I can't stop swallowing. Like his blood is water and I'm dying of thirst. I surrender myself to it entirely, my eyes closing. I don't know if I could ever quit on my own.

But then, much too soon, he says, "All right, Little Fish. That's enough. Sleep now," and I feel my body falling limp in his arms.

II

WINTER

6

My dreams are filled with crimson sprays of blood. Gavron's blood, flooding my mouth, black, chill, and delicious. And Gavron himself, his bleeding wrist pressed to my lips. His strong arms cradling me. His cold, elegant fingers caressing my cheek. His tender kisses atop my head.

The damned bastard. I don't want him in my dreams.

I wake in my own bed—though it's still odd to think of this massive, ornate stone room as *mine*—with late afternoon light slanting through the stained-glass windows. Even the strange, filtered light is overly bright, making me flinch and squint. I scrub at my eyes and kick free of my sheets. I hear fabric tear as I stumble out of bed with more force than I intended, slamming into my washstand and nearly toppling with it. I grip the carved edge, its intricate patterns biting into my skin, and I stare over the porcelain washbasin and into the mirror above.

My eyes are no longer their nondescript brownish gray, but pale—the color of raw fat just exposed by a butcher's knife. Ringing what were once my irises is a black circle, with tendrils beginning to crawl inward like a sickness. No, like Gavron's blood in me. They could still pass as human eyes, but they look diseased.

As I inspect my irises, a bubble of panic rising in my chest, my pupils shrink to pinpoints and the colors of the room return to normal brightness. And yet, everything is still richer and sharper than I remember it being before. I'm so distracted by my improved eyesight that it takes me a moment to notice the other changes in my appearance.

The dark hollows under my eyes and cheeks are gone. My skin is clear and smooth where it was dull and chapped. I let my hair swing into place, and I feel its thickness, less like dead straw and more like living wheat now, falling in a straight sheath to my shoulders.

I hate to admit, not all the changes are bad.

If Gavron's blood healed me from a mortal wound, then ingesting it has done even more. It's starting to make me *im*mortal. At that disturbing thought, I lift my upper lip to check my teeth. They, at least, are the same as I remember.

Despite my eyes, these new improvements could suit my purposes. Before, I only wanted to hide. To stay alive in the shadows. Now I need to be strong if I'm going to survive this place. Instead of being translucent and flimsy as parchment, I need to hone my edges. Make myself a blade.

And maybe that's already starting to happen. Something springs to life in my chest at the thought, climbing over the fear that there might be no coming back from this, no hope of escape.

I look over my shoulder and catch sight of the ragged edge of silk I left behind. I'm apparently strong enough to tear my bedsheets just getting out of bed.

"That's definitely different," I say. Even my voice sounds stronger.

My door bursts open, and Marai's own powerful voice precedes her inside. "Isn't it great? You can hear better, too! I heard you say that out in the hallway!"

Marai was already strong and healthy, but her dark brown skin practically glows with a new luster, and her hair bounces in a cloud of even more perfect spirals around her head, her motions vibrant. Almost too vibrant—manic. Her eyes, like mine, have turned so pale their original color is nearly gone. Except they're ringed in red, with veinlike lines streaking inward.

"Pretty sure I'd be able to hear *you* out in the hallway without better ears," I grumble.

"I project, remember? You don't. Although, now . . ." She eyes me up and down. "You look incredible."

I look away to fight a blush. No one has *ever* told me I look incredible.

"So do you," I mumble.

"Still think this is the worst thing that could ever happen to us?" she asks with a smirk.

"Maybe not, but we're not through it yet." My stomach clenches as I turn back to my reflection. "We have a long way to go, and where we end up might be worse than we could ever imagine."

You can still escape, I tell myself silently. I don't sound convincing, not even to my own mind.

"If you mean ending up as a corpse or as a thrall, sure. But if all you mean is what we'll need to eat someday, I see that as a small price to pay."

"Blood," I enunciate, meeting her eyes in the mirror. "We'll have to drink human blood, Marai."

Call dung dung. The thought of drinking human blood is barely more appealing than consuming *that*. At least that hasn't changed with our small transformations. I don't have a sudden urge to bite someone.

As long as that someone isn't Gavron, comes the unbidden thought.

"If human blood tastes anything like Claudia's blood, I'll consider myself supremely lucky." Marai sighs dreamily. "I've never drunk anything that delicious."

My stomach gives another twist. Except this time it's out of hunger, not revulsion.

Which is disgusting in its own right.

Gavron and my wanting to drink his blood *now* weigh heavily on the wrong side of the scale. Would that I could forget about him—

that arrogant bastard—but my connection to him is the source of all this, good and bad.

Maybe the fact that he has a dread blade is worth ignoring the bad.

And yet, if he thinks I'm going to treat him like the Father Incarnate, he has another think coming. That he seems as burdened by me as I am by him only makes my teeth grind. He didn't have to take me on, and I certainly didn't ask him to.

At the same time, I'm probably better off with him than I would be with the likes of Kashire, Maudon, or Claudia, who seem to have crueler streaks. Only Maudon among them might have a dread blade like Gavron, if my suspicion about the Black Court is correct, and I'm not sure it would be worth getting close to him, even for that.

For my purposes, Gavron might be the best of bad options.

And yet, Marai looks intoxicated, despite who her maker is.

"How was Claudia?" I ask reluctantly, turning to face her.

Marai stares at me with wide, pale eyes. I definitely preferred her warm brown, *human* eye color—not that mine are any better now. "She's amazing. She's so powerful and confident. And when she . . ." Now she looks away, unexpectedly bashful. "It was very nice," she says. "How was it for you?"

I scowl at my torn sheets. "Now that I'm stronger, I can try to hit him harder next time. Not that I landed a single blow."

Marai gapes at me. "You *fought* him? Why would you do that?"

"Not all of us found the experience *very nice*," I snap, except, as soon as the words are out of my mouth, I know they're not entirely true. My jaw clenches so hard I actually hear a creak.

Marai sobers. "Oh. I'm sorry. Are you . . . okay?"

I sigh, suddenly wishing I hadn't brought down her mood. "I've had worse treatment."

What I'm not even admitting to her, or even myself, is how damnably *good* it felt with Gavron, despite the fear and anger and helplessness. How much I want to do it *again*.

No, don't think about that. Focus on how much you hate him.

"Was he nicer this morning?" Marai asks. "Well, before first light? I guess we're supposed to think of that as bedtime now."

I blink. "I haven't seen him since . . . you know."

"Oh!" Marai's surprise is written on her face, but she quickly erases it. "Claudia came to see me before dawn, to see how I was adjusting to the changes." She hesitates. "If you didn't enjoy your time with Gavron, perhaps it's better that he didn't come."

All I remember is Gavron telling me to go to sleep. Claudia evidently wasn't that abrupt with Marai.

I can't tell if I'm relieved or affronted that Gavron didn't check on me. He did this to me, after all. Even if he had no choice. And even if I don't hate *everything* about it.

I still hate *him*.

His words echo Silvea's in my mind: *I should have let you die.*

Too late, I think with grim satisfaction.

"So, you're stronger now?" Marai asks. "Does that mean I am? I hadn't tried much of anything new yet."

Just then there's a knock at the door.

"Come in!" Marai calls, before I can suggest anything else.

It's a male servant with a gilded tray of food, which he deposits at my bedside table. "Since you didn't attend in the main hall, I was sent to deliver your breakfast, my lady."

"Don't call me that," I snap, folding my arms tight against my chest. "I'm not a lady."

Marai raises her eyebrows. "You *are* above him as a novice, according to vampire etiquette."

"Still," I insist. "Not a lady."

"All right." Marai eyes him, head to toe. He's tall and well-built. "I wonder if I can test my strength on him. Hey, sir," she addresses him. "Would you arm wrestle me, as if we're sailors in a tavern?" She gives a high, giddy laugh, and I remember the breathlessness with which she said, *We can do whatever we want.* "Wait, maybe I can even . . ." She stares deep into his eyes. Her voice changes, sounding more commanding and melodic at the same time. "*Arm wrestle me.*"

"Your wish is my command," he responds tonelessly.

"Marai!" I cry. "Don't enthrall him!"

"Why not? We have to learn how to do it sooner or later."

"Then *later*," I nearly shriek, "and not in my bedroom!"

She holds up placating hands. "Calm down! I'm not sure it even worked. Did it?" she asks the servant.

All he does is bow. "It is my nature to serve."

She frowns. "Hmm, he's already enthralled. That doesn't really clarify things. *Fine.*" She sighs and gestures at him. "Please leave."

He bows again and backs out the door. Marai regards me, irked at first and then a little sheepish. "I'm sorry," she says. "I forget enthrallment is so horrible to you. Even if I'm used to it, that doesn't mean I love it. But we *are* going to have to learn it, so you might as well get used to it, too."

The thought stops me cold. "I don't know if I can."

She grimaces. "Then you might end up a thrall yourself." She pauses, softening. "Come on, Fin. You're a survivor. You can manage."

Can I? I wonder. If I'd rather die than become a thrall, could I enthrall others to stay alive? I'm not sure. What I do know is the longer I stay here, trying to discover how to kill monsters, the more monstrous I'll become.

As I'm pondering that morbid thought, there's another knock at the door. This time, a female servant enters, bearing a swath of black fabric in her arms.

"Your clothes, my—"

"Don't call her *my lady*," Marai interrupts, and I shoot her a grateful look.

The servant appears mildly startled behind the faint glow in her eyes. "As you wish. Here are your garments for today, sent by your maker, Gavron."

"Don't call him my *maker*," I spit.

Now the servant looks so thoroughly confused that Marai takes pity on her. "Please leave," she tells her, too.

The servant sets the clothes on the bed and backs away slowly as if we're dangerous.

Maybe we are.

"We're probably never going to get good service with you, are we?" Marai exclaims, exasperated, spinning on me after the door closes again.

It draws a grim laugh from me, despite myself.

She smiles back at me, and then glances at the pile of fabric. "What's this?" Without waiting for an answer, she picks up the garment, shaking it out.

It's black like Gavron promised, and it's a gown. It's less voluminous than my last one, but I can see the familiar bone stays of a corset.

"I'm not wearing it," I declare.

Marai's eyes pop. "But won't that anger him?"

"I don't care." That only alarms her further. I smile reassuringly, and even force myself to joke, "I wonder who I have to enthrall to get a pair of pants?"

I wore woolen pants under my skirts in the village for warmth, and would have rather lost the skirts altogether, since they tangled up my legs as I walked. But extra layers were preferable to freezing to death.

"I'm sure I can help with clothes," Marai says, "and I daresay without any enthralling, since *I* know how to interact with servants. Maybe I can find what you're looking for even before lessons."

I blink. "When are those?"

"You didn't see? Oh, yours is right here." Before I can ask, *My what?*, she bends down and scoops up a folded piece of parchment off the floor. "The schedule was delivered to us while we were sleeping. You must not have noticed." She unfolds it and hands it to me.

I'm glad she didn't assume I was illiterate. I try to shake the memory of Silvea hunched over her herbalists journals with me, explaining how to sound out each letter to make words, and then eventually sentences. It was boring reading, but I didn't care, sitting at her fuller table, in front of her bigger hearth . . . and especially next to her, the firelight playing over her soft features. Making her glow.

I swallow the sudden tightness in my throat.

"Here, you look at this and I'll go speak to the necessary people about clothes," Marai says. I don't know what she's seen in my face, but she slips out quickly as I turn to the piece of parchment.

It reveals a grid laid out in spidery black ink. *Winter Season* is written atop it, the days of the week under that, and various lessons speckled throughout. Shortly after sunset, I have Red Court Basic with Claudia—*lucky me*—followed by Gold Court Basic with Pavella, later in the . . . evening? It'll be early morning by that point, but like Marai just reminded me, it won't help us adjust to think of it like that. So I settle on *night*.

The Silver and Blue Courts' lessons are tomorrow with Jaen and Kashire, and then the schedule repeats over the following two days. *Nights.*

I should be more focused on who's teaching half of my lessons, since Claudia and Kashire will no doubt make things unpleasant for me. But before I realize it, I'm scanning for *his* name. On the fifth day before we take our weekly break—*(For the purpose of doing as you see fit and integrating in your leisure time)*—I find it: Black Court Basic, Gavron. *(Optional.)*

I've had no intention of going—neither of risking death more than I already am nor of being around Gavron any more than I have to. But I keep staring at his name.

69

The thought of seeing him again is more intriguing than it should be. I tell myself it's because of the dread blade he wields.

But then I spot something else. For Black Court Basic, the schedule instructs us to meet at the Black Gates. If I want to maintain a hope of escaping, it would pay to know my exit better. It might be worth the risk. It's certainly worth pondering.

Not long after I've finished my breakfast—the entire tray, since I was ravenous—Marai returns with a stack of clothes draped over her arms. She glances at the empty plates.

"You, too, huh? I felt like I could have gone for seconds. It's probably the changes making us so hungry, like growing children."

I'm abruptly ill. Normal food won't be what my body wants for long, unlike a child's.

"Here we are," she declares, dumping the clothes on my bed. "You'll look like a stable boy, but some people like that." She gives me an exaggerated wink, and I can't help but smile. There are finely woven breeches to tuck into tall black boots, and a loose white shirt with a trim black vest. "The shirt was the biggest problem since I couldn't find one slight enough," she adds, "but the vest will hold it in. A corset would look better, but I can't imagine—"

"No. Thank you." I've had enough of those after only wearing one.

Over the top of all of this will go my fur-lined cloak. Somehow I doubt a stable boy would have a garment as nice as that. But as long as I'm warm and I no longer look like someone you could address as *my lady*, I honestly don't care what I look like.

"Why are you helping me?" I ask suddenly, turning to Marai.

She shrugs. "You don't like being forced into a corner that doesn't fit you. I don't, either."

The ways I don't fit in are entirely different from hers, even if we're both here to pursue our dreams, in a sense. She wants to become a vampire. I want to kill them.

"That still doesn't mean you should help me," I say. "So, why are you?"

She looks taken aback. "We're friends, remember? Friends help each other."

"So, you're expecting me to help you," I say, suspicion leaking into my tone. "What do you want in return?"

She throws up her arms. "Blood and piss, Fin! I want *nothing* right now, except maybe someone to watch my back while I have theirs." She raises one eyebrow and glares. "Have you ever *had* a friend?"

I open my mouth, then close it. I shake my head. Silvea wasn't my friend.

"Sorry," I say. "Truly, Marai. I'm *not* used to friendship or getting something for nothing. The only time I have, everything went . . . wrong."

Marai looks somewhat assuaged. And pitying. "Well, don't poison the well because you're afraid to drink from it. Especially not if you're thirsty."

"Who says I'm thirsty?" I mutter, but a smile is creeping back onto my face.

Her expression turns sly. "I don't know. Maybe we should ask Gavron. Are you *sure* you didn't like the taste of his blood? Maybe *he* can tell me how much you actually——"

She can't finish because I've hurled a pillow at her. Just as fast, Marai chops it from the air before it can hit her, wielding her arm as powerfully as an axe. The pillow bursts, raining feathers around us like snowflakes.

We're both startled into silence, white tufts drifting between us.

"That was entirely your fault," Marai says.

And then we're both doubled over, laughing too hard to speak.

7

After sunset, Marai and I wind our way through the elaborate maze of Courtsheart's halls to our first lesson. She loops her arm through mine as we walk, exclaiming about various pieces of art we pass. I'm not used to someone casually touching me, but her sonorous stream of information keeps my attention elsewhere. In addition to singing, she's studied painting, history, vampire society . . .

My eyes mostly dart around, sharper and quicker than they've ever been, looking for danger. It's how I used to walk alone in my village.

This isn't what you're used to, I remind myself.

It might be worse, despite Marai's company and our luxurious surroundings. Even with enhanced senses, I might not be able to sense any danger coming. The interior design of the castle is like spiderwebs of stone, intricately carved lines gathering in every corner and draping over our heads. Even the hallways themselves are laid out in a weblike fashion, widening outward. Maybe these patterns are meant to capture our attention so we don't notice what's sneaking up behind us.

Which makes vampires the spiders, and the rest of us flies.

Despite the seeming frivolity of some of Marai's tutoring, she's far more prepared for Courtsheart than I am. After she mentions something about vampire philosophy, I say, "You sound like you're on the path to join the Silver Court."

She scoffs. "All of *that* is just what I was forced to study by my parents and tutors. That's not what I want as a vampire."

"What do you want, other than your *wildest dreams?*" I quote, nudging her with a smirk.

"Pretty much that." She sighs deeply. "I want to explore and fight . . . *love*."

It's essentially the motto of the Red Court: *Blaze and Bleed.* Maybe she's somehow in the right place with Claudia, though I find that hard to imagine. My dislike for Claudia aside, I'm not sure why anyone would want to expose themselves like that, blazing and bleeding for all the world to see. Shadows are comforting. Concealing. Marai has obviously come from a far richer family than I have, so perhaps she feels safe.

"Don't you miss your family?"

She frowns. "Not really. They never really saw me."

Her words hit me like a blow to a still-healing wound.

"I mean, they always paraded me around," she says, "made sure I learned all the subjects they thought I should know. Didn't get too attached to me. Perhaps because they wanted me to become favored. I was just another piece on the game board for them. I don't know if they were happy or disappointed that I drew the white feather, if that played into their schemes or hindered them. They certainly didn't care if I was happy or not. It was never about me, you see. I was always supposed to become a vampire. Probably under the Gold Court." She makes a disgusted face.

"I see," I say. At least I'm starting to. Marai is making her new life about *her* now—her happiness. It's hard to fault her for that, especially since she's never had much choice but to become a vampire. And especially since she's still trying to be a good friend.

I vaguely wonder if I should follow her lead. Seek *happiness*. It's an unfamiliar word, a strange shape in my mind. Maybe more of an absence. The fishing line of my dreams is tangled, to be sure. Before I can unravel these knots any further in my head, we arrive where our first lesson will be held.

Claudia stands in a wide courtyard sheltered by arching stone pillars, her impressive longsword strapped to her back, daggers on her hips and thighs. No skirts impede her now. She's wearing soft tan leather with only subtle red accents and her long brown curls are pulled back in a tight tail. I'm somewhat relieved to see that outside of events like Findings and Beginnings, vampires don't *only* adhere to the color of their court. To be so bound for eternity would be tedious.

Though perhaps Gavron is as tedious as the reputation of his court. *We'll have to dress you in black*, I hear him say in that dreamy voice.

The thought makes me flush, and I furiously swear to myself that I'll never wear any of the items he sends me . . . unless a dread blade is included.

Focus.

Red Court Basic has a title so *basic* I have no idea what it will entail. Judging by Claudia's manner of dress and that it looks like we're trapped in a finely wrought cage, I have a clue. A troupe of traveling performers once visiting our village set up an enclosure like this for a dogfight. This is far more expansive, though I hope it will be less bloody. Somehow, I doubt it.

Marai doesn't seem nearly as nervous as I am. She's once again dancing on the balls of her feet, eager at the sight of the Red Court vampire.

"Welcome to Blades." Claudia starts speaking before we've barely assembled with the other novices, fewer than the seventeen at our Beginning—only nine of us, in fact. "The Red Court teaches the arts of seduction and weapons. Your maker will have chosen your focus. If you're here to learn the sword and dagger, you're in the right place. If you hoped to study seduction, you're most assuredly in the wrong place. You'll want Havere, my Red Court brother, down the hall."

There are a few snickers, though this is all new to me. Seduction is where the other novices must be. I'm relieved they haven't already died. And I'm also relieved, against all odds and despite Gavron not consulting me, that I'm here in Claudia's lesson and not the other. Seduction sounds like a nightmare.

"However," Claudia continues, "unlike other House skills that have a more linear progression, you'll be expected to take a basic lesson in both Blades and Seduction. You only need advance in a single track, but if you were hoping to avoid one entirely, you can't. Not without losing the Red Court's mark of approval—also known as *failing*."

Blood and piss. I wonder how long I can put off Seduction. Maybe I can save it till the final season. With any luck, I'll have escaped by then.

A novice raises her hand. She was among the favored, though I can't remember by which House. When Claudia nods her permission to speak, the novice says, "My lady, I've only ever wanted to kill people. Not the *other* thing."

Claudia smiles indulgently. "You only have to get by—you don't have to excel. Even knowing how to fake it can be exceedingly useful." She lifts a delicate-looking hand and shrugs, graceful as a dancer. "It's all I've ever done."

I glance at Marai, wondering if she's bothered by such an unromantic admission, but she's only gazing at Claudia with admiration. Maybe it's their bond. I can't imagine ever looking at Gavron like that, despite certain errant thoughts of mine.

"Let's begin," Claudia says, and gestures to the weapon racks. "We'll start small, and work up to bigger weapons as your arm strength increases. Everyone take a dagger."

I have my fillet knife at my hip, but I select a dagger along with the rest of the novices, the leather-bound grip unfamiliar in my hand. We gather back in the center of the courtyard, where Claudia begins to pair us up. I do a quick sum and find we have an odd number.

My stomach plummets when Claudia says, "Fin, with me, if you please."

I do not *please*, but I don't say that. Surprisingly, Marai makes a noise of protest.

"My dear." Claudia cups her cheek. "We can practice all you like, just the two of us. I should focus more on other novices, in session." Her red eyes flicker to me in disdain. "Especially those who need it most."

Those she wants to murder the most, she probably means. Or to beat senseless, at least—which she proceeds to do with great alacrity and skill.

She bats aside my first clumsy thrust with her bare hand and trips me onto my back before I can blink. She stares down at me, waiting for me to get up. Unsurprisingly, she doesn't offer me a hand.

Once I'm up, she does it again.

Only every so often does she point out what I'm doing wrong. She most delights in *showing* me. Over and over.

Truth is, I *am* behind most everyone in combat. Even Marai has had basic self-defense training. The only one worse off than me is the foundling boy who was chosen last at our Beginning. His name is Lief. He's paired now with the self-professed killer-at-heart— Gabriella—and already has tears running down his face. *Poor kid,* I think, never mind that he's only a couple of years younger than me, at most.

Poor me, I revise, as Claudia violently twists my arm behind my back and my knife drops from my nerveless fingers.

"Always keep your knife on you," she hisses. "You never know what's coming."

A threat, no doubt. How kind of her to warn me. I still have my fillet knife, but I think she'll appreciate it about as much as Kashire did if I stab her with it.

Bent over like I am, I suddenly spot Maudon, watching us from the shadows between an arch. I can't spare him much attention, but the next time I glance in his direction, he's gone.

"Does Maudon often observe your lessons?" I gasp at Claudia as she traps my arm again.

She lifts me off my feet, the bones in my arm creaking and my toes dangling. "Maudon doesn't concern you, little one, and it would be best for you to avoid his attention," she snarls. "It's worse than mine."

And then she knees me in the stomach and drops me in a heap.

<hr />

Needless to say, I'm sore during Gold Court lessons later that night.

The Gold Court teaches the skills of governance, mind reading, and enthrallment, our instructor Pavella tells us. While she isn't violent, she doesn't make me feel any less humiliated than Claudia. Much as in Blades, I'm far behind before I even begin.

Gold Court Basic's true, long-winded title is *Codes of Conduct: Etiquette and Leadership*—Conduct, for short—which covers the laws binding both the rulers and the ruled of our land. In other words, vampires of all ranks and their decidedly lesser human counterparts.

Growing up in my remote village as I have, I don't know the first thing about any of that. Marai whispers information to me when she can. But Pavella, a golden-eyed, bronze-skinned beauty with a braided crown of blond hair, tells her to be silent.

You would think Pavella would be twice as tall with such a towering impression of herself, but she's actually shorter than my middling height. Maybe that's why she chooses me first for a demonstration, standing me up in front of the novices to tear me down. I half wonder if Claudia or Gavron put her up to it. She tells me my assigned role, which I must then properly act out according to whatever rank of vampire she pretends to be, making a fool out of myself since I have no chance of getting it right. She pairs up the rest of the novices and constantly gives the foundlings the worst treatment, though none so much as me.

We're like puppets made to dance on her invisible strings of rules, and I already hate her for it.

Before dawn, I'm ready to collapse into bed and cry. I refuse to. I fall asleep with my jaw clenched so hard, it's a wonder I don't wake up with broken teeth.

When my eyes next open to twilight, I feel broken everywhere else. Thoughts of escape are louder than they've ever been. But at least these lessons promise to teach me *something*. I just need to be strong. Or wait long enough to *get* stronger.

Besides, I don't think I can escape right now. This is a fortress swarming with vampires, the exit barred by the Black Gates. I'd never make it out. Not yet.

I haul myself out of bed, muscles aching, to eat breakfast, and then walk to Silver Court Basic with Marai.

While the topic is as tedious as Conduct—*The Unavoidably Simplified and Yet Nonetheless Hallowed Journey of Our Kind*, or the actually simplified Vampire History—the instructor, Jaen, doesn't shame anyone for what they don't know.

Of course, Jaen is lovely, with straight black hair that falls to her waist like a silken cape, tawny skin, and hooded silver eyes. Marai can barely keep her own eyes off her as soon as we enter the sprawling study scattered with tables and chairs. The walls are lined in maps, charts of the stars, and shelves holding jars containing strange forms submerged in liquid, among other things.

The Silver Court is primarily concerned with the sciences of preservation and healing, Jaen tells us. Somehow, history is a part of this. She neither asks many questions so we can prove our knowledge or our lack thereof, nor pits us against one another. She simply passes out books to each of us and starts recounting vampiric history in a fluid, calming voice.

We're supposed to remember what she's saying, but the lesson is downright relaxing—too much so. I start to drift, and when Jaen clears her throat and I stammer my apologies, she only gives me a smile and continues.

Perhaps I shouldn't be surprised that Revar's pupil and one-time apprentice is as calm and informative as they are, but I never expected *kindness* from a vampire.

I tell Marai as much as we walk to the most dreaded of our lessons—Blue Court Basic under Kashire's direction.

"Vampires can be kind," Marai says. "Claudia is kind to me."

"Are you sure she's not enthralling you to think that?" I ask wryly, remembering all too keenly my treatment at her hands yestereve.

Marai glares at me. "She wouldn't do that. I trust her. And if you won't respect her, at least respect *my* judgment." I've clearly hit a nerve. Before I can respond with any sort of apology, she snaps, "Just because *your* maker is terrible doesn't mean everyone's is."

I shut my mouth abruptly.

She groans. "Sorry. It's just that you have a similar outlook on vampires as you do on friends. They're not all terrible, Fin. And Gavron is mostly awful for ignoring you at a time like this."

I don't answer, wanting to leave all talk of Claudia *or* Gavron behind. Although, it does beg the question that I hardly want to ask myself:

Where *is* he?

———————⋆✵⋆———————

Kashire's lessons are held in a small dining hall—small by Courtsheart's standards, anyway—that has high ceilings that arch over a massive dining table stretching the length of the room. Side tables line the lamplit walls, their contents covered in cloths.

Kashire stands at the head of the table and wastes no time, clapping his hands. "Be seated, my sweet, tender novices! It's time to learn how to crush and rebuild yourselves."

I'm still sore from Blades, so I don't like the sound of that, but I take a seat next to Marai.

When we're settled, Kashire begins. "Your lessons from the Blue Court in these next undying seasons involve the techniques of masking and shapeshifting. Namely, they're all going to be about *change*. Not change that moves *away* from yourself, but inward. It's more about getting in touch with our deeper natures, as we of the Blue Court are wont to do. There are some aspects of yourselves that will be forever difficult to change, those that are our strongest outer layers. This varies from person to person, but they tend to include things like your basic temperament, your skin color or height, or the markers of human sex—unless, of course, you have a misalignment or, shall we say, *flexibility* in that area, and then it comes quite easily. Some vampires will have a hard time even changing their cheekbones. So don't try to look as beautiful as *me*"—he gestures at himself with a flourish—"because you won't succeed."

"Then what *can* we do?" someone asks sulkily. Thank the Father they're not sitting next to me. I have no desire to draw any special attention from Kashire.

But the Blue Court vampire only shrugs. "Maybe nothing, if you don't have it in you. Just as there are those who will never shadowstep or become master enthrallers, you might never succeed at this. While you must only excel in one House, you still need to become proficient in at least two other Houses' skill sets. Since studying under the Black Court is optional—and I don't recommend it— this allows you to be abominable in only *one* of the Houses. But you shouldn't get complacent, because you never know where you might fail. That *should* scare you, children." He levels a look at all of us, so blue and so cold that we all freeze.

"So," he continues, breezy again, "if you want to surpass the Blue Court's base standard, you must first be able to change your face such that another can't recognize you for yourself. It's a very important tool for survival, if you ever find yourself surrounded by a human mob, for example. We call each face you master a *mask*, even though it's as much your own face as the one you wear now. For your purposes as a novice, you only need a firm grasp on one. But there are those in the Blue Court who have dozens."

His own face suddenly shifts. One second, Kashire is before us, frighteningly beautiful, the next is a man with the same warm brown skin but completely different features and short-cropped hair instead of a cloud of curls. Before we can blink, the usual Kashire is back.

"And," he continues as if nothing happened, "later in the seasons, for your final test, you must be able to shapeshift into your inner animal."

We all stare at him, and then glance at each other. *Inner animal?*

Kashire melts again, but this time, it's not just his face. His entire body blurs and then seems to collapse in on itself—leaving a raven standing on the back of a chair, one with impossibly blue eyes. It caws brightly and flaps enormous wings, launching into the air. It takes a turn about the room, diving low enough over novices' heads to ruffle their hair and make them duck. Me it actually clips with its talons, yanking off a few strands of my hair.

Once the raven is back where it started, it blurs, elongates, and then Kashire is standing there once more.

"Such as with masks," he says, "some Blue Court members can shift into dozens of animals. Most of you—unless you're miserable failures—will only manage one. Your truest animal reflection."

Everyone seems thoroughly bedazzled by Kashire's transformation, but all I can see in my mind's eye is the cat from my childhood, sitting by my cot and looking at me with gleaming eyes. *Forget your mother. She has forgotten you.* Was that a vampire, then? It must have been. Perhaps a messenger from my mother . . . Or is there any way the cat itself could have been—

I sever my racing thoughts. Revar told me not to think of her, that it could be dangerous. And I'm seated in front of one of the most dangerous vampires I know, one who's already tried to kill me once.

Despite not wanting his attention, I force myself to ask, "What about your . . . other . . . transformation?"

"Ah." Kashire gives me a knowing smile, as if we share a secret between us. "That is the Blue Court specialty, which we'll teach someone only after they join the House of Winter Night. But to answer your question, my dear, that is called a *night terror*. I won't show you now because I fear my own poor novice would faint on the spot, and I am nothing if not a caring maker."

He grins at Lief, who does indeed look ready to collapse. He's worse off here than he was in Blades or Conduct. Perhaps Kashire picked him because he had to, or maybe he did it for sport. In any case, I doubt it was out of any sense of pity for the boy.

Kashire turns back to the rest of us. "None of this is illusion. These are not images you put into someone else's mind, like a Gold Court vampire would. It's not even a disguise. This is truly changing yourself. You have to believe it of yourself so strongly that the truth bursts out from inside you. But before you can learn how to do so . . ." He pauses, raising his brows.

We novices are hanging on his every word, and he knows it. Even I am. He's a charismatic showman when he's not being evil, I'll grant him that.

"You have to learn how to *let go*," he says finally. "And this, my dears, is the entire subject of your first undying season under my tutelage. For now, forget about masks and inner animals, and focus on . . . *revelry*."

We wait for something more. When nothing else is forthcoming, we look at one another in puzzlement.

"Come now, it's in the House motto, after all: *Revel and Remember.* And yet, remembrance is for the past. For your deepest selves. As for your present limitations, you need to *forget.*" He whips a cloth off a side table behind him, like a magician unveiling some trick.

All he reveals is wine. Bottle after bottle of it. I blink. He only wants us to *drink*? He can't be serious.

I'm not the only one who's baffled. Low murmurs hum all around, and no one moves.

Kashire's blue eyes narrow. "Well, drink up, unless you want to lose my House's mark of approval here and now."

Chairs scrape back and we rush for the table.

"Where are the cups?" someone asks.

"No cups," Kashire says. "You each better have a bottle empty in the next five minutes or else failure, and all that."

Marai and I quickly snatch up open bottles and raise them to each other. It's heavy in my hand. I've never had more than a sip of ale or wine before, and now I'm supposed to drink *all* of this? Marai looks nervous, but also giddy. Like this is something new and exciting and against the rules. Except we're being *told* to do it. We clink our bottles together shakily, argument in the hall long forgotten.

As it turns out, it's the first of *three* we're forced to down. Our bodies work through alcohol faster than they did before we drank vampire blood, Kashire tells us as we gulp and choke and cough and gag, but we still can get intoxicated. *Very* intoxicated, we find.

Soon, the room starts to blur and spin. My stomach is full and burning. Marai and I practically cling to each other as the effects of the wine sink deeper into us.

"Now," Kashire cries, "for the feast!"

At his words, the doors to the dining hall open and in walk . . . a parade of animals. A bear, a badger, and a cougar are first. A magpie flies overhead, and I even hear the hiss of a snake and the playful bark of a dog as they file around the table.

"Are we supposed to eat the animals?" a novice slurs, laughing.

"No, my dears." Kashire smiles, and then spreads his arms. "*You are the feast!*"

And then the night terrors come out. Dogs and snakes and badgers turn into horned creatures with massive wings and claws, just as horrifying as the first night I saw them. The other novices are less prepared than I am. I lose sight of Marai as she cries out, ducking under the table and trying to drag me with her.

But I resist. I need to see them coming, so I can be ready for them. Amid the screams and cackling laughter, I grip the hilt of my fillet knife unsteadily. Kashire actually catches my eye before horns sprout from his head, wings from his back, and claws from his fingertips. He grins at me.

"Care to dance?" he asks.

And then he seizes me, yanks me off my feet, and flies me around the room, dodging and weaving other night terrors who are twirling their own terrified novices through the air. My breath seizes in my chest, the dining hall a swirl of color and chaos and noise. I'm tempted to start screaming myself, until I realize the night terrors aren't drinking from us or hurting any of us. They're *actually* dancing with us as they fly, while we're too drunk to do more than get extremely dizzy. Already I spot one stream of vomit raining down, and I hope Kashire doesn't let me get hit with any. Or drop me. I decide to jam my fillet knife back in its sheath instead of between his ribs again.

His bright eyes track the movement. "Smart decision, love," he hisses through elongated fangs.

Absurdly, I begin to laugh. At least Kashire looks amused . . . before all the night terrors start tossing novices back and forth between one another, and he joins in.

Then I start screaming.

8

⟿

On the third day of lessons, when the two-day schedule repeats, I show up sore *and* hungover to another one of Claudia's beatings. She doesn't go any easier on me. In fact, she pushes me harder, going so far as to slice me a couple of times when I'm too slow. At first it's shocking, but then my bleeding stops quickly. By the end of class, my skin has knitted.

Despite the ache, I'm already feeling stronger.

I wonder when I'll be strong enough to make a move. The problem is, more vampire blood is the one thing that will surely make me more powerful. But Gavron hasn't offered me any again.

So I keep going to my lessons. And yet, the more I learn, I realize how little I know.

The next session of Conduct is just as horrible and embarrassing, even if it doesn't leave any marks. If only the sting of Pavella's humiliation could vanish as quickly as a cut.

At our second session of Vampire History, we walk into the strange study to find someone who looks like Jaen's male twin. Same long black hair, same skin tone, same eyes, just more masculine lines and proportions.

"Hello, sir," Marai greets, sounding disappointed. "May I ask who might you be?"

The vampire smiles. "Jaen, of course."

To Marai's credit, her jaw doesn't drop like mine does. She's been around vampires before, seen what they can do. We even just heard about it from Kashire. But, later in the lesson, when we're writing down a summary of how vampires migrated to this continent, she mutters, "I liked him better when he was *her*."

"I'm always changing, like night to day," Jaen says, suddenly leaning over us. Neither of us heard him approach. "You just have to wait for your hour."

He drifts on, checking on other novices' work. Marai buries her face in her hands, mortified.

"I thought you were too busy being enamored with Claudia, anyway," I joke, trying to distract her.

She laughs. "I am fully capable of admiring more than one woman, my friend." Then she says softer, "But it's not really like that, how I feel about Claudia. She's beautiful, impressive . . . terrifying. I'm more in awe of her than anything. And she doesn't seem like the romantic type, anyway, despite belonging to the Red Court." Marai sighs. "I just hope I don't disappoint her."

I'm not exactly sure what Claudia has done to earn such respect from Marai, but then, I haven't been privy to their private training.

I haven't been privy to *my* private training, either. I've been waiting for Gavron to appear, both dreading it and wanting . . . something . . . from him. Not only another glimpse of a dread blade, but some sort of acknowledgment. *Instruction*. Marai's accusation that he's ignoring me keeps ringing in my ears.

First he forces his blood down my throat, and then he just abandons me while all the other novices are getting coddled? Well, perhaps not Kashire's novice.

By the time my first week of lessons is at its end, I make up my mind to attend Black Court Basic, even though it's optional. Even though I hate Gavron.

He must hate me, too. But I need him to acknowledge me. To teach me what he knows. I've learned more from Claudia—some of it secondhand through Marai—than him. Here, knowledge is life. It's the means to survive. It's the shield against becoming a thrall. It's the blade in our hands. And Gavron is denying me. My resentment—and my fear—is getting harder to swallow.

And so, I'm going to see him at the one place I know I can.

Before I go, I find Marai after dusk, curled up on a plush chair in her room. She's reading a novel with the aid of only a single candle, about a vampire on a quest to save her lover from a marauding band of evil humans. Earlier, she described the story to me with bright-eyed enthusiasm, while insisting she's merely using her free time to *integrate*, as suggested. I declined when she offered to let me borrow the book after her.

Now, when I ask Marai if she wants to join me for Black Court Basic, she shakes her head, her tight spirals of hair waving emphatically. "I want people to see me coming when I'm closing in." Her wicked grin falls as she shudders. "Besides, who wants to risk ending up as mist forever? I also have a wretched headache."

I don't want to end up as mist, either, and I have a headache, too, courtesy of Kashire's second round of Revelry. But I go anyway, setting out alone, the night chilly and quiet. My breath clouds the air, and as it disperses, I try not to imagine disappearing with it.

I exit Courtsheart proper, making my way through the colonnade and toward the Black Gates. It's my first time approaching them since my arrival, and I can't help my curiosity. My desperation, even, to see what might be my only avenue of escape. I don't see any novices heading my direction, only a few servants and couriers, moving through the deepening dark and the thin crust of snow. Though I do spot one novice hurrying in the *opposite* direction—killer-girl, Gabriella.

Odd. Of all the novices, I would have thought she'd be the most interested in what the Black Court has to offer. Anything that would make her attacks more effective. So why does she look like she's running away?

87

Somehow, I'm not surprised when I arrive at the drawbridge to the Black Gates, where we were instructed to meet, and Gavron isn't there. But Kashire is. The very last vampire I want to see more of. Fitting, as far as my week has been going.

He grins at me as I approach. "How's the head?"

Revelry last night was no more directed than the first night, though it was less terrifying. This time, he had us drink ourselves blind out in the courtyard during a snowfall, and I ended up making snow spirits with Marai, laughing hysterically as we flung white powder everywhere at inhuman speeds with our flapping limbs. That was actually fun, but I ended the evening by vomiting. I half think Kashire doesn't know what he's doing, other than wanting to toy with us like rats in a barrel. Drunken rats.

"It's stuffed with wool, thanks to you," I say, before I can check my tone.

"Maybe everything is too tightly wound in there." He moves like lightning and flicks my forehead, making my headache rebound tenfold. "Like I've said, you need to loosen up. Let go. Enjoy yourself a little, like I *so* hope you do tonight."

I hiss, clapping a hand to my brow, and glance around. "Where is everyone?"

He shrugs nonchalantly. "Perhaps they're not interested. My own novice certainly wasn't. Practically wet himself at the suggestion of coming." He shivers in mock horror. "*Human bodily functions.* So unnecessary. Still, I thought I would be here to see how my dearest Gav's first lesson starts off. You know, *supervise*, since I'm so much more experienced."

I narrow my eyes at him. Aside from his casual discouragement in class, I have the sneaking suspicion that the Blue Court vampire has scared everyone away from this potentially dangerous training, using threats or bribes or simply his mere presence. He even chased off Gabriella.

Leaving only me.

It's obvious why he would do such a thing. He deliberately foisted me as a novice upon Gavron to torment him, and Gavron has successfully avoided me all week. I nearly laugh. For the first time and probably the last, Kashire and I actually have a shared interest. I'm not eager for this particular lesson, either, but I want to force Gavron to at least look at me.

And I wouldn't mind getting another look at *him*—his weapons, at least, I tell myself.

"Kashire, I must ask you to never lay a hand on her again," says a pleasant, deep voice behind me, making me jump. "She's my novice, not yours."

I spin around to find Gavron smiling, though his expression looks as painted on as it did before. Frustratingly, he's even more handsome than I remember, his jaw and cheekbones a sharp frame for those sensual lips. He doesn't meet my eyes, his dark gaze on Kashire. My heart immediately picks up speed, in both fear and anticipation—because *finally*, here he is. I hope neither of them can hear it.

Kashire puts a hand to his chest. "I swear I won't, outside of the necessity of my own lessons." He grins. "Unless you ask me to."

"I won't," Gavron says, and I swallow something disagreeably close to gratitude. His smile grows sharper, deeper, more carved with a knife than limned with a brush. "Speaking of your lessons, you've taught all of two sessions more than me, and now you think you're an expert? Why *are* you here? I didn't expect many to show—except my own novice, of course," he adds quickly, tossing an arm around my shoulders—as if trying to keep up appearances. "This lesson is for novices only, my friend, even if you failed to gain the Black Court's mark of approval. Are you even allowed to attend?"

Kashire waves Gavron away. "I don't know, don't care, and have no interest in attending your gruesomely boring lecture, my love. I just wanted to make sure it got off to a good start." And with that, he gives us a wink and then strolls off into the night, whistling.

Gavron stares after him, then turns on me, still under his arm. I keep my back straight under the withering force of his look. I throw off his weight as soon as Kashire is out of sight.

"Well?" I say, glowering up at him. "Are you planning on teaching me anything *ever*, O Great Maker? You're doing a piss-poor job of it."

I must not have learned my lesson from Kashire's flick. I hope Gavron doesn't respond in kind, because I doubt my skull could withstand it.

He only folds his arms. "Are you sure you want to do this? I can't convince you otherwise?"

I don't let myself think of what I might truly want or even look in the direction of his blades. He might see the truth on my face. "Why have you been avoiding me?" I demand instead.

"Because thoughts of you are too consuming as it is," he says simply, and I nearly choke. "Before you flatter yourself," he adds, "it's only part of the blood claim. You're a distraction I can't afford right now."

I make my voice firm, try to project like Marai. "If you're as bad at your other duties as you are at giving me guidance, then I don't think I'm the problem."

His eyes flash. "Watch yourself, Little Fish."

"Yes," I enunciate in answer to his previous question. "I want to be here."

He looks me up and down. "You're not wearing any of the clothes I sent you."

I don't expect that turn in the conversation. "And?"

"*And* if you'd bothered to glance at them, you would have noticed I sent you an outfit with pants as well as skirts, rendering *this* clumsy disaster you're wearing unnecessary. I also included instructions on how best to equip yourself. Trust me, it involved more than that fish-poker." He glances disdainfully at my fillet knife. "At least you didn't show up in a dress, even if you look like a stable boy."

"Better than a vampire's doll," I fire right back at him. I can't believe the servants *tattled* on me. Actually, I can. He is supposedly my *maker*, after all, and they're enthralled to obey. What I can't believe is that he bothered to check on me even from a distance.

Gavron's smile bares two very particular teeth. "Trust me, Little Fish, I don't play with dolls."

"Oh?" I try to make my voice unconcerned. "What do you play with?"

"Life and death."

That makes my stomach flutter, and not in a good way. But maybe this is something I can use, if his lessons cover vampire death.

He must see enough in my expression to think that I'm cowed. "In the future, I'll not have you dressed like this. And, dear Founders, please eat something so you don't look like you're nigh starving."

"What do you care?" I snap.

"Like it or not, you're my novice. It's my duty to provide for you."

My blood goes from simmer to boil. "I'm afraid providing for me involves more than fancy clothes and food. I managed well enough without those before I got here. You need to teach me about your world if I'm going to survive it, and that involves suffering my odious presence longer than it takes to fool Kashire. Whom you *haven't* fooled, in case it's not obvious."

Gavron looks around, as if noting all those who aren't in attendance. "I see that."

"I wanted to get you alone, anyway," I add, before I can think better of it.

He arches a brow. "Why?"

Because I need you, is my immediate thought, but I don't say that. "So you can teach me!" I say, fighting a blush. I gesture at him violently. "If *this* is all it takes for you to be my maker, please tell me the rest of this has all been a nightmare. Tell me I'm not actually bound to you through your blood." My voice gets a little ragged at the end. "Tell me I can *leave*."

He tosses his head impatiently. "Of course you're bound to me, and of course you can't leave." Now it's his turn to sneer. "You say you want to learn from me, and yet you've just admitted you don't want this life."

Something in his tone says *you don't deserve it, either*, and it makes me snarl, "But I want to *live*. And, right now, without any help, my chances don't look promising." I step right up to him and poke his chest with a finger. "So stop pretending and actually do your duty!"

For a second, I worry he might erupt with anger, but instead he grows calm, still. He steps even closer to me, my face level with his chest. His hand reaches up to touch my cheek in a gentle downward stroke, like a falling tear.

The feeling between us is tangible, nearly a vibration in the air. A *pull* toward each other.

"You're so fragile," he says, his voice soft. "So fickle. You'll accept becoming a vampire, just to stay alive? You realize that means the human part of you will die, all the same? That to survive as a vampire you need to *consume* the life force you're so pathetically clinging to? This is a cost you're willing to pay?"

His touch—so impossibly *right* and *good*—isn't enough to distract me from his disturbing questions, all of which I've begun to ask myself as I've tossed and turned in bed.

Except I wouldn't become a vampire just to survive. I only would if it was the last path open to me. And even then death is always an option. At least, I hope.

Even that choice might be taken from me if I'm made into a vampire. It certainly would be taken from me as a thrall, where I would die only when my body gave out or someone killed me.

Is Gavron asking why I don't make the decision to die now, while I still can?

The absolute bastard. Easy for him to ask, from his position.

I know why I can't die yet, but I don't owe him any answers and I wouldn't be wise to give them. He owes *me*.

"*You* must have been willing to pay the price." My voice comes out hoarse. I refuse to retreat. Or worse, lean closer to him.

His black eyes are flat. "I didn't have a choice. I was born to this life."

I dredge up enough fire to brush his hand away from me. "That's absurd. You can't be born a vampire."

He smiles grimly. "But you can be born *marked* as one. The Black Court understands this better than the other Houses with their favored pets, coddled from childhood. We're not coddled; we're forged. And we certainly know what a farce the Finding is. At best, it's a death sentence. Worse, an insult to our kind. All you are good for is practice fodder."

Logs to the flame. Grain for the mill. Straw dummies for the sword.

I want to slap the smug look from his face, but I don't. He's given me all the more incentive to learn what he knows. To arm myself however I can. Which means I can't drive him away. I need to get closer to him, no matter how maddening a task that is.

"And you might as well be asleep, leaving me to face this alone." I hardly recognize my own voice through the fury. At least Gavron's capacity to provoke me is good for something; it pushes the fear away. "You want me to cower while you ignore me? Accept my fate and simply give up and die? No, thank you."

A chuckle escapes him. "I can see you won't go easily." He touches my cheek again, this time holding my gaze. "Death suits you."

My teeth are clenched so tightly, the words come out grated.

"If you mean it suits me by dying, you're mistaken. If you mean by *killing*, then yes, it does." I don't specify by killing *what*. "And I could say the same to you. Death suits you." I emphasize this with a look that combs over his black-clad, knife-covered form. He raises an eyebrow, and I glance away, embarrassed. "And I would like to learn from you."

You bastard, I add silently.

For a moment, I think I have him with my flattery, but then his expression shifts. "I thought you *hated* me," he says with a mocking sneer. "I'm a *bastard*, after all."

A panicky feeling seizes me. Revar said that after our Beginning, the blood we drank was supposed to better shield our minds from vampires.

"The blood claim only shields you from vampires less skilled at mind reading and gives you a *measure* of protection against skilled vampires—and not much from me," Gavron says, as if it's not a terrible violation.

My cheeks light on fire. "Why? Do you excel at mind reading, too, like everything else?"

I desperately hope he hasn't heard anything else I've been thinking.

To my surprise, he scoffs. "No, I'm actually middling at mind reading. It's my very claim on you that, while cloaking your thoughts from others, grants me better access. It's still by no means perfect, and it'll end when my claim does or when you become a full vampire. Until then, you need to practice being quieter, both inside and out, my disapproving novice."

No harm actually saying what's on my mind now, Conduct be damned. All the better to bury anything else.

"So teach me, you useless arse," I hiss.

His expression hardens instantly. "Fine, you bloody fool." And then he moves faster than Kashire did. Perhaps he doesn't move at all, and simply shadowsteps right next to me. He seizes me in his arms, and then he shadowsteps *far* more noticeably, me in tow.

Blink, we're over the drawbridge. *Blink*, we're in the middle of the road bisecting the Black Gates. *Blink*, we're outside the gates. *Blink*, we're in the forest. *Blink*, deeper forest. *Blink*.

It's worse than last time, probably because we've done it six times in a row. As soon as he releases me, I bend over beneath towering trees and vomit across the snow-dusted pine needles.

Gavron steps away from me and wrinkles his nose in distaste. "Be thankful I didn't mist us. You'd probably feel worse, unaccustomed to it as you are."

I hope it smells terribly unpleasant for him. I hope he hears that in my thoughts, too.

He smirks at me. "Think you're sharp, do you, with your silent jabs? Let's see how sharp and silent you can be without the boots I sent you, without the daggers I selected. After all, this is what Black Court Basic covers: Stillness. Silence. *Stalking*."

"We're outside the castle?" I can't hide the excitement in my voice. I take a deep breath of pine-and snow-scented air. I definitely prefer being under trees to the looming stone walls of Courtsheart.

"Don't sound so thrilled. You're not going to enjoy yourself, ill-prepared as you are."

Even so, I'm relieved to hear we won't jump straight into shadow-stepping, that we'll be stalking, instead—whatever that entails. I figured there must be preliminary stages in learning the Black Court's dangerous arts, but I didn't trust Gavron not to throw me headfirst into the well, so to speak.

"Nor should you," he says. "Just because you're not shadowstepping doesn't mean it's not serious."

I spit, wiping my mouth. "I suppose it couldn't have anything to do with the Black Court if it wasn't serious."

"Oh, look, Kashire has taught you *something*—insolence." He stares at me, eyes dark and hard. "And yet he's a vampire, and you're a pathetic human child without a bit of sense. Be careful whom you taunt."

Perhaps he's right about my lack of sense, because I immediately snap, "I'm not a child, you fossilized piece of scat."

I expect anger, but instead he barks a laugh. "I'm not old, nor is age an insult among vampires. It's prestige. Alas, I was only turned a few years ago."

Which makes him only a few years older than me, at least as humans measure it. "That doesn't mean you're not a piece of scat."

I feel some satisfaction, if also fear, when his eyes narrow to slits.

"You think you're so clever?" he asks, his voice dangerously low. "Allow me to teach you something for your impudence." He crouches down, one palm on the ground, the other draping over his knee. His gaze is decidedly predatory.

A sense of danger prickles my skin. "What?"

His smile is as cold and hard as his eyes. "The question is: What are *you* going to do? Here's your answer: Return to Courtsheart in one piece, if you can. On foot, of course."

"Wait—" I start, fear climbing inside me.

"Might I suggest you try being quiet? Holding still will also be wise if you want to avoid detection."

It sounds like a parting salvo. I expect him to charge, or maybe shadowstep, but instead his form blurs . . . *melts*. Then a wolf is standing before me, staring at me with black eyes. Its fur is mostly gray, but there are startling accents of white on its face and breast, as well as deepest black lining its back and tipping its ears, paws, and tail.

I would hardly need to see Gavron change to know it was him. So *this* is his inner animal—unless he's learned others, which I somehow doubt. He's too inflexible.

I wonder if he's indeed going to hunt me, until he sends up a howl loud enough to make me cover my newly sensitive ears.

The howls that answer him—too many and too close—chill me to my core.

I've seen what a pack of wolves can do. They eat almost everything. Bone. Fur. *Hair*, if their prey is human. Oftentimes they eat even the bloodied snow.

I spin on Gavron's wolf-form in a panic. "What if they attack me?"

His words prickle in my head. They're uncomfortable, itchy to have where they don't belong, like burs in clothing. *You're strong enough to fight. You'll heal quickly.*

That's not comforting, either. "What if they *eat* me?"

Then you'll be dead.

Blood and piss, I think.

The wolf inclines his head to me, in agreement or farewell, I don't know. And then he lopes off into the trees back toward Courtsheart, swift as a shadow in the night.

I hear the howls again. Closer now. Spreading out around me. A discordant, answering noise makes me jump: the cackling of a raven, as if it's laughing at me.

Maybe it's *actually* laughing, because maybe it's not truly a raven. I can't see Kashire—if indeed it is Kashire—within the inkblots of pines looming against the night sky.

"Bloody bastards, all of you!" I scream into the trees.

I wish I could disappear into mist now.

Instead, I start running as fast as I can, whipping though the trees. I'm swifter than I've ever been before, but the howls pursue me.

Already I know I won't be fast enough.

9

The wolves close in.

My breath burns in my lungs. My energy is quicker to return now, but I'm not giving it much chance. I run at full tilt through the trees, heedless of the branches that whip my cheeks.

I can hear my hunters getting ever closer. Courtsheart remains far away. I spot glimmers of light in the distance, its windows like welcoming campfires through the tangle of the forest. Impossibly out of reach. Despite not yet learning what I've hoped, maybe I should take my chances running *away*.

But then all of this will have been for nothing.

I stop, neither going forward nor back, my gasps loud as I stand in indecision.

Echoing howls send fear spiking through me. Whether I return or not, the wolves are a problem I have to face, right now.

Silence. Stillness. Those were the tools Gavron said I would need. All I've used is speed. I catch my breath, gathering my other senses. The snowy forest smells like ice and pine and danger.

It doesn't matter that I try to hold entirely still, drop my breathing to the quietest possible hiss. The wolves still come. I hear the snap of a twig with my sharp ears, the whisper of their movements in the underbrush. Circling around me. Gavron's advice only seems to have made the situation worse.

I remember the wisdom of my village, when it comes to wolves.

It's the opposite of stillness. You shout and make a lot of noise, preferably waving around a burning torch as you do.

I leap out of hiding, drawing my fillet knife, lift my arms over my head to make myself as big as possible, and screech, "*Get away from me.*"

I can see their reflective eyes and shaggy shapes among the trees. To my relief, none move closer.

And then something slams into my back like a battering ram. I feel claws rake my sides, tearing skin, teeth digging deep into my shoulder. Terror streaks through me with the pain.

I hear a raven cawing. *Laughing.*

A flash of rage brings me clarity. I only have my fillet knife, but it might be enough. I thrust behind me and hear an immediate yelp. I keep stabbing until the beast leaps away and I can stand, clutching my bleeding side. I raise my knife to the darkness, hold it like Claudia has been drilling into me, as little as I want to credit her for anything. My hand shakes violently, and I choke down a sob.

And then a monstrous form with glowing eyes comes lunging out of the underbrush, straight for me.

I stumble back and barely keep hold of my knife. Right before the creature can flatten me, something *else* hits it with a yowl, something small. They both go tumbling off into the shadows and scrub. I scrabble away, my panicked breath roaring like the ocean in my ears. With fully human eyes, I would have seen nothing; now I see vague shapes. The smaller of the two continues screeching and hissing, the bigger creature snarling and snapping. There's another yelp, and then they both careen off into the trees.

Leaving me alone, just like that.

I wait for a long moment in silence, clutching my wound. I don't dare move or make another sound. The rest of the pack seems to have gone, too.

I'm ready to embrace stillness so much that I want to lie down. But my blood is running through my fingers—I'm not healing.

I have no choice now but to go back.

Desperation sets my feet stumbling in the direction of Courtsheart. My blood patters over the snow, tapping out my remaining time in a terrible rhythm that makes me try to move faster, except my legs won't cooperate. I keep the windows in my sight, even when they begin to blur.

Eventually, I start to feel hot and cold at once. Shivering and burning. My knees feel weak. I've felt like this before, from the fever that near killed me. The one from which Silvea saved me.

Maybe fate is catching up with me. Death outstripping me before I can leave it behind.

I struggle onward for as long as I can, feeling like I'm trudging through curdling cream, but eventually my knees buckle. I hit the ground hard, landing on my uninjured shoulder. I wonder if I'll ever get up again.

A hand grips me. Death's icy fingers, perhaps. But then the hand *shakes* my wounded shoulder, jostling me back to full consciousness and making me cry out in pain.

"What's the matter with you?" Gavron demands.

Of course, he would blame *me* for this.

"You tell me, arsehole," I mutter into the snowy earth.

I sense him drop on all fours above me, hear him *sniff* the wound at my shoulder. "This is a werewolf bite."

I open my eyes in incredulity, twisting my head to look up at him. "You're kidding."

He's infuriatingly handsome, even as he frowns down at me. He's back in human form, his hair pulled away from his face, belts tight over his muscles, not a knife out of place. He's the honed edge of a blade in the night.

"I don't mean the werewolves of the ridiculous stories you've no doubt heard," he says, "about humans who change into wolves under the light of the full moon or some other nonsense. Those are probably shapeshifting vampires like me, mistaken for something else."

The real monster mistaken for a nightmare, I think deliriously. *Yes, how nonsensical.*

If Gavron has heard my sarcasm, he ignores it. "True werewolves aren't like that. They're only bigger and smarter than normal wolves, and they're toxic to vampires. Humans, too, of course," he adds as an afterthought, pulling the fabric away from the wound and inspecting it, even though it makes me hiss. His eyes narrow. "It's keeping your skin from knitting, despite my blood. I didn't think one would be out here, so close to Courtsheart. They usually steer far wider of the castle, because we kill them on sight."

I giggle up at him, which earns me a raised eyebrow. "I'm glad it wasn't you, at least, murdering me in wolf-form. A pretty obvious disguise, if you ask me."

He looks taken aback. "I would never do that. You're my novice."

The laughter bursts out of me, making me wheeze in pain. "You left me to get *eaten*!"

"No, you fool," he growls, leaning lower, "I left you to learn a lesson. Without the werewolf, you would have managed."

"Thank you, then, for imparting your wisdom." I try to hold in my laughter and snort instead. "I've learned I'm all alone in this."

He sighs through his teeth. "You're not alone. I'll . . . be there . . . more, for you." It sounds as if the words cost him. "This shouldn't have happened. I should have stayed nearby. But you angered me. You *disrespected* me."

That's probably as close to an apology as he's going to give.

"So I'm poisoned." That explains the burning. The dizziness and giggles. "Just let me die, then, if that's what you want."

I should have let you die.

But the memory of those words only revives my anger. Death would be the easier choice, but I don't want to die.

I want to live. I want to *fight*.

"I don't want you to die." My surprise at his declaration is cut short when he hauls me halfway onto his lap. Fire tears through me, and he speaks calmly over my outcry. "And based on how your heart sounds, you're not dying—yet. I can fix this."

"With more of your blood?" I wish I sounded more disgusted at the thought. I blame it on the pain I'm in, not my sudden intense craving.

Gavron doesn't move for his wrist, only looks down at me steadily. "Yes. But if I remove the toxin from your system first, you'll need less of my blood to heal. I don't want to risk turning you before you're ready."

I don't want to be turned into a vampire right now, either. But by *remove* does he mean—

Then he leans down and *licks* me, one long stroke of his tongue along the ragged gash in my shoulder. I yelp in shock, ready for a wave of fiery pain to wash over me. But where his tongue runs, it leaves blissful cool behind. I shudder in relief rather than horror. The only other time I've felt his tongue—in my mouth—I'd been dying too much to notice any numbing effect.

Despite what he just did, Gavron is all efficiency, passionless, like he was after Kashire stabbed me in the woods. "Vampire saliva isn't only a numbing agent, it also has healing properties. Not as much as our blood, but still something. You'll learn this in your more advanced Silver lessons. But the toxin is too deep in you now to try to remove from your skin alone."

His cold, hard fingers find the collar of my shirt and rip it away from my throat, popping seams and tearing fabric. Fear thrills through me, and when his strong arms pull me into a closer embrace, another feeling does, too—and not just pain. Something primal and excited. He dips his head toward my neck, lips parting. *Fangs* showing.

"Wait!" I cry.

He pulls back only enough to snap, "I'm helping you, you—"

"*Fool*," I say, turning his own word against him as I twist in his grasp, wincing. "I know. But won't the toxin hurt you, if you drink it?"

His eyes widen a fraction, as if he's surprised I care. "I'll be able to process it, especially since I'm not actively trying to heal. I recommend you stop squirming."

He's already tried to teach me one lesson about ignoring his recommendations. I don't care for another.

"Fine," I say, turning away so he doesn't see my face flush—and exposing my throat. My skin prickles from the chill air. I'm not used to having my neck uncovered—protection from more than the cold, of course, though I've never felt the sting of vampire teeth. I can't help but ask, "Will it hurt me? Your bite?"

I can hear his frown. "I can make it not hurt. I figured there were more important things—"

"Please." My voice is small, and I hate it. I refuse to look at him. "I'm scared."

I think he might chide me for admitting it, or call me weak. Instead he only mutters, "You might hate *this* just as much."

Before I can ask what he means, his fingers grip my chin, turning my face toward him. He meets my eyes and holds them. His gaze swallows mine, his voice all I can hear.

"You have nothing to fear from me, Fin." It's the first time he's said my name beyond confirming it was mine at my Beginning. It's been *Little Fish* or *fool* ever since. "You're safe, and this won't hurt. It's going to feel . . . good," he adds grudgingly, as his hand slips into my hair, surprisingly gentle.

And I believe him. Even when he turns my head back to the side and he bends toward my neck, I'm entirely calm. His arms around me are all I need to feel secure. At his command, I've given myself to him—in my mind, at least.

And soon through the veins in my neck.

Gavron's whole demeanor changes abruptly. He's no longer cool and methodical. His body melts around mine until he's embracing me like a lover might. Vampiric feeding must not be all violence. This is another side to it I've never seen.

He licks the skin of my neck slowly, lingeringly, inhaling deeply as he does and sending shivers down my spine with a wash of tingling relief and something closer to pleasure. I feel the sharp points of his teeth, and I gasp in anticipation. I can't help tensing as they break skin, sinking in slowly, but all I feel is a strange pressure, a burst of wetness around the bite, and then a piercing sweetness as he begins to draw from me.

It's bliss. His lips on my neck, his tongue gently lapping my skin, his teeth *inside* me. As he drinks, I can feel the poison draining out of me, taking its horrible burn. This is the best thing I've ever felt, aside from drinking Gavron's blood. I don't mind that he's taking mine now; I only want to give him more. I moan and arch into him, exposing myself further. That might have been embarrassing—horrifying, even—if he weren't pressing into me even harder, sucking on my throat like it was the most delicious piece of fruit. And if I didn't want it more than anything. *Almost* anything.

At some point, my eyes start to roll back into my head. He pulls away with a ragged breath. Good thing, because I wouldn't have wanted him to stop. Not until it was too late.

For a moment, we just pause there, him holding me, me drifting. He's clutching me tighter, I realize foggily, as if reluctant to let go. He keeps his head bent close. Maybe protectively, or maybe he wishes he could keep feeding. And yet, he licks over the holes he made in my skin, able to heal me now that the toxin is mostly gone.

It takes a while for my mind to focus enough to speak. But when it does, I feel different. I'm scared of dying again. Scared of *him* again. It's like waking up from a trance, even as I want to pass out.

He's a monster who just drank my blood, as pleasureful as it may have felt. He's keeping his immense strength in check, but I can feel it in his grip: He could snap me in half. Worse, he could tell me it felt good while he was at it, and I would believe him.

"Did you—did you enthrall me?" I rasp.

"No," he murmurs. My blood glistens red on his lips. "It's just the power of suggestion. Entrancing rather than enthralling. It fades quickly. But you'll tend to want to listen to my suggestions."

"As a human?"

"As my novice."

Of course. "Am I still . . . suggestible?" It's not that I don't appreciate his taking my pain and fear away. But I need to know when I'm me and when I'm not, even if he's helping me.

"As long as you're mine, you're open to it."

Mine. I shiver, and it's not only horror. Something in me appreciates his claim. Wants the protection. Craves the power in his blood. I need him to survive, after all. If such proximity to him gets me what I need, perhaps being his novice doesn't have to be so bad.

Or maybe such sentiment isn't my own.

"I'm not entrancing you anymore," he continues, as if in response to my thoughts. "I won't, unless absolutely necessary. Or unless you ask me to."

I want to believe him, but I don't trust *that* feeling entirely, either. "Why not?"

"Because it's lazy. You should want to listen to me of your own volition."

He wants to *earn* my respect. At least that's a step in the right direction.

"Never enthralling," I say. It's not a question.

"Never," he says, and then with a fervor that leaves me no doubt, he adds, "I hate enthrallment."

A deep tension in me loosens.

"I thought you said my blood wasn't to your taste," I quip drowsily. "Didn't seem like it, just now."

I don't know why I'm prodding him. Maybe I'm near senseless from blood loss.

"It's different now that I've claimed you. It's . . . very much to my taste." He frowns as though he's not happy about that.

I grin crookedly. "Does that mean you like the taste of *your* blood in me? That's rather vain."

"Hush, please," he says. But it's not a command like *that*, and there's a slight smile tugging at one corner of his mouth. "I know what will shut you up, other than dying. Which you're doing in earnest now. Your heart is stuttering."

Thanks to him.

He bites his wrist in what is becoming a familiar gesture. Even though I need his blood to stay alive, I want its power, and it's the best thing I've ever tasted besides, I want to recoil. But it's drink or die at this point.

My disgust doesn't last long. When he lowers his bleeding wrist to my lips, he doesn't need to encourage me to drink. I'm desperate for it. If I were strong enough to seize his arm, I would. As it is, he holds it in place for me with gentle pressure.

Impossibly, the flood of his blood tastes better than I remember it, despite my craving it since it first touched my tongue. The focus of my entire being narrows to my mouth against his wrist and the cool, viscous liquid sliding down my throat. As I gain a burning hot surge of strength, I cling tighter to him. He hoists me higher against his chest, the easier for me to swallow. I'm too engrossed to be embarrassed that I'm curled up in his lap, rocking back and forth over his arm.

As far as I'm concerned, I could stay like this forever.

"Founders," he breathes like a curse. "Me too."

And yet, too soon, he leans against my head, rubbing his temple against my hair like a dog would. Or a wolf, maybe. "Fin, you have to stop." My name again. It makes him sound serious, and yet . . . his breathless, ragged tone indicates that he'd rather I do anything but stop. "We can't risk turning you too soon, remember? It would be very hard on you. And you shouldn't get too far ahead of the other novices."

It's like he's trying to convince himself.

He lets me carry on for a few more seconds, until he says, "Fin, the more you drink, the stronger you'll be . . . but the more suscep-tible to my control you'll be."

That gets me to stop.

I become fully aware of my surroundings, like coming out of a dream. I open my eyes to find myself cradled in his arms, still clutch-ing his wrist to my closed lips. Like I'm kissing it. I let go and stare awkwardly up at him, acutely aware of our intimate embrace. His mouth is still stained red with my blood, his eyes blacker than ever. He looks like he wants to kiss me, bite me, rip my clothes off, tear me limb from limb. It's hard to say.

I can only imagine what I look like. I want to do all those things to him and more, right now.

He slides out from under me, standing brusquely. He wipes his mouth and dusts the snow and pine needles off his clothes.

"We can walk instead of shadowstepping, so you don't vomit all of that up," he says without looking at me.

I belatedly remember he could probably read all my inappropriate thoughts. I almost wish he'd just knocked me out again after feeding me so we wouldn't have to suffer through the awkward aftermath.

I think of something, anything, to say, and then remember I actu-ally have a question I'm almost scared to ask. "Would—?" I swallow. "Would Kashire somehow have something to do with this?"

"No," Gavron says shortly.

"I'm pretty sure I saw him in raven form, and he's tried to kill me once already."

"That was before you were my novice. He wouldn't do that now."

"How do you know for sure?"

"Because I know *him*," he snaps.

It's a hard thing to accept on faith, even if he and Kashire were once lovers by the sounds of it. Even so, what saved me? It was a smaller, spitting creature.

Before I can wonder at it, Gavron says, "I'll be just ahead of you. I promise."

And with that, he strides away.

Leaving me on my back, staring at the night sky. I touch my lips numbly. My fingers come away black. I resist the urge to lick them.

Part of me wants to sink into the earth and vanish. Maybe I feel like anyone who's done something under cover of darkness that they might soon regret. Uncertain. Vulnerable. My deepest desires laid bare. But, unlike how a person probably looks after a typical scenario like that—unless they're a murderer instead of a secret lover—I'm absolutely covered in blood. Black, red, it doesn't matter. It's one big mess all over me. And yet my skin is smooth and firm, horrible wounds gone.

Maybe I will start wearing black, I think, as I haul myself to my feet and start in the direction Gavron went.

Not away from him. Not anymore. Because the *other* part of me wants to sprint after Gavron. Seize him. *Drink* him.

I don't entirely trust the compulsion, let alone surrender to it. At the same time, my urge to escape Courtsheart is muffled, as if buried under a blanket of snow. It's not just Gavron's watchful proximity that discourages me from running, or even the more comforting presence of Marai—or even Revar and Jaen—back at Courtsheart. Not even my desire for revenge.

Maybe it's something inside me. Something I'm becoming.

I've tasted power, and I want more of it.

I look forward to seeing what you will become, Revar said.

Maybe the fact that I'm studying how to become a monster should give me a clue as to what that will be. The thought should frighten me.

Maybe, a quiet thought creeps into my mind as I walk, *maybe I'm somehow meant for Courtsheart.* I didn't have a true place in my own village, after all. My very existence was resented. I'm not exactly welcome here, and the lessons are brutal and the inhabitants dangerous, but I might have choices, chances, I never had before. *Strength* I never had before.

Someday, I might be a match for them. Use their own blood against them.

Like a guiding rope, I cling to the thought of the Black Court. They kill vampires, and they're vampires themselves. I can learn from them. Keep my goals clear, as I get deeper into this world. Stay human, even as I become more and more like them.

I might even enjoy parts of the journey. I just don't want to look too closely at *which* parts.

Following Gavron's lead, I stumble back to Courtsheart in a heady daze.

10

After falling into bed before dawn and sleeping like I did indeed die, the first thing I do when I wake up the next evening is look in the gilded mirror above my washstand. The nonlight left behind after dusk is enough for me to see myself with crystalline clarity.

What was once hazel and then pale and raw looking in my eyes is entirely gone, with ever-more black eating into now-eerie pure white around my pupils. It's as if between the black center and the surrounding black ring of my iris, I have a tendriled white star.

Even though I anticipated this, the sight of it still hits me like a blow. I've crossed a threshold. I couldn't go back to my village, even if I wanted to. I would be branded as something *else*. A freak. They would see me either as something to be hunted . . . or the hunter.

I wonder—

I feel my teeth with my tongue and gasp. They're definitely sharper. I raise my lips, and I startle myself with my animal-like snarl. My canines aren't quite as long and pointed as a vampire's, but nigh longer than any human's I've ever seen. My gums ache to the touch.

My teeth are growing.

The realization isn't as horrifying as I would have thought. Maybe these changes could fade over time without more infusions of blood—I don't know for sure. But I do know there's something that won't change: After tasting such power in Gavron's blood, I crave more of it.

You won't want *to leave, soon enough*, Revar said.

That doesn't mean I can't do what I came here to do. Instead of bringing some sort of secret knowledge or weapon against vampires back to a human population, *I* can become the weapon.

As long as I don't die or become a thrall before then.

I'm more frightened, now, at the thought of failing at Courtsheart than I am at succeeding. It's as if the changes overtaking my body are trying to get me used to the thought.

As odd as my eyes and teeth are, I can't help but admire the fact that I'm already more solid looking, if not more filled out. Still no breasts or hips to speak of, and I'm inexplicably relieved that hasn't changed. I have more lean muscle, nothing else. But something in my bones makes them feel made of steel. I'm strong enough to break the wood of my washstand under my fingers. I pull away quickly at the first creak.

A knock at the door makes me jump, as if I've been caught doing something wrong. It's true that I've hardly admired myself before. And maybe now, with what I'm becoming, I especially shouldn't.

Before I can respond, a servant bustles in carrying a tray of food. Followed by another. And another. They fill up every flat surface, save for my bed, with steaming plates and bowls. I'm still staring at it all, utterly confused, when they leave me alone again, surrounded by an absurd feast.

"What's——?" I start to say aloud, and then I feel chill fingers wrap gently around my throat from behind.

"You're dead," Gavron whispers in my ear. Fear spikes through me like an iron rod. "Or you would be, if I wanted to kill you. Lucky for you, Little Fish, I don't."

I'm suddenly all too aware I'm only wearing my black silk nightgown. I step away from him quickly, despite feeling that same pull between us.

He regards me for a moment, his black eyes betraying nothing. And then he smiles as if he likes what he sees.

Maybe, I think, *as much as he likes the taste of his blood in mine, it tickles his vanity to see me becoming more like him.*

His smile flattens. "That you assume I couldn't appreciate you for reasons to do with *you* says more about how you see yourself than how I do."

I blink as his words settle in. And then I'm embarrassed to realize he might be right. I *was* just ashamed to be admiring myself— something I've hardly ever done. I've never felt I deserved it before.

"Good morning—evening," I blurt, just for something to say. And then I add, "How is your health?" An even sillier, more human thing to ask. It's not as if vampires get sick.

He raises that eyebrow of his. "Indeed, I should be asking *you* that. At least my blood will soon make that question moot. You look good. Healthier," he clarifies.

"Is that why you're here?" I ask, resisting the urge to hide. I square my shoulders and feel a mingled rush of self-consciousness and satisfaction when his gaze wanders over me again. "To ask after my health?"

"Do I need a reason to look in on my *dear* novice?" he says breezily. Before I can snort, he adds, "I brought you something, and I wanted to make sure you opened it this time." He pulls a cloth-wrapped package from behind his back. It's large, but he carries it looped around his little finger by a string, as if it weighs nothing.

I snatch it for something to cover me. It's lumpy and heavy, but I clutch the package to my chest like a shield and say, "Thank you," perhaps too loudly.

His lips twitch. "Are you going to open it?"

"Oh!" I turn and trip over the rug getting to the bed, spilling the package on the covers.

Keep yourself together, Fin, I snap at myself. *This is entirely normal. You only have a vampire in your bedchamber. One who has claimed you by blood.*

Each justification only makes me more aware of his palpable presence behind me as I untie the package. Sleek black material slithers out. I hold up a long-sleeved silk shirt, cut trim enough to fit me well, and then a pair of slim leather pants. This is Black Court garb. An array of belts and buckles accompanies it all.

"For your daggers," he explains. "When we strap them to your chest and thighs."

When I only stare at the clothes with an inexplicable mix of disquiet and yearning, he says impatiently, "Go ahead. Put it on."

I spin around to gape at him. "I'm not dressing in front of you!"

"You really think I care?"

"*I* care!"

He rolls his eyes, leaning against my carved bedpost. "Little Fish, I've drunk your blood, you've drunk mine, and yet you're bothered over the sight of flesh?"

I wonder if blood sharing is the most intimate thing a vampire can do. It certainly felt intimate to me. It occurs to me, for the first time, that this blood claim is something akin to an arranged marriage, one that neither of us wanted, and one that we've already . . . *consummated*, on more than one occasion. At least it didn't require any clothing removal, unlike the human ritual.

As strange as that is to consider, what I *don't* want is to imagine myself as a lump of clay he's forming into his own image. Awkward intimacy is preferable to losing myself—losing sight of my goals.

I silence the thought quickly.

"There's not even that much of you to see," Gavron adds. "Therefore, I've ensured you have enough food."

I gesture at the bowls and platters. "Have you forgotten how eating works? You realize I can't actually fit all of that in my belly at once, yes?"

But he's not listening. He's turned away, long-fingered hands on his narrow hips, gazing around at my room. My own eyes can't help dropping to his waist, where his own leather pants are low slung. I

113

snap them back up when he turns on me in disgust. "I should have come sooner. This is a disastrous arrangement. You need better curtains, thicker, and this bed is in an unsafe placement. Better yet, you need a covered bed *with* curtains——"

"I like my bed!" I interrupt, gesturing at the thick castle walls. "I don't want to be even more closed in."

"Come now, you can't imagine you could continue sleeping *exposed*, for all the light-loving world to approach." He almost makes it sound scandalous rather than dangerous.

"And yet exposing myself to you is fine?" I demand.

He gives me an incredulous look. "That's entirely different. Those are petty human concerns. Try to think better." My jaw drops at his sheer arrogance, before he adds with a wave, "Now, get changed."

"First, get *out*! Please," I add in a lower, more pleading tone. "And don't tell the servants to do anything to my bed."

He purses his lips in disapproval, sighs, and then vanishes, not bothering with the door.

As soon as he's gone, I sag against my bed. First he ignores me entirely, and now *this*. I wonder if I'm going to regret securing his attention. I look around at all the food and the clothes. I picture his eyes on me and experience a rush of giddiness. It's all a bit . . . much. Even if not all of it is bad, I feel unsure of my footing.

I shake myself and turn to the clothes piled on my blankets, conscious that I might not have much time. I hurriedly strip off my nightgown and toss the shirt over my head, nearly getting stuck at the neck because I didn't unlace it first. The pants almost trip me in my haste to stuff my legs inside. These clothes are tighter than I'm used to——they fit like a glove.

Thank the Father I made Gavron leave first.

Thank the Father, I muse. No doubt that's another lowly, too-human phrase, never mind that it's referencing the father of all the gods, albeit ones I've never much respected.

Try to think better.

I glare at the door, as if I can see him through it. *Bloody arrogant vampires.* And then I catch sight of myself in the mirror and stop dead. The outfit is sleeker, darker, and an altogether superior version of what Marai and I cobbled together for me at first. It's perfect for the day-to-day. *Night-to-night*, rather. Perfect for hunting. I have to admit, I love it. And I haven't even added the belts and straps yet.

"Do you need help?"

I nearly jump out of my new clothes, spinning to find Gavron in the room once again. "Can you *knock?*" I sputter.

"I could," he says, without promising to do so in the future. Instead, he steps up to me to straighten the laces on my shirt. The casual contact makes me freeze despite a sudden rush of heat. While I stand still, he scoops up one of the belts from my bed, threading his arms around me to strap it across my shoulders. For a moment, we could almost be embracing.

His proximity is a torch igniting my thoughts, and I try to stamp them out as quickly as possible.

Too close, too close. At least my silent chant will keep Gavron from hearing anything else I might be thinking.

He scoffs as he carries on buckling a belt around my upper arm. "You realize both your sense of shame and preciousness regarding your flesh, your fear of being seen or touched, is damage inflicted upon you by centuries of horribly misguided human practices."

I'm glad he thinks it's *only* fear and not excitement. I grimace up at him, showing my teeth. "What about my fear of vampires? How have centuries of their horribly violent practices damaged me?"

"Point taken," he says. "But you're going to be one of us, so try to start thinking like us." His hands still for a moment, and he holds my eyes. "Please. If you don't, it will not end well."

It's the same warning Revar gave me. At least Gavron doesn't tell me to *think better* again. I try to ignore the feeling of his arms as he threads yet another belt around my hips.

"If I'm not precious about my flesh, then it's going to get destroyed before I *can* become one of you," I grumble. "That's not a great end for me, either."

He cinches the belt, jerking me into him such that I have to steady myself with both hands against his chest. I expect him to push me back, but instead he lifts his own hands to my shoulders, giving me a light squeeze.

"That's why I'm here. To protect you."

My mouth is suddenly dry, and I find I don't have the inclination to pull away. "Why the change of heart?" I force myself to ask.

"Do I need a reason to care about my novice?"

"Seems like you did, before," I murmur, keeping my eyes downcast.

We're still standing face-to-face, our hands on each other. Then Gavron does the unthinkable. He tips my chin up with a crook of his finger and runs his thumb gently over my bottom lip, studying it with those fathomless eyes, his lashes a dark fan. Almost as if he's about to kiss me.

Panic rises in me . . . but so does a delicious anticipation, like when he was about to bite me.

And then he pushes up my top lip to *examine* my pointed tooth.

"Coming along nicely," he says. I jerk away, smacking him in the chest as I do. He lifts his hands in mock surrender. "Founders, what now?"

"I'm not your bloody *horse!*" I spit back at him.

He stares at me for a moment. And then he starts *laughing*. It's a startling, unfettered, *heart-stopping* sound, much to my irritation.

He covers his mouth with a hand, as if to hide his fangs—I wonder if that's a courtesy to other vampires or only to humans—his obsidian eyes gleaming. "You"—he clears his throat, dropping his hand to speak seriously—"would make a *terrible* horse. You are the least obedient creature I've ever met."

"Get used to it," I snap, and I shove by him and out of the room. I slam the door behind me before I realize I don't recall where I'm going. I grope for the answer while marching; I only know I need to go somewhere *away* from him.

I can't believe I thought he was about to . . . that I would have *wanted* him to . . .

I must be losing my mind. That or the blood claim is stealing my wits.

"Let me accompany you on the way to Blades," Gavron says, suddenly alongside me, matching my stride. So he knows my schedule.

I scoff, trying to bury my mortification. "Why the sudden concern? Has an errant werewolf been sighted in Courtsheart?" When he doesn't answer, I look at him. "Truly, why?"

He avoided my question earlier. *Is it Kashire?* I can't help but wonder, fear sparking in my chest.

"No," Gavron says. "But it would do us well for Kashire to see us together. To see that I'm making a fuss over you."

I gape at him, nearly tripping. "That's all this has been about? Getting Kashire off your back?"

He turns on me impatiently. "You know as well as I that he's thrown you in my path to torment me. Leaving you alone will only encourage him to get more creative."

"So this is all for your benefit, not mine?"

"Not entirely."

I try to outpace him in my fury. Gavron's right: I *am* a fool, especially for thinking I'm anything but an annoyance to him. One he can use to quench his thirst, on occasion. That's probably the only reason I'm worth keeping alive, for him.

I try to tell myself it doesn't matter how he sees me, as long as I get what I need from him.

Knowledge. Strength. *Weapons.*

Gavron catches up to me with ease. "At least I'll be able to bloody sleep again."

"Why haven't you been sleeping?" I sneer. "*Kashire* haunting your dreams?"

He glances at me. "*You* are, obviously."

"Am I annoying you there, too?"

"That's putting it lightly." I open my mouth in indignation, but then he says, "You're often sick or dying or starving or in some other nightmarishly mortal predicament I'm helpless to protect you against." He carries on as if I haven't stopped in my tracks. "At least awake, my worry for you consumes me slightly less because I have some control over the situation. I need control. It's the only thing that makes this tolerable."

I start forward again, trying to make sense of everything in a way that won't reaffirm my foolishness. "So you only want to outmaneuver Kashire *and* to play the all-powerful Father Incarnate at the same time. Clearly, you're worried about me for my sake."

Frustration flashes across his face. "Fin, don't you understand—"

Before he can finish, we nearly walk straight into Kashire.

Speak of the vampire, as they say, *and it'll come.* Gavron slips a protective arm around my shoulders. I nearly bite it.

"'Evening, Kashire," Gavron says, guiding me past him. "I'd stop, but I'm escorting Fin to lessons."

Kashire smiles as if he knows what game we're playing, but then he takes in our matching attire with his startling blue eyes. His brows lift in surprise. "I see. Don't let me keep you."

He sounds sincere, but I wonder if he's playing a deeper game—pretending to believe Gavron cares for me, only to later pull a knife from his sleeve.

Gavron keeps his arm around me as we move on, though I know it's only for show. It's an internal struggle not to shrug it off. As if he can read my mind—*ha ha*—he whips his arm away when we reach the practice yard.

But then he surprises me by taking my hand. Maybe he'll inspect my nails this time. Make sure they're becoming suitably clawlike.

Instead, he brushes a kiss across my knuckles, leaving me speechless.

"Don't get yourself killed," he says, more command than entreaty, and then he's gone.

———————

Easier ordered than done. My lessons get more challenging in stride with my growing strength, never giving me a moment to drop my guard. At least as winter season wears on, Claudia pays me less attention, and I don't spot Maudon lurking in the shadows anymore. But Claudia often pairs me with killer-girl, Gabriella, whose eyes, I soon see, are as pinkish red as Marai's, and the lessons are painful enough in the end.

Pavella remains Pavella, and I scramble to bow and scrape at her command. I imagine breaking her bones as I do.

Kashire also remains Kashire. *Perhaps I'm noticing a pattern with vampires*, I think ironically: *They don't change much.* In Revelry, I get so drunk I go blind. I hallucinate. He guides us up to the highest towers of Courtsheart and drops us off them, only to have other Blue Court vampires catch us midair before we splatter on the ground. He also takes us down to the deepest dungeons. I don't want to remember what happened there, though I still have nightmares about being locked up alone and intoxicated in a pitch-black cell with crawling rats and long-decayed corpses, while listening to screams for help echoing in the darkness—perhaps the other novices, perhaps other prisoners. But I bury the memories upon waking. Kashire claims his lessons are all about *forgetting*, after all. Or is it remembering? Sometimes it's hard to say.

I can't forget one thing I saw on the *way* to the dungeons. *The other kitchen*, Kashire called it with a wink as we passed. Of course Courtsheart has kitchens to feed its servants and still-human novices, so I didn't understand the purpose of another kind until I got a glimpse inside. Alcoves lined the walls with curtains half-pulled aside. In most of them were humans, waiting on cushioned seats. All were thralls, not putting up a fight, but the iron rings and manacles embedded in the stone around them hinted at less willing "guests."

The other kitchen—where the vampires of Courtsheart feed when they're in residence. Better than hunting humans for sport, perhaps.

This is what I'll have to face, if I ever become one of them—or even if I fail. I'll simply be waiting on the other side of the curtain as a thrall, for those teeth to pierce my throat.

Marai is my primary comfort during these strange and exhausting times, though Jaen also shows us constant kindness despite two different faces. If only Vampire History was as comforting. Vampires seem to consume other lands and cultures like locusts, devouring them and leaving something else in their wake, though they insist what they provide is better. Maybe it is, in some ways. Some, it's decidedly not. But we have no choice but to accept it, because they have all the power.

We, others keep correcting me. *We have all the power.*

I can't think of myself as one of them. Despite my reflection in the mirror, I'm here to learn about vampire vulnerabilities, not their strength. Not *human* weaknesses. But that's all that our lessons seem to be about.

My culture is considered a Nordic one, I learn. These lands are particularly favorable to vampires because they don't mind the cold, which tends to hinder human armies. It's why they've positioned their most powerful strongholds up here, so invasion would be inconvenient for the more sensitive skinned.

Lucky *us*.

In truth, cold no longer bothers me. I don't need much more than my long-sleeved silk shirt to be out all night in freezing weather, or supple leather boots to trek through the deepening winter snow. My muscles no longer ache, and they're as hard as stone. I can run nigh as fast as a horse on flat ground. Lighter wounds start to vanish within minutes, especially if I'm well-fed and rested. My other senses keep growing more and more sensitive.

Too sensitive, sometimes. Light hurts my eyes. The sun also burns my skin easier than ever before. I start to hide from the daylight more for my own sake than I do to adhere to the vampires' schedule. My teeth continue to hurt. To grow.

And yet, I'm still mortal. I tell myself that with relief, even as I appreciate my new strength.

Gavron doesn't feed me his blood again because I'm already leaps and bounds ahead of the other novices after the werewolf attack, he says. He doesn't drink my blood, either, despite admitting it's to his taste now. In the next couple of weekly lessons going forward, he teaches me techniques for stillness and moving silently to sneak up on prey—or vampires, I hope, though he never states it so directly. It pleases him greatly to sneak up on *me*. He often wraps his fingers around my throat, though gently. He reverts to calling me *Little Fish* and *fool*, sometimes *bumbling fool* if I fail to be quiet enough. No more *Fin*.

And yet, he never strays too far from me when we're training in the forest outside Courtsheart. He certainly never abandons me out there again. Too much food keeps arriving in my room, and he makes a particular effort to appear with me before others, occasionally even putting an arm around me when he's not too busy sneaking up on me. Once, even, he runs his fingers through the hair at the nape of my neck. I'm not even sure he's aware of doing it.

But never more than that. I can't tell if I'm relieved or disappointed.

I assume I've just about learned whatever painful surprises winter season has in store for me when a thick vellum envelope is slipped under my chamber door.

It has *Novice Fin, care of Master Gavron* written on the outside, and inside is an ornate invitation for both of us to something called Winter Sol, hosted by the House of Winter Night. Before I can much more than puzzle over it, Marai bursts into my room.

"It's a ball!" she practically shouts. "Any vampire of import will be attending, even if they dwell far away from Courtsheart. Apparently, the highest-ranking lines from every House will leave their strongholds to be *here* on the night of the solstice. Exciting, isn't it?"

In my village, we had the Midwinter Festival. It was always a bright spot in the darkness for me. Somehow, I doubt Winter Sol will be anything like that, not with the Blue Court's involvement.

She scowls at the expression on my face. "Let me guess, you hate balls."

"I've never been to one." I stare at her in dawning horror. "Will I have to *dance?*"

She throws up her hands. "You're hopeless."

I should have known after Kashire's "feast" and aerial acrobatics that dancing would be more his court's specialty. This sounds like another one of their revelries, only grander and more intimidating.

"As hopeful additions to vampire society, we need to make a good impression, Fin. Do you know how to dance?"

My grimace is answer enough.

"I figured as much. Which is why I'm here." She spreads her arms, beckoning me into her embrace. When I hesitate, she says, "Come on, just pretend I'm Gavron. You'll have to dance with him, after all. He'll be your escort."

Something in her tone sours on that last part. I told her everything that's happened between me and Gavron, of course. While she's pleased he's finally taken an interest in me, she still seems to distrust him. I wonder if she's simply being a good friend, looking out for me.

And yet, at the mention of Gavron, Winter Sol suddenly doesn't sound so horrifying. I remind myself I should probably know better.

When I reluctantly take Marai's hand, her smile is like a sunrise.

I wonder how many of those I have left to see.

11

The evening of Winter Sol arrives after a flurry of preparations, with servants and vampires alike scurrying about the castle. Fortunately, I have nothing to do with most of it.

Though, when my gown arrives, I wonder if perhaps I should have.

Gavron has chosen it, no doubt. It's made of palest gray silk, with black embroidery clawing its way up from the hem in stark, overlapping lines. The design looks like a tangle of bare branches against a cloud-covered sky, backlit by a full moon . . . or like my eyes and the changes overtaking them. It comes with black satin gloves that go up past my elbow, and a wide black ribbon to tie about my neck. As if my throat is a gift to unwrap.

No, thank you, I think.

Despite looking strikingly beautiful, complementing my hair and complexion, the gown is still . . . not me. And yet, I put it on without complaint. Outward complaint, anyway, though I even practice keeping quiet in my head. Gavron *did* bring me the pants and the knives. So if he misses the mark sometimes, I feel like I owe it to him to be polite.

Or maybe Conduct is getting to me more than I've guessed.

Worse, perhaps something else is changing my disposition toward him—whatever this thing is between Gavron and me. My body keeps wanting to lean into his—blood calling to blood, perhaps. I don't know how he feels about me. If it's only his blood claim drawing me to him, it would be best to ignore the feeling. I can't trust it, and it's only a distraction, as Gavron once accused me of being, from both my studies and my true goals.

A desire for revenge, I can trust.

Claudia, Marai tells me, is coming to her room to escort her to the ball, but I receive a note in Gavron's thin, elegant scrawl that he's going to be late and that I should escort myself.

I'm irritated, if not shocked. There always seems to be something keeping him away.

Oddly, there's a postscript from him: *Wear the neck ribbon and the boots. Don't argue.*

I've indeed left off the neck ribbon. And the boots are a black leather pair that came with the dress. Not only do they have too much silvery embroidery and too many ribbons lacing them up, the heels are high and the sole is thick and heavy. I was planning on trading them out for simple satin slippers since they seemed like a tripping hazard more than anything.

Still, I follow Gavron's instructions. Feeling like a fool—rather, a delectably wrapped treat—I escort *myself*, with my beribboned neck and excessive dress and boots, down the spiderweb halls of Courtsheart to Winter Sol. Somehow, I manage not to trip.

Two servants open the towering double doors for me, revealing the grandest ballroom I've ever seen—which isn't saying much, but I can't imagine anything grander. White stone pillars line the walls and split high overhead like towering trees, supporting a roof that looks like the night sky. The domed ceiling and walls themselves are deep black stone inset with diamonds and silver and gilt filigree—constellations mapped out. All around are stars and wisps of cloud and so much darkness. It's as if we're atop the highest tower of Courtsheart, exposed to the night air through branches of stone, minus the wind and snow and cold. Even the floor sparkles like fallen snow, covered in metallic flakes that glitter in the faint candlelight.

For a moment I gape, and then snap my mouth closed when I remember the vampire leaders of the world are likely in attendance. I know better than to draw attention by looking like an ignorant peasant. I slip into the shadows like Gavron has taught me. My dress, all branches and frost, actually matches the decor rather well. I try to take everything in discreetly, tracing the boundaries of what I know.

To look for cracks, if there are any.

Unfortunately, I see only power on display. The immortals here look stunning and invincible.

I search for vaguely familiar faces. It probably helps that my eyesight is significantly sharper. It's so dim in the ballroom that a normal human would have a hard time navigating without bumping into anyone. Indeed, the servants walk with small lanterns attached to chest harnesses, soft orbs of light hanging above their heads like will-o'-the-wisps, marking them for all to see.

So does the trail of blood behind them. The glittery shards on the floor cut their feet, and all the servants are barefoot. They're like lonely fishing boats in a sea of darkness, leaving wakes of blood behind as chum for the sharks. All their eyes have that vacant glow. I hope they're feeling no pain, at least. While some of the servants are being harassed—their wrists and necks even bitten—more are ignored, simply leaving what must be the lovely perfume of human blood behind them.

It's like "the other kitchen" all over again, only more finely dressed.

I feel sick to my stomach. At least I heeded Gavron and wore the boots. I'm certain the servants will be healed—maybe even during the ball so they can come back out again with fresh feet—but it's still an unsettling sight. I wonder about Gavron's insistence on the neck ribbon as well . . . but I don't have to for long.

There are humans in attendance who *aren't* Courtsheart servants, and while some are clearly barefoot and wincing as they walk, one man even led by the neck on a chain, others have thick shoes and seem to be adored. Ribbons in various House colors adorn the necks of chosen humans, marking them as off-limits, I realize. Those with bare necks must be fair game. Some vampires even laughingly carry their human charges on their backs like children, if their shoes are thin. Some *are* children, I realize with horror, no doubt being groomed as favored novices, much as one would select a choice pup before it's weaned. Or even—I shudder to think it—after having already selected the dam and sire. Vampires can't have children, after all. They can only choose from among ours.

And yet . . . perhaps it's something, at least, that these children are fed and pampered and protected, albeit by monsters. Sometimes *something* is better than *nothing*. But not always.

I push down the memory of standing hungry, waiting for my hot-cake in line with the other children at Midwinter Festival, getting shoved to the back.

My stomach growls as if in remembered hunger. But it's more than that. I ate before coming, and yet there's a rich, heady scent that I waved away as I imagined what human blood must smell like to vampires.

I can smell it, too—the blood. And it smells *good*.

Unconsciously, I press my tongue against my growing teeth and wince. I'm becoming more and more like them every passing night.

I would suddenly rather be anywhere else, but I'm sure leaving will draw more notice than if I just wait for Gavron. I try to find Marai in the crowd and fail. I spot Revar, who looks to be having as much fun as I am in their formal silver robes. Their attendance has likely been forced as one of the Council of Twelve. They only give me the slightest of nods, not inviting me to approach, and I'm not foolhardy enough to try.

Nervousness stabs me as I wait, gutting me as I continue standing aimlessly by myself. Will I be left here, empty armed and alone, to look the fool? Unwanted? Although perhaps I shouldn't want company in this massive hall swarming with vampires, especially those of the Blue Court. This is *their* night, after all. I'm probably better off alone.

"If you pity yourself more, you might do us all a favor and die of it." From behind, I feel a swift kiss on my cheek, there and gone, as if to take the sting out of the words.

"You're here!" I exclaim, spinning to find Gavron. I'm too relieved to be irritated. He's dressed in black, as usual, except his vest and coat are of fine silk and there's a cravat at his throat. His loose hair is a dark curtain framing the perfection of his pale face. Kohl lines his eyes, making them all the deeper and more striking. I've never seen him dressed so formally, and I look away before I'm caught staring.

I can still feel the cool press of his lips on my cheek. *Not that it's special*, I tell myself. I've seen other vampires greet their novices like that. It's a formality. Just one that I'd yet to experience.

"Of course I'm here. I wouldn't miss it." He pauses, dark eyes flickering over me. "You look lovely."

"I appreciate the boots the most," I say earnestly.

He glances at a servant leaving bloody footprints. "That part of the decor isn't to my taste. The Blue Court loves its extravagances."

As if blood were like ribbons or flower bouquets. Still, I appreciate that he doesn't approve.

I can still smell it. I'm still hungry. But I choke down the feeling. I don't know what Gavron would say, and I'm not sure I could bear his mockery over something so horrifying. Or worse, his encouragement.

"I'm not fond, either," I say, my voice a little hoarse. "You're *late*."

"Some of us have more important things to do than dance with clumsy novices all night."

I try to keep my face blank along with my thoughts, but I feel winded.

His expression softens in a way I've rarely seen. "I'm teasing. I was helping Maudon with a task. I came as soon as I could."

"What task?"

"None of your concern, Little Fish."

"When you abandon me in a giant ballroom filled with Blue Court vampires, it is my concern," I say, smiling through gritted teeth.

He sighs. "Fine. I've been especially occupied because the Black Court provides protection for Courtsheart at times like this. Also enforcement of our laws. Many different vampires are arriving, including someone entirely unexpected, whose mere existence is a problem."

"*Who?*" I ask, wondering who could be worse than those I've already read about.

"Nobody infamous. Quite the opposite. She's a new vampire, Red Court, with no maker we can find. It's a breach of our laws, though no fault of hers. At least, she's not at fault *yet*. Turned too quickly like that, with no guidance, she's a danger to others. Killed her entire village," he adds, almost as an afterthought. A *human* village, he must mean. That's not a mark against her, to vampires. "She needs to apprentice under a mentor soon, which is something we've been trying to arrange with the Red Court. They need to take her off our hands, or else . . ."

"Or else what?"

Gavron only narrows his eyes in seeming thoughtfulness and taps his chin. "If you keep prying, maybe I'll start calling you Nosy Fish." He taps me on—of all things—the nose.

I want to bite his finger. Instead, I glower at him, assuming he'll hear my violent desire, anyway.

Against all expectations, Gavron laughs, suddenly sweeping me up in his arms and twirling me in a circle, my gown fanning out around us. I'm dizzy when he sets me down. And not just from all the spinning. I'm not sure where his cheery mood has come from, but then it hits me . . .

Maybe he's happy to see me. Just like somewhere beyond my raw relief that I'm not alone, I'm happy to see *him*.

I don't think his reaction is simply for appearances, despite where we are. But that doesn't mean it's a good thing. Before I have a chance to wonder if either of us has a choice in how we feel, his smile falls.

Blood and piss, my thoughts were too loud.

"Yes, they were," he says, as if he just took a sip of something sour. "Why can't I be pleased to see you without there being something no-doubt insidious behind it? Why can't you *trust* me, even the slightest bit? Haven't I earned that much, at least?"

Beneath his exasperation, he almost sounds imploring. Like he *needs* me to trust him. The realization sends a shock through me. I didn't think he needed anything from me.

"Of course I do," he says instantly.

"What, my undying obedience?" I say, masking my surprise with sarcasm.

He rolls his eyes. "As if that would ever materialize. Look, I . . . apologize . . . that I wasn't there for you at the start. Something held me back. But I'm here now."

"*Why?*" I repeat, for what feels like the hundredth time. "Did the blood claim finally become too much to ignore?"

"No." He grimaces and looks away. "I need . . . *you*. And it's more than the blood claim. Before I took you on as a novice, I needed something in my life that was mine."

"Yours?" I bark a laugh. "So this *is* about you playing the Father."

"*No*," he snaps again. And then his voice drops. Softens. "I mean, I needed something to care about. I didn't know it at the time, but I felt asleep. Encased in stone. This has woken me up. *You* have," he adds, looking at me as if surprised himself. "Being forced to care for you has . . . It's given me something unexpected. Something *real*."

I'm beyond surprised. He could knock me over with a flick of his finger.

He shrugs, a mischievous gleam coming back into his eyes. "Still, you probably overestimate my regard for you, insidious as it is."

I scowl at him until his lips press together to ward off a smile. I realize I'm staring at his mouth, so I look off to the side, making my voice nonchalant. "So . . . you *didn't* miss me?"

"No. I merely enjoy vexing you."

"Mm-hmm," I say. I can't keep a straight face, either.

He groans in mock despair and holds out a hand. "I'm fairly certain we must dance as maker and novice on your first Winter Sol or else we'll be breaking thirty-five codes of Gold Court conduct. Shall we get this over with?"

I'm not horrified by the thought now. More . . . *excited.*

I take his hand. "Maybe. Are you as high and mighty about dancing as you are everything else?"

"To be honest, I despised it at first, but I *am* a quick study," he says with a sly glance that makes my stomach flop.

I make a noise of disgust. He grins fully, and it's a beautiful thing, fangs and all. The sight tugs something even deeper inside me—a hook and line inexorably pulling me toward him. I don't dwell on it, so he can't hear.

Gavron dances like he stalks through the woods: precise, smooth, and silent, practically floating. I'm better off than I was before Marai's instruction, but I'm still not great. Gavron even laughs again in that loud, unfettered way when I trip over his feet.

"I haven't heard you laugh like that in a long time, love." Suddenly Kashire is alongside us, startling me.

His short robe, which would look nearly indecent on someone less flamboyant than him, is blue silk embroidered with black ravens, belted low to expose the warm brown skin of his sculpted chest, strands of gems and pearls coiling around his neck. Beneath bare, muscled legs, he wears towering black-heeled boots that make mine look meant for beginners. His kohl-lined eyes are just as striking as Gavron's, though they gleam their bright jewel tone, and while his hair curls in its same brown cloud, I spot the iridescent glimmer of needle-thin feathers woven throughout. I have to admit that he's quite the vision. Not that I would ever tell him that.

"Where's Lief?" I ask pointedly.

Kashire puts on a regretful face. "Poor dear, I don't think he could handle it." And then he flashes a wicked smile. "But it frees me to enjoy more interesting company. Care to dance, my love?"

He holds out a hand to Gavron, and something sinks inside me.

Gavron hesitates, but Kashire waggles his fingers, jewels winking on his nails. "Come now, it's Winter Sol, and you owe me." *For what?* I wonder. He smirks at me. "Besides, I'll only ask you for this once a year, if you're lucky."

Rolling his eyes, Gavron takes his hand. Then they're off, leaving me behind and looking inhumanly gorgeous while they're at it.

I remember I'm still standing in the middle of the dance floor when a couple swoops past me in a blur of speed. I back away quickly, retreating to an upper balcony where I don't have to see the bloodied feet of the servants.

For a time, I watch Gavron and Kashire, even though it hollows my chest for some reason I don't want to examine too closely. I tell myself it's simply that *I'll* never look that graceful, and I force my eyes elsewhere.

I glimpse Jaen, a female vampire now, dancing with Marai. The sight brightens a few of the dark corners inside me, even if I pity Jaen, no doubt a victim of Marai's irrepressible enthusiasm. I'm surprised the Silver Court vampire even came, since Jaen seems like she'd enjoy dancing about as much as Revar, and yet she doesn't hold the kind of prominent position Revar does that would make her attendance mandatory. Perhaps someone dragged her. I vaguely wonder where Claudia is. I can't spot her—happily, since I have half a mind to go ask Marai for her next dance so I can rescue Jaen.

But then, my gaze drawn like a moth to the consuming flame, I see Kashire spin to a stop with Gavron in the center of the floor, and then lean in with that wicked grin on his face.

And then Kashire kisses him.

For a moment, at least, Gavron kisses him back.

The bottom drops entirely out of my stomach, and I realize with horror what the feeling means.

No, no, no, no.

I don't wait to see for how long Gavron returns Kashire's affections. Before I realize it, I'm backing away from the railing.

And I run.

12

My heeled boots nearly topple me as I weave through stone pillars and find a hidden hallway leading away from the upper story of the ballroom and vanishing into the castle. I follow it, not knowing where it leads. Only that I need to get away.

Fool, fool, fool, I chant, using Gavron's favorite word for me. *What are you doing? What are you thinking? This is just a mask you're wearing. You don't truly belong here. You'll never belong with him like that. You don't even want that! You hate Gavron! You want to use him!*

Do I? I don't know what I want anymore.

I soon come upon a small alcove with a narrow window looking out into darkness. The glass has been broken out and snow blows through the open stone frame, heaping in a small drift underneath. Two marble benches face opposite each other, and I take one, resting my forehead on the heels of my hands.

Even that doesn't give me much reprieve once I feel the material against my skin. I used to twine scraps of filthy cloth around my fingers for warmth. Now I have satin gloves, and I'm not cold even though I'm sitting before an open window in the middle of winter's deepest night. I'm at Winter Sol instead of the Midwinter Festival. There's blood instead of hotcakes. And the blood smells *good*.

How things have changed.

It's not that I want to go back to my old life. But this new one is *wrong*, even though it's trying to pull me into its dark embrace with its silk and shadows, knives and blood.

Rather, *Gavron* is drawing me in, providing me all of that and more. And then turning around and kissing Kashire. The vampire who has tried to murder me on at least one occasion. Probably more.

And yet, I don't think Gavron's seeming disregard for my *safety* is what sent me running. Something else did. Something that I've been trying to ignore as the weeks have passed.

How can I be jealous over someone I'm supposed to hate? Maybe I *do* still hate Gavron, just like he must hate me, but his blood claim is forcing us closer, making him protective of his novice and me eager for his attention, despite ourselves.

And yet, Marai said she doesn't feel that way about Claudia. And Claudia certainly never felt that way for Maudon if she switched from the Black Court to the Red after her noviceship under him. Maybe this strange new feeling isn't because of the blood claim.

The thought doesn't leave me reassured. I don't know what to trust. Certainly not myself.

Bloody fool. Jealous of a vampire's affections.

Gavron doesn't want me like that. I absolutely shouldn't want him. It should be simple.

But it's not.

I sit on the cold bench for a long while, an hour maybe, my gown pooled around me. At some point, I hear a bell outside ringing the hour and realize I should probably return to the ball, if only to bid Marai good evening.

And Gavron, I suppose.

Or maybe I should ignore Gavron. Forever, if possible. Quitting Black Court lessons would probably be an excellent start.

But then how will I get my hands on a dread blade or some other weapon that can kill vampires? Perhaps staying close to Gavron is worth the risk, so long as I can ignore how I feel about him.

What do you want, Fin?

To be alone in my room, to start.

I stand, no stiffness in my limbs, only my gown and boots to encumber me. My eyes are so well-adjusted to the darkness I barely need to look where I'm headed as I return to the ballroom.

Maybe that's how I almost trip over the body.

I stop myself just in time. It takes my brain a moment to piece together what I'm staring at: Lief's utterly bloodless corpse. Even his eyes are drained of all color, leaving only the black pinpricks of his pupils staring at the carved ceiling. There's not a drop of blood around him. It's like someone simply set his body here.

Or dropped it, when they heard me coming.

I press my lips together, choking down a shriek. My breath slows automatically, following the lessons I've been learning from Gavron, and I try to back away as quickly and quietly as possible.

I bump into someone. A hand clamps over my mouth. *Now* I try to shriek.

Which does absolutely nothing to stop the knife that slashes across my neck from behind. It parts both the black ribbon there and my skin like butter. *My* blood, unlike Lief's, sprays everywhere in a dark ruby arc, splattering across the entire hallway.

I barely feel it. My terror is too great. I stumble away from my attacker, falling to my knees, one hand clenched to my squirting throat.

So much blood. Why isn't it stopping?

Help, I need help. I try to cry out, but the words are only a rasp.

I scrabble away. Before I get far, harsh fingers fist in my hair, hauling my head back. I feel the damage that's already been done, the burning line of fire. I try to scream again, agonized, clawing at the hand.

I stop when my attacker releases me, dropping me facedown on top of Lief. I hear a grunt behind me, a scuffling and hissing, and then nothing. No footsteps retreating. Although maybe a faint pattering of what sounds like small feet?

All I can do is wrap sticky fingers as tight as I can around my neck and curl into a ball. When nothing comes lunging out of the darkness to finish the job, I nearly sob with relief.

Then I hear Kashire's voice: "Fin?"

I throw myself away from him, scuttling backward across the floor as fast as I can one handed. My back hits the wall, and I stare at Kashire, wild-eyed, while he looks from me to Lief's body.

For his part, he looks disturbed. If it's feigned, it's a good act. But then, this is Kashire, who puts on masks as real as his own face.

"Who did this?" he asks quietly.

I nearly laugh, gasping instead. "You?"

It's the only word I can get out. And then I slip sideways down the wall, my blood making a waterfall over my bare shoulder. It looks a lot darker than it used to, I think hazily. Like old blood. Somewhere between red and black.

Kashire's eyes widen at the sight. In a blink, he's at my side, laying me on my back. He wrenches my hand away from my neck—*to let me bleed out faster*, I wonder?

When he bends toward me, I think, *To feed, then.* His tongue confirms it, tracing over the burning wound in my neck. Leaving soothing cool behind. Taking nothing.

He straightens, glaring at me. "It's not healing. This was made with a dread blade."

I try to say something. Blood gurgles in my throat. My eyes widen as I choke, panic flaring in my chest.

Kashire lifts his wrist to his mouth, ready to bite it. Before he can, Gavron is suddenly above us both, shoving him out of the way. Gavron looks oddly disheveled, taken off guard. *Were they still spinning together on the dance floor*, I wonder vaguely? Or had they retreated somewhere more private?

As bitter as the thought is, it would prove Kashire didn't do this.

The castle hallway, already dark, begins to sink deeper into shadow, my vision dimming. My eyes begin to flutter closed.

I lurch awake at the press of a bleeding wrist against my lips. Gavron's blood—I would recognize it anywhere—floods my mouth. But I don't gulp it down, not this time. I only swallow a little, no matter how delicious the taste. It nauseates me now. I hurl his arm away, shoving myself upright, and press my back into the wall, clutching my still-bleeding throat.

For some reason, I don't want anyone near me. Not even him, not even to heal me. My other hand scrabbles for a dagger until I remember I don't have one.

Gavron's dark eyes flicker between me, Lief, and Kashire. "How did this happen?" he demands.

"Kashire?" I rasp.

Kashire narrows those blue eyes at me. "I hope you're asking my opinion, my dear, and not accusing me."

I swallow painfully. "Your arrival is quite the coincidence, then."

"I sensed him," he says, nodding at the body. "I didn't know something was truly wrong until I felt him die. He went peacefully, I think, though it took his heart a while to stop beating even without any blood."

"So you just happened to know exactly where his body was?"

"I told you, I could feel it," he says, irritation seeping into his tone. "This is new to me, too, sweetness. I've never lost a novice before."

Sweetness. For a blinding second I wish I could light Kashire on fire.

Since I've left my village, my heart has been stabbed through—by Kashire—my spine severed—by Kashire—and my shoulder and side shredded—possibly by Kashire. Now, I've just had my throat cut. Also possibly by Kashire.

He glares at Gavron. "And before you judge me for this, love, you're not so fantastic at looking after your novice, either. Fin appears to have stumbled across his body *and* his attacker. That's the second time you haven't been there for her."

Which means he knows about the time in the woods, with the werewolf. Because he *was* there, in raven form, laughing at me. I knew it.

"Never mind that your novice is *dead*," I grate, spitting blood, "and that you were the one to lure Gavron away from me tonight."

"Jealous?" Kashire cocks an eyebrow at me. "Our dance was done ages ago. We parted, bickering as usual. This is on him. And, indeed, my novice is on me," he adds, looking down at the body again. "I guess that's why they give those like me foundlings as a learning experience."

"Fin, let me finish healing your neck——" Gavron starts. He tries to move for me, but I halt him with a furious glare.

"Why was Lief wandering alone?" I ask Kashire.

"Probably looking for me," he admits.

"And did he find you?"

"Obviously not——I told you."

"Why is your word or his body evidence that he *didn't* find you?"

"Fin——" Gavron says warningly.

I ignore him. "If you were no longer dancing, where have you been?"

"I don't answer to you," Kashire says coldly. "And you might as well ask your maker where *he* was while you were meeting the nasty end of a dread blade."

"It's been an hour since your dance," I say to Kashire. "Maybe you were looking for me, too, after you killed Lief. You *do* like to follow me around as a raven and watch me suffer."

Kashire's eyes narrow even farther, into icy slivers. "You're lucky I came upon you. Your maker might not have before it was too late.

Same as before. I *warned* Gavron of the werewolf, you little ingrate. He only came in time to save you because of me."

"He's telling the truth," Gavron states, exasperated. "I told you that he had no hand in the attack."

"But why would you do that?" I ask, trying to drag myself higher up the wall from my slump. "You tried to kill me the moment we met! You couldn't possibly regret that?"

Kashire smiles murderously. "Not at all. But since I arranged this torture scene between the two of you," he says, pointing between me and Gavron with a long, elegant finger, "I've endeavored to keep it going. Why would I give it up so soon by letting you die? It's far too entertaining."

And yet he's proved he doesn't have any qualms about risking my life, and he might be arranging these attacks to make the situation more entertaining—forcing Gavron to come to my aid—even if the goal isn't actually my death. Or else, perhaps now, after tonight . . .

I haven't heard you laugh like that in a long time, love.

"Maybe I'm not as torturous as you might have hoped," I say. My pain is making me reckless. "Maybe I'm becoming less entertaining to you." *Because* you're *jealous*, I think, but don't say aloud. If it's loud enough for Gavron to hear, he doesn't let on.

I groan as I adjust my hold on my neck. Gavron tries to come to me again, but I wave him away. Kashire and I share a hard look. "So, where were you?"

He opens his mouth, eyes blazing. But then he freezes, and then spins on something I can't sense. "Come out, come out, whoever you are," he says, his voice singsong.

Claudia detaches herself from the shadows farther down the hall. Gavron's eyes narrow in suspicion, though I'm not sure why he's not looking at Kashire like that, as well.

This is nearly everyone who would want me dead. If Maudon

were to suddenly arrive, it *would* be everyone. If Gavron weren't around to stop them, they could have a bloody toast over my corpse.

"What are *you* doing here?" I demand, hoping my harsh tone is enough to mask my fear.

"Looking for her." Claudia's red eyes flicker down the hall opposite her. I hear who she means before I see her.

"Fin!" Marai cries. "Where have you been? I went all the way back to your room, and I've been combing the halls since." She lurches to a stop when she finally takes me in, sitting in a massive pool of my own blood next to Lief's corpse, my neck partially held together by my hand. Her vibrant pink eyes widen.

Yet another person looking for me. Perhaps it's best that Marai didn't find me until now. I shudder to think of what could have happened to her, as well—another novice, a foundling, even.

Claudia seems to agree, barely glancing my way before starting in on her. "Don't go running off like that, or you could end up like her." She nods at me. "Or worse, *him*." She doesn't look at Lief at all.

"Foundlings do seem to be going quickly around here," Kashire says. When we all stare at him, he asks, "Too soon?"

I can only glare at him from my hunched position against the wall. All this talk is starting to wear on me. The only reason I'm able to speak at all is because of Gavron's fresh blood. Without it, I'd be dead. To heal completely, I know I need more of it, but right now, I can't stomach the thought.

"Why is no one helping her?" Marai demands.

Gavron scrapes his hand through his hair, his irritation plain. "She's been resistant."

Marai spins on him, evidently ready to tell him what she feels about such an excuse, when Claudia interrupts her. "Entrance her," she says simply.

"I promised her I wouldn't," Gavron snaps.

She snorts. "Come, Marai, she'll be fine with Gavron here. Let's return to the ball and be done with such foolishness."

Marai sputters, but no one listens to her.

"Can you send word to Maudon of what happened here?" Gavron asks as Claudia departs, her arm through Marai's.

Claudia sneers at him over her shoulder. "I'm not the Black Court's messenger. But yes, I can."

"We'll talk later, Fin!" Marai calls, and then, "Let him heal your bloody neck!"

Bloody, indeed.

Kashire waves in my direction soon after they're gone. "I, too, will leave you to clean up this little mess." He bends over Lief's body. I'm surprised he doesn't just abandon it for servants to take care of, but Kashire covers it with his jacket before he lifts it—gently—and walks it out of sight.

Probably the least he can do is show Lief's body respect, if he murdered him.

"Fin, don't," Gavron says. "I don't want to hear it."

"Then why don't you stop eavesdropping on my thoughts and go follow him, since he's *that* important to you," I hiss up at him. I don't want to lift my head and open the cut more than it is.

Gavron crouches down in front of me. "You're a mess."

I laugh stickily. "Probably should've worn black."

"Stop moving and let me help."

"Stop pretending you give a rat's piece of scat about me."

He ignores me, lifting his wrist to his mouth.

I whack his arm away with my free hand and instantly regret it. Even that was too much movement. "I don't want it. I don't want *anything* from you." My voice strains at the end.

Worse, my eyes start to fill with tears.

It's not just that he let something like this happen to me *again*. Or the kiss he gave my likely attacker just an hour before. It's Lief, a novice, yet another foundling like me . . . dead. Someone tried to kill *me*. Again. I feel sick, not hungry.

Perhaps my village *is* a better place for me, after all. I was only bruised there, not cut half to death.

"I get that you're afraid, but don't be ridiculous. *Drink*," Gavron insists. "You were due for another feeding soon, anyway. The other novices are catching up."

"Shouldn't I stay at their pace and not get ahead again?" I hate that my voice is choked with tears.

Gavron winces. "Just drink, damn it. After dancing with Kashire, I was searching for you—"

I choke down another laugh. "You teach Stalking. It's your House's mission to hunt errant vampires. I can't imagine you were searching for your novice for that long, or else you would have found me."

He glares but doesn't deny it. If he was only with Kashire for one dance, then where *was* he? Probably fulfilling yet another task for Maudon. I doubt he'll tell me the truth, but I know all I need to: I'm *not* his primary concern.

And it's going to get me killed, especially if he can't see a murderer right in front of him.

"Despite what little esteem you seem to hold me in," he hisses, "I'm not going to let you just sit here and bleed to death to get back at me."

"I'm fine," I insist.

He snorts. "You probably can't even stand on your own, let alone make it back to your room."

"Can, too." I start struggling to my feet one handed. I get halfway there, but I'm dizzy, my soaked gown weighing me down, and my heeled boots slip on my own blood.

Gavron catches me before I hit the ground. Reflex makes me flail and grab on to him, exposing my neck and the mess there.

143

His eyes alight as they latch onto it. His expression transforms entirely.

For a moment, he looks like the monster he is.

"Have it your way," he says, and then he's clamped into my neck and drinking.

There's nothing to calm my fear now, but at least his tongue numbs the pain from both the gash and his teeth. I still gasp and struggle, punching at his ribs, his neck, his head. I'm a lot stronger now, even injured and weak with blood loss. But I realize how far I still have to go when I barely shift him.

And then my remaining strength starts ebbing rapidly. My fist drops to my side. As much as I hate to admit it, it's almost relaxing. It doesn't feel quite as good as it did before when he *told* me it would feel good, but it's not terrible. It's like drifting away on a cloud. My knees buckle, and he catches me.

When he eventually pulls away, keeping one arm looped under my shoulders to hold me up, I have to struggle to open my eyes. I'm too drained to glare at him.

"*Now* you can't stand," he says smugly, back to usual Gavron. Except his lips are stained with my blood and there's a gleam in his dark eyes. He's almost cheerful as he says, "I didn't even entrance you. Will you accept my help now, or would you rather die?"

At least *one* of us is in a good mood. Maybe because he knows my answer already, the bloody bastard. I'm having a piss-poor night, but not one so bad as that.

"Such language," he chides mildly.

I wonder if he'll bite his wrist here and now, with me hanging like a rag doll. The thought reminds me of Lief's limp form again, and I feel even emptier.

"No," Gavron says, his voice softer. Gentle. "Let's find somewhere more comfortable."

For a moment I worry he'll shadowstep, because vomiting might just kill me. Instead, he scoops me up in his arms, blood-soaked gown and all, and carries me down the hall as if I weigh nothing. I vaguely wonder where he's headed.

He takes me to the bench where I spent a good hour before the attack.

"*This* is where you were?" he says, sitting down with me nestled against his shoulder. My gown blankets us both in a layer of bloody silk. "It's where I used to come to escape Winter Sol myself."

"Did *you* break the window?" I murmur.

He blinks down at me. "How in the Founders' names did you know that?"

"Just a wild guess," I say. "It seems like you would have wanted the fresh air. And that you probably had a temper." My eyes start drifting closed on his bemused half smile.

They fly wide a moment later when he presses his bleeding wrist to my mouth. At least, until the hunger takes me. After which, I close them again, clinging to his arm like a cat on a kill.

Cat, I think, but I can't hold the thought much longer as I drink.

This time, I can't resist. Perhaps my body needs it too much. As usual, his blood is bliss.

"Drink, Little Fish, drink," Gavron hums above me. Based on the direction of his voice, he's facing the open window. "Embrace the night, and let it embrace you." He almost sounds entranced himself. But then he holds me closer, tighter. I feel him drop a kiss on the top of my head. He bends toward my ear where he whispers, "This isn't so bad, is it?"

Is it?

I force myself to stop drinking this time, before he has to. I lie still for a while after, resting against his chest. He keeps his arms lazily wrapped around me, uncaring of the blood everywhere. He even rocks me gently back and forth.

I don't think about how good it feels to be in his embrace. If I did,

I might as well shout it out loud, because that's how good it is. So I keep my thoughts very carefully blank. As white as a field of snow. As smooth as the crust of a fresh hotcake steaming in the chill air.

"Why are you thinking of hotcakes?" Gavron asks suddenly.

"I'm hungry," I say quickly.

He chuckles. "You shouldn't be, not after what you just drank."

"Maybe *you're* not all the world has to offer someone like me, despite what you might think," I say stiffly.

Gavron only grunts, perhaps in agreement. "Let's go." I assume he means back to the ball, which is a horrible thought, but then he says, "I'll take you back to your room, make sure you get there safely. And I'll stand guard until just before sunrise. You should get some rest. And food."

When he stands, he lifts me with him, carrying me in his arms as he starts down the hallway.

"I can walk," I say crossly, trying to shuffle my legs out of the crook of his elbow. It's like trying to budge a marble statue.

"Relax. Give my blood a chance to work. Wounds from dread blades take time to fully heal, and you need to regenerate a lot of your own blood."

It took his heart a while to stop beating even without any blood, I hear Kashire say.

I shudder and lie still.

"Who else possesses dread blades?" I whisper into Gavron's shoulder. It's the first time I've ever asked about them. I don't think it's odd for me to do so now, seeing as one nearly severed my neck.

I catch the dark flicker of his eyes as he glances down at me. "Only the Black Court. But no member of my House would have done this, I assure you. Dread blades have been stolen over the centuries. Not many, but this must have been one of those."

"Why would someone use it on me? Or Lief?"

What did Lief do to anyone? I try to silence my next thought before it fully forms: *To anyone but Kashire?*

"I don't know." I can hear the disquiet in Gavron's voice. "Why would anyone hunt foundlings? Disregard is the norm."

"Yes, we're too unimportant to even bother murdering," I snap, "except Lief's corpse and my neck say otherwise. That's *two* foundlings dead now. The first was the boy in the woods, before our Beginning, and we know Kashire did it because we both watched him do it. He nearly killed me then, too, if you recall. And he was there in the forest with the wolves."

"Aside from the fact that he *warned* me you were in danger then, he—what? Had a chat with the werewolf and talked it into biting you? Werewolves aren't like that, *if you recall*," he echoes me. "They're not rational creatures."

"He could have enthralled it and then warned you I was in danger to cover for himself. He either thought you'd be too late to save me, or he only wanted a show. The creature's eyes were funny, though I didn't get a good look," I admit.

Gavron shakes his head above me. "Kashire has never been decent at enthralling. He's too direct for that."

It suddenly occurs to me that animals don't have strange eyes only when they're enthralled . . . but when they're not truly animals at all. "Maybe he can turn *into* a werewolf."

"Kashire has many talents, especially in the realm of shapeshifting, but that's not one of them."

Something in his voice gives me pause. "Are there vampires who can?"

His eyes flicker down and away from me. "Don't concern yourself with that. My point is, it wasn't Kashire, and that's the whole argument you're trying to make when you should be resting."

There's something he's not telling me. "How can you argue that what just happened tonight isn't suspicious? Kashire made no secret that Lief irritated him. He wouldn't say where he was when the murder happened, and he *winked* at me after I accused him. He's obviously murdering foundlings!"

"Kashire merely likes to play games. I hate to agree with his crass assessment, but foundlings do tend to die the easiest of all novices. Two deaths don't make a pattern. Besides, *everyone* irritates Kashire. It's not cause for him to murder. And whether a vampire likes their novice or not"—Gavron smirks down at me—"the death of a novice would feel something like losing your own arm."

I blink. That's news to me, to hear my death would hurt him.

"As far as foundlings go," Gavron continues, "you heard Kashire when we first met. Despite what he did to you and that boy on the way to Courtsheart, he was criticizing *me* for resenting you as a burden, pointing out the Black Court's . . . prejudice," he admits grudgingly. "As ironic as it may seem, he probably did all of that to try to get me to care. So why on earth would he be killing you all now?"

"I don't know, for fun? Because you *still* don't seem to care about foundlings?"

"I don't, do I?" he says softly, dangerously.

I don't have the energy to argue anymore, so I fall silent for a moment as he walks. The stiff fabric of my gown, rustling against his legs, makes more noise than he does. "Is *anyone* even going to care?"

"I'm going to report to Maudon. I'm sure he'll look into it."

I doubt that. But then I tense as I realize we *are* headed back to the ballroom.

"Don't worry," Gavron says, sweeping me quickly back through the doors to the upper balcony and setting me on my somewhat unsteady feet. "You don't have to come down. I'll shadowstep from here and just be a second."

He vanishes. I'm tempted to remain exactly where I am, maybe lean against a pillar and let it take some of the weight off. But the stringed instruments, the faintly bobbing lights, and the tinkling laughter down below are too intoxicating. I can't help shuffling over to the railing for one last look at Winter Sol.

Just in time to see *them*.

Gavron appears next to Maudon, who is arm in arm with the woman at his side. She's willowy, with pale skin and golden hair. No ribbon around her throat, because she doesn't need one to protect her. Where her eyes would have been blue, I can see with my own keen sight that they're now bloodred.

This must be the new Red Court vampire, the one without a maker, or at least insofar as anyone can identify. The one nobody seems to know.

Except I know her.

It's Silvea.

13

---

er eyes like Claudia's. Her arm in Maudon's. I fall back from the railing, clutching my chest as if I've been stabbed. *Silvea.*

The strange new vampire taking up the Black Court's attention is *Silvea.*

The pain in my heart is a visceral thing, making me gasp.

"Fin?" Gavron says. He's reappeared next to me on the balcony above the ballroom floor, and he places a concerned hand on my shoulder. "What is it?"

There's more tenderness in his voice than usual, not to mention he's still using my name. The intimacy of our blood sharing hasn't yet faded, I suppose. I spin away from him, a hand over my mouth.

Maybe Gavron doesn't know who Silvea is to me. I genuinely don't think so, based on how innocently he relayed the information about her: *Turned too quickly like that, with no guidance, she's a danger to others. Killed her entire village.*

I close my eyes.

Her.

Entire.

Village.

The words I heard earlier are entirely new. They slam into me like ocean waves, leaving me cold and staggering.

My entire village is dead.

It's hard to breathe around the force of the truth. I never belonged in my village, but it's entirely different to know that they're all gone. I was the least loved or important among them, the one destined to be discarded. And yet I'm the only one left. And Silvea, who used to be the best of them, their healer-in-training, the one I sacrificed myself for . . . she's the one who killed them all.

And now she's here. Maudon and Gavron have been the ones shepherding her into this life.

"Fin?"

It's *her* voice. She must have watched Gavron vanish and reappear in the balcony over her head. Must have caught sight of me up there and followed on inhumanly fast feet. I turn to find her at the top of the balcony stairs, an apparition in scarlet. Her dress is as red as mine, except hers is from dye, not blood. Her new, matching eyes drink me in.

"Not curious as to why I'm here, Fin?" she asks lightly. "You haven't even said hello yet."

"Hello, Silvea," I say, a bitter laugh escaping me. I feel some of the dried blood at my throat crack. "How are you? How's the village?"

"It's changed quite a lot since you last saw it. As have I, since you last saw me." She takes a few gliding steps toward me.

Gavron shifts subtly closer. He must have a hint of what's going on from what he can read in my mind, and yet he's keeping quiet. On guard.

"Oh, Gavron, *this* is your novice?" Silvea asks in apparent sympathy. "You deserve so much better."

He doesn't respond. No protest. Maybe he's focusing, but it still stings.

Maudon suddenly appears behind Silvea, looking irate. "There you are."

She doesn't seem to notice him. Only me. She's still staring at me when Claudia arrives at the top of the stairs. Marai isn't with her this time, and I wonder vaguely why she's come.

Unless she has something to do with Silvea's arrival at Courtsheart.

Silvea suddenly giggles, covering her mouth with a delicate hand—at least, it used to be delicate. I can't imagine what that hand has done now. "You told me you'd kill me the next time you saw me. But now I'm immortal, and you're the only person from our village I have *yet* to kill. That was a nice try, though." She nods at my gown, her gaze lingering on the blood.

I have no words. I can only gape at her.

Gavron looks to Maudon, hard and fast.

"Silvea has been with me the entire time, until just a moment ago," Maudon says. "I wouldn't be so lax in my duties as to risk cutting her loose. And I *won't* let her out from under our watch until she has a Red Court mentor." His dark eyes flicker in Claudia's direction. "Though she should be your own House's charge, they're being less than forthcoming with her care."

"Don't look to me." Claudia's words are defensive. "Just because someone in the Red Court couldn't control themselves, that doesn't mean she's *my* responsibility."

Something in Maudon's demeanor sparks a question in my mind: Does he think *Claudia* may have turned her, perhaps behind his back? Could she have? They both seemed to want Silvea at the Finding, before Revar thwarted them. I thought Maudon was obsessed with her, but he doesn't look that way now. Her presence seems to be more of a nuisance than anything. It's his job to uphold the rules of the vampire world—Maudon would probably be reluctant to break them so thoroughly.

But Claudia might not have such restraint.

If either one of them was angry at me for taking Silvea's place, a fitting way to repay me would be by either trying to kill me or by turning her anyway—or *both*. And right now, Maudon seems to be pointing at Claudia.

She folds her arms, as if warding off suspicion. "I already have a novice, besides."

Even though Silvea is watching the exchange between them, she hardly seems to be paying attention. She's inching closer to me, her nose turned my way—or at least to the blood covering me.

Maudon notices and takes her arm forcefully. "Time for us to leave, I think."

"Indeed," Claudia says, turning on her heel and marching back down the stairs.

Right before Maudon vanishes, shadowstepping her away from the apparently delectable meal I would make, Silvea grins at me. Showing her long, pointed canines. It's the last I see of her before I'm left alone with Gavron.

I'm barely aware of him. As soon as Silvea is gone, I bend over and throw up a voluminous amount of black blood all over the sparkling floor. I lose my strength with it, my limbs instantly feeling a thousand times heavier.

Perhaps it's because of the blood loss—both his and mine—and now *this* shock, but my body abruptly decides it's had enough.

I faint dead away. I'm not even sure Gavron catches me.

<hr />

When I wake up in my massive bed the next evening, I'm alone. My bloody gown has been stripped away, and I'm in a clean black nightgown.

I don't get up. As I lie there in my dark nest of silk sheets and pillows, I force myself to picture their faces: The headman and his wife. Silvea's mother, the village healer. Gregor, the baker's boy. The baker, Harald. The butcher, Frell. The fishermen who used to go out to sea with my father. Gone now, like he is.

I wonder if anyone bothered to bury them, or if that was left up to the winter snow.

I didn't love any of them. But I never wished any of them death. And now *she's* a vampire.

I loved her once.

I don't know if I can face what Silvea has done, who she is now. What could I even say to her?

Tell her to forget about my threat? That I don't care what she did?

Tell her how I felt about her?

I feel the *No, No,* and *No* coat my heart like burning-hot wax, hardening around it.

Resolved, I finally sit up. I catch my eyes in the washstand mirror. They're far darker. Gavron must have fed me again in my sleep.

It's like they're not my eyes anymore, his blood written all over them. And for a moment I despise them as much as Silvea's red gaze. With my disgusted sneer, I catch sight of my teeth. Not quite as long as Silvea's yet, but longer. Still human, but barely. Clinging to it with my weakening human grip. Clawing away from it with blood-fueled strength.

Maybe I should just let go of being human. It would be easy.

It would feel *good*.

I picture it against my will: Gavron in my bed. With me. Even asleep, I likely curled around that magnetizing source at his wrist and pressed into him. Maybe I even bit him myself this time.

The guilty pleasure of that thought, the delicious shame of it, isn't even why I'm furious. I'm furious because, even now, when I should despise him most, I want him here with me. His dark form cupped around me, as if made to fit me. Or me, him.

For a moment, I hate myself more than I hate him.

It doesn't help that I still have the faint flavor of his blood in my mouth, tantalizing my tongue.

There's a note nearby, the scrap of parchment pinned under a plate heaped with cold hotcakes—what I said I was craving most. His spidery writing gouges almost all the way through, forming only two words.

I'm sorry.

For what, exactly? Not being there when my neck got slashed? For returning Kashire's kiss? For feeding on me when I was unwilling? For Silvea, turned? For the demise of my entire village? For making me crave his blood? For making me feel *other* things?

The list is long.

Maybe he's apologizing for all of it, which is why he pressed so hard with the quill.

I hurl the note, and then my pillow, at the wall. Then the plate with the hotcakes and my candlestick from the bedside table. Then the table itself. And then I lift my *entire bed* and shatter it against stone in an earsplitting, wood-shrieking crash before I realize what I'm doing.

I'm left standing in the wreckage of my own room.

I have no parents. No home to return to. No friends, save Marai. And now I don't even have a bed.

I quite liked that bed.

If you pity yourself more, you might do us all a favor and die of it.

Before I realize it, I'm grinning. Because I'm not going to do anyone a favor by dying. I'm going to *live*. I'm going to *learn*. And I'm going to *remember*.

And I don't even need to avoid Gavron while doing it. He's going to help me, both with his blood and his knowledge.

I'm not afraid of becoming a vampire, not anymore. Not all vampires are my enemies, but my enemies are all vampires. I need their strength. And while their blood will remake me, it won't change what I want. I won't forget, any more than I'd forget my mother. Even if it hurts to remember my humanity, I'll use my pain to drive me.

I might indeed be becoming a monster. But I'm going to find

out who attacked me, who killed Lief, and even who turned Silvea, destroying my village as a result. Even if I'm the only one who cares, it means I'll be best suited for the task.

I'm going to learn how to hunt monsters. Even if I become one.

And I know just the monster to teach me. He already hunts vampires, after all.

<hr />

While the servants are replacing my ruined bed, I crawl into Marai's with her the next morning to sleep. I tell her about Silvea and my village—though I leave out my past feelings for her, as well as any suspicions about Claudia. Marai is as comforting as I hoped she would be, and doesn't ask many questions. I think she can tell how much Silvea's arrival has hurt me.

And then I tell her that someone might be killing off the foundling novices, and that we might be the only ones who care . . . and quite possibly next on the short list. There are only two left besides us now. Both of the others were claimed by the Silver and Red Courts.

"But what can we do?" Marai whispers, her silk-wrapped head ducked under the covers with me, where we're hiding from even the weak winter sun. Her eyes nearly glow in the darkness. The red in them isn't as strong as the black in mine, but she still looks far from human. Her sharper teeth glint in the shadows as she talks. "If we find the vampire trying to murder us, it's not as if we can stop them."

"What if we can?" I say breathlessly.

"How?"

"Gavron is a Black Court vampire and . . . my . . . maker," I say sourly, clutching a pillow tighter to my chest. The word still tastes horrible on my tongue, no matter how many times I've heard it. "He knows how to kill vampires. He'll teach me."

Marai shudders. "Even *vampires* think of killing other vampires as monstrous. I thought you were only learning how to mist yourself."

"Shadowstepping comes well before mistwalking, and I haven't even gotten to *that* yet. That's next season, if I continue. Mistwalking, I'm not sure, but it doesn't matter. He's been teaching me how to *stalk*. Animals right now, but then once we combine it with shadowstepping . . . Marai, I think the Black Court lessons are all about killing vampires. Their House has skills the others don't. And weapons. They're the only ones with *dread blades*." I whisper the name even quieter and rub at my throat. There's no scar, but I can still feel the memory of the cut. "Trust me, they work. And Gavron has at least one. Maybe I can convince him to let me borrow one." My tone is too casual.

"Fin, do *not* steal," Marai hisses, "from your *maker*."

Her use of the title makes me all the more willing. I smile. "He's stolen from me, so why not?"

"He's also given you much—"

"Maybe I won't have to steal," I interrupt, and then add less hopefully, "Maybe I can charm him." The words make me flush when I realize how they sound. I hope it's too dark for Marai to see.

She snorts. "We haven't taken Seduction yet. Your skills in particular might be lacking there."

"*Hey*," I say with exaggerated insult and flap the blanket at her. "I mean I'll charm him by being the perfect, diligent student, not by seducing him."

"Good," she says. I don't have a chance to ask her to clarify before she asks, "Why can't you just tell him the truth and ask for help?"

"I already tried," I say shortly. "He won't listen." I don't say, *My main suspect is his maybe-not-former lover.*

She groans and flops on her back. "I should *not* be helping you with this ridiculous scheme. So, once you miraculously come to possess a dread blade and you know how to shadowstep without killing yourself, whom do you plan to stalk?"

"Whom do *we* plan to stalk, you mean?"

She groans again.

"Kashire," I say.

She looks at me incredulously. "Do you have a death wish? I wouldn't have become friends with you if you had a death wish."

"It's precisely because I *don't* have a death wish that we need to follow him. He's already killed one foundling, nearly killed me, and now his own foundling novice is dead. Maybe we can lay a trap for him with one of us as bait." I take a deep breath. "And then I'll kill him, if I have to."

She blinks. "Okay, if you don't have a death wish, you're mad."

I give her shoulder a light jab. "Listen to me! Kashire failed the Black Court's lessons—Gavron said so himself. The Blue Court can't match this type of training. When the night terrors attacked the carriages on the way to Courtsheart, Gavron fought them off by *himself*."

"That's Gavron, you're you, and Kashire is Kashire—"

"He's still only a young blood!" I don't have a perfect grasp of what this means, since it encompasses the time after apprenticeship until being considered "mature," which Gavron described as up to fifty years. But I hope Kashire, like Gavron, is on the younger side of "young blood," since they're . . . *friends*. "We can do this, especially with a dread blade." I forestall further interruption. "We have to do something, or else Kashire might kill *us*."

Marai's eyes are wide, but I can tell she's considering the plan. "But what if it's not him? Who else might want us dead?"

I know who might want *me* dead: Claudia. And perhaps Maudon, though I'm becoming less certain there. Mentioning Claudia will complicate things with Marai. She's already defensive of her maker, and I haven't even come close to accusing Claudia of murder yet. As for Maudon, if he wants me dead, there's probably little I can do about it. He's no young blood, and he's the commander of the Black Court.

There might be one newborn vampire who wouldn't mind seeing me go, and she's even tied to these two somehow. But she only just arrived here.

"Maybe we won't have to use the dread blade for anything but a threat, if Kashire can prove to us that he's not responsible. But he's still the obvious suspect," I say. "Even if we fail to find the killer, it's better than simply waiting around to be murdered. We might avoid a sticky end, at the very least. You said you wanted to be a wolf, not a sheep for the slaughter. It's time for us to be wolves."

Marai frowns. "Are you just saying that because a certain gentleman vampire can turn into a wolf?"

"Don't make me destroy another pillow over you, please."

She sighs wistfully up at the blanket tent above our heads. "I guess I wouldn't mind not having to attend Revelry anymore."

"Actually," I say with some reluctance, "we have to finish out this season and start the next before we act. I need to learn more from Gavron. More from Claudia, too," I add, as eagerly as possible, "and get my hands on a dread blade. And we need Kashire to suspect nothing coming his way. If we move against him too soon, he'll know."

"No avoiding Revelry, then," Marai grumbles. "But why can't we simply wait until someone else finds the killer? Such as the vampires whose *duty* it is? Also known as the Black Court?"

I frown. "Gavron reported everything to Maudon, so we'll see what happens. We can only wait until I've been able to get what I need, or else we risk too much." I can't imagine a vampire will care as much about this as I do, especially Maudon. But maybe he'll surprise me. "Either the Black Court finds the killer or we do ourselves. Unless we want to end up like Lief. Like I *nearly* did."

I won't let Marai or myself fall next. And if Kashire isn't responsible, then I'll move down my list of likeliest suspects:

159

Claudia.

Maudon.

I don't even let myself think the last name. She couldn't have.

Could she? After what she's already done in her new life as a vampire, maybe the real question is: What *wouldn't* she do now?

"You *are* mad," Marai says eventually, chewing on her lip with one especially sharp tooth. "But that doesn't mean you don't have a point. I'll help you, however I can."

I smile. "I know. You're terribly predictable."

It's her turn to break open a pillow over *my* head!

III

SPRING

14

The night air outside is still cold. Winter hardly seems to have departed, even if spring is here. As usual, I no longer feel the chill.

The only change in scenery to indicate a new season is thanks to Gavron taking me to a different location outside Courtsheart for our first session of Black Court Intermediate. When I arrived at the allotted time in front of the bridge, he looked thoroughly surprised I showed up at all.

We've hardly spoken outside of Winter's final lessons, and only during them to discuss the finer points of what he was trying to teach me. He no doubt heard what I did to my bed—another massive, curtain-swathed bed, which I hate, arrived in my room afterward—and yet he's never mentioned it or his apology note. And so I haven't.

None of our awkward silences have detracted from his teaching. He's been as exacting as ever, just as I need him to be. I've tried to learn as much as possible from him. My life, and maybe others' lives, depends on it.

For my final test of Stalking, I took down the entire wolf pack that had once hunted me. Not at his direction; he allowed me to choose my own target. *Subtle*, Marai said. Really I did it to save a village the loss of their sheep or one of their children—more a response to Silvea than to Gavron, though I haven't seen her since Winter Sol. I came out of that last lesson half-mauled, but I healed in a night.

Tonight, I'm once again the only student. Marai told me that

Claudia told *her* that Silvea tried to join us, since she's been permitted to partake in certain lessons, but Maudon forbade it because she didn't have the base knowledge necessary—not to mention she's unstable.

Thank the Founders. It's the first time I've thought that instead of *Thank the Father.* I never imagined I'd be grateful to either the mysterious vampire Founders *or* Maudon. Then again, no fathers, real or divine, have ever been particularly deserving of my gratitude.

"Are you sure you want to do this?" Gavron asks, echoing his words the first time I showed up for his lessons.

"I don't think there's anything I want to learn more than this," I tell him truthfully.

I need to find out who killed Lief, who has been trying to kill me, and to prove it. Or else they might succeed next time. Or go after Marai.

And if it's the same vampire that turned Silvea and destroyed my village, I need to destroy *them.* I don't know quite how I'll manage, but that won't stop me from trying.

In any case, I need Gavron's skills and weapons more than ever. *Especially* the dangerous ones.

Gavron gives me a wry look. "I think your stomach might say otherwise. Shadowstepping has never agreed with you."

"It's fine. I'm ready to learn."

And then we lapse back into silence as I look around the wide clearing we're standing in, skeletal trees lining the perimeter, snow glittering in the moonlight. There's not a breath of wind. Stars sparkle in a stretching expanse overhead. Whenever I'm with Gavron, we're usually in dense shadowy forest or dark hallways. Constrained. Now it feels like we're the only two people in the world, free of everyone and everything. For a brief second, I wish appearances weren't deceiving.

"This is different," I say.

"You need the open space now, so you don't end up bouncing off trees. Shadowstepping isn't quite as dangerous as mistwalking, where you could end up with half or more of you *in* the tree. But trust me, you don't want to risk miscalculating here, either, until you're more experienced. If you try to take the place of something else when there isn't any room to allow you, it responds with violence. *Bone-breaking* violence. Even for a vampire."

"And I can do this now?" I say dubiously. "Even as a not-quite-vampire?"

"My blood should give you enough power to *try*."

I smirk at him, and he smirks right back. It almost feels normal between us. Whatever normal is—and if only for a moment.

Gavron shifts next to me, almost hesitantly. "I'll start by taking you with me. It will be easier if I'm behind you, so you can see exactly as I see." He shadowsteps then, and I instinctively feel him at my back. He doesn't touch me, and I don't turn.

"Not exactly as you see. You're taller," I say, a weak jest.

He remains silent, but I know he's there. The back of my neck prickles in warning, but I'm not going to give him the satisfaction of looking over my shoulder like I'm in my first season.

"Are we using our imaginations only?" When I feel his breath on my neck, I ask, "And is your imagination—or *your* stomach—running away with you?" I toss my hair, wafting whatever my neck smells like right in his face. "Hungry?"

I feel his short laugh more than hear it. "Always."

Still, I wait, my senses tingling. And then there it is: the softest touch through the fabric of my silk shirt, his fingertips tracing my arms. It's been so long since he's touched me; I have to resist leaning into him. Even when he steps up to me fully, his chest only presses whisper-light against my back. It's like the most delicate of dances. I would have hardly noticed any of this before drinking his blood, but now my skin is alight with sensation—a recognition of him, my body crying out for his. My eyes flutter. I want to shut out my sight so I can feel *more* of him.

Except, *no*, this is not what we're supposed to be doing right now. We're supposed to be shadowstepping.

Gavron's hands abruptly close over mine, holding me firm, as if he were showing me a swing of the sword. It's no longer intimate; Claudia has held me the same. He must have heard me. I feel a brief flare of regret before I tamp it out. He dips his head lower over my shoulder, a lock of dark brown hair escaping his ponytail to brush my cheek.

"You need to know where you want to go," he says, his voice wholly practical now, "by direct line of sight or having been there before and memorized the spot. *Perfectly*." He raises my hand with his, pointing. "See that rock? We're going to step there. Only without moving our feet."

I clear my throat, reaching for a tone of casual wryness but still sounding a little strangled. "That's the part I don't understand."

His words gain in intensity, humming low in my ear. "You need to feel the shadows. The darkness. Find its edges, grip it, and then use it to cut through as if with a blade. Follow through the opening you've made, folding yourself into it. The greater the distance, the harder it is to cleave. That's why we're starting small."

I can feel it now, a sharpness in him that suddenly slices forward, indeed like an invisible sword. It leaves an absence where it just was, sucking air into its wake—and then us.

Blink. And then we're standing halfway across the moonlit field, by the rock. No footprints behind us. My stomach lurches.

"Did you feel that?" he asks, his head still bent alongside mine.

"Oh, I felt it," I mutter.

His laughter shakes against my back. "I meant what I did, not the aftereffect. As for that, you'd better get used to it."

"I'm accustomed to being nauseous around vampires, so no need to concern yourself."

His laughter cuts off, and I want to take back my words. But it isn't as if they're untrue, and I'm not here to amuse him, anyway.

"We go again," Gavron says, and he points to a snowcapped hummock.

At the end of the lesson, my stomach feels like a rag beaten against a river rock, and despite having shadowstepped a lot—far too much—I didn't do any of it myself.

Afterward, Gavron steps away from me, putting distance between us once again.

So much for becoming his prize pupil.

———◦◦◦———

I do much better in Intermediate Blades. After all my training with Gavron, I find following the strike of a weapon much easier than cuts made by shadow, and turning to dodge much simpler than folding myself into a space that should be impossible. Claudia regularly pits me against other novices to show them what to do correctly.

I soon move to the top of the class with Gabriella and Marai—one favored by the Red Court and the other the chosen novice of our instructor. When we duel one another, the rest often stop to watch. Once, after Claudia gives me a nod of approval for a particularly well-executed disarming, I briefly catch a flash of jealousy in Marai's eyes. I hope I imagined it.

Thank the Founders that Silvea isn't in this lesson, either. Rather than it being too dangerous for Silvea, Claudia deemed her too dangerous for the rest of us as a full vampire, inexperienced though she may be. Instead, Silvea joined Seduction with Havere, who finally volunteered as her mentor, since her maker is nowhere to be found.

I've put off Seduction for as long as I can, and now I'm doubly glad I did. It means I'll avoid Silvea entirely—at least in my Red Court instruction.

I can't avoid her in the rest of my lessons. Luckily, in Immortal Anatomy and Physiology, we sit far apart from each other in Jaen's study and are rarely forced to interact. I appreciate the lack of distraction, since I'm finally learning what makes vampires hum. Jaen teaches us the theory behind how vampires heal themselves or others with blood and saliva, how they preserve themselves for so long with their strange anatomical functions. But I'm far more interested in what makes them vulnerable: sunlight; confinement to the point of starvation; and those weak spots that, when attacked, will hinder movement or healing speed, or will actually kill a vampire if one is using a dread blade.

The choicest targets are the heart and the neck—the latter only if severed entirely and the body given no chance to retrieve the head. The best solution is burning, or exposing them to sunlight. Piercing the skull can be effective but not always wise. The vampire might lose all rational abilities but not its life, and thus become a mindless beast trying to kill everything in sight. I take as many notes as possible, though Jaen tends to skim over these topics. After all, vampires killing other vampires is supposedly monstrous.

Killing humans, on the other hand, is nothing much. Or even a cause for accolades, as the Blue Court proves with Silvea.

They deemed her to have understood the nature of Revelry well enough in slaughtering her entire village and so granted her access to Kashire's Blue Court Intermediate, Masks, where the goal is to change our faces. She doesn't manage to change hers any faster than the rest of us, but if the aim were to shift one's temperament as if turning a heel, Silvea would be advanced beyond this lesson, too. She's nothing like the person I once knew. Her darker mood swings unfold like sudden storms, her laughter bursting like the sun from behind clouds. I try not to let the warmth of her smile touch me, because I know it's false.

There's more substance to Blue Court training this season. We now sit separately at desks with beautiful silver-framed mirrors propped before each of us. Wine still plays a role, as do small bits of some kind of mushroom that makes my features swim when I stare at myself. Not only must we learn to "let go" like last season's Revelry, but we must learn to let go of our own faces.

I'm excited by the possibilities of disguising myself, even if I don't yet have much luck. It would be useful if my potential killer couldn't spot their intended prey or recognize who might be hunting them in return.

My outlook on this lesson also improves for another reason entirely. The first moment Kashire strides into the room, he sets eyes on Silvea and sneers, "Ugh, a newborn vampire without training. It's like clay that's been allowed to set too long. And trust me, you'll want to change *that* face."

While Silvea's features briefly twist into a snarl, I sit stunned. It's not just that Silvea's face is fine. More than fine. Both her and Kashire seem to be like-mindedly capricious and, well, *evil*. And yet, he seems to have found in her a new target. Same as Jaen, he keeps Silvea well away from me, and I begin to wonder if Gavron has had anything to do with the seating arrangements. Or even with Kashire's jibing, which distracts Silvea and consequently allows me to focus on what we're learning.

Instruction by way of the Gold Court and Pavella is far and above the worst. Not only is the subject, Mind Reading, of no use to me against a killer vampire and appalling to boot, but Silvea is impossible to avoid.

At first, we novices are made to stand in a line across from enthralled servants in a wide ballroom, as if we're about to dance. Marai takes her place on one side of me, and Pavella doesn't object when Silvea skips over to my other side, my one-time friend winking at me like we share a secret, her blond waves swaying around her slender shoulders. The servants have been told to imagine specific things, and we must stare into their oddly glowing eyes and glean the information from their heads. As reluctant as I am, the thralls' minds are exceedingly exposed. We all soon find reading them as easy as reaching out to pluck a juicy tidbit from a table.

I can already imagine how easy it would be to put a thought back *into* their heads. It makes me shiver.

To Silvea, with her enhanced senses, it's child's play. Which is why Pavella, after only a couple of weeks of lessons, announces, "Silvea, pair with Fin."

At Pavella's words, cold that I thought I could no longer feel ices over my chest. Marai spins from where she's standing in front of the enthralled servant to shoot me a concerned glance.

It's not just that it's Silvea. Our differences in power are such that if this were Blades I would be like a straw dummy for her to strike at will. I have no hope of reading her thoughts; I'd have better luck with a stone wall. This is for her edification, not mine.

I don't pause to wonder why Pavella has chosen me among the novices. The sneering Gold Court vampire hates me because I'm a foundling, and she suspects there's history between Silvea and me—unshed blood. And when a vampire smells blood, they want it to flow.

And so I find myself standing across from Silvea, staring into her red eyes. She smiles prettily at me. If I could get over the horror of seeing her like this, I would have to admit she looks stunning as a vampire.

"Oh, I know how you see me," Silvea says with a light laugh.

Already I've forgotten to wall off my thoughts. Gavron warned me I only have *some* protection against full vampires, and I would need to be on my guard. Especially, I imagine, with someone who knows me so well.

"I must say," she continues, "it amuses me. You're trying so hard to hate me, but I know there's something else underneath all of that.

Show me." She tugs at the laces of my black shirt, and the way she looks at me makes my cheeks burn. "How did you once feel about me, Fin?"

I never expected her to ask that, and I'm as thrown off balance as if her question were a surprise dagger thrust. For just a split second a crack opens to those feelings sealed within my hardened heart. I don't even have a chance to respond aloud.

"I *knew* it," Silvea crows, causing heads to turn. "I almost don't need to read your mind. Havere's lessons have taught me so much already. Some part of me always suspected you might feel that way about me. Of course, I ignored it as best I could because you were *revolting*." Her blithe tone twists into something hateful. "You filthy little thing."

I stagger back.

She taps her chin with a long nail. "Maybe I *could* try women now. It doesn't seem so strange anymore. Everything has changed. Nothing is as it was." She pauses meaningfully. "Except you, of course. You're still disgusting."

She's mad, I try to tell myself, a hand clutched to my stomach as if to staunch a wound. *She's mad.*

And yet, she probably felt this way back then. Only now she has the mind to speak such things. She's breaking my heart all over again.

I grope for words, coming up empty-handed. But Marai is suddenly standing right in front of me.

"Fin isn't disgusting," she spits, stabbing at Silvea's chest with a finger, "but *you* are, if you enjoy spilling someone's private secrets. Get away from her, you poisonous bitch."

Those red eyes focus on Marai. "It's your secret, too, hmm?"

"Careful," Marai says threateningly.

"And what else are you keeping secret? Oh, I see, you're jealous of—"

Silvea doesn't have the chance to finish because Marai punches her square in the nose, all of Claudia's training behind the strike. It still doesn't do much damage, but the shock on Silvea's face as she stumbles back is beautiful.

I don't wait around to see what Silvea might do. I haul Marai back, tugging her across the ballroom floor and out into the hall, Pavella's remonstrations and Silvea's sudden, wild laughter ringing behind us.

The only thing that makes me pause are Pavella's final words: "Marai, I grant you leave for your own safety. But, Fin, if you don't return immediately, don't bother coming back."

I keep going.

Once we've made what I think is a safe distance from the ballroom, I throw myself against a wall, breathing hard, still clutching Marai's hand in a white-knuckled grip. I look at her. Her face is set in murderous rage. But not for me. There's no trace of the jealousy I saw there earlier in the season during Blades, even if Silvea's prying almost betrayed it.

I take a deep breath. "I can't go back," I say shakily. "I'm done with the Gold Court. I suppose that means I've lost their mark of approval."

Marai nods, her expression still set. "You might as well save yourself the pain of Enthrallment come summer season. I can't imagine you'd make it through that, anyway."

I grimace. "I can't imagine I would."

"But, Fin, this means you can't lose the approval of any other House or else you'll end up a thrall yourself."

I shake my head. "I'm studying under the Black Court. We only need to gain the approval of three Houses. A majority. With Gavron's lessons, I still have one other I can fail."

"That's assuming you don't give up on shadowstepping. I was somewhat hoping you would abandon your mad plan."

A chuckle wheezes out of me. "You think *that's* mad? You just hit a murderous vampire in the nose."

A reluctant smile cracks her lips. "Better than plotting to hunt down and stab one. Though I guess I could have stabbed her, too."

"Marai, you are the best," I say, and her face glows. "I don't know what I would do without you."

I don't say it to further bury the jealousy I saw there. It's true. Now that I have a friend like her, I can see how what I had with Silvea was bare tolerance, not friendship. I was so lacking in love and attention that anything I could even mistake as that, I built a shrine to.

And now it's time to tear it down. Even if I have to take Silvea down to do it. But she'll have to wait her turn—assuming, as Marai said, that I can manage to shadowstep.

"Without me, you'd probably get yourself killed in no time," my friend says, sighing theatrically. "You're *terribly predictable*, after all," she adds.

I grin, though it feels sharp in my face. I might end up dead no matter what, if I can't learn to defend myself and the other foundlings. At least failure there won't mean a lifetime under enthrallment.

If not the best way to end my studies at Courtsheart, death wouldn't be the worst.

15

If only my resolution to hunt my enemies translated into shadow-stepping ability or a way to finesse, whether by charm or theft, a dread blade from Gavron.

Perhaps it's my constant nausea in reaction to the Black Court's special skill, but shadowstepping comes to me *least* naturally of all vampiric abilities, even the abhorrent mind reading—which I'm relieved I never have to practice again, despite the added risk of failing at Courtsheart. I don't regret leaving Pavella's torture chamber for a moment, especially since I've seen far less of Silvea as a result.

As for the dread blade, Gavron keeps two on his person at all times, buckled tightly into black leather sheaths, but I'd never be able to take one from under his nose. It doesn't help that Gavron has maintained the distance between us—if I move in his direction he usually withdraws or shadowsteps. Even when we practice now, he no longer holds me close to demonstrate. He's still doing the cutting, but he forces me to follow him—to fold myself—through the gaps he makes on my own. I can manage that much, at least. But even with his back to me, there's no sneaking up on him.

Although he does still enjoy sneaking up on *me*.

One chilly spring evening a couple of weeks after I abandoned my Gold Court lessons, I arrive in our clearing to find it empty. The once-fluffy snow now sags like melting wax. The only sound I hear is the pitter-patter of water dripping from the drooping trees and the occasional gust of wind.

And then I feel chill fingers slip around my throat, gentle but firm. I know it's him, otherwise I might be frightened. Even *this* contact, I like. I want to lean back into him.

Instead, I snake my hand behind my back, reaching for one of his dread blades like I would any one of his weapons in a true fight. Gavron deftly blocks me and cuts an escape before I can fully turn, but I manage to squeeze myself into the shadow gap before it closes. And yet, when I come out the other side—following his footsteps, in a sense—he's already gone again. I give chase among the snowy hummocks. We're like the last two fighting in a battlefield of the fallen, or perhaps morbid dancers among freshly mounded graves. I can feel the edges of his shadows like the brush of a silken garment. So close, and yet so far.

As usual. I can't resist chasing him, and not just for what I might steal. I want to truly touch him. But I can only keep up my pursuit for so long.

He reappears out of reach and crooks his finger almost playfully, a slight smile on his lips. "Come and get me."

I'm too nauseous to smile back, let alone to go to him. My sense of failure drags at me like the half-frozen bog sucking at my feet.

His smile turns quizzical. "Fin, you're doing incredibly well, your Gold Court misadventure aside. Haven't I told you that?"

"No," I say. And it doesn't matter if I'm doing well enough for him. At this pace, I'll never be good enough at shadowstepping to be able to hunt . . . *on behalf of the Black Court*, I force myself to think quickly.

"You're thinking of joining the Black Court?" Gavron asks, shocked.

"Where else would I go?" I say, and *I'm* shocked that the admission is true. I flap my arms, the wind slicing through me. I feel as substantial as a cut in shadow. "I don't belong in the other courts. I'm not exactly proving I belong in yours, either, but it's the one that interests me the most. If only for the skills it might provide me."

Belatedly, I realize it might sound like it's because *he's* not providing me with enough.

Gavron regards me with a crease between his brow. He looks oddly tired. "I'm glad you came back to my lessons, Fin. I want you to learn what I know. I want you safe, believe it or not, whatever you may think about me. Or about Kashire."

"I try to think as little as possible about Kashire," I say shortly. Or at least I try not to around Gavron. It's a good sign Gavron wants to help me, despite knowing how I feel about his . . . *friend*. That might mean he's willing to help me in *other* ways.

Or at least drop his guard enough so I can steal one of his dread blades.

That thought doesn't even surface in my mind enough to cause a ripple. If being used as Silvea's practice dummy did one thing for me, it helped me better hide my intentions from others.

"You're not still convinced he's trying to kill you?" he asks with a quirk of his lips.

"I certainly haven't let it disturb my sleep," I lie.

"Your broken bed tells a different tale."

I flush in anger and embarrassment, and I'm spitting words before I can think better of them. "No, you arrogant arse, you can't hear sense because all you can hear is yourself! How are you so convinced he's innocent? How well do you really know your past lover?" I pause only for a moment before taking the plunge. "Maybe you can't see him clearly because he's not exactly a *past* lover."

Gavron's black eyes flash. "Not that I owe you an explanation, but I returned Kashire's impertinent kiss at Winter Sol to distract him from the knife I pulled on him a moment later to deter future such advances. Our shared past—yes, *past*—isn't clouding my judgment."

Oh. A fist loosens in my chest, one that has been squeezing somewhere under my lungs ever since that night. Before I can appreciate the relief, Gavron's words strike me anew:

"How are you so sure it wasn't *your* mad erstwhile lover who tried to kill you?"

The reminder of Silvea cuts to the bone. Not because he's stabbing at the heart of something that he's not privy to, like I did with him. Rather, he's piercing what *isn't* there. And, ever the hunter, he knew how badly such a blow would hurt, even if he didn't exactly know why.

"She *wasn't my lover!*" I nearly shriek. Tears sting my eyes, and I dash them away impatiently.

"But you wanted her," Gavron murmurs, studying me across the gap between us.

"Why don't you just read my mind to find out?" I snarl.

He drags a hand through his hair in frustration, hard enough to reveal the twin shaved sides of his head. "Fin, can we stop striking at each other long enough for you to listen to me? Silvea could have been so disappointed that she wasn't chosen in the Finding that she enticed a vampire to turn her. She became one of us far too quickly for her sanity. Who's to say she didn't try to hunt you at Winter Sol out of resentment, and then, when that failed, murder another foundling instead?"

"Maudon said he was with her the entire time," I say. "Don't you trust him?"

"Of course," Gavron says quickly. "I'm trying to say that Kashire and Silvea are *equally* as likely to have done it—by which I mean, equally likely to have *not.*"

Kashire is by far the likeliest suspect, in my eyes. But I know I won't be able convince Gavron.

I trudge rather than march out of the clearing, since there's no way I'll be able to focus enough for shadowstepping now. Once more, I've failed to accomplish anything toward my goals of gaining the skills or the weapons I need. For that, I figure I've earned myself the long slog back to Courtsheart.

———————

It's only too perfect that Silvea is standing in the central courtyard when I get back. Maybe she knew I was out and has been waiting for me to return. Surrounded by an expanse of dark cobbles, she looks small, cold, and somewhat lost within the billowing folds of her gauzy dress. If I didn't know any better, she would almost appear vulnerable. She's alone, neither Maudon nor Havere anywhere in sight. No one to keep her under control.

Which is especially unfortunate, since I can't seem to control myself. Gavron's suspicion still rings sharp and clear in my mind.

"So is it true?" I snap, striding up to her. "Did you walk around in the woods after dark without a scarf or whatever, trying to get yourself turned?"

She smiles mysteriously. "I didn't need to go to such extremes. But yes, the impulse was mine."

"Why?" I nearly shout. "Why did you want to be a vampire?"

Why did you take my sacrifice for you and throw it back at me, poisoned?

She raises her hands dramatically, the wind whipping her blond hair around her. "I wanted to be the world's greatest healer, if you can believe it!" She giggles, dropping her arms and staring off into the darkness. "I realize now that what I truly wanted was to become something *more*. But back then, I wanted to impress my mother. Best her, deep down."

"What happened to that?"

She meets my eyes. "I killed my mother and I'm not much into healing anymore."

My mouth is suddenly dry. "Probably don't join the Silver Court, then."

"Oh, I won't. I'm leaning toward Blue."

"Not Red?" They're a touch more human friendly, at least, but judging by what she did to our village, I don't think that's what she's striving for. "You've already got the eyes."

"They can change that. It hurts, I hear, but what's a little pain to get what you want?"

"What *do* you want now?" I'm almost afraid to ask.

Her mouth curves into a smile, and I spot the point of one of her fangs. "More. And I know what you want." She runs a hand down her dress.

I sneer. "Not anymore."

She raises her eyebrows. "Ah, do you want someone with . . . darker eyes, perhaps?" Her caw of laughter tears through the empty courtyard. "To think *anyone*, let alone him, could ever want someone like—"

Before she can finish, cold hands sweep me up. I can barely believe it when I realize it's Gavron, spinning me around like he did at the ball. Even less believable, he presses a long kiss to my forehead as he sets me back on my feet. He's hardly touched me in weeks. I'm completely thrown off guard, but he only smiles down at me until I catch my balance.

No words come to mind until he somewhat exaggeratedly winks at me.

He's putting on this show for Silvea.

I force myself to say, only somewhat shyly, "Hello, Gav." As much as I hate to admit it, Kashire is my inspiration for the name.

Gavron cocks an eyebrow Silvea blessedly can't see. He doesn't break character otherwise.

I can only imagine how we must look. More importantly, how absurdly handsome Gavron looks every waking minute, and it's a picture he just painted in this dark, dank courtyard with me in the frame.

Silvea's mouth forms a sour pucker.

He glances at her like an afterthought, his own lips flattening in distaste. "Oh, it's *you*. I'm afraid Fin has more important things to do right now, and you've already taken up too much of her time. Move along, apprentice." He waves her away like she's a fly or a bad smell. "Go find your mentor. I'm sure he has much more to teach you about making yourself appealing to others. Such a *useful* skill, Seduction," he adds as if, in the end, it's not very useful at all.

For an insane newborn vampire who wants to be *more*, it's probably the worst thing he could have said to her.

Which he knows. Ever the hunter.

For a moment, Silvea looks like she's about to charge him. I would have dearly loved to watch that play out, but she manages to get herself under control. She stiffly bows her head to Gavron, and to me she says with a coy glance, "I'll be seeing you, Fin."

"No, you won't," I say. One second, I'm staring at her hateful face, and the next, I feel the shadows' edge in my grip. I seize it and make the cut, just like I've practiced—and failed—a hundred times.

Then I'm looking at the back of her head. I've shadowstepped.

Dizzying nausea slows me for a second, as does dizzying joy—*I did it*—but not long enough for Silvea to see where I've gone. I bring the point of my fillet knife to her neck.

"You'll only feel *this*," I whisper in her ear, pricking her skin.

She spins around, her face twisted in a snarl, her hand raised to strike me.

Gavron catches her wrist. He squeezes so hard I actually hear her bones snap. Her scream is far louder, nearly piercing enough for me to wince.

Gavron's expression doesn't contain a speck of pity. "I said *move along, apprentice*," he growls in her ear. "Before I mist you away. And then who knows where you might end up, hmm? Maybe encased in a long-lost tomb."

Impressively, Silvea wrestles her features under control. When Gavron tosses her arm away, she realigns her bones with only a casual flick of her wrist. She bobs her head without meeting his eyes, and then shoots me a glare that would spear me straight through if it could.

I meet it levelly. "Some here call me Little Fish. Maybe because of this." I flip my fillet knife around in my grip and present her with the handle. "You might be needing it now. Something to remember me and our village by."

Her smile could cut stone as she takes it. "I can practically see your name on it."

Gavron stares after her even once she's exited the courtyard, as if to make sure she doesn't make a sudden return. He speaks out of the corner of his mouth without turning. "Did you just shadow-step, threaten the life of a newborn vampire when you're still human, and then give her your *knife* to stab you with later?"

I nod, but he can't see me. I don't trust myself to speak. My knees suddenly feel weak, all pride and joy at having finally succeeded at shadowstepping draining out of me.

To my surprise, a guffaw bursts out of him. "Founders, you incredible creature. But how could you let her taunt you like—" He turns. Sees my face. And stops.

I look away before he can catch my eyes brimming with tears, but his hand cups my cheek gently. He doesn't force me to face him, instead ducking his own head to meet my eyes. He fills my vision, only the empty, cloud-dark sky behind him. "You know the little finger of your left hand has more merit in it than she has in her entire rotten corpse, yes?"

I hiccup. "I thought I was Little Fish. Fin. Parchment thin. Invisible. Nothing."

One side of his mouth curves up as I speak. Almost as if he can't believe what I'm saying. I expect him to call me a fool again, but instead he says, "Being so quiet and so still, moving as if you are nothing until you strike like you just did, is something indeed." His smile grows with unmistakable pride. "You've even taken *my* diminutive name for you and given it teeth."

"You're only saying that because those are *your* qualities," I say stubbornly. "Because I'm becoming like *you*."

"This quiet strength has always been in you, too," he says softly. "*I* was a fool not to spot it the first moment I laid eyes on you. I see you now, Fin, even if others can't." His eyes are still locked on mine, giving me something without words. Something I want to lean into. He laughs. "Even *Kashire* sees it."

I do *not* want to think about Kashire right now. I only want to focus on Gavron, focusing on me like that, but it's too late. I scoff and turn away. "Maybe that's why he's jealous."

"Founders, please don't start that again." But instead of growing irate, Gavron abruptly laughs, seizes my arms, and twirls me around again. "You just *shadowstepped*. I've never seen a novice progress so quickly."

Maybe all his enthusiasm wasn't just a show for Silvea. I allow myself to share a little of it, again. *I did it.*

"Has the Black Court even *had* many novices?" I grumble as he sets me on my feet. When he takes his arms away, I feel their loss keenly. Why does he always feel so damnably good?

He groans. "For all you disparage Kashire, you sure do sound disturbingly like him sometimes."

Which reminds me . . . I shove the thought down before it can arise fully. "Maybe you're right, and I shouldn't suspect him," I say reluctantly. "And maybe you were right to suggest Silvea."

As close to an apology as I'm going to give. If I started now, Gavron would grow suspicious. And he should be suspicious, if he knew where I was truly going with this.

"I said she's *just* as likely to have done it," he says, frowning.

"Though she's beginning to rise in my estimation, if only in that regard."

"And now I lost my favorite means of protecting myself," I say with a grim laugh. "*Gave* it to her. Perhaps that was foolish of me, contrary to what your smug flattery would have me believe."

"That knife couldn't have hurt her much, so it wasn't much protection to lose. Remember when you stabbed Kashire?" His fond smile in recalling my violence makes me forgive him for bringing up Kashire yet again. "As fun as that was to watch, it didn't harm him."

"But it *can* harm me, and now Silvea has it and many other advantages besides. Maybe even a dread blade, if she was truly the one to attack me at Winter Sol."

"Then you simply need to gain the advantage."

I couldn't have said it better myself. This is the moment I've been waiting for, since I came to Courtsheart. The *opportunity*. "Can you lend me one of your blades?" I ask.

He cocks his head. "I've given you plenty. Unless you've somehow given all of those away, too," he adds wryly.

"That's not the kind I mean."

Gavron stares at me for a long moment, pursing his lips, while I hold my breath, not daring to say anything else. And then he takes my arm, guiding me over to an alcove beyond the courtyard's colonnade, shrouding us in stone and shadow.

"And that's not what I meant as far as the advantage you should gain," he murmurs, his hand still on my elbow. "You should continue to practice your shadowstepping. You shouldn't ask for more."

"Without a weapon truly capable of letting me hold my own against a vampire, I can only use shadowstepping to *flee*," I hiss quietly. "Silvea, or whoever is killing foundlings, could probably catch me even then."

"I'll protect you," Gavron insists. "I did tonight."

"Thank you," I say sincerely. "But what if you're not there, next time?" I poke at his chest with a finger. "You haven't been in the past. Twice, remember?" I ignore the fact that I'm echoing Kashire's own words yet again. "Once more might be one time too many. This is the only thing that can truly protect me."

Gavron grimaces. Hesitates. I can see the war within him play out in the minute changes on his face. I'm suddenly more aware than ever of our proximity.

"Come, Gavron," I say softly. Probably one of the first times I've used his name, at least in this tone. I drop my hand to grip his wrist, giving it a light squeeze. We're only a subtle shift away from an embrace, but he doesn't pull away. "You can't be there for me always, not with your duty to Maudon. I'm not asking you to tell me what it is. But I am asking you not to leave me helpless while you fulfill it."

His jaw hardens. "Promise me you'll only use it in defense."

"I promise," I say immediately, excitement spiking within me. After getting nowhere for weeks, *both* of my goals are suddenly within reach.

"You absolutely cannot lose it," Gavron continues, "or *my* honor with my House will be lost. You know firsthand how unfortunate it is when these things go missing. That's half the reason I'm even considering this."

I nod, rubbing my throat for good measure, and he takes a deep breath. But instead of reaching for one of his dread blades, he says, "We can't do this here," and wraps his arms around me. He barely needs to move to tuck me against his chest, but suddenly there's a chasm of difference from where I stood before. It feels like I fit here, in his arms—like a homecoming, even though this isn't exactly a familiar place.

I don't get to sink into his embrace for long before I utterly come apart.

Literally. My body dissolves. Into mist.

It's not like shadowstepping, folding myself through a cut that should be way too small for me. This is like someone found the seam of my very being and unraveled it, throwing my stuffing to the wind.

I *am* wind, carried in a gust over the courtyard, and the soaring up the side of a castle wall to a dark window many stories above. I don't even realize the window is mine until I'm standing in my room, Gavron's arms still about me.

I'm dizzy, every bit of me tingling. It's like that feeling of mind-numbing, buzzing blankness right before you faint. Except, rather than falling unconscious, this is more like slowly falling back into my body, one small piece at a time.

Gavron just holds me for a moment, and I'm grateful. If he'd stepped away I would have dropped like an empty sack.

"Let me guess," I say, when my lips and tongue can form words again, "we just mistwalked."

He rubs my arms, perhaps unconsciously. "It was the quickest route, and the most difficult to trace. Are you all right?"

Surprisingly, I am. I'm not even nauseous, just disoriented. Maybe all my shadowstepping has helped me grow more accustomed to inhuman ways of traveling. I nod.

He steps back, still keeping his hands on me to be sure. When it's clear I'm not going to keel over, he begins reaching for one of his dread blades. And stops.

"What is this?" He gestures at my bed—the bed from which I've torn away the thick curtains, leaving the weighty fabric piled in the corner. "Do you detest everything I give you that much?"

"Of course not," I blurt. Since he was just about to give me a dread blade, I feel it's wise to speak up. "It's just . . . You'll just call me a fool, if I tell you."

His expression softens. "What?"

I wave at the bed. "With the curtains closed, it's . . . so *dark*."

His eyebrows climb. "You're training to become a vampire, and you're . . . afraid of the dark?"

"No!" The high pitch of my voice betrays me. "It's just . . . I need to see what's coming. I've always been able to run and hide if I sensed danger at night. Especially once my father died."

"I'm sorry?" It's a question, as if he doesn't quite remember how to feel normal human sympathy. He's squinting at me like I'm a strange object.

I shake my head. "*He* was the danger, half the time. His death was a good thing, save for my nearly starving to death after."

"Ah," Gavron says, understanding dawning. Reading more in me, as usual, than I probably want him to. "You would feel vulnerable inside it. Blindfolded. It's also why you like being outside the castle so much. Out in the open."

"I suppose," I say, turning away. I'm about to change the subject back to what's far more important—the dread blade—when he catches my hand, stopping me in place.

"Fin, you can tell me these things without shame. Your concerns. Your fears."

"So you can mock me?"

"So I can *help* you. I need to know you to do that. I don't know all of you yet, but at least I have more of a map."

Yet. He doesn't let go of me.

I'm having a hard time focusing on anything but his hand around mine. Anchoring me here with him.

"I *need* to help you," he insists.

"Why?" The word comes out a near whisper.

"If you want the insidious answer," he says with a lopsided smile, "it's to help myself. Like I said, *I* wasn't sleeping well."

I know that's only half the truth, but I'm scared to hear the rest. Still, I ask, "How are you sleeping now?"

He meets my eyes, and I know the answer. There's actual *pain* in his look. I remember his note, written with such force the words broke through the parchment in places. *I'm sorry.*

He's been distant . . . but maybe because I have. He's giving me the space he probably assumed I wanted.

Honestly, I didn't really want to see him, beyond his lessons. To enjoy a vampire's company felt like too much of a betrayal of my species after Lief's murder and Silvea's destruction of my village.

Never mind that I'm becoming one. And that not *all* vampires are terrible. This one, especially, doesn't seem to be.

Not to mention I can't seem to help enjoying his company.

"I . . ." I choke on the words, but force them out. "I've missed you. I know I haven't acted like it, but I have."

He purses his lips. "I've managed to stop short of stalking you just to see how you're doing, but the idea occurred to me on more than one occasion."

I bark a laugh. "I know the feeling."

He frowns. "No, you don't know. It's . . . different on this end. I've been where you are now, and it's not like this. Everything else in my life that used to govern me . . . it's been overtaken. You're all I think about, even though I still have my other duties. Sometimes it's like you're tearing me in half."

I stare in stunned silence after his admission. Suddenly, this feels too big. Like I'm getting myself in too deep.

Before I can try to change the subject, Gavron slips onto the bed, stretching out like a lounging wolf and patting the space next to him. "Come, I'll demonstrate something."

I goggle at him. "You can't be serious."

"Fin, get over here." His tone brooks no argument. And he used my name. *And* I still need to get the dread blade from him.

I step over to the bed and gingerly crawl onto it beside him, awkwardly lying on my back to avoid facing him and leaving as much space between us as possible.

"So . . . ," I say, as stiff as a corpse. "I'm here. Can I go—"

He slides closer to me, putting his body flush with mine and covering my eyes with his hand.

My breath catches in my chest. I can feel my heart pounding in my throat.

"Don't panic," he whispers in my ear. "I'm right here."

That's part of the problem.

"Now," he continues, "I want you to focus on your other senses beyond your sight. What can you tell me?"

Unfortunately, I can only focus on him, lying right next to me, various points of our bodies touching. Even his cool hand over my face, blocking my vision, is a sensation that's not entirely unpleasant.

"I feel . . . *you*," I murmur, trying to keep my voice even.

His laugh is low, and I feel it in my bones. "What else?"

"My heart is a lot louder than yours," I joke. His, of course, isn't beating.

"Go on. You're on the right track."

"I . . ." I focus, and then say in surprise, "I hear other things. A servant out in the hallway. Voices down the corridor. Footsteps in the room below."

"Exactly. There are other ways to sense danger coming. Sight isn't everything. Sometimes it's worth nothing. Now, tell me what you see." The pressure of his hand suddenly vanishes.

I open my eyes, blinking.

He's gone.

"Gavron?" Instinct makes me freeze, my back rigid against the covers.

His face appears right above mine, his entire body braced on the bed around me. I barely stifle a scream.

"You wouldn't see me coming," he says, his dark eyes holding mine with a mischievous gleam.

"I get your point," I gasp. Fear isn't all I'm feeling. My body is thrilling with excitement.

I will him to pull away before my thoughts can betray me, but he only drops back alongside me and says, "I'll sleep in here with you, until you feel comfortable."

I nearly choke. "That's not necessary."

He frowns down at me. "It's no bother. It's my place to guide you. If I had before now, you might not have been afraid."

Once again, he doesn't understand, as a vampire. Where I come from, unmarried girls simply don't do things like lie in bed with strangers.

But, then again, he's not exactly a stranger, I'm no lady, and there's no one left alive in my village to judge, for better or worse. Maybe I should care less about human rules.

Gavron continues in the wake of my hesitation. "If you wake and feel cornered, you'll know that I'm here, in this corner with you." He smiles. "And I'm probably more frightening than anything that would be coming for you."

He's likely correct. But he still can't stay with me like this, his body lining the length of mine. I wouldn't be able to sleep, let alone control my thoughts. I might want to do something *else*. Even if he's thinking along a similar path . . . I don't know if I want this. Not when I'm unsure what *this* is.

"No, I'll be fine." Forestalling any objection, I add, "And I'll sleep with the curtains closed, I promise. You won't have to worry."

"Oh, I'll worry," he says under his breath, but he pulls slightly away from me, giving me room to breathe. For a moment, he leans on one elbow, looking down at me, his dark gaze unreadable. I have the irrational urge to brush the hair out of his eyes, trace the sharp lines of his cheekbones with my thumbs, run my palms over the tendons standing out in his powerful forearms. "But I trust your word. You promised me something else, as well, to only use this in defense."

He removes one of his dread blades from his belt, unbuckling the entire sheath, and sets it atop my chest. I tear my eyes away from it— and his hand on me—to look up at him.

His stare hasn't wavered. "Fin, I'm trusting you an inordinate amount. Don't make me regret it."

That last part hurts as I clutch the dagger, grazing his fingers with mine. But I haven't exactly lied to him. Only after he kisses my forehead and slips off the bed as quietly as a shadow, vanishing into darkness as if before he can change his mind, do I let myself think it:

Hunting down a killer *is* defending myself. And Marai. And the worth of foundlings, both alive and dead.

16

Any immediate plan of mine to stalk a killer is thwarted by the bustle leading up to Spring Nox—a celebration held on the equinox by the Red Court, their version of Winter Sol. Rather than a ball like the one to showcase the Blue Court's sense of revelry, this will be a series of competitions, a festival of sorts, to honor what is most valued by the House upholding the motto *Blaze and Bleed*—namely, the Arena, an arms tournament any vampire can enter, and the Salon, a grand display of painting, dramatic arts, and musical performances. I vaguely wonder if there will be a competition in seduction, and I cringe at the thought.

This time, I manage to avoid the commotion better than I did before Winter Sol, even though Claudia tries to drag us into it.

"There is room for two novices to compete in the Arena," she declares one evening in Blades, two weeks before Spring Nox. "Only the best from this class, and only against each other. No one expects you to go up against full vampires."

Thank the Founders for that.

"I've not heard of novices ever partaking," a haughty Gold-favored boy, Yuhan, pronounces.

"Because it was my idea to give you the chance, and my wish was granted." Claudia shrugs. "You don't want to? I will not force you to enter. As I said, there's only room for two. The *best*," she emphasizes.

Marai, Gabriella, and I glance at one another, then look away quickly.

Yuhan's expression turns wily. "What's in it for us? What will the winner receive?"

"So rapacious, like a grasping Gold already," Claudia muses, tapping her chin with a long, sharp-nailed finger. "Here is your prize: If you win, you *can't* fail your lessons insofar as the Red Court is concerned. You will preemptively gain our mark of approval before the conclusion of your noviceship, as well as our special favor. Useful, if you plan to join our House."

I'm not planning to, so that last bit isn't as useful to me. But being unable to fail Red Court lessons would mean I won't have to succeed at Seduction.

I can't imagine anyone less interested in that particular subject than I am, until I catch Gabriella's knifelike red gaze once again. I remember her words to Claudia our first day in Blades:

My lady, I've only ever wanted to kill people. Not the other *thing.* And yet, somehow, she wholeheartedly wants to join the Red Court.

Just like Claudia, I think.

As if to prove her eagerness, Gabriella begins adeptly spinning the sword in her hands, and I find myself wondering if shadowstepping might be useful against more than the likes of Silvea and Kashire. I could win in the Arena. Just like that, I'd have no chance of losing the Red Court's approval. I might not have to attend Seduction *at all*. But then, using my new skill during Blades will mean revealing it to everyone. Even if that keeps me a step ahead of a half-life as a thrall, it won't keep me ahead of a killer's dagger.

Winning in the Arena won't keep me *or* Marai from dying.

And if I don't compete, I can stalk Kashire or even Claudia while everyone else is distracted by preparations. I won't have to reveal that I can shadowstep. But I'll still have Seduction to face, come summer, and the strong possibility of failure. I might have to risk it.

Besides, I can't let Marai and me be pitted against each other, either in Blades or the Arena. It would drive us apart. I'm already wary of her jealousy. Without me in the running, it would surely only be her and Gabriella competing at Spring Nox. No one else compares.

I come to a decision. Perhaps I'm a fool, but I didn't steal the white feather from Silvea because I was particularly wise.

"Time for warm-up exercises," Claudia says. "After those, we'll start our practice trials to determine the two who will represent you in the Arena. Your fellow novices are now your competitors."

I slip over to Marai as we ready our weapons. "I'm not going to try for it."

Her shoulders relax like she's just released a great breath. "I'm sorry to be glad," she says, "but I don't want to fight you, Fin. Besides, you don't even want to join the Red Court, as far as I know." She bites her lip. "Even so, I thought you still might compete."

I grimace. "It crossed my mind. I already lost the Gold Court's approval, so——"

"So, you can still lose one more House with your Black Court boon. You're like the rest of us now. You'll be fine. This is my chance to prove myself. You don't have to take it from me when you don't need it."

I frown at *like the rest of us now*. "It's not like I've gotten some special treatment or like I haven't worked my arse off under Gavron. His lessons have nearly killed me. I've had *more* on my plate to swallow than any other novice until I abandoned Gold."

"Yes, you're amazing. That's my point." Her words sound only slightly bitter. "Remember, that's why I'm sticking with you, *knife girl*."

It's what she said to me our first day in Courtsheart, back when we were still awake while the sun was up. But, this time, Marai nods at the new addition strapped to one of my belts, inconspicuous among the other knives Gavron has given me. You'd have to remove it from its sheath to know that the blade is black.

And, this time, I blink at *girl*. It fits me awkwardly now, perhaps

192

because I feel older. Perhaps because I'm less human. Perhaps it's something else. But I don't entirely mind the word. Paired with *knife*, it's everything *my lady* isn't, cutting away the parts I don't like.

In becoming a vampire, I'm less than a girl. And more.

Or maybe I'm becoming what I always have been, deep inside.

A blade.

Marai notices my hesitation and misunderstands. "I'm not staying by your side for a *knife*, you goose, not anymore. I was against your whole plan, if you recall?" She adds excitedly, "But I have to admit, you of anyone might be able to pull it off. I can't believe he gave you—"

I silence her with a quick hiss, and she gives me a sheepish grimace. I've told only her about the dread blade, and that I can shadow-step. Silvea already knows about the latter, of course, but I'm hoping she'll be too embarrassed to speak of it, and I've asked Gavron not to tell anyone. He agreed that a secret way to maneuver in a fight is just as advantageous as a secret weapon. He just doesn't know whom I may use it against.

"Thank you for believing in me," I say. "I'm not going to let anything bad happen to us. To you."

Marai smiles almost shyly.

Claudia's voice behind me startles me. "In the Arena, you have no one to rely on but yourself. Fin cannot fight for you, Marai. She's now your competition. Understood?"

Definitely not a ploy to drive a wedge between us, I think sarcastically.

I don't bother to hide my satisfaction when I turn on her and say, "In point of fact, I'm not competing."

Marai sidles away, slowly at first, and then with increasing speed, to spar with someone else. The last place she would want to be caught is between her maker and me.

Claudia stares at me with those murderous eyes. "So you're decided, then? You would choose the Black Court over Red?"

I hold my ground without dropping my gaze. "Maybe, if they'll have me."

"A foolish decision, child."

"Jealous because I'm learning things you don't know?"

Claudia shadowsteps and disarms me before I can blink, leaving my fingers numb and empty. "I was a novice under a Black Court vampire, too, my dear," she whispers in my ear, "and I gained the Nameless House's approval."

My surprised gasp is genuine. I've never seen her shadowstep before, either out of convenience or in a fight. She walks and runs, dodges and lunges, however inhumanly fast, like the rest of us. And she's just admitted she knows even *more* than me of their skills.

"Why don't you use what you've learned, then?"

"Because I *hate*——" She cuts off. I don't think she was going to say shadowstepping. By the expression on her face, I think she hates the Black Court.

"Why?" I ask, turning to look at her fully.

In response, she throws me to the ground with a twist of her arm and glares down at me. "Foolish child!" she hisses. "Do not tread where you shouldn't, or else you may live to regret it. Or maybe you won't live long enough to be able to."

And then she stalks away, leaving me winded in the dirt.

———————

I linger after Immortal Anatomy and Physiology, waiting for the study to clear and to leave behind only Jaen—a female vampire tonight.

While Gavron is drawing something of a map to me, I wonder if I'll ever know exactly where I stand with him. Or if I even *want* to know. But if I can face Silvea, if I can face my fear of failure and enthrallment just so I can face a killer . . . maybe I can face whatever is growing between Gavron and me, too.

I'm so nervous that I hardly notice Marai's surprised nod as I bid her to go on ahead, or Silvea's red-eyed wink as she passes me.

"Can I ask you something?" I say, once Jaen and I are alone. I'm suddenly unsure how long we *have* been alone, how long she's been waiting for me to speak as I fidgeted with the corner of my desk, picking at an invisible flaw in the perfectly polished wood. Before she can open her mouth, I babble, "It's just that you seem to know about more than a few topics *other* than history and healing—it might even involve vampire physiology—and I thought you might be able to help me."

"I might," she says with a slight smile, coming to stand in front of me and clasping her hands loosely before her. Like Revar, she often wears flowing silver robes such as this one tonight. Her mouth is painted a deep plum that looks lovely with her long black hair. "That is, if you ever tell me what you want to know."

Suddenly I'm looking at my own hands, fingers twisting around one another. I drop them. "I'm worried that I have no choice but to feel certain things," I begin hesitantly. "That something else, in particular, is causing them. It feels almost . . . wrong. Out of my control."

Jaen raises an eyebrow, and I know what that look means from her lessons.

"Okay, *specifics*." I decide to just jump into it face-first. "Is the blood claim . . . romantic? I mean, can it make me feel something . . . *else* . . . for Gavron?"

I'm fumbling my words an embarrassing amount in front of a Silver Court vampire, but Jaen doesn't look bothered or surprised in the slightest. "It's not always romantic—though don't tell that to the Red Court. They're so saccharine. Except for Claudia," she says with a soft chuckle, and I can't help a grim smile in response. "A blood claim *can* involve such things. It's also more basic than that, and yet more complex at the same time. It's similar to the primal animal or human instinct to cleave and create, but it comes from intelligent, *inhuman* instinct on our part. At its simplest, it's still a power exchange—a trade of blood and knowledge for obedience and potential. A gift of life for the 'gift of *becoming*."

"So . . . ," I say, only having understood some of that. "Then the blood claim wouldn't *necessarily* make me want to remove Gavron's clothes? I mean, if that was something I wanted? All hypothetical, of course."

She presses dark lips together, perhaps to keep from smiling. "It isn't necessarily the cause of such an impulse, no. Many maker-novice or maker-apprentice dynamics occur without those urges. Revar's and mine, for instance, and I'm sure you've noted examples of others already. But your desire for clothing removal is no better or worse a connection, my dear. No purer or tawdrier. It's similar, but different. While the Red Court elevates the delights of the body and puts them on a pedestal, many here view coupling as driven by a similarly basic and yet *human* instinct to reproduce that is no longer imperative, since we manage through blood exchange. A minority might even view such dalliances as lesser because of that, but feel free to ignore them."

"So what is it for you?" I can't help but ask. *What is it to Gavron?* I wonder.

"Fun," Jaen says with a sharp-toothed grin. "I don't need intercourse, like many of us don't. But I still enjoy it, like a bit of wine mixed with blood. Some of us *do* yet feel the need, perhaps a remnant of our human roots. And often, though not always, the humans we interact with possess such a desire, too, which can encourage our own interest." She shrugs elegant shoulders. "In any case, knowledge of such skills can be useful."

"Wow," I say. "How romantic."

"Indeed." It's evident she's responding to my sarcasm more than my words when she continues, "Even love, the oft-exalted counterweight to all this instinctual hunger, can be looked at as a chemical reaction that leaves you little choice but to—"

I hold up a hand to interrupt her. "Jaen, please don't ruin love for me. I have the rest of my life for that."

She bows her head. "As you wish. I'm pleased you seem optimistic about your life span. What I'm trying to say is, it's all how you want to—"

"—see it," I finish. "Yes. Marai told me much the same thing, despite being an overly romantic Red Court vampire in the making."

"I like Marai," Jaen says sincerely.

"And she likes you," I say, before I realize I'm verging into dangerous, personal territory. "As her instructor," I add quickly, before I also realize how indifferent *that* sounds. *Marai is going to murder me,* I think despairingly. "So, you're telling me it's difficult to distinguish what I might be feeling for Gavron independent from the blood claim, but it's not caused by it. And yet, even if I separate the two, the feelings are not all that different anyway?"

"My dear, with an oversimplification like that, you would make a terrible Silver Court vampire. But, basically, yes."

"I'm fairly sure I'm not destined for the Silver Court," I mutter, and then I wince. "Sorry."

Jaen doesn't look the least bit offended by my admission. "No need to be. Do you know which court you wish to join, given the chance?"

"Black, possibly." I bare my teeth in half grimace, half smile. "But if I murder Gavron, maybe Red. Silver, less likely. But even Blue is likelier than Gold." I sigh, shoulders drooping. "And all of this allowing that I don't fail or die before then, as you've pointed out."

"Yes, that's important to consider," she says, nodding seriously.

"Because Founders forbid I indulge in wishful thinking," I grumble, and gather my cloak around me before I awkwardly flee from the room. I toss a hurried "Thank you!" over my shoulder as I go.

At least what Jaen said is *something,* I muse as I make my way down the hall, back to my room. It's both a comfort and a concern to know that this . . . attraction . . . to Gavron isn't forced on me by an outside influence. But that means I can't blame anyone or anything but myself for my foolishness. And even if my feelings are mine to own, they don't seem to be under my control at the moment—unless I can somehow manage to wrestle them into submission.

And I should. Soon.

Better be careful, I warn myself. *Or else your heart is going to end up on the ground next to your guts before you know it.*

17

I change my face in Masks not long after my conversation with Jaen.

It's as if knowing myself better and trusting that my feelings are mine, even if they're unwise, relaxes something deep inside me. Maybe I understand myself well enough that I can loosen my grip, let go as Kashire always tells us, and yet not lose track of what makes me *me*.

It happens while I'm staring into the mirror at my desk, as usual. Except this time I'm not concentrating on my face and trying to imagine something different, even as my features swim with the help of wine and mushrooms. Rather, I'm lost in a daydream, imagining myself wandering through an unknown land, flowers blooming around me, confident where I tread and yet wanting to explore. In my surreal vision, I find a rippling pool of quicksilver water at my feet and peer down into it with the same open curiosity.

I want to see *who* I can become as much as where I can go.

Distantly, I hear Revar's words that first evening on the way to Courtsheart: *I look forward to seeing what you will become.*

Me too, I think dazedly, for the first time. For once, I'm not fearing—or even feeding—the vengeful creature inside me. Or the starving child. Or the weak foundling. I just let them be, all of them like shards in a stained-glass window, no longer broken fragments, but together shaping something complex and difficult to make out from too close. Maybe even something beautiful. I've never wanted to be beautiful, but maybe I can find it in me as I piece myself into something newer and fuller.

I'm just *becoming*, in each new moment. Unfolding like a blossom. But instead of parchment or petals, I'm made of knife edges that become a work of art when moonlight hits it just right.

That's when I change. The boundaries of my self ripple outward in the water's surface at my feet. Suddenly the quicksilver pool in my daydream becomes the mirror on my desk in Masks, its movement stilling to a smooth glass reflection. The face within is different from what it was before. It's still mine, but something entirely new at the same time.

My wheat-colored hair now appears silvered by moonlight, the color of frost in the darkness, shaved on one side and falling in a straight blade past my shoulder on the other. My features are neither particularly feminine nor masculine. Just . . . me. My jaw and chin are stronger, more angular, my nose and cheekbones sharper and bolder. And yet there are softer accents about my fuller mouth and my near-black eyes where long, dark lashes fan against luminous skin.

I'm beautiful—or handsome—or *something* fascinating, like I never have been before. I'm myself, and yet not like the Fin who was sitting here a moment ago. I also recognize others in the more superficial touches—vampires. My lips are a deep plum color, borrowed from Jaen, and my eyes are lined in kohl like I've seen on both Gavron and Kashire. My hairstyle is half-Gavron's, half-mine. I wonder if I'm looking at the vampire version of myself. Is this a window to the monster, or a mirror image of what's inside me?

How did Jaen describe the blood claim? *A gift of life for the gift of becoming.* This isn't only what vampire blood is giving me. It's about potential. About what *I* allow myself to be.

It gives me hope I can become a vampire and still be myself.

I want to keep this face, wear it like a crown jewel, but I put it away quickly, blinking back at my human-looking self with the unshaven, wheat-colored hair and narrower, softer features. I've already thought Gavron's blood was making me into something newer, sharper, brighter, but I had no idea what *I*, myself, could do.

I almost wish I could thank Kashire. Soon, I'll bring my other face back, appreciate it, wear it as much as I want. But right now, it's another secret weapon for my arsenal.

Kashire comes up behind me and taps me on the shoulder. "No luck yet? I thought I sensed something."

I shake my head, muttering about strange daydreams.

"Good. Dreams are often where you find yourself." And then he strolls on to the next desk to torment someone else.

That was close. He almost saw. It's the point of this lesson, but I don't need to succeed at Masks yet, not until the end of the season.

And I might have to stalk my instructor before then. If he can't recognize my face, he'll be less likely to see me coming with a dread blade. Especially if I shadowstep first.

———✦———

Marai is too busy training for her competition to help me with any of the half-cooked plans we've come up with to stalk our killer. I practice sparring with her when I can, but mostly I try to discreetly follow vampires on my own, using my new skills. Mostly Kashire, since he's the one I suspect the most.

But I'm mostly unsuccessful. I only manage to see him in Masks, where he usually leaves me alone. He vanishes like smoke on the wind outside of that. Not even Gavron has seen much of him, but that's not surprising for a vampire who can change his face like clothes. Soon, I realize if I'm going to confront Kashire on my terms, it will have to involve a carefully laid trap.

If he's the killer, the best time for him to strike at me or another foundling would be during the chaos of Spring Nox, just like Winter

Sol. Marai will be under many pairs of watchful eyes, so she should be safe. But I won't. Which is how I want it.

I bide my time until then. In Blades, everyone is focused on Marai and Gabriella, who of course come out on top in the trials. I don't mind that my budding skills in combat are overshadowed. The better for my shadowstepping to go unnoticed.

In Immortal Anatomy and Physiology, I can describe, word for word, the inner workings of a vampire from head to toe. Jaen seems largely pleased with me and my prospects for the final exam, even if I care more about how the teachings apply to killing than healing. Healing is for next season, anyway.

Gavron is something more than pleased. I shadowstep with more and more fluidity. I could almost imagine how to keep going, to take smaller and smaller steps until I become one with the shadows—dissolve into mist—but drawing close to that edge makes me pull away in fear. It feels like oblivion. Or maybe eternity. It's hard to tell which. Becoming or unbecoming?

It helps, much to my growing pleasure, that Gavron is always behind me to steady me. He doesn't pull away anymore, his hands lingering on my body more and more. I find myself leaning into him, anchoring myself, before I manage to withdraw. He never tugs me back or pushes himself on me. But somehow I know we can both feel the space between us like a taut band, wanting to spring back together.

And then Spring Nox is upon us. The Arena will last two full nights, the equinox falling on the third and final night, when the Salon's performances will be held.

A plan arrives, as well. There are seating arrangements for the audience to behold the various festivities in the least conflictual way possible—namely, divided by House and ranked according to one's standing within each court. Novices have their own small box, the highest above either the Arena or the main stage of the Salon.

The Black Court's novice box is empty and remote. The perfect place to murder me. I'll be the only one up there, after all. My hopeful murderer might just be surprised by what they find.

I make regular appearances up in the box, not bothering to hide myself as I watch the competitions with unfeigned interest, chin perched in my hands while I lean to get a better look—and to better put myself on display.

The fights are astonishing. Aside from barely seeing Gavron and Kashire's tussle during my fateful journey to Courtsheart, I haven't seen two full vampires face off with each other. These fights aren't to the death, but they leave me as breathless and clenching the railing as if they were. The combatants move in blurs too fast to trace, their clashes of steel leaving sparks behind them and hurting my sensitive ears even from so high up.

I don't see any shadowstepping or mistwalking used in combat. And, of course, not a single dread blade makes an appearance. The Black Court doesn't compete at all.

They do watch. I catch sight of Gavron, Maudon, and a few more shadowy figures I've never met, cloaked in the typical dark attire of the Nameless House. In the boxes reserved for the highest ranks, I see only one man, his pale blond hair hanging long around his shoulders and glowing against a black velvet cape.

I wonder who he is. The members of the Black Court seem as murky and mysterious as their powers, hidden from the view of the other Houses. *To keep their advantage?* I wonder.

I feel less nervous and more ready as the competitions in the Arena progress, but my readiness goes unanswered. No one tries to murder me. When it comes time for the novices' match, I think I've figured out why.

I've watched the box reserved for Blue Court young bloods avidly, without catching a glimpse of Kashire. However, just before Marai and Gabriella face each other in the Arena, I spot him in the

Silver Court section, taking a seat next to Jaen as if that's nothing out of the ordinary. I've never seen him with Jaen.

And then it hits me: He's trying to disguise his interest in the match. In *Marai*. Kashire hasn't paid her much attention outside his class, but this is a special occasion. She's not only a foundling but a Red Court novice. Lief was a Blue Court foundling murdered during Winter Sol—the Blue Court's celebration of their season. Now it's Spring Nox, the Red Court's. I don't have a season as a Black Court foundling, but Marai does.

Lief died *precisely* on the winter solstice. It's not the spring equinox until tomorrow, the last night of festivities, when the Salon's final performances are held. If any killer would have a flair for dramatic timing, it would be Kashire.

If that's the case, his target isn't me—it's Marai. He's watching her and waiting, like a spider at the center of his web.

Except I have a web of my own. Even if I'm no longer the bait as his intended target, I still have hidden fangs.

When Kashire moves, I do, too. My gaze is locked on him, not Marai's fight. His eyes are predatory as he watches the match, and when he slips away from Jaen's side, I have a hunch where he's headed.

I follow, unseen and silent, wearing my new, unknown face and shadowstepping most of the way to the outer stairs leading from the battlefield to the Red Court seating area. There, I wait for any sign of him. Trying to get a closer look at his victim, to taunt her? Or is he even hoping to snatch her while no one is looking, in preparation for tomorrow's night?

A voice I wasn't expecting makes me freeze outside the stairwell and press myself against a wall. *Two* voices, on the Red Court's upper landing.

"I don't have time for you right now. My novice—" Claudia says impatiently.

"If you don't keep your promises to teach me what you know," Silvea cuts in, "then I might just spill what *I* know."

I hear a hiss—Claudia, presumably—then that tinkling laugh of Silvea's I've grown to despise. Light footsteps retreat upward, back to the Red Court boxes.

What was *that*? What does Silvea know about Claudia that could be so damning?

Before I can turn my attention to that question, that's when I spot him, in the shadows down the hall. His face is different, like I imagined it would be. Maybe he can change that *easier* than he can clothes, because I recognize his white silk cravat, pinned with a diamond about the size of my thumb knuckle. His stylish flair is betraying him as much as his dramatic flair.

Kashire. My suspicions were correct all along. It's *him*. He's the one. There's no other reason for him to be here.

Loud cheers swell from outside. Moments later, Marai comes bursting in through the hall that leads from the Arena, tears streaking her face. The roar continues outside. Which means Gabriella is still out there, basking in the crowd's praise. And that means . . .

My heart sinks.

Kashire doesn't move. Probably because Claudia descends to meet her novice at the base of the stairs, while he and I both remain discreet.

I hate to see it, but Marai throws herself at her maker, holding her tight and sobbing. Surprisingly, after a moment Claudia raises her hand to pat her novice on the back, though she looks much less fluid than when trying to cleave something in half.

Kashire slips away, and I silently curse Claudia's timing. I've confirmed his involvement, but learning more about his intentions would have been useful.

I let my own mask vanish, and I slip out of the shadows, breathing hard as if I've just run down from my Black Court novice box, not shadowstepped the whole way. "Marai, I'm so sorry."

I expect her to put on a tough face, but instead she pulls away from Claudia and throws her arms around me, her sobs renewed.

Claudia withdraws, looking unmistakably awkward. "We can talk later, Marai. I'll give you two some privacy."

Privacy. Perfect.

As soon as she's gone, I whisper in Marai's ear, "He's after you, the one I've always suspected. I followed him here." Her glistening eyes widen, and I hasten to add, "Keep crying like before. But, Marai, this is *great*. We know enough now to trap him. We can use your defeat as an excuse to leave Gavron and Claudia tomorrow night at the Salon's performance and go up to the Black Court's novice box for privacy—"

Marai jerks away from me. "I'm glad this is great for *you*," she says, wiping her cheeks with the back of her hand. "All my hopes and dreams were on the line, but I guess you were too busy to notice."

"I don't mean *that's* great," I mutter, raising a cautioning hand and glancing around for eavesdroppers. "I'm sorry about that. You're still fine—"

"Fine? I had the chance to secure my future House's approval, and I just failed!"

"You'll still earn it. You're amazing in Blades, and I'm sure you'll do well in Seduction. Come on, you're a born romantic! And even you have to admit that Gabriella needed this. Seduction would have been too much for her."

"Since when do you care about *her*?" Marai sneers, tears vanishing. "And that's no guarantee for me. You've been so obsessed with this plan of yours that you've completely ignored me. You've only been focusing on your own goals."

"*My* goals?" Anger lights my tone in turn. "I didn't even compete in the Arena. Yes, for my own reasons, but also for you, so you would have a better chance!"

Her nostrils flare as she draws in a breath. "Now you think you're better than me?"

"*No.* I've been trying to protect you," I growl. "Myself, too. But, Marai"—my voice drops to the barest whisper—"you're the one he's after."

"Maybe he'll be doing me a favor, if I fail to gain the Red Court's approval." I gape at that, but she only draws herself up. "And yes, I'll join you in your box tomorrow night, even though I would be smarter to keep Claudia's company." She eyes me bitterly. "She'd probably be *better* company, too."

I continue to stare after her as she leaves me alone in the hallway. I sag against the wall.

She's right, I realize, at least in a sense. I've been so focused on what I thought of as *our* problems—the risk to us foundlings—that I not only neglected my own interests, but hers, too. I've even driven her to *Claudia* for hope and support.

But I don't chase after Marai, apologize for my disregard, and tell her to forget about Kashire.

Because, in the end, it'll be hard for either of us to achieve anything if we're dead.

———— ·◦◦⟨∩⟩◦· ————

I'm nervous for more than one reason the night of the spring equinox. I stand in front of my mirror, turning back to front in the candlelight, eyeing my outfit.

I'm wearing a dress, but it's like none I've ever seen. I designed it, with the help of the servants, and it fits me like a glove. Rather, it looks made to encase a blade more than a hand. It's a sleeveless, elegant sheath of black silk, deceptively simple, slit up the sides for ease of movement. Sturdy black leather boots protect my calves up to my knees, and belts strap my waist, thighs, and upper arms, many of my daggers still in place. Including *that* one.

I'm wearing my original face, of course, but I'm still surprised—impressed—by what I'm becoming. I lift my upper lip to spot canines still shy of a vampire's, but not far off.

I still can't imagine drinking human blood to sustain myself, but right now I have bigger problems. I need to survive the night.

A knock at the door makes my breath catch. I haven't received a note or other message like I was half expecting, informing me that Gavron wasn't coming. Which means . . .

I open the door, still expecting to see no one, if only because he's already behind me, ready to wrap his fingers around my throat. But, no, Gavron is leaning in the doorway this time, in black and gray silk brocade, an onyx stone cut in the shape of a dagger pinning the cravat at his throat. His hair hangs sleek and dark to his broad shoulders.

Founders, the sight of him makes me *hungry*.

He's looking down at what he's holding—a black rose. "I pinched it from the glasshouse in the Autumn Hall." He frowns at it, twisting the stem gently in his long fingers. "Hopefully it doesn't spit acid or something. Those Silvers do like to experiment. *And* they're fond of acid."

I smirk. "Then maybe you shouldn't steal." I'm aware of the irony of this, coming from me.

"Oh? Then you also won't be pleased to receive this." He pulls something out from behind his back and presents it to me.

It's my fillet knife, in a new, fine black leather sheath. He somehow got it back from Silvea. Stole it, by the sounds of it. It's basically useless next to a dread blade. But I don't care. It's all I have left of my old life.

"I'm—" I swallow the hard lump in my throat. "Thank you."

He looks up—truly looks at me for the first time this evening—some reply ready on his lips, and freezes. It's just about the first time I've seen him stunned. Especially at the sight of me.

"Fin . . . ," he starts. "You look amazing." His dark eyes trace me, lingering, and then he blinks. "You're wearing a dress? I was getting the impression you hated them."

I swish the silken black tails of my slitted skirt, pleased to know that he doesn't know *everything*. I want him to understand me, but he can also just be so damn sure of himself sometimes that I like to catch him off guard.

"I like dresses," I admit, "if they're like this. I'm just—"

"You're just you." Gavron smiles crookedly. He looks nigh drunk at the sight of me.

Which makes *me* feel drunk. "I'm glad you're here," I say, taking the knife from him. I slide it onto one of my belts. He snips the rose's stem shorter with a flick of his thumbnail and tucks the black bloom behind my ear.

He holds out his arm. "Are you ready?"

I thread my hand through his elbow, ignoring the thrill as my fingers rest on his sleeve, the fear churning in my stomach. I wish this night could just be about him. Spending time together. *Drinking* each other in.

Like he said with regard to me and his other duties, it feels like he's tearing me in half.

But I have to stop a killer. This is all I've ever wanted—to fight back. To put a stop to those who wronged my mother, who wronged me. To save my friend—once Silvea, now Marai.

It doesn't matter that I might want other things. Because, right now, I have a target.

"I'm ready," I say.

18

As Gavron and I move closer to the stage where the Salon's grand performance will be held, we cross paths with more and more vampires in the hallways. We're like inkblots in a sea of blood, everyone gleaming scarlet in the candlelight. There's an excess of red fabric in honor of the occasion—or not much, considering how much skin is showing. In contrast to the Arena, there's a distinct lack of armor and weapons. Tonight isn't about fighting; that seems clear. It looks like a night for lovers' trysts.

"Remember, I promised to meet Marai in my novice box, since it's empty and we can talk." An arrangement that's looking less appealing the longer I'm standing next to Gavron.

Stay focused.

"All right," he says, sounding just as reluctant. He leans closer to me, as if sharing a secret. My skin prickles as his words stir my hair. "But just so you know, young bloods from the Black Court are nigh as rare here as favored novices. There are others of my rank, of course, but most are away from Courtsheart, on missions or advanced training. Only I was assigned teaching duty here, which is why we'd have *my* box to ourselves, as well. The better for you to see and hear," he adds, as if not to give me the exact idea he already has.

The two of us. Alone. In the dark.

"I don't want Marai to be by herself." I don't need to fake sincerity.

"You could tell her to meet you at a later time. Ah, here she is right now."

Down the hall from us, I spot Marai in a corseted red gown with voluminous skirts. I expect to see Claudia at her side, but instead, her escort's hair gleams golden in the lamplight.

Havere?

As they reach us, the handsome Red Court vampire whom I usually avoid, because he's the Seduction instructor and Silvea's new mentor, smiles at what must be the obvious question on my face. "Claudia asked me to escort Marai in her stead, as she has something pressing. Since Silvea didn't wish to attend tonight's grand performance, there was no conflict."

Two Red Court vampires not coming to the finale of Spring Nox? Strange.

I hope I'm not following the wrong set of tracks here. It *has* to be Kashire.

I'll know soon enough.

I stare hard at Marai. "Remember, though, meet me in my box soon? We won't have to contend for seats up there, and it's a fine view. Promise."

"But I must steal Fin for a moment, before that," Gavron asserts. "Duty calls."

The word *duty* strengthens my resolve. My smile hardens. "I'll only be a moment," I tell Marai.

"Yes, I'm only briefly imposing upon Havere's generosity myself," she says. She sounds lower than usual. She reminds me of a drooping rose in her red dress. When she laughs, it's shallow. "Only insofar as *his* duty requires."

She turns away to greet someone else, and Havere graciously nods to us, following her lead. I feel oddly alone as Gavron pulls me in the opposite direction. I hardly hear what he's saying; Marai's distance leaves a hole in my chest.

The young bloods' boxes are all arrayed on the same level, so it's not surprising to bump into those from other Houses in the halls curving outside. But I *am* surprised to see both Kashire and Jaen—a man tonight—strolling together. I assume they're going to pass by, but Kashire heads right for us.

Perhaps he's already tailing Marai. Or at least looking for her. He's used Jaen as a mask for that before.

Kashire flashes a dazzling smile and says, "What a pair the two of you make! Let's celebrate."

"We were just headed in——" Gavron starts.

"Nonsense, you can spare a moment before the show begins." Kashire halts a passing servant bearing a tray of crystalline glasses that hold red liquid. "A toast to you and to a hopefully entertaining finale to Spring Nox!"

"I truly hope there won't be singing this time," Jaen mutters.

"Jaen, it's an *opera*." Kashire laughs. "This is why I find you a more delightfully terrible creature than I am. Who hates singing?"

"Many, you'll find, if you trace the lineage of the——"

"Come now, let's drink before he murders us with boredom," Kashire interrupts, seizing a glass from the tray.

I suspiciously eye the beverage offered to me. Gavron accepts his cup but doesn't drink immediately, watching me.

"What is it?" I ask.

"Bloodwine. A Red Court specialty," Jaen says, his voice kindly. "But you should know . . ."

I can smell it before he can finish. It has actual blood in it. Even more horrifying, I'm not revolted by the smell. My stomach growls.

"*Whose?*" I nearly squeak.

"Fin, you don't have to drink," Gavron says, at the same time Kashire says, "What does it matter? Try it. It's delicious. And the effect is *so* lovely."

I watch all three vampires toss back their small cups and then groan in pleasure. I have to admit, those sounds only make me hungrier.

I *am* supposed to join them someday. It's a small gesture. And maybe if I seem relaxed, Kashire will be less suspecting. I toss back my cup, too, hoping I won't regret it.

At first, the bloodwine burns down my throat like any strong alcohol. But then the richness explodes across my tongue and spreads like velvet over my limbs, giving them a soft, delicious weight. My knees wobble, and Gavron catches my arm.

"I've got you," he says. "You'll be fine, I promise. It wears off quickly."

Kashire laughs. "I love watching novices drink bloodwine for the first time."

Of course he would, based on his lessons. I try to glare, but my eyes don't want to cooperate with something so . . . unpleasant. Even Jaen and Gavron are smiling at me. The intended effect can't be all that malicious. It's a Red Court beverage, after all. *Blaze and Bleed.* The drink has the taste and feel of their motto, but the softer side. I want to leap to someone's aid, proclaim my goals passionately—*no, don't do that*—or . . . I glance at Gavron and flush.

Which is probably exactly what Kashire wanted. I look at him, looking at me and Gavron, and I suddenly understand. He wants to distract me so much that he's willing to throw Gavron in my path. It's just about the only thing that could sidetrack me. With the heat pulsing through my veins from the bloodwine, Gavron is . . . irresistible.

Marai will be safe as long as Kashire is in my sight. And my trap can be more convincingly set if he thinks I'm occupied.

"It's nice," I make myself say. My words sound loose in my mouth. "I just need to be able to walk. I'm meeting Marai up in my novice box later."

"Of course you are." Kashire's blue eyes flicker between me and Gavron wickedly. He doesn't believe I'll make it up there. He waggles his fingers at us. "Enjoy the show. We'll be enjoying ours."

Jaen sighs. "At least one of us will."

Kashire winks and saunters off, arm in arm with Jaen. So much for keeping him within sight. But he's still with Jaen, whom I trust. They turn onto the stairs that lead to the Silver Court section before Gavron guides me to our own entrance.

He was right. We're absolutely alone in here. But I *can* see Kashire and Jaen arriving at their seats, from a distance. I can't see much of my novice box above our heads—if Marai were already there, she would have to lean out to be seen. I spot her across the way, with Havere in the Red Court section, and I breathe a sigh of relief.

And yet, while I can keep an eye on Kashire, he can do the same for me to know exactly how well his distraction is working. Which means I might actually have to let myself get distracted. Risky indeed, since he'll know better than I will when Marai arrives up top.

"If you need to sit . . . ?" Gavron holds his hand out toward an ornate chair, and I follow gratefully. My knees, besides wanting to leap and bound, otherwise want to buckle.

"What was *in* that stuff?" I mutter, sinking onto the plush cushion, trying not to focus on how close Gavron is as he sits beside me.

"Blood, like you smelled, and wine," he says, "but what you're feeling most is the Red Court's own special mix of tonics. It's infamous, as you can imagine. Many a popular story has started with a few too many glasses of that."

No doubt Marai's romantic adventure novels are laced with it. Which is why I shouldn't be leaning toward Gavron in my seat, if I want to keep my wits about me. I should be excusing myself to go up to my box alone. But I can't, not with Kashire watching me. And . . . I don't want to. I feel wreathed in warmth, silk, and the safety of shadows. Gavron leans toward me until our shoulders rest lightly against each other.

Neither of us moves farther, as if not to scare the other away, or tip our precarious position into something more dangerous. I'm barely breathing. Him, not at all.

Then the show begins.

The lamps below dim, and a red velvet curtain rises on a sprawling stage below. Intricate wooden props begin to shift in the background, forming the shape of a storm-churned sea.

A woman takes the stage, ferried by a long ship like my people use, rotating paddles rowing her across. She's also wearing a hammered brass helmet like we once wore, back when we used to fight other humans. Before vampires first came. She begins to sing. Her voice raises the hair on my arms, it's so crystalline and beautiful. I try to follow the words.

She's a vampire looking for her lover, one that humans have stolen from her.

I stifle a laugh. This is the popular story among vampires that Marai was reading this past winter "to integrate"—though she actually found it terribly romantic, despite its blatant fear of humans.

My urge to laugh gives way to a near trance as the vampire keeps singing. I can feel her voice in my bones, ringing through me, making a bell of my body. My skin tingles, my flesh begins to heat . . .

And then I feel the tip of Gavron's knuckle graze the side of my leg, just above the knee, where it's bare between silk and leather straps. The resonance of my body falls completely still, as if he's silenced it on command with only the crook of his finger. For a moment, all I can feel is his touch, before he pulls away a hairbreadth—a question waiting for a response.

I know what I want. But I also know what I need to accomplish tonight. Can I have both? I glance over at Gavron. He's looking sideways at me with heavy, dark eyes.

I move without thought, my body knowing what to do. What it's been wanting to do since I laid eyes on him.

He moves at the same time. We turn to meet, crashing into each other more forcefully than ocean waves. Our mouths find each other, lips making way for tongues. Our hands invade our clothes as smooth as water.

We are a storm incarnate. Ready to break each other, or rise together.

I climb onto his lap as he lifts me onto it, the high slits in my skirt keeping the silk from tearing. One of his hands crushes my hips down to his, while the other finds my breast. I've never much thought about my breasts before, other than to be happy they weren't terribly obvious. But now I'm glad they're there. Especially when he squeezes.

I feel heat where I rarely have before, down between my legs, which I've also often wanted to ignore. Now I want to stoke the fire. I want *him* to touch down there—until he bites into my neck, his teeth a delicious pressure.

I gasp, arching against him. He curves over me, drinking deeply, as I shudder in his arms. Waves building on each other. I start to groan, loud—too loud—and his hand covers my mouth. When I lick his palm, he cranks my head sideways, gaining better access to my neck, while also wedging that pad of flesh spanning thumb and forefinger between my teeth, leveraging it up against those sharp points in my mouth.

He wants me to bite him.

I oblige. My teeth are finally long enough. Sharp enough.

His rich blood floods into my mouth, as the fount of my neck gushes between his lips. My hips grind rhythmically against his, involuntarily, with every beat of my heart.

I could be tossed on this sea forever. Either until I broke, or until I exhausted the storm.

He wrenches his hand away from me and withdraws from my throat enough to gasp, "Fin, you'll be too strong. Soon you won't be able to resist human blood. Too soon, for you."

He's *stopped* too soon for me. But then his freed hand cups my shoulders, catching me as he leans me back. He supports my weight with one arm while his other hand, the one on my hip, slides around front, parting the silk of my skirt, to seek between my legs. He must have read my previous, unfettered thought that I forgot as soon as he fed me his blood. I remember an entirely different need. I gasp, melting at his touch, my head falling back, my eyes fluttering.

It's still enough to see that Marai is no longer in the Red Court's box. Havere is sitting with someone else. I jerk my gaze over to the Silver Court section. Jaen is alone.

Kashire is gone. Knowing full well I was occupied.

I press into my knees and practically leap off Gavron. As easy as it is physically, the willpower required is violent. Tearing.

For his part, he looks bewildered. He reaches out a hand as if to stop me, my blood staining his lips. "Did I do something wrong?"

"No, I——" I wipe my own lips with the back of my hand, smoothing my skirt over my thighs from where it had ridden up. "I'm just . . . not ready for this. I need to go."

"Wait, Fin——!"

I shove outside our box before he can convince me. It's a close thing, even with my friend's life at risk. Kashire knew what he was doing.

But his diversion cost him. My limbs are no longer warm and velvet cloaked, but cold and hard as steel from Gavron's blood. I never intended to use him like that, but if this helps me, so much the better.

As long as I'm not too late. I shadowstep so quickly, I wonder if I nearly mist myself. My body tingles as I appear in the Black Court's novice box.

Right behind Kashire.

Marai is facing him in the dark booth, standing from her chair, looking startled by his arrival. He must have just gotten here. Her near-red eyes flicker to me, almost betraying my presence.

Not before I press the point of a dread blade to Kashire's back, positioned between his ribs and directly behind his heart.

217

19

Just as I face the enemy I've been hunting, the vampire woman onstage sings in low threatening tones as she approaches what appears to be a human settlement. It's background noise, cloaking us all the more. This perch where Kashire is cornering Marai is almost too well hidden from the rest of the audience. If I make a mistake now, the privacy I wanted for this confrontation might just mask our own murders.

I prod Kashire with the dagger. "Tell me what you're doing here," I spit, every muscle in my body taut. "*Now.*"

Kashire glances back, his brow raised in surprise. And then he scoffs. "Ugh, Fin? I didn't think you would be here."

"Complicates things, does it?"

"It certainly makes them more awkward." He turns back to Marai as if I'm no bother at all. "Shall we resume this in privacy?"

Marai opens her mouth, but I snarl before she can respond, "Thought you could take her without a fight, did you? That we foundlings couldn't defend ourselves?"

Kashire blinks back at me. "I was rather hoping she would come with me willingly. And why would you dare fight me?"

"Because you've stabbed me one too many times. What do you want with her?"

He shrugs, as if there's not a dread blade pressed to his back. "*I* want nothing with her. Not to my taste. But she is to the taste of the evil mastermind of this foul plan."

My heart plummets. Are he, Claudia, and Silvea somehow a team? "And what do *they* want with her?"

"Oh, probably to devour her." He waves like it's nothing. As if her life is nothing.

Just like mine isn't. Or Lief's. Or the other, nameless foundling's before he could even arrive at Courtsheart. Or my mother's.

That's more than enough justification for me. I thrust the dread blade with all my might.

Kashire dodges sideways in a blur. I catch one of his blue eyes widening in shock as the black tip pierces his shoulder. He staggers, arm wrapped across his chest to staunch his wound. When he pulls his hand away, dark blue blood is visible on his fingers.

"Tell me the truth about Winter Sol," I snarl, readying my weapon. "Why are you murdering foundlings?"

"Foundlings?" Kashire gasps. "Murdering——?" And then he begins to laugh. He abruptly swallows the sound, meeting my stare with icy blue death in his own. "You used a dread blade against me."

And then he lunges. Miraculously, I manage to shadowstep away from his first strike, leaving him reeling in surprise. I slice him again across the ribs with grim satisfaction.

This time, I'm not fast enough to evade his counterattack. A blow from his fist sends me flying into a chair. The wood shatters beneath me from the force.

I don't know if it's good or bad that fake cannons fire onstage at just that moment, with the vampire woman singing at her highest pitch. No one could have heard us. We're alone in this. I scrabble away as Kashire advances. He kicks a wooden shard up into his hand.

"It's an exaggeration that wood in the heart is as effective as a dread blade," he muses, "but it's what humans use against us." He stares down at me. "With you, it will be more than enough."

"Thanks for the lesson," Marai spits.

And then she's charging him with her own splintered chair leg. I don't even stand, just shadowstep to reach Kashire one step after her, dread blade in hand.

Kashire catches us *both* in midair, his wooden stake clattering on the ground, his hands around our necks. Marai rasps, kicks, just as hard as I do as his fingers tighten. Her own stake drops.

"My *hands* will be enough, you fools," Kashire snarls.

I manage one more slice with the dread blade before my own grip loosens too much to hold it. The cut I inflict on his arm doesn't seem to make a difference. Kashire looks absolutely inhuman, blue eyes glowing, fangs elongating as he snarls. His grip tightens as he draws us closer to him, mouth opening wider, never mind his own blue blood pattering on the floor. My vision begins to darken at the edges.

Then I spot something strange over his shoulder, crouched underneath a chair. A creature with glowing eyes, looking ready to pounce. I wonder if I'm hallucinating.

Everything goes dark.

I hear Kashire gasp before I see what's happening. His grip loosens, and Marai and I fall to the ground at his feet. I look up, coughing, half wondering if I'll see the strange creature attacking him.

Gavron stands behind him. Kashire's back is arched in agony around the dagger plunged into it. When Gavron rips it out, I see the black blade gleaming blue with blood. Kashire collapses as if boneless. Gavron must have gotten him in the spine—one of the better spots, unlike I managed.

But Gavron looks anything but triumphant. He catches Kashire before his head hits the ground, settling him down gently, his voice frantic. "No, no, not again—"

Again?

Gavron's hands shake as he turns Kashire over to find the wounds in his back. He bends over him. I can't quite see what is happening; I only know that Gavron is healing him.

"No——!" I wheeze, scrabbling toward them with my dread blade.

I don't even see what Gavron does. His form only blurs for a moment, and the blade spins from my numb fingertips to clatter away from me.

Gavron snarls at me like a beast where he crouches protectively above Kashire, baring more teeth than I've ever seen. "Fin, if you know what is good for you, stay away from him."

"I don't understand——"

"No, you don't understand a thing. Now shut up and let me fix this." He bends back over Kashire.

Stunned, Marai and I gather into a huddle, holding each other. Gavron keeps working over Kashire for several long moments, finding the worst of his wounds and biting his own wrist to spill his black blood. I begin to wonder if it's too late——and perhaps if I've made a horrible mistake.

But then Kashire sits upright with a rasp of pain, shoving Gavron back from him.

"Kash, I'm sorry, I had to." Gavron tries to reach for him, but Kashire bats his hand away.

I expect Kashire to come flying at me next, tear me limb from limb, but he only hauls himself laboriously to his feet, his clothes stained in blue and black.

"You pathetic imbeciles," he hisses, holding his side. "You want to know my reason for being here? My excuse for Winter Sol? Well, come with me."

When he starts to limp for the door, no one else moves. Gavron, Marai, and I are all somewhat ridiculously sitting on the ground in a wreckage of chairs.

Kashire stops, glaring at us. "If you don't come now, I will go straight to the Blue Court seats of power and report this as a slight against my House. Fin is not a Black Court vampire yet. She's not allowed to use dread blades with impunity. But she is *your* novice, my love," he says, turning his icy gaze on Gavron. "Her mistakes might—and I stress *might*—be excusable, because she's young and inexperienced. Which makes you more the fool than her for letting her cloud your judgment."

I can't see Gavron's face, turned away from me, but whatever Kashire sees there softens his tone for a moment. "I know how you feel about her. I even welcomed it." *Not anymore*, seem to be the unspoken words. "But she's used that against you, and you let her."

Gavron looks at me then. Gone is what I saw in him earlier this evening. The warmth. The *need*.

Now there's only cold, fathomless darkness in his eyes.

Kashire snaps his fingers, drawing our attention back to him. "Despite my regard for you, my love, if you don't come with me now—and drag these two little chits with you—then I will not protect you from the consequences."

"Wait, *Gavron* . . . ," I start.

But he only nods at Kashire. "Where?"

My heart trips, and Marai digs her nails into my arm.

"Jaen's study. I told him to meet me there soon." With that, Kashire turns into a bat and wings off.

"What?" I say, confused. "*Jaen?* Why—?"

But before I can say more, Gavron is upon us. He seizes Marai and me by the scruffs of our gowns like children.

And then we're mist. Flying out of the box, down flights of stairs, through a web of dark stone hallways.

And then we're in front of a dark gray door, inlaid with silver scrollwork. Jaen's study. I'm steady on my feet, but Marai nearly falls over, gagging.

Kashire arrives a few moments later, straightening his lapels and heading for the door. "I didn't want to kiss and tell before I got permission to do so, but you're all being insufferable."

He knocks sharply.

Jaen opens it. I could have told the truth of the situation by the look on his face, alone, when he sets eyes on Kashire.

The two of them are . . . *a pair*. And I am indeed a fool.

Jaen's softness vanishes when he takes in the rest of us, and the blood on Kashire. Those silver eyes narrow into something razor-sharp and deadly. "I think you'd better come inside."

He holds the door wide enough for us to follow. Gavron's grip on my shoulder doesn't leave me any choice. He shoves both Marai and me through after Kashire and kicks the door closed behind himself.

The study looks the same as it always has, except fewer candles light the polished desks, books, maps, strange instruments, and specimens sealed in jars. I'm used to this place feeling like a comforting haven. Now Jaen turns on us in a slow but distinctly menacing fashion.

"What is the meaning of this?" he asks flatly.

Kashire raises an eyebrow at me. "Care to share with the class, Fin?"

I still can't believe what this means. "*You* were the one Kashire wanted to bring Marai to?" I ask him incredulously. "*You* were with Kashire during Winter Sol? He dragged you there to dance? You're . . . *together?*"

Jaen nods once, a coldly efficient gesture. "I deduce that you thought otherwise and stabbed Kashire based on your assumptions?" He sighs, his disappointment cutting deeper than anything. "I've taught you better reasoning than that. *Gavron* has taught you better."

"Don't be so sure," Gavron mutters, massaging his forehead with his fingertips.

I can't bear to look at him, so I turn on Kashire. "Why didn't you just say so?"

"Because it's none of your business," Kashire says tartly, leaning against a desk. "And since there was already suspicion cast upon me with Lief's death, I didn't want any to fall on Jaen. Alliances forming

223

outside of Houses can be viewed with . . . distrust, especially under unusual circumstances."

"Untrustworthy is all you've *been!*" I cry.

"Whatever do you mean?" Kashire scoffs. "Since Winter Sol, I have gone out of my way to avoid you, or to at least avoid antagonizing you. I daresay I've been *nice*, on occasion."

He's right about that much, even I have to admit. I just thought it was for a dubious reason.

"But I saw you there at the Arena," I insist stubbornly, "waiting for Marai in disguise after her match. You were watching her. I thought you wanted to kill her!"

"I wasn't sure Jaen wanted me blabbing it about." Kashire glances at him, waiting for a nod of permission. "While his male side rather fancies me—whose wouldn't?—her female side is partial to women. Women *perhaps* like Marai. I was going to invite her to celebrate her victory with Jaen and me. I was there early to catch her before any other admirers, and yet in the end there wasn't much to celebrate, was there? The mood spoiled, I figured it was best to wait until—"

"Tonight." I groan. "Can't you go about matchmaking in a less suspicious fashion?"

"Maybe suspicion is what you've always held me in, and therefore suspicious is what you see," Kashire snaps. "If I was being sneaky, it's because I didn't want to let on to Jaen what I was planning. I wanted to surprise him with a small gathering here. If I asked his permission he probably would have denied me on the grounds of my being rash and inappropriate, but really he—*she*, in particular—is shy. And, what can I say, I love misusing this stuffy place. At the very least I wanted to get us all drunk and make a mess and have Jaen chide me for it the next day."

Jaen smiles at Kashire, and I'm suddenly struck by the sweetness of it all. Marai, herself, even murmurs, "That would have been fun."

Her cheeks are warmer toned than usual, and she's distinctly not looking at Jaen.

I flap my arms at Kashire. "After what you've done, how could I have known any better? Much less guessed *this*?" My gesture takes in Jaen, as well.

Jaen glances wryly at Kashire. "He's really not all that bad. He's more bark than bite."

My jaw drops. "He killed a foundling with his *teeth* and stabbed me through the chest!"

"Well . . . ," Jaen hedges. "We've all killed people with our teeth."

"I haven't!" I nearly shout.

"Not for long," he says seriously. "Unless you prefer a worse fate."

I stare around, incredulous. Marai—and Gavron, lurking by the door—won't even look at me. "You all just see us as no better than livestock."

"*Us?*" Kashire tsk-tsks. "You're closer to being one of us now. Not part of that world anymore, but on the threshold of ours. So try to act like it."

When I don't respond, Kashire prods, "Why so hesitant? Would you rather be back in your village, half starving and covered in fish guts?" I begin to snarl at him, but he adds, "As *annoying* as you are, you belong here." He pokes at one of the holes I made in his dress shirt. "Why, if you didn't irritate me so much, I might actually like you."

The last part takes a moment to sink in. "You can't be serious."

He smiles, but it's mocking. "Of course, how could the *horrible* Kashire care enough to like anyone? Well, despite your occasional bouts of foolishness, you've impressed me since my first lesson with you. Which is why I helped you that night. Yes," he insists when I open my mouth, "*helped* you. If you'd drawn your knife on one of my fellow night terrors, it would have ended poorly for you. Never mind all the rest I've done for you that you pretend I haven't."

He *did* save me later with the werewolf, too—even Gavron corroborated his story there. "But why keep helping me after you tried to kill me?"

"As I said, you have qualities I admire. But most importantly, you belong to Gavron. Despite all we've been through, I would never want to hurt him *that* badly." He eyes Gavron, who remains stone-faced. "Although you don't look like you'd be in much pain, my love." He raises a brow. "Not smug that I'm aiding and praising your novice? Or are you yourself still too stubborn to admit that mere peasants can be worthy of this life?"

I swallow. Gavron still won't look at me.

Kashire turns back to me, shrugging. "It is unfortunate about Lief, by the way. I didn't dislike him because he was a foundling. I disliked him because he was afraid of his own shadow. I'm more frightening than a shadow, and that resulted in a lot of pants-pissing at the sight of me. Unappealing. Un*flattering*, to say the least." His smirk falls. "But I didn't kill him."

"I'm sorry, Kash," Gavron murmurs. "For Lief, and for attacking you. But I had to save *her*," he spits at me, "for reasons you understand all too well."

I finally understand how much losing a novice must hurt a vampire. Akin to losing a limb, Gavron said, even if they dislike their novice.

Kashire has been trying to spare him that pain. At least until I stabbed him with a dread blade. I don't entirely blame him for retaliating. No wonder Gavron is so ashamed. Of himself.

Of me.

My stomach drops when he says, "Fin. A word. Now." He gestures outside the study.

I follow, wishing I could be anywhere else.

When it's just the two of us in the hallway, door closed, he spins on me. I hope to see something else in his eyes with just the two of us alone—some echo of what was between us earlier. But it's worse than I could have imagined.

"You used me," he says bluntly. "You knew how I felt about you, and you used it to get *this*." He flips my dread blade in his hands. He must have retrieved it in the box. "And then you forced me to attack one of my oldest friends in your defense. Was everything with me earlier all just a show to fool Kashire?"

"No, I—"

"Don't lie to me, Fin."

"I'm . . . not sure," I stammer, my stomach sinking further at the look on his face. "I wanted to kiss you, but I also knew Kashire was watching—"

His lips twist in disgust. "Just stop. It's over."

The air leaves my lungs. "What?"

"This"—he gestures between himself and me—"is finished. Don't bother showing up to my lessons anymore."

"*What?*" I gasp. My chest feels hollowed out. "You can't just do that!"

"I can. You've betrayed my trust. You don't deserve my favor or that of my House, and you certainly don't deserve *this*"—he raises the dread blade—"after how you've misused it."

I shake my head frantically. "How could you do this to me? You know what will happen if I fail here at Courtsheart. I'll be made a thrall!"

"Most novices never even have the chance to *lose* the Black Court's favor. You're still ahead of them there. You only have to earn the approval of three other Houses to succeed."

"I've already lost Gold's, and I'm *not* going to succeed at Seduction," I cry. "If I fail that, it's over!"

He smirks. "You'll be more than capable there. If all else fails, you just have to be able to *lie*. You're already adept at that."

"Gavron—" I begin, a distinct note of begging in my voice.

"I want you to stay away from me," he interrupts coldly, taking a step back. A step that feels like a chasm. "Stay away from the Black Court. You can find a maker from another House, come autumn. Or not. It's not my concern."

He's as distant as a stranger. "I thought you cared about me! This isn't you."

He shakes his head slowly. "You don't know me, Fin. At all."

"What about your *duty*?" I demand desperately. I've hated thinking of myself like that, but if it's all I have now to throw at him, I'm going to use it. "I'm still your responsibility."

"I'll keep an eye on you. That doesn't mean you'll see me." He shrugs. "Besides, you've proved you don't need my guidance. You can manage on your own for a while—like you've been doing already, under my nose. Kashire won't betray what you've done to him, because he's more decent than you could ever understand. I won't report it, either, as long as you heed what I've just told you—for once." He begins to turn away.

"I'm *sorry*!" I nearly sob. "I was wrong—"

He spins on me, chopping his arm down. "I told you to trust me. You think you're so wise sometimes, but you're not. So listen to me now." His voice has a weight to it I've never heard. "*Stay away from me.*"

I feel as if I've been stabbed, but from the inside, somehow, pain blossoming outward from a hot knife under my ribs.

And then he's gone, vanishing into darkness. I stare after him for a long moment, as if he might come back.

He doesn't.

I sink to my knees. Alone.

I don't know how long I kneel there, tears running down my face, feeling emptier and more discarded than I ever have, when I hear a voice behind me:

"Fin? What are you doing out here alone?"

Claudia. I leap to my feet, scrubbing my cheeks. She's the last person I want to see me cry.

"What are *you* doing here?" I demand.

I expect anger at my lack of decorum, but she only says, "Looking for Marai. It's dangerous for her to be alone, too. Gavron told me she was here after he heard the news. You must already know," she adds, nodding at me. Perhaps at my wet cheeks. "He told you, made sure you were safe?" There's a hint of doubt in her tone as she glances around the dark, empty hallway.

He abandoned me, I think. "Told me what?" The only "news" I know is the attempt by two foolish novices on Kashire's life. This doesn't sound like that.

Her brows lift a fraction, and her gaze darts away. "I don't wish to be the bearer of bad news. I didn't think it would be, until I saw your . . . tears." She frowns in distaste.

"*What?*" I repeat, feeling slightly breathless.

She looks at me squarely, her eyes like blood. "Silvea is dead."

20

F ound bloodless," Marai repeats to both Jaen and Kashire, back
in the study. The words wash over me like rain. Cold but
meaningless.

I'm numb, seated at one of the desks, staring at its gleaming surface. I barely heard what Claudia said after she gave me the news in
the hallway. She only made sure Marai and I were together and safe
under the watchful eyes of Kashire and Jaen, and then left us with
them, because she was needed elsewhere. She was too distracted to
even notice Kashire's shirt, torn and stained. It's an odd twist of fate
that I'm now being looked after by the vampire whom I just tried to
kill—who I thought was trying to kill *me*.

The Red Court is in an uproar. On Spring Nox, one of their newborn apprentices was found dead, entirely drained of blood. Sure,
she was an unsanctioned addition to their ranks and a murderer
herself, but it's still an affront to the House of Spring Dawn.

I don't know how I feel. I'm not sure I feel anything. Claudia
seemed uncomfortable with whatever she saw on my face. Maybe
because she knows that I suspect she had something to do with Silvea's death.

It doesn't matter that she was the one to deliver the news. It was
either an incidental result of her checking on Marai, or Claudia did
it intentionally, perhaps to appear less suspicious. In any case, she
seemed especially eager to leave.

"Fin, why do you look poleaxed?" Kashire asks from where he's lying sprawled on top of one of the desks. "I would think you would be celebratory. Silvea was an insufferable bitch."

Jaen clears his throat, glaring at him, but Kashire is right.

Silvea massacred nearly everyone I've ever known. Nonetheless, I loved her once, and what she did wasn't entirely her fault. She was turned into a vampire too quickly. Even if she wanted it, someone did that to her, knowing the potential consequences. Making a monster of her.

Now she's gone. And Gavron's as good as gone. The hole his absence has left is shocking, considering I hated him only a few months ago. Now, I only have Marai . . . and I'm afraid I won't for long.

Marai speaks up next to me, making me wince at the kindness I'm not sure I deserve. "Fin's relationship with Silvea was . . . complicated."

"Complicated enough to drain her of blood?" When we all stare at Kashire, he plucks at his shirt. "What? You did just stab *me*."

"No, I didn't kill her," I say woodenly, unable to come up with a more biting response.

But I might know who did.

I was too busy noticing where Kashire was that I hardly noticed who *wasn't* around during the Salon: Claudia. Marai's own maker. Whom Silvea threatened with blackmail. Silvea was oddly absent from tonight's grand performance just like Claudia, and now she's dead.

What might Silvea have known that was worth it to Claudia to silence? Maybe Claudia *did* turn Silvea against the rules, like Maudon seemed to suspect. Maybe Claudia did it in order to get back at Maudon. Maybe they were in some competition over her during the Finding that I thwarted and Claudia finally ended by turning her, if only so Maudon couldn't have her. And then, after Silvea threatened to reveal what Claudia had done, Claudia ended *her*.

Whatever the story, if Claudia had something to do with Silvea's

231

death, what else might she be capable of? With Kashire proven innocent—well, innocent enough—she's my main suspect. She was there right after I was attacked outside the ballroom. That doesn't entirely explain Lief, since my foundling theory has fallen apart, but there must be some way he fits into this puzzle.

"I think I know what's happening," Jaen says. All eyes fly to him. "If not who is doing the killings, I might know *why*."

Kashire tosses his head. "Well? Do tell!"

"Lief was a Blue Court novice," Jaen begins, "drained entirely of blood on Winter Sol. And now a vampire apprentice of the Red Court has been murdered in the same fashion, on Spring Nox."

A vampire apprentice. It's easier to think of her like that. A nameless target.

"Can you even kill a full vampire by draining their blood, newborn or not?" Marai asks, frowning.

"Not easily, which is why I don't mention it as a true danger in class," Jaen says. "Vampire flesh heals and our blood regenerates too quickly for most humans to manage killing us that way. But another vampire perhaps could try."

"Was she *drunk* dry?" I whisper.

"That's hard to say. It's not difficult, physiologically speaking, for one vampire to bite another, but we usually don't. And it's mostly unheard of to go so far as to *drain* another vampire unless such a thing is meticulously and lawfully conducted by the Black Court to allow a vampire to switch courts. They have a . . . tool for the job, one most of us don't have access to. And I don't mean a dread blade. Nothing so portable," he adds. "And even then, it's rare, and the drained blood certainly isn't consumed but carefully disposed of with witnesses to confirm."

It hurts, I hear, I remember Silvea saying about switching courts, *but what's a little pain to get what you want?*

I shudder.

"You notice we don't drink from one another, for fun or nefarious purposes?" Kashire says with a raised brow.

I hadn't noticed, actually. But now that I think about it, I've usually only seen vampires drinking from humans—or humans, in the case of novices, drinking from their vampire makers.

Jaen taps his wrist with a fingernail. "A vampire's blood is power. It's why drinking your maker's binds you to them. It gives you strength, yes, but it also gives them a strong sway over you. Your blood, as a human, doesn't give you much of an edge over a vampire when they drink it. But once you turn into a vampire, it's a different story. Your blood would gain its own potency then."

Kashire grins. "This is why we prefer humans as prey instead of other vampires."

"So," Marai says, "drinking from another vampire might make a vampire stronger, but it's too risky because that blood . . . intoxicates them?"

Kashire shrugs. "More highly influences them. Even vampire intimates who trust each other immensely don't often indulge in blood sharing. As for an enemy, if you didn't subdue your victim well enough to kill them by draining them, you might end up utterly under their power."

Jaen nods. "Coercing—or forcing—another vampire to drink your blood is the closest thing we have to enthralling one another. Much like the blood claim that lies between a maker and their novice, you're blood *bound* to another vampire if you feed on them. Made subordinate even as you gain some of their strength."

"Unless you drain them dry," Kashire adds, "which is still challenging even for a vampire because of the aforementioned healing and regeneration."

Blood bound. It dawns on me, what this could mean for me. "So after being made into a vampire, Gavron won't want to drink from me? And I can't drink from him?"

I remember it's a moot point if he hates me.

"Call it a preservation instinct," Jaen says. "We don't crave vampire blood—or even that of another's novice who is too far advanced—in the same way we do a human's. Perhaps that, and the immeasurable risk you take by feeding on another vampire, is what keeps us from driving our species to extinction through cannibalism."

That explains that while human blood has become more appealing, none of the novices' around me has, and certainly no vampire's—other than Gavron's, of course. His, I could almost kill for.

Kashire snaps his fingers. "And *that's* why Silvea's death is strange. Lief's would be less so—any overly enthusiastic vampire could have done it, since he was still weak—had Fin not been so brutally attacked when she found him."

So, who would kill for Lief's or Silvea's blood? And why?

"These deaths have a ritualistic air about them," Jaen says, "and I'm afraid I might know the ritual." He smiles faintly. "We Silver Court vampires make it our business to learn about these things, but even this one has nearly been lost to time."

"I sense a lecture coming," Kashire mutters, dropping his head onto the desk.

"What do you remember about the Founders, Fin?" Jaen asks, ignoring him. I'm surprised he's asking me. Maybe it's habit as a teacher. Or maybe he's trying to break me out of my daze.

"Back when the Houses were only the old, original families, each family had a singular head, the one who started that vampire line," I say dutifully. "The Founders, four in total."

"Where are they now?"

"Gone?" The histories never addressed that part. It was so long ago, I've gotten the impression that no one really knows exactly what happened to them. Only that they went away, and the more recent Council was established to make a ruling body of twelve. Each House still has their own hierarchies and leadership, but the Council of Twelve is how they cooperate among one another at Courtsheart.

Jaen perches against the back of a chair as if settling in. "Legend has it—a legend so old it's nearly dust, even among our kind—that the Founders were entombed here underneath Courtsheart after vampires migrated here, to be watched over by future generations."

"So they're dead?" Marai asks.

"I didn't say that. At least, not any more dead than some humans might consider vampires."

Kashire clicks his tongue. "How rude. I'm more alive than half the world together."

"I prefer to think of us as *advanced*," Jaen says, ignoring Kashire.

I ignore them both. "So if the Founders aren't *dead* dead, then they're . . ."

"Asleep," Jaen supplies, "or so the legend goes. Hibernating in a dehydrated state that they can yet be woken from. But it's not as simple as shaking them awake, or even giving them blood. Their current state isn't due to the natural functioning of a vampire. They were *put* there by a complex ritual. And it would take an equally complex ritual to wake them."

"Why?" Marai asks. I'm glad she's more alert than I am, to help ask the important questions. "The Founders are like gods to vampires. Who would put them to sleep?"

"That's the question, isn't it?" Jaen says, holding up both hands like a balancing scale. "Was it for their own good or for the good of others? Was it at their bidding or against their will? Remember, vampires, unlike humans, never attribute a false sense of morality and righteousness to our revered figures. They, like us, just *are*."

Vampires. *Monsters*. Or so I thought. I look at Jaen, even Kashire.

I think of Gavron. Revar. They *can* be monsters. And sometimes they can be creatures of great beauty and compassion. Often, as Jaen says, they're somewhere in the middle.

Almost like humans, I can't help but think. It seems traitorous.

In any case, were the Founders monsters or miracles? Demons or gods? Neither or both?

I have no clue, and I don't think Jaen does, either. But I think I understand where he's going with this.

"You think these murders are an attempt to raise the Founders?" It seems absurd even to me.

"It's less about *who* was murdered than it is *what*, *when*, and *how*."

"What do you mean *what*?" I ask. "They were people. Or a vampire, in Silvea's case."

"I mean what stage of vampire. A novice. A newborn apprentice." Jaen ticks the two off on his fingers. "As for when, Winter Sol is often considered the rebirth of the new year during the first of the undying seasons, if there can be a first. It's certainly the height of significance for the House of Winter Night. And the one murdered was a Blue Court vampire-in-the-making. A seedling yet to sprout, if you will. A beginning. Spring Nox holds equal importance for the House of Spring Dawn, as does the fact that Silvea was the youngest of vampires belonging to the Red Court—a vibrant new bloom, as fresh as the season itself." *Vibrant* was indeed one way to describe her. "Exactly the type of blood most appropriate for its sleeping Founder."

"So the blood is meant *for* each Founder?" I can't help but grimace.

Lief. Silvea. Their lives distilled down to nothing more than a rousing tonic.

"But only to be ingested at the appropriate moment—the type of blood harvested at the most potent time for each, but delivered to them all at once. Thus, I believe, the ritual to wake them will be complete."

236

"That means, come summer and autumn . . ." I trail off, feeling numb all over again.

"We can expect more murders. Two more, to be precise: vampires of increasing age, the younger of the two belonging to the Gold Court and the eldest to the Silver, occurring at Summer Sol and Autumn Nox, respectively."

"How do you know this?" Marai demands. "I've read a *lot*, and I haven't heard of anything remotely like this."

Jaen gives her an indulgent smile, but Kashire shrugs. "Likewise, to be quite honest."

"While I *do* know more than the average vampire or, needless to say, novice," Jaen says, politely not looking Marai's way, "I only learned about this ritual by proximity to Revar, one of the most learned among the Silver Court, as their apprentice. They instructed me to guard the information closely."

I can't help but blurt, "Then why are you telling any of us?"

Jaen pursues his lips. "I'm not sure who else to trust. But you and Marai have been so bent on discovering who killed a foundling that you nearly killed my lover. And I trust him. So, here you all are."

Marai sighs. "To be fair—or unkind, however you wish to see it—that was mostly Fin's idea."

"And now someone Fin once cared about has become the next sacrifice." Jaen turns back to me. "So I trust you'll continue to investigate these ritualistic murders with equal dedication and *far* more caution."

He says it matter-of-factly, and yet it almost sounds like a threat.

My jaw drops. "You want our *help*? Marai and I are just novices!"

And I *failed* to find the killer. Badly.

"Kashire, Revar, and Gavron all see great potential in you. So do I," Jaen says.

I scrub a hand over my face. "I don't think Revar remembers I exist, I nearly killed Kashire"—Kashire snorts—"and Gavron just abandoned me," I say, slumping lower.

Marai gasps. "Gavron did *what?*"

Even Kashire looks up sharply at that.

"I assure you, Revar forgets nothing," Jaen says calmly. "And you didn't nearly kill Kashire, you only tried, and he will forgive you—"

"Will I?" Kashire interjects.

"You already have," Jaen says. "As for Gavron, until we know more about this situation, perhaps it's best that we keep this core group as small as possible. It's precisely *because* you're a foundling novice that you're perfect for this task. No one pays you much mind, making you ideal for ferreting out information. Moreover, because you're not a full vampire, I can still impel you."

I abruptly stand, my chair scraping back with the force. "Do *what* to me?"

Jaen smiles apologetically. "I know what you're thinking. It's less severe than enthrallment, which is taking control over someone entirely. It's not even as mind altering as entrancement temporarily is—though it has far more staying power. Rest assured, this type of influence pertains only to select instructions. Such as . . ." He trails off, nodding at Kashire.

Who moves faster than lightning off the top of the desk. He's behind me before I can even think of shadowstepping, gripping both Marai and me by the backs of our necks, forcing us to face Jaen.

"Still think you're faster than me?" Kashire whispers gleefully in my ear.

Before I can respond, Jaen's eyes fill my vision like that quicksilver pool in my dreams. His voice invades my head.

"You will not speak of this to anyone but this group. If and when you do speak with us, you will ensure to the best of your ability that you are not being overheard. You will tell me, especially, anything of import that you learn."

Kashire releases us then, and both Marai and I fall forward against the desk, unsteady on our feet. I lean onto my hands, breathing hard. My head feels strangely heavy.

As if something was just put inside it.

When I can speak again, my words are bitter. "How do you know I'll help you? Why didn't you just *impel* me to do that, too?"

I look up to catch Jaen's slight smile. "Because I know *you*. I see how diligently you pursued Kashire. It must be like a splinter under your skin to know you were so wrong about him. The killer is still loose. And there's even more at stake now."

Even if he's right, I'm still angry. Apparently, so is Marai.

"Explain what's at stake, then!" she snaps before I can. I'm surprised she's willing to take that tone with him. He's her instructor, and he—or at least *she*—has been of even greater interest to Marai, at least in the past. I wonder if this has ruined that. "If the Founders wake, what happens then?"

Jaen looks grave as Kashire strolls back around our desks to lean next to him. "Honestly, I'm not entirely sure," Jaen begins.

"It would probably be terrible," Kashire adds almost cheerfully.

"In any case, it would be a massive upset of power. I'm not sure how the Council of Twelve would survive the transition. And what would our new—ancient—rulers desire after being asleep for so long? The old ways were . . . harsher."

"My House is famous for remembering and celebrating such things, so I second that," Kashire says. "It might be excessive even for us."

Jaen nods. "Perhaps the Founders were deemed too old for a newer world. Their sleep might appear to be something like peaceful retirement, but it may have actually been something a previous faction of vampires decided for them and kept quiet. I've wondered myself if the Black Court—the enforcers of balance among us—played that very role and that's why we know next to nothing about their history."

Curiosity about the Black Court aside, my mouth goes dry. Four vampires who've been asleep for a myriad, suddenly rising to find the human world at their feet? It would be a slaughter.

"Who would want that?" I whisper.

"That's what we need to discover, and ideally put a stop to their plan," Jaen says.

Jaen was right. I *do* want to help, no impelling necessary. If the Founders were raised, that could be a blow to humanity the likes of which hasn't been seen since the vampires' first arrival. Not to mention what might yet happen to Marai, if Claudia has something to do with this.

I can still find the killer, and at the same time shield both humanity and those closest to me in a way I never imagined before. And perhaps even regain favor with the Black Court, if Jaen's suspicion about their origins is correct.

Really, this is a gift from Jaen, impelling aside. And other than assuring that I won't betray our group, the impelling hasn't affected me much or hurt me at all.

"So, who's behind this?" Kashire asks. "The boring ole Black Court should want to stop any plan to raise the Founders, whatever their past or bloodletting tools. They're insufferable when it comes to the balance of power."

"Blue *does* want things to return to the old ways," Marai says suddenly, sounding sharp. I wonder if there's any jealousy there over Jaen, or if it's just her usual dislike for Kashire. "Raising the Founders is as old as it comes."

Kashire shrugs. "But we wouldn't necessarily want *all* the Founders back. Some were probably insufferable, too."

"I'm not trying to flatter my hopeful future House here," Marai says, "but it doesn't seem like a very Red thing to do. They want to be more and more involved in humanity, not bring back old hierarchies."

I have my serious doubts about the Red Court. *Silvea.* Her name flashes through me like a phantom pain. But Jaen considers her words and nods. Marai looks so relieved I can't quite yet bring myself to accuse Claudia.

"Gold wants to control humanity more than they already do," I say. "That could involve bringing the Founders back."

"Don't allow your prejudice to blind your eyes to their shining light!" Kashire exclaims, but there's a smirk on his lips. "Gold wouldn't want to raise the Founders for the same reasons as Blue—the Founders might hinder their rule, not advance it, and in even more bothersome fashion." He taps his chin. "Who else? Silver? They're all about preservation and restoration, so you could make an argument there."

He says it as if it's far-fetched, but it gives me pause. I turn to Jaen. "Who else knows about this ritual to raise the Founders in the Silver Court?"

"Likely only Revar and a few of the oldest among us," Jaen says. "Probably so that other courts didn't get any ideas," he adds, but he sounds uncertain.

"Or maybe so the other courts wouldn't know how to *stop* the ritual," Kashire says. "And here you are, blabbing it all over the place."

Jaen narrows silver eyes at him. "Remind me to quit loving you."

"I will," Marai mutters.

Kashire throws up his hands. "Point being, all of this is conjecture. It could be any of the Houses. Or none at all."

Jaen meets his gaze. "Revar was serious, Kash, when they told me about the danger of this. Well, in that entirely preoccupied way they have."

Kashire grimaces.

Marai glances back and forth between us. "Likeliest candidates?"

We all look at one another then, especially Kashire and I, who hold each other's eyes the longest. At first it seems surreal that these vampires are even humoring Marai's and my presence in this conversation, despite impelling us to keep it a secret. And yet, as young bloods, they might have only a handful of years on us. I don't know how long Jaen and Kashire have remained at such status after their apprenticeships without yet being considered mature. A few years, like Gavron? Twenty? Forty? *Young*, still, as vampires go. They might truly not know what's brewing in their own Houses, and feel isolated against it.

"The Blue Court is a possibility," Kashire says first, ever direct, "as much as I might rue admitting it. We do like to cause a ruckus, and this would certainly be that."

"Silver," Jaen says, smiling faintly. "We like ancient theories and rituals, and we're very smart."

"Gold," I say, "because it's a path to greater domination. And Red," I add reluctantly, bracing myself. "If only because of Claudia."

"*What?*" Marai spits, rounding on me.

I finally admit what I overheard between Silvea and Claudia during the Arena, and how they were both absent during the Salon. "She was also nearby when Lief was murdered and I was attacked. She was the first to arrive after Kashire."

"She was looking for me!" cries Marai.

But Kashire's expression is thoughtful. "Claudia was there in the woods when the werewolf attacked Fin. I saw her. Maudon was there, too, but I figured he was only supervising Gav's first lesson. She was the odd one out."

The news hits me like a bucket of ice water. "Why didn't you tell me?" I gasp.

"I wanted to see what she would do—if she would try something against you. I was looking out for you, for Gav's sake. That's why I was suspicious of her, myself, the night that Lief died. But she hasn't made any ripples since. Until now, if what you say is true about Silvea threatening blackmail."

I nod blankly. Claudia was *there*, with the werewolf—I trust Kashire enough, finally, to believe him. Maudon was, too, but as Kashire said, he could have been watching Gavron's lesson. Not that the thought of his presence is comforting.

But Claudia had absolutely no reason to be there. Unless she was trying to kill me. Or at least was playing some part in the attempt.

Jaen frowns. "I don't know exactly what killing Fin would have to do with these sacrifices, other than to remove her as a potential obstacle. But, I'm sorry, Marai, it does appear that Claudia could be involved."

"There's something between Maudon and Claudia," Marai insists, somewhat desperately. "I know he's her one-time maker. But like you said, he was there at the attempt on Fin's life, too. He could be tricking her or using her!" When no one says anything, she spins on me, venom in her voice. "Funny how you blame every last House but the one *you* want to join. What about the Black Court, Fin?"

Never mind that I likely *can't* join the Black Court anymore.

"Why would they be behind such a thing?" Kashire asks dubiously.

"I don't know, but like Jaen said, they even have the tool for the job!"

"Tools can always be borrowed, stolen, or improvised," Kashire says, giving my daggers a meaningful glance.

"Perhaps they think raising the Founders would *restore* balance, somehow?" Jaen suggests. "Especially if they had no part in putting them to sleep originally?" He doesn't sound convinced. I wonder if he's saying it simply for Marai's sake.

"How is four more balanced than the Council of Twelve?" Kashire asks.

Jaen shrugs. For a moment, we all just stand there. Marai's silence is frosty, Jaen and Kashire contemplative. I'm restless. I want to move.

"Well, bloody hell," Kashire says. "The accused are many. Though

I still mostly disagree on Black," he adds. "If only for Gav's sake." His tone is uncharacteristically grim.

"Yes, let's go easy on Gavron, Fin's maker, and not *mine*," Marai says sarcastically.

"We don't even know if this is truly what's happening," Kashire says with a note of impatience. "So let's not get too excited for such a party yet. Right, Jaen?"

"Correct. We might even have to wait until Summer Sol before we can know more."

"And what, we just do nothing in the meantime?" Marai says, exasperated.

Jaen nods. "That would be wise. You still have your lessons to pass, and your House's approval to gain. You still run the risk of failure at Courtsheart."

Of course. And now my risk is far greater, without Gavron and the Black Court's favor.

"But this might be more important than your futures," Jaen muses. "Than *all* our futures."

He lapses into silence, chin perched on his fist. Kashire frowns, looking almost disturbed by what he sees in Jaen's expression. But he blows out a great breath and pushes off from the desk, heading for the door.

"You can all worry about this while I go have a drink. Let me know if or when the fun is going to start."

Leaving Marai, Jaen, and me. I wonder if Marai will want time with just Jaen, now that Kashire is gone. But before I can excuse myself, she shoves by me, bumping my shoulder with more force than necessary, leaving without a word.

Jaen's so deep in contemplation, he doesn't respond when I bid him good night.

Claudia, I think as I slip into the shadows. She may be behind the murders. And maybe even a plot to raise the Founders. I have no idea what it all means.

But I want to find out. To prove it's her—or prove it's someone else. Not only to stop a potential catastrophe, but so Marai won't hate me once she sees the truth. Gavron already does, and I can't lose her, too. I've already lost Silvea, even if her presence was more wound than balm.

I need to win *both* Marai and Gavron back, somehow. Because, without them, I don't know how I'll survive Courtsheart.

IV

SUMMER

21

Summer begins with blood.

I stare at the gaping knife wound in the chest of the enthralled human strapped to the table. Hunger mixes with revulsion in my stomach, and I want to vomit. The woman's eyes are serene behind their glowing sheen, but that only makes my nausea worse. I thought I'd escaped thralls being used in class for demonstration purposes. And yet Healing with Jaen might be worse than actual Enthrallment with Pavella.

Not that I'm attending the latter. I've only seen the insufferable Gold Court vampire once, when she passed me in the hall.

"I'm sorry for your loss," she told me with an oily smile. "I know how important Silvea was to you."

I didn't say anything in response, only made a rude gesture and stalked away as she sputtered in outrage. It felt especially satisfying—I've long lost the Gold Court's favor, anyway.

I might be about to lose the Silver Court's, along with my breakfast.

"She's enthralled not to feel pain," Jaen reminds me, stepping around the table, her bright silvery robes spattered with blood. "As all the others who contribute to this class will be. I assure you, she, at least, will fully recover without memory of this."

All the others. The wooden desks of the study have been removed to make way for iron platforms draped in white sheets. Jaen did the enthralling herself. She's quite good at it.

I've comforted myself with the thought that it's kindhearted Jaen who impelled me to secrecy with regard to the Founders, that I'm safe in her—or his—hands. I'm less sure now.

She did the cutting, as well, to show us what we'll be learning this season—healing, though the study looks more like a torture chamber. We'll have to injure the thralls ourselves in the future. Which means our failure at healing will be carved into someone else's flesh.

No pressure. They're only humans, after all.

I've seen a lot of blood since my Beginning, including my own, and yet my ears buzz almost too loudly for me to hear. My head spins. I can feel Marai looking at me, but I don't meet her eyes. Heat rushes to my face.

Yuhan, the haughty Gold-favored boy, asks snidely, "Something wrong, Fin?"

I barely make it out of the study before I'm bent over, spilling my insides.

An enthralled servant will no doubt clean this up. Which makes me throw up again.

I feel a hand on my shoulder and straighten in a rush, ready to cringe away from that pleasant expression, those faintly glowing eyes, the calm voice asking me if I need anything.

Any one of these thralls could be my mother. It's the worst irony now that I now have to cut them open.

Instead, it's Jaen. "Fin? Are you all right?"

"I'm not sure if I can do this." To not sound weak, I add, "I don't think I'm built for healing." Which is also true. But I'm not sure I can *hurt* the thralls, either.

Jaen's expression grows more concerned. She doesn't have to tell me why.

If I fail at Healing, perhaps *I'll* be the body on the table next summer.

A smile replaces her concern as if it was never there. "We'll talk after class. Take some time to recover. I expect no more absences, though."

Kashire brings us to an entirely new space for his summer lesson, a room more like the one we used in Blades, except it's set down in a huge pit in the floor, deep in the bowels of Courtsheart somewhere near the dungeons. I'm not sure I like the look of it.

Kashire raises his arms in his usual dramatic fashion. Several novices flinch away from him. "Here is where you will unleash your inner animals!" he declares.

"Why does it look like we'll be *fighting* them instead?" Gabriella mutters to me.

Marai isn't talking to me anymore. In her absence, Gabriella has felt more comfortable approaching me. I think she appreciates the fact that I didn't compete in the Arena, giving her a better chance to escape Seduction.

Never mind that I now wish I had competed. Marai lost to Gabriella anyway, and if I'd been busy training with the two of them, I wouldn't have had time to enact my ill-considered plan against Kashire. And I might not have to face Seduction myself.

"Or maybe we'll be battling something *else* while trying to unleash our inner animal?" I mutter back to Gabriella.

"Fin, you guessed it!" Kashire claps. "That's why you're my favorite student."

A dubious honor not even the Blue Court novices would challenge me for, I imagine.

"This class is still about letting go," Kashire continues, pressing his palms together. "But unlike Masks, where it was more akin to you trying to sneak up on yourself, this is more about change under pressure. Your inner animal prefers to *erupt*, let's say. And to allow it, this time you need to let go of your entire bodies." He spreads his hands, waggling his fingers.

Somehow, I doubt it will be that easy, and I wonder what sort of intoxicant we'll have to swallow this time. Probably an even stronger one to match the challenge.

"Fin!" Kashire calls again. "Since you are my favorite student, you go first. Come here."

A dubious honor, indeed. I don't hear a snide comment now, not even from Yuhan. No one wants to draw Kashire's attention from me. I drag myself over to our instructor.

"Do you trust me?" he asks, sounding almost kindly.

"Yes?" I say, only a half question. Perhaps I owe him that much.

"Then turn around."

I obey—only to have Kashire cuff my wrists tight behind my back with massive iron manacles and then kick me over the edge into the fighting pit. I land hard, spitting sand and blood.

I'm not sure why I hoped Shapeshifting would be any more pleasant. Maybe it's because I succeeded so well in Masks and because Kashire and I, while nowhere near friends, have something of a new understanding.

The pack of wolves that files into the pit through a raised portcullis says otherwise. Their shoulders hunch, golden eyes trained on me as they gather. Perhaps this is Kashire's revenge, finally, for my stabbing him.

Never mind that I did it because *he* attacked first.

"*Wolves?*" I screech, scrabbling upright. I try to face all the beasts at once, but they fan out around me, flanking me.

Out of the corner of my eye, I catch Kashire's shrug. "I thought they might be inspiring?"

Because of Gavron, of course.

Bloody bastard.

I back toward the nearest wall. The stone is ancient and covered in slime. Unscalable with my hands bound. "How am I supposed to fight them like this?"

The other novices are whispering overhead. Probably grateful they're not me. Dreading their turn. I can't see Marai's face well enough to know what she's thinking. Perhaps that's for the best.

"You're not supposed to fight *like that*," Kashire calls. "Remember, you're supposed to meet them on their footing, so to speak."

"*That's* all you're giving me?"

His silence is answer enough.

I stare at the wolf pack circling around me, their teeth wickedly sharp in their slavering jaws. I remember the feeling of those teeth tearing into me all too clearly.

Fear must be the intoxicant this time.

I try to reach for something deep inside, something that's hopefully trying to reach back, to help get me out of this mess. But I feel nothing. No animalistic pressure building, only panic.

I almost wish I was blind drunk. At least I wouldn't know what hit me and I'd be numb to the pain.

The wolves charge.

I run. As fast as I am now, there's no escaping them in the pit. With my arms bound, I'm wrapped like a sausage for the taking.

Eventually Kashire scares them off, using his night terror form to help convince them. I've been thoroughly chewed upon by then—a warning for the other novices of what's to come.

So much for Kashire helping me during his lessons. I suppose those days are done. Of course, something like this would have killed me in our first season, and perhaps it's a strange sign of his *trust* that he thinks I'm ready now. Even so, I need Jaen's healing to survive the mauling I've taken.

Better that it's *my* blood all over Jaen this time.

I know Seduction will be by far the worst. One would think a wolf pack would be less appealing, but they'd be wrong.

Standing in the center of a salon, surrounded by plush settees and chairs and backed by a roaring fireplace, Havere looks as handsome as ever. He's dressed in red brocade and velvet, none the worse for wear for losing Silvea. I imagine the death of a vampire apprentice is more painful even than a still-human novice, but one wouldn't know it to look at him.

He teaches what Gavron calls *lying*, so perhaps that's why. *Maybe I will be good at Seduction*, I think with a grim little laugh.

I actually miss Claudia and Blades, and not just because she would be easier to track if I saw her regularly. I'd happily take a knife in the gut over this.

"Fin," Havere says, "can you repeat what I just said?"

Blood and piss. I shake my head.

"Come here, then, and help me demonstrate."

For someone who's skilled at hiding in the shadows, I'm having a miserable time of it this season. First vomiting in Healing, then bleeding nigh to death in Shapeshifting; now I'm the center of attention in the last lesson I ever wanted to attend.

Yuhan snickers. Because of course he does.

I approach Havere in the center of the salon. "Closer," he says, beckoning. "Closer," he repeats, until I'm standing right in front of him. His golden curls are immaculate.

I feel short, scrawny, and squirmy. The fireplace is so hot, especially in summer like this.

"May I?" he asks, raising his hand and waggling his fingers.

I already let Kashire bind me and throw me into a pit of ravenous beasts, so I nod.

Havere reaches to tuck my hair behind my ear, first dragging his nails across my cheek, and then down my neck. My eyes pop. He cups my chin with the same hand, brushing his thumb across my lower lip. He bends close, bringing his wicked smile with him.

"You are magnificent," he whispers, his cool, sweet-smelling breath a caress.

I've had next to no one but Gavron touch me like this. My knees nearly give out. It's like I've tossed back another cup of bloodwine.

Havere pulls away from me then, thank the Founders. I don't know what the other novices can see in my face. Some are blushing, some snickering, most watching avidly.

"I will teach you the places to touch—beyond the obvious—that will have skin aflame and flesh melting," Havere says. "The perfumed scents to beguile the senses. The drape of clothing to flatter your shape. The instruments to play and the songs to sing to entrance the listener. Most importantly, I will teach you the words to make a human *yours*, either for a quick feeding or for their lifetime. And when you know everything, you'll barely need to speak. It will take but a glance. You can have queens or emperors, beggars or courtesans. All you have to do is *listen to me*," he emphasizes, shooting me a red glance. "And practice."

I nod wordlessly. Such skills sound dangerous, potentially abused. But like fire, which can burn but also warm, all of this has a side to it that makes me flush pleasantly from scalp to toes.

Marai clears her throat. "Can such things be used on other vampires, or only humans?"

Havere smiles faintly. "Vampires are not immune, I assure you, though we require more talent."

It's already occurred to me that blood sharing is like the vampire equivalent of coupling, and probably more pleasurable and satisfying. But what if vampires also enjoyed—and improved upon—*actual* coupling, like Jaen seemed to suggest?

I remember climbing onto Gavron's lap, writhing against him as we drank each other's blood, the opera singer's voice rising in the background, higher and higher. I wanted to climb to new heights myself, to reach the crescendo I somehow knew was waiting for me. But then I ruined it.

I can barely breathe at the memory. I wonder if it haunts Gavron, too.

No wonder the Red Court values such skills, and insists that novices learn the basics. There's a lot of power in it, indeed, as much as in a deftly-wielded sword, as well as potential for control and manipulation that rivals the Gold Court. *When you sit* upon *the person seated on the throne, I believe that makes you superior*, I remember someone saying.

Like the Red Court's bloodwine, the potency is intoxicating.

And this is exactly what Gavron accused me of using against him. I wasn't trying anything like it at the time. But since he already thinks I'm guilty, I wouldn't mind the practice.

Perhaps it would get his attention.

I miss him more than I imagined I could. And I also *need* him, desperately, for the chance to earn the Black Court's favor once again. Taking most every other court's instruction but his has made me realize where I belong. And his mark of approval might keep me from something far worse than an ill-fitting apprenticeship.

———————

While I've secretly been enlisted to hunt the killer attempting to raise the Founders, there's not much for me to do during the summer aside from wait, watch, and listen. And *struggle*.

Outside of lessons, I don't even have much time to spy on Claudia, and Marai is no help at all. She won't tell me where she is, and actively bars my way when I try to follow her maker.

This season's lessons are by far the most difficult, beyond anything I ever expected. Fitting, I suppose, since they're the final challenge to determine if we deserve immortality.

And yet, as grueling as lessons are, I still wish I had one more.

When I first show up at the Black Gates for my summer training outside, Gavron's not there. I can't say I'm surprised, though I hoped he would be.

Even so, my foolish hope must be as long-lived as a vampire, because I keep showing up. A few weeks and many bloody and ego-bruising lessons into summer, I even decide to shadowstep out to the clearing where we trained last spring.

No one much cares if I leave Courtsheart anymore, because they know I don't belong anywhere else. That I'll come back. Besides, if I left for long, a Black Court vampire would likely hunt me down eventually.

I wish a certain Black Court vampire would come after me now.

Insects hum in the night, the tall grass glowing a vivid green in the moonlight, and wildflowers create a soft carpet of purple in the center. The sky overhead isn't as dark as I remember, and I eye it warily. The days have grown longer, the nights shorter, making vampires move cautiously. The summer season here is like winter for humans—more time spent indoors hiding from the elements. Even as a novice, I can feel the threat of the sun lurking below the horizon.

Gavron isn't here, either. I sigh, turning, ready to head back for Courtsheart. I freeze in my tracks when I see a dark figure looming at the edge of the clearing.

I hold my breath, hardly daring to believe.

And then Maudon steps out of the shadows. "Fin," he says. "I've been waiting for you."

So, is all I can think at first. *This season* can *get worse*.

My instinctual side is already at work. I shift my weight in the tall grass, pivoting my hips but keeping my shoulders perfectly still to hide the movement of my hand, drifting to one of my daggers strapped to my outer thigh. Not that a normal dagger could do anything against Maudon. Gavron kept the dread blade he'd given me, of course.

"Maudon," I say with a nod. I keep my voice polite. "What are you doing here?"

"Such caution? I would hope that you would fear me less by now." He puts a palm to his black-belted chest. "You insult me." He smiles to show he isn't serious. But then he starts into the clearing toward me. He drops his hands loose at his sides, making a show of being unarmed.

He could still kill me in a heartbeat.

I smile back, refusing to retreat. "I'm not afraid. But I respect you. So how could I ever think you harmless? That seems more insulting, to me."

His smile sinks deeper. He looks like a cat, staring at a particularly plump mouse. "You've learned much in the ways of flattery. In the past you would have snarled and snapped."

"I've learned how to survive," I say.

"I'm not here to hurt you, Fin." He folds both arms to his chest, bowing deep. "We're nearly kin," he adds as he straightens.

I bark a bitter laugh. "Hardly. I'm sure you know by now that I'm not destined for the Black Court."

"That's not what I mean. I'm from near your village originally. North of it."

I blink at that.

"Does that surprise you?" He turns, meandering farther into the clearing, his hands folded innocently behind his back. To an untrained eye, it would look like he's walking away from me.

My eye isn't untrained. He's circling closer.

I *am* surprised by what he's saying, but not enough to be distracted. "You're of my people?" I ask. I wonder what that means to a vampire. "Do you believe in the gods, then? The promised land?"

I don't, but I want to keep him talking.

He shrugs. "I don't believe that *promise* is a place. It is a state of being. We fight, we drink, we love"—he gestures down at himself—"and then we do everything again the next night, our wounds healed, ever thirsty, ever passionate. *This* is the promised land. Right here. *We* are the gods." He holds his arms wide, tipping his head back, breathing in the night sky.

"What about the Founders?" I ask carefully. "Aren't they the most godlike of all?"

Jaen said the Black Court might have had a hand in putting the Founders to sleep. I don't know if Maudon genuinely thinks he's like a god or equal to the Founders, or if he's trying to bait me into blasphemy against them. In any case, I can try to find out what he feels about them.

"Of course they are superior," Maudon says, but his tone is indifferent. He nods back toward Courtsheart, glowing in the distance. "They're entombed somewhere here, if you believe the stories. But they are not *of* here. We are. The very roots of the Black Court are buried deep in this soil, too."

That gets my attention.

"They run just as deep as the other Houses," he continues, "and more widely up here. The Black Court began here, unlike the other courts. We were likewise a part of the Great Southern Spread, but when we returned to build Courtsheart, it was a homecoming. They call the south the Old Lands, but we're more ancient up here."

"We don't learn that in Vampire History," I say.

"Not all secrets are intentionally left unspoken," he says. "Did you know that Courtsheart was built on the bones of the oldest Black Court fortress? I know what the other Houses consider this place: a monument to our greatness, a grand stage, a diplomatic mission, a tower of learning . . . but it's also a tomb. Perhaps for the Founders. *Definitely* for the Nameless House."

I shudder. I want to ask about the Black Court's past, but I know that it's secret—intentional or not. Their banner is clue enough—the tower split by lightning. A House sundered. A name forgotten. Something new, nameless, and fragmented lurking in the shadows, watching over the other Houses.

For some reason, that's never bothered me. As gloomy as the Black Court seems, I find myself drawn to it. I like things rebuilt from broken shards. Especially if they're sharp.

And if their only crime is that they helped put the Founders to sleep in the first place . . .

Once again, I find myself wishing I hadn't ruined my chances to join. I crave the belonging I felt there. I miss . . . I don't let myself think his name.

"Did you know Gavron is from this region, too?" Maudon asks casually.

I gape. Vampires don't usually talk much about human connections.

"I'll let you in on a little secret," Maudon says in a stage whisper. Still circling ever closer to me. "All of us in the Black Court are from here. We're very selective about who we take."

"So I've heard," I murmur. "But I thought my own village was in Red Court territory." I pivot with Maudon, refusing to give any ground or let him flank me. He moves in time with me.

Is he a dance partner or a predator on the hunt? Perhaps *he* doesn't even know yet.

"Now it is by and large Red Court land, since the Black Court doesn't possess much of its own anymore. But those who rule here aren't necessarily *from* here. And those of us belonging to the Black Court all share blood." Maudon pauses. "And not only the vampire blood that makes us who we are now. *Human* blood."

"Gavron said you were born to be vampires in the Black Court. Marked."

"Those meant to join us are usually selected from a specific place where they're raised to know their path. An old temple, in the mountains near your village."

"I haven't heard of it."

"You wouldn't have. It's an old family secret."

Somehow, I fear what he's telling me. These are deep secrets. Dark secrets. The kind that can get you killed.

I realize something. "You said *they*, not *we*."

He smiles again, but it's brittle. "I wasn't born at the temple, no. I was adopted into the family, so to speak. It can happen every once in a while, with northerners such as ourselves, if we prove we belong."

Ourselves. Just as he was excluding himself before, he's including me now.

"Were you a—a foundling?" I can't keep the surprise out of my voice.

He bows again. "I was. And if you think proving yourself at Courtsheart is hard, making it beyond the Black Gates is more difficult. *Infinitely* harder as a foundling. Even as we share the same roots as the Black Court, you and I are cut from a different, sturdier vine. And I respect that about you now, even if I didn't at first."

I squint at him. "Why?"

"We have it the hardest. It's not just that Black Court novices are only usually selected from those raised in the temple, but apprentices are made from only the best among them, not merely the survivors. You won't benefit from those advantages, just as I didn't. And we will lack more beyond that. Few within the Black Court are allowed to become makers. Human *and* vampire bloodlines are important, you see."

"You aren't allowed?" Perhaps it's an impertinent question, but I ask before I can think better of it.

He cocks his head at me. "No. Any novice of mine would go on to be made by another."

Just when I think he might finally be close enough to lunge for me, Maudon instead adjusts the sword at his hip and sits on a log. He gestures to the spot next to him.

I approach slowly, thinking wildly. Maybe that's what happened with Claudia. Maybe she *wanted* Maudon as her final maker, and since she couldn't have him, she went to the Red Court. Or perhaps she wasn't good enough for the Black Court. And she couldn't allow Silvea to be, either.

The thought fills me with some petty satisfaction. Then I pause.

"If Claudia was your novice, does that mean she's from this area, too?"

Maudon gives a jerk of his head. "I made a mistake with Claudia. One I wish to forget."

Maybe their falling out is why she's plotting something terrible. Maudon might have told her about the Founders' tomb—maybe the Black Court knows more about it even than the Silver, because this is their ancestral home. Perhaps that's why Claudia would want to raise the Founders—in revenge, defying the Black Court's purpose.

She as good as admitted that she hates the Black Court, after all. Perhaps she wants a new authority here at Courtsheart.

Right before I sit, I ask, "Is Gavron allowed to be a maker?"

Maudon smiles at me knowingly. "Yes. The youngest among us. He was carefully cultivated—as pure Black Court as we come. One would be fortunate to have him."

I try to make myself sound nonchalant as I take my seat. "I think I lost my chance there."

Maudon glances around the clearing. "I see he's absent from his teaching duty, yes." He looks directly at me. "Do you still want to be one of us, Fin?"

"Can I try?" I can't hide the breathlessness of my voice. Despite my wariness of Maudon, a strange warmth blossoms in my chest at the thought.

The Black Court sounds more like a family than anything. And I realize I crave that about as much as I crave blood now.

Of even vaster significance is the fact that, if I still have a chance to earn the Black Court's approval, it might save me from becoming a thrall. And if I don't have to worry so much about failing, perhaps I can find the killer. Stop the Founders from rising. Protect the human world and Marai—and even other vampires who might deserve it.

All as a Black Court vampire.

"I've never seen even a temple-raised novice shadowstep as quickly as you did," Maudon says seriously, no mockery on his face. "I think you have marvelous potential. You belong with us. And Gavron knows it. He's only being stubborn."

"He would accuse me of the same," I mutter.

"A trait among those of us belonging to the Black Court."

Belonging. The word cuts as deep as family.

"He's also dutiful nigh to a fault," Maudon continues. "You must have made him very angry, indeed."

I wait for him to ask about it, but he doesn't. Instead, he passes me the hilt of a dagger. The blade is cloaked in a black leather sheath. I don't need to withdraw it to know it's a dread blade. I gape at Maudon, not yet taking it.

"Why?" I ask bluntly.

"You already had one," Maudon says simply. "Gavron told me what happened. You used it on another vampire."

"Then why would you give one back to me?"

"Because I think it belongs to you. Just as I think you belong in the Black Court. And I want you to prove it." He lifts the hilt until I take it, and then he stands.

All I can do is hold the dread blade, baffled, looking up at him in shock. The stars frame him like he is indeed a god.

"So." He gestures for me to rise. To join him. "Show me what you know."

22

M audon begins to train me in what he calls shadowfighting, a deadly combination of stalking and shadowstepping. Mistwalking, I learn, is for next season, only after I become a member of the Black Court as an apprentice—a carefully guarded skill, like shifting into a night terror is for the Blue Court.

I'm not sure how I feel about his training, beyond exhilarated. It's dangerous, secretive, and yet he's offering me something akin to what Gavron once did, something almost too much to hope for: a home.

Even if Maudon has given me this chance to still earn the Black Court's favor, I might not be able to take advantage of it. Before, I was sure I could manage to gain the approval of three Houses if I had "my Black Court boon," as Marai once called it. Now, I'm not so sure.

Seduction, contrary to all expectations—the lesson I was most afraid of—is my favorite. It's not always easy, but it's fascinating and I'm improving. My other lessons remain unforgiving. I'm worried I won't gain the Silver *or* Blue Court's favor, at this rate. The Red and Black Court's marks of approval won't be enough to save me from enthrallment.

At the very least, I need to shapeshift, and I need to *now*. I'm not surprised to find that Jaen can change into a silver-tipped fox at the snap of a finger—never mind the menagerie that Kashire holds within him. But it's with increasing despair that I watch every novice favored by the Blue Court find their inner animal, followed by Marai and Gabriella, who explode into a falcon and a hooded serpent, respectively, while trapped in the pit.

I'm especially bitter when even the Golden ass, Yulan, manages to transform—until I realize he's a ferret and I laugh hysterically. But Kashire informs me that small, sharp-toothed, sneaking creatures are quite useful. He then throws me into the pit where a thousand rats nearly eat me alive. Yulan gets the last laugh, there.

I begin to wonder if I'm so bound by my pathetic past that I would turn into a fish if I let myself, and so out of some sense of self-preservation I'm saving myself the embarrassment of flopping about on the sand until feral cats eat me. Kashire's way of cheering me up is clapping me on the back and saying, "I occasionally have glimpses of liking you, Fin, but don't get me wrong—if you don't succeed in this, you're as good as dead to me. As much as I admire you, you have a lot to prove. You did wound me deeply, after all."

"You tried to kill me first," I spit. "Fair is fair. Can't we be even now?"

When he only smiles at me, I think better of my words. "I'm sorry, by the way. Truly."

He makes a noise of disgust. "Don't start that now, or else you might turn into a fluffy bunny rabbit." He whacks me upside the head. "Find your inner animal, Fin. I know you can."

Somehow, his confidence fails to reassure me.

———·◦∈∩ℵ·◦·———

I fail Healing entirely, a short while later.

I've even managed to "properly" injure my thrall this time. I've fallen short with many others, going too shallow with my cuts or barely cracking bone when we're supposed to be healing serious fractures. I'm about to slice my own wrist—which equally goes against all instinct—in order to use my blood in the healing process. But then, my victim—*subject*—begins groaning.

He's not supposed to do that. They've been thoroughly enthralled by Jaen to not feel what's happening.

Just as my subject begins to scream—like I would if half my guts were on the table—I see the ferret scurrying away across the floor.

Yuhan. Either he's already better at enthralling than Jaen, or he's enthralled my subject to feel something that's *not* happening, but just as bad.

Or worse.

The screams pierce my brain. I can't think. I just move.

My dagger strikes out, burying itself to the hilt in the thrall's temple.

He falls silent.

And then I remember it was a *man's* temple, not just a thrall's. My dagger is piercing his *skull*. And my dagger didn't do it. *I* did, without thinking. To spare him the pain, yes. But to do so, I ended his life instead of healing him.

I release the hilt and step away from the table in shock. There's a spray of blood up my arm. It's all I can see as my hands begin to shake.

I've never killed anyone before. I've wanted to—especially vampires. And yet, the first person I've killed is someone who didn't deserve it at all. He was the most pitiable, least dangerous, among us.

A scream builds in my throat as shame swallows me. Maybe it's appropriate that I'm about to take one step closer—maybe the final step—to becoming a thrall myself.

"Fin," Jaen says, approaching me slowly, his hand upraised. "Don't go. Remember what I said . . ."

No more absences. I can see the resolution in his silver eyes. He'll stand by it. Now, more than ever, I understand Jaen will leave me to a fate worse than death, just like Kashire. The two of them are as unforgiving as the lessons they teach.

But I can't do this. I can't heal. I wasn't meant to. I know this now.

I dash from the study. Yuhan's grin is the last thing I see. Maybe

Pavella put him up to it, after I insulted her. But it doesn't matter. This only illuminated the truth: I was born to hurt people.

I've been slowly realizing not all vampires are bad. But what if I'm *worse*?

Tears blur my eyes as I begin to shadowstep, farther and farther away from the castle proper. Soon, I'm out of Courtsheart, in the woods.

I wish I had Gavron or Marai to comfort me. But they're as distant as ever.

I end up in the clearing. It's empty of all but grass, flowers, and starlight. Maudon is nowhere in sight, of course. It isn't time for our lessons.

And yet, I realize I'm looking for him.

It doesn't take Maudon long to appear. I have no idea how he knew to find me here.

"Fin?" he asks. "What's wrong?"

His words are direct, plain, no mockery or malice in them. It's his consideration that gets to me. Seeping like water into the chinks of my armor. I never realized I wanted this so badly—someone like him to care about me. Someone like a father.

My voice breaks as I tell him what happened. I sound weak. Vulnerable. But I can't help it. I can't stop the flood of tears.

"I killed someone," I start. "I've never been afraid of killing, but it wasn't supposed to happen like that. What if I'm becoming someone I don't recognize?"

"I recognize you," Maudon says.

That can't be right. As I explain, my pitch gets higher and more ragged. Maudon moves closer to me, slowly. Like I'm an animal that might flee.

Or one he's about to stab. Maybe he's here to put *me* out of my misery.

Kashire is right. All I expect is violence. Which is why I'm stunned into silence when Maudon sits next to me on the log, pulling out a black handkerchief. With it, he wipes the blood off my arm. I must have been staring at it as I wrung my hands. He even dabs at the tears on my cheek.

"I think you're perfect," he says. "Death is the only mercy some of us know how to give. It's normal that you can't heal. Beautiful, even, when you understand the rest of what you can do. Fin, you are a wondrous creature of edges and darkness."

I open my mouth. Close it. I feel like a fish out of water more than ever before. *I'm* pouring my heart out to *Maudon* that I'm broken, and he's telling me I'm *perfect*? Nothing in my life makes sense anymore.

"You'll get the Blue Court's mark of approval. I promise." He taps my chin with his finger until I look at him. "You have a ferocious beast inside you. I can see it. And that will earn you the favor of the three Houses needed, because you have my favor already, and I'm sure my House will agree."

Oddly, I feel better. Reassured by him, of all people.

"But I think you should try talking to someone else, too," he says, as if reading my mind. "Follow me." He stands, and then smiles down at me. "If you can."

It's his usual challenge, one that spurs me. Numbly, I follow him as he grips the shadow, cutting deeper than I've ever seen him do before. Deeper even than Gavron has.

Somehow, I cling to the edges in his wake and squeeze my way through the tightest gap I've ever managed. One that gets tighter as I go.

I feel like I barely make it out the other side. I find myself gasping for breath in a dark stone courtyard. It's nondescript, no torches to light the darkness. The starry sky is far overhead, and only two barred gates lead out either end.

Maudon is already gone. But someone else is here.

Gavron turns, frowning at me.

A clear note of pain rings through me at the sight of him, as if from a string only he can pluck.

"Maudon ordered me to meet you," he says before I can open my mouth. "I have no idea why."

Which means he doesn't know—I silence the thought before I can finish forming it. *He doesn't know Maudon is training me.*

"Where are we?" I ask.

"The Black Gates. One of the outer courtyards."

From the clearing, that distance would have taken me at least six shadowsteps, and I wouldn't have known this place well enough to cut my way inside, anyway. Maudon is revealing how powerful he is, at the same time showing me something private of the Black Court's.

Proving that he trusts me.

"Very welcoming, as you can see," Gavron adds, his lips twisting.

Meaning that I'm not welcome—by him, at least. For a long, stretched moment, we simply stare at each other. I drink in the sight of him, wishing I could go to him. I crave the feeling of his arms around me more than ever before.

Gavron only folds his arms, regarding me flatly.

I have the urge to cry again, but I choke it down. Tears had no effect on him last time. And I refuse to beg a second time.

Finally, he sighs, dragging a hand through his hair. "I don't know why I'm here. Why are *you* here, Fin? You betrayed my trust. And maybe you were right to think I can't keep you safe. Maybe I can't do this anymore. I can't do"—he waves at me—"*you*. You're too much. Not enough."

I step closer to him until I'm right in front of him. I force him to meet my eyes. "What if you were too much for me? *And* not enough? That might make us a good match for each other." I shift my weight, so my knee bumps his. "I miss you."

I keep the words soft. Smooth. Not as raw and bloody as they feel inside.

Gavron's dark eyes abruptly narrow. "Are you . . . are you trying to *seduce* me?" He covers his mouth. A guffaw bursts out from behind his hand. He folds over entirely, shaking with laughter.

My face burns like a forge. "You're the one who told me I would be good at it, you insufferable arse. And, you know, I'm actually not bad."

Abruptly, Gavron stops laughing and straightens, seizing my shoulders. Before I know it, he's pushed me up against the wall, pinning my hands above my head with one of his. The other traces my neck, gentle, threatening, our hair an entangled curtain alongside our faces. The length of his body is flush with mine, all hard muscle.

"I said you were a good liar." He leans in to nudge my forehead with his, his lips dancing perilously close to mine as he whispers, "But I am of the Black Court. You'll get nothing of me that I don't want to give. Especially not in exchange for lies. I told you to stay away from me." His voice drops even lower. "If you try this with me, you might get more than you want."

If it's supposed to be a threat, it isn't working. My heart is pounding, my skin laced in tingling shivers, but not from fear. I feel more alive, keener, *hungrier* than ever.

"Who says I don't want this?" I whisper.

His hand lifts to cup my cheek. He tips up my chin, his black eyes searching my face. Reading it like a book. Realizing I'm not scared. Quite the opposite.

He drops his hand and steps back.

My face grows hot again, humiliation threatening to swallow me. "All teeth and no jaws when it comes to *that* threat, I see," I snap. "Aren't you hungry, at least, wolf pup?"

Are you mad? a part of me shrieks. *Taunting a vampire with feeding on you and belittling him at the same time?*

Maybe I am mad. I feel like I'm unraveling at the seams.

Gavron holds my eyes for a long second. "Always," he says simply.

And then, he shadowsteps away from me. Leaving me alone once again.

I groan and sag against the wall. Why is the bloody bastard being so unforgiving? Yes, I stabbed his friend. But his friend has mostly—sort of—forgiven me.

Which means I wounded Gavron far worse.

Maybe, just as I can't heal, I can't manage other, more delicate things, like loving someone, without stabbing them to death at the same time.

Joining the other dark clouds over my head—my now-official failure at Healing, my lack of success in Shapeshifting, and the coldness of Gavron and Marai—is the approach of Summer Sol. Unlike Winter Sol or Spring Nox, the Gold Court's favorite time to *Shine and Steward*, as their motto dictates, has nothing to appeal to me. It's also known as the Summit, where vampire leaders from all over the land meet to discuss how best to rule. Needless to say, I don't mind skipping the proceedings entirely.

Jaen said it might take until Summer Sol for us to learn something new about the sacrifices, but I was hoping to make more progress before now. Waiting for something to happen means waiting for someone to die. And even if the sacrifice is supposed to be a Gold Court vampire this time, that doesn't mean that others can't die as well.

Especially among those trying to *stop* the killer tonight. I'm less afraid for myself, but I worry about Marai with her proximity to Claudia, who is still the likeliest suspect. Marai is also still human, if barely. She could get killed just by being in the way. I don't care that she hates me. She's still *my* best friend, whether she likes it or not.

The fact that I don't have lessons during Summer Sol is one less worry, at least. I'm doing as well in Seduction as anyone else, I don't have Healing anymore, and Maudon keeps assuring me I'll secure the Black Court's favor, but Shapeshifting weighs on me such that I'm about to collapse. I'm the only one who hasn't managed to change form yet.

Which makes it especially awkward that Kashire finds me at the start of the Summit as I slip out of my room, heading in the opposite direction from everyone else, in order to better stalk where a killer might be lurking on the fringes.

"You're with me," he says, making me jump. He's leaning against the wall outside my door.

"What?" I snap.

"Jaen and Marai are partnering up, since Marai didn't want to be with you and two novices together are liable to get killed or try to kill someone they shouldn't," he says pointedly. "And Jaen thought you might be upset with him . . . So, you're with me."

"Pairing the two who have tried to kill each other is the best idea?"

"The better to find a killer, right, if we have experience killing?" Kashire says cheerfully.

"That doesn't make sense at all," I say. But when I think about it, Marai and I *are* perhaps safer with full vampires alongside us. At least, I hope I'm safe with Kashire.

"How's this for stalking?" Kashire says. When I turn to him, he's become a wolf at my side.

I groan. "Please, no more wolves, as much as it might amuse you." I wave him away. "Yes, Gavron, Stalking, I get it. It's not amusing to *me*."

The wolf melts away, turning into a striped serpent slithering over the stone floor.

"Because no one will notice *that*," I snap.

Kashire—the snake—looks up at me with those same icy blue eyes. Before I can leap away, he coils around my ankle, shooting up my leg.

I barely stifle a shriek as he twines his way up my waist. And then he's wrapped around my neck, forked tongue tickling my cheek. I freeze.

"Kashire," I say, as calmly as possible. "We're not going to be terribly subtle in our stalking if I start screaming."

And then he's a more familiar raven, talons digging into my shoulder. When I try to brush him off, he pecks my finger with his enormous beak, making me hiss in pain.

Kashire makes a clicking noise, sounding suspiciously like a rider would make for a horse. *Let's go.*

I start off down the hallway, scowling. It's as simple as breathing to find my way in the dark halls of Courtsheart. My eyes are nearly black now, only a few spikes of white lancing outward from the center. Not that the vampires attending the Summit would need to use their inhuman sight. Closer to where the gathering will be held, the Gold Court has hung their banners everywhere, the gold thread reflecting the excessive torchlight glowing on every wall. It's as if they're trying to prove something about how much they can shine.

If I wanted to kill someone, I would stay well away from all of that.

And yet, Kashire and I don't find anything unusual. I cover miles throughout the night, catching glimpses of light and snatches of boisterous conversation when I cross courtyards or open windows. Kashire lets me do all the stalking. I think he even falls asleep on my shoulder at one point.

It's nearing dawn when I lean against a wall in frustration, glaring out at the main courtyard through a window. I haven't found a single thing, and I don't have much more time. The sun comes up far quicker at this time of year. I spot servants dragging heavy black drapes over the windows that encase the halls of the Summit. I step to the side, away from where a lance of sun could hit me.

That's when my eye catches something strange outside, high against the tallest tower looming above the courtyard. It looks like a flicker of gold. Odd, since the stone of Courtsheart is a dark, dripping gray. The gold spreads downward, rippling. Unfurling.

It's a huge banner. The Gold Court's, with the all-seeing eye atop the staff. And something is rolled up in the middle of it, the weight causing the banner to unspool with greater speed. Just as the words *Shine and Steward* are revealed at the bottom, a body comes tumbling out, arms pinwheeling. It plummets toward the courtyard cobbles.

Even from here, I can see it's Pavella. Her blond hair lights like a torch in the dawn. And then so does her body, burning as sunlight hits it.

My mouth falls open in shock.

"I do appreciate the poetry of it," Kashire says, sounding impressed. I barely notice that he's abandoned raven form in favor of his night terror. Ready for battle. I'm too fixated on the scene outside to even flinch away.

Pavella's body drops like a flaming comet to crash in a smoldering pile far below. The banner follows her, fluttering and glittering as it snakes its way down to land in a heap atop her, smothering the fire.

Not that it helps her. I don't imagine Pavella survived. If I had to guess, I would say she was dead and bloodless before her body was thrown out the window.

My gaze shoots upward, tracing her path. There, through the window, I spot someone moving in the safety of the wall's shadows. I think I see a mass of long curly hair, but it's hard to tell at this distance.

"*Claudia?*" I breathe.

23

Claudia can shadowstep, so I need to reach her before she vanishes. The fastest path is my direct line of sight—or flight, for Kashire, but the sunrise prevents him from taking to the air outside. From where we are, I can't shadowstep directly through that window into the high tower, because I need to *see* where I'm going. But maybe I can be fast enough to try to cut across the courtyard. Besides, I'm still a little bit human. I hope it's enough, against the sun.

"Meet me over there," I blurt at Kashire. "I'm not strong enough to take you with me."

"What——?" But he doesn't have time for more before I shadow-step out the window and high above the courtyard—into midair. The burning in my eyes distracts me enough that I begin to fall, my stomach lurching, before I can shadowstep again, this time level with the tower window. I'm glad I don't have time to look down. I'm a dizzying distance above the cobbles and Pavella's gold-cloaked ruin down below.

It's enough to glimpse Claudia through the open window and an empty space, plenty big enough for me to occupy, before I begin to plummet downward.

I land on a giant circular rug after shadowstepping once more, breath whooshing out of me.

I made it. I'm too exhilarated to care that my skin feels like it's on fire for a moment before it heals. But there's no time to celebrate.

I was so quick, Kashire hasn't had time to follow me. I'm alone. With her. A full vampire who taught me everything I know about fighting. And we're surrounded by empty suits of armor ringing the room, every manner of weapon held in the grip of the empty gauntlets.

Blood and piss. I shadowstepped myself into an armory with a weapons master.

Claudia leaps away from me, surprised. "*Fin?*"

"Murderer," I wheeze, launching to my feet and unsheathing my dread blade.

Her red eyes widen. I have no doubt she's going to fight me; I'm still no match for her, not even with the black blade. I just need to stay alive long enough for Kashire to get here.

But then Claudia tries to shadowstep. I feel her grip those nigh-intangible edges for just a moment—before I seize them myself, tearing them away from her. She blinks at me in shock.

And then she *runs*. I don't have time to wonder at it. She's fast. Her form blurs as she takes to the stairs spiraling down around the tower. The hallway curves just the right amount to keep me from leaping ahead of her. I careen after her, smashing violently into the walls, my shadowstepping sometimes tripping me or hurling me too far.

We burst out onto a lower floor, this one filled with all manner of taxidermied animals. It reminds me uncomfortably of the pit. A moose and bear are frozen in spectacular combat, and an enormous creature that I vaguely recall is an elephant raises its long nose between monstrous tusks in a strange salute. I even spot what looks like a werewolf before chasing after Claudia.

But then she freezes, and I almost slam into her, dodging around her at the last second. She catches my shirt, dragging me to a halt. Before I can strike out at her, I also freeze.

Because the werewolves, plural, *aren't* frozen. They're moving slowly, creeping between the other taxidermied animals. They're alive. Stalking us.

"Fin, get behind me," Claudia murmurs.

She wants to *protect* me?

When I don't respond, she hurls me behind her with all her strength. I fly into an unmoving stag, my body nearly mounting itself on its antlers. She's just in time to meet the werewolf strike. All of them lunging for her, not me.

What in the Founders' names is happening? I wonder, hanging upside down across the stag's neck. But I fling myself upright and, of all things, rush to Claudia's defense.

Miraculously, she manages to hold off all six werewolves. She's a blur again, ducking and weaving around the snapping jaws. Avoiding the venom that can kill her, landing powerful, bone-breaking kicks and lethal strikes with her longsword. One werewolf falls dead.

But as I get closer to help, she turns to growl at me, "I told you to get *back*." A kick straight to my sternum sends me flying back into the stag. This time, it goes toppling with me.

I hear Claudia's cry of pain and drag myself into a crouch. I can't let her get shredded by werewolves, no matter how weirdly she's acting. If anything, we need her alive to question her. She's tucking her arm tight to her chest, red blood dripping to the floor. She's been bitten.

As the werewolves circle her once again, I can already see her speed flagging.

But then Kashire bursts through double doors, wings spread behind him. As a night terror, he's by far the most frightening creature in the room.

"Hello, my pretties," he snarls through fanged jaws, horns twisting above his head. But then he blinks glowing blue eyes. "Who or what am I fighting?"

"The *werewolves*," I shout.

The werewolves scatter when Kashire flies at them. They're already vanishing among the other creatures, slinking away into shadows, when Jaen and Marai come dashing into the room. They stop dead.

"*Claudia?*" Marai cries, seeing her maker in the center of the wreckage with her bleeding arm, and immediately spins on *me*. "What did you do to her?"

"Me?" I demand, but it's a fair question. I turn to Claudia, opening my mouth for the question that's been nearly choking me. *Who are you?*

But she's not there anymore. I worry she shadowstepped—though I think I would have felt it—until I spot a large bobtailed cat slipping between the legs of the moose, limping away.

Cat, I think, remembering.

This creature is striped like one, at least, with pointed, black-tipped ears. But it's too big to be a cat, its tail too short. I recognize it nonetheless.

That short tail is something I might not have noticed as a child. When the *lynx* came to me in what I thought were my dreams.

This is the cat I saw long ago.

Forget your mother, it said. *She has forgotten you.*

Claudia said that. A vampire likely originally from this region, if the Black Court once took her on as a novice. I don't have time to consider the implications.

"Wait!" I cry, dashing after the lynx. "Please, wait!"

Vaguely I hear the others coming after me, but I scan the room frantically, heedless of any werewolves that might still be lurking. *Please don't vanish again.*

I round the elephant just in time to see a short, stubby tail disappear into a vent near the ceiling, at the top of a real tree growing against the wall. I can already see, despairingly, that the bark of the trunk is too smooth for me to climb, the vent up there too small for me to even try to shadowstep up to it.

And then I'm running forward. There's a truth too vast to contain trying to rip through my chest. Too strong to outrun. Rather, I ride the wave of it, my speed suddenly doubling.

Or perhaps what's doubled is the number of my limbs striking the ground.

A strange yowl tears out of my throat, and I'm climbing up the tree. My nails—claws—grip the bark like they were made to, sprouting from wide gray and black paws. Four of them. I'm to the top almost before I know it. I glance back at the others down on the ground, but I'm distracted by what else I see. Over my furry shoulders and lithe back speckled with spots, there's a long, lashing tail, tufted white at the end.

Kashire and Jaen are both grinning at me. Even Marai's eyes are wide.

"You did it!" Kashire says.

"And a lovely snow leopard you are," Jaen adds, his voice kind.

All I can appreciate is that I'm not a fish. I don't wait around for more. I dive into the stone vent, having to claw my way forward on my belly. Even like this, I'm almost too big.

I nearly tumble headfirst down a long stone shaft. My claws keep me from falling, slowing my descent with earsplitting scratching. I drop onto all four paws into an old furnace room, unlit. It must heat the tower in winter to keep the greenery alive.

There, I find Claudia—the lynx—curled up in a pile of ancient rags, panting and bleeding. Her red eye rolls to look at me, but that's about all she can do.

I change back to human form to shout, "We're down here!" I hope the others will be able to follow the sound of my voice, using their own shapeshifting to navigate the vent.

When I spin back to the lynx, I find myself looking at a strange woman instead. She's lying on her side, clutching her bleeding arm to her chest, staring at me with a distant, feverish gaze. No, she's not so strange, though I barely remember her face. It's like wiping a thick layer of dust from a painting, and then I recognize her.

My mother.

Except her eyes weren't red back then.

In a blink, she's Claudia again. She always *has* been Claudia, just with a new face. Her vampire face.

Claudia is my mother. I wouldn't have been able to put the two together if I hadn't seen it with my own eyes.

I don't know what to feel, other than panic that rises to a fever pitch within me.

I can't let her die. It doesn't matter that she's a vampire now, and not a very nice one. She's still at the root of everything I've ever wanted to avenge. To shield. To *save*.

I can't breathe at first, and then I'm breathing too hard, too fast.

When she passes out, I stop staring at her in shock and scream at the top of my lungs for Jaen.

It's Marai who arrives first, as a falcon tumbling out of the chute, flapping awkwardly until she takes her human shape again. And then a long-limbed, long-clawed creature I've never seen, carrying a silver-tipped fox under one arm, comes dropping down with much more grace, landing in a crouch. And it's Kashire and Jaen, standing and dusting themselves off.

"You found her?" Kashire asks. And yet, he doesn't know the weight of that question. It's trying to bring me to the ground.

I found her—my *mother*.

I fall back, shaking, to kneel on the ground as Jaen goes to work over Claudia's unconscious form. I bite my hand until it bleeds from my fangs, watching. Marai seems just as concerned about me as she is about Claudia, anxiously shifting her attention between the two of us. I must look unhinged, rocking back and forth. Kashire crouches down next to me, slapping my cheek lightly until I look at him.

"Fin, what on earth is going on? What did she say to you?"

"Nothing. I—She—" I can barely form the words, my teeth chattering. "She's my mother. Claudia is my *mother*. Please, Jaen," I say, beginning to sob like a child. "Please save her."

24

Okay, now that no one is dying *or* trying to kill anyone . . . *explain*," Kashire says, seating himself on an overturned metal bucket, somehow looking like royalty as he does.

Claudia is conscious and upright with her back against the wall, if a little slumped, Jaen still tending to her arm. Claudia has been eyeing me occasionally, looking both weary *and* wary.

I've managed to get myself under control, but now I don't know what to do with myself. I don't know what to ask, where to look. I don't even know where to *sit*, until Marai guides me to the furnace where she's lit a small fire, wrapping a musty, half-rotten blanket around my shoulders. I must still be shivering, even though I'm not cold. The flames cast a flickering orange light over us all. Making Claudia's eyes glow like embers.

Just like the cat's of my childhood. It was too hard to tell they were red back then, just like I couldn't tell she was actually a lynx. *Or* that she was my mother, telling me to forget about her. As if I *could* forget her.

"She's my mother," I croak.

"Yes, you said that already," Kashire says. "But I'm hoping Claudia can explain how this could possibly be true. Did *you* know?" he asks her.

Claudia nods minutely. Marai, despite her helpful bustle, still looks like she's been hit over the head.

I can barely believe it myself. If I hadn't glimpsed the half-forgotten face of my mother, I might never have known. Claudia has certainly hidden it well.

She's *hated* me.

I realize I must have spoken the thought aloud when Claudia says, "I haven't hated you. I've been protecting you your entire life. Mostly from Maudon."

"Maudon?" I echo. "He's been the only one *helping* me, lately."

Claudia swallows a bitter laugh. "He wants you to believe that, at least."

"Oh my, this is getting entertaining," Kashire says delightedly. "But first, and then we can get back to the interesting part . . ." He points at Claudia. "Did you kill Pavella?"

Claudia shakes her head. "I was trailing the person who did. I couldn't get a look at their face. They were shadowstepping, and then misted away after dropping Pavella's body out the window."

"Was Pavella bloodless?" Jaen asks, settling into a crouch.

The corner of Claudia's mouth curves humorlessly. "It was a little hard to tell with her body shrouded in a banner. Why?"

Kashire waves the question away. "We'll get back to that later. But first, Maudon. Why is he after Fin?"

"It's a long story."

"Do tell." He spreads his arms. "We're a captive audience."

Claudia sighs in resignation. "Maudon was on the Finding that brought me to Courtsheart," she begins, "and he grew obsessed with me from the moment he saw me. He chose me at my Beginning like I knew he would, but then I fled from him and the Black Court, because he wanted more than I was willing to give." She holds my eyes. "He wanted *you*."

"Me?" I repeat dizzily.

"Or, at least, my child. He didn't see you at my Finding, but he gleaned I had one. Family is everything to him. *Building* his family is everything to him." She grimaces, looking away. "I told him you were dead. He suspected I was lying. It's difficult to lie to your maker."

"How did you manage?" I ask.

"I used your old name when I said you were dead." She shrugs. "A name that no longer fit you. You were already Fin by then, when he was pressing me. But it had an element of truth."

She doesn't mention the name. I don't want her to. Because it truly is dead. I'm Fin and only Fin.

She *knows* me. And yet she never came back to me.

"You abandoned me," I say.

"Oh, Fin, I didn't," Claudia says remotely. "I watched you and protected you often, if at a distance. I killed your father so he couldn't hurt you anymore. He never even saw me coming."

Kashire whistles. I don't have the breath to make a sound. Everyone else is silent.

When I can speak again, all I can think to shout is, "I nearly starved to death after that!" My voice reverberates in the small room, and Kashire puts a finger to his lips to shush me, though he's still watching this play out like we're at the opera.

"You were better off without him," Claudia says simply. "And you had Silvea to look after you."

"No thanks to you. She healed me when I would have died of infection. Gave me food. Let me sit in on her reading lessons, despite hating me—" I freeze. I stare at Claudia.

She smiles faintly at me. "Fin, back then I would have burned down this castle if it would have helped you, and done many other distasteful things besides. Some of which I *have* done. And I don't mean drowning your father, which I would do a thousand times over."

"You're the reason Silvea saved me," I say, aghast.

A laugh burbles out of Kashire, though he has the barest shred of decency to cover his mouth. I shoot him a glare.

"It only took a little convincing for her to watch over you," Claudia says.

I shake my head. "She was never my friend. She was only nice to me because you *bribed* her. Or did you enthrall her?"

"Bribery was enough. I promised her immortality and hidden knowledge. And enlisting her served more than one purpose. Maudon knew I was visiting the village in secret, knew I was somehow lying about not having a child. By then your father was dead, so he couldn't betray your existence. I planted rumors that Silvea was adopted by her mother, and that I felt bad for her, because she reminded me of my dead daughter. Whether or not he believed she was truly my daughter didn't matter."

Her cold, utter lack of humanity shouldn't be surprising. "Silvea served her purpose, I suppose," I say weakly.

"Indeed. She helped you survive, and Maudon turned to her instead of you."

"As the next member of his family." I feel sick. "And then I thwarted his plans—and Silvea's—by taking her place in the Finding."

"My plans, as well. I was very angry with you," Claudia says. Her lack of emotion somehow makes it worse, sending a chill down my spine. "I was trying to keep you away from this life. Away from him."

No wonder I thought she hated me. I quickly shift the focus. "So Maudon found a way to turn Silvea into a vampire anyway."

"Not by his own blood, so no one would know he'd broken the rules. He either called in a favor or made a threat. It was someone from the Red Court, obviously—rulers of those lands, so it would seem less suspicious, and so she'd be closer to me at Courtsheart. A gift." She smiles without mirth. "One he could take away. I knew her arrival was his doing. He no doubt intended for me to cast aside Marai to make Silvea my apprentice."

I glance at Marai. She looks slightly ill. I feel unsteady, as well. Like the ground is shifting under me.

"I've continued to protect you from Maudon," Claudia continues. "When you had your first lesson with Gavron, Maudon followed you into the woods, and I followed him. He was furious you took Silvea's place, and frustrated that his best pupil had been burdened with you as a novice."

"You're welcome!" Kashire sings.

"Maudon must have enthralled the werewolf and then mist-walked. I didn't see precisely because I was tracking him at a distance. He no doubt thought he was doing Gavron a favor by eliminating you. And probably a favor for me," Claudia adds wryly, "after he watched us interact in Blades. I wanted to speed your training, but without showing you favoritism that would make Maudon suspicious. I must have done too fine a job throwing him off the scent with how harshly I treated you. Luckily Kashire was there that night in raven form, and he flew off to warn Gavron when the werewolf attacked you."

"You're welcome!" Kashire sings again.

Claudia nods at him and says, "Kashire's actions were doubly fortunate, because it meant he wasn't there to see me fight off the werewolf. My secret interest in you was safe."

"But I *did* see you before that," Kashire says. "And mentioned it to Fin."

"That's partly why I suspected you were responsible for the murders," I say to Claudia, grimacing.

"I saw Maudon, too," he adds, "but I didn't know what he was up to. Only supervising Gav's lesson, I thought."

"I knew what he was about, of course," Claudia says, "but I couldn't confront him, because then he would realize what you were to me. I was careful to hide my tracks, even when I fought off your attacker at Winter Sol."

"*You*——?" But then I remember the scuffle outside the ballroom after my throat had been slit, just like with the werewolf in the forest—hissing and the faint sound of paws scampering away. A cat, I thought. But it was a lynx. *Claudia*. "Do you know who attacked me?"

She shakes her head. "Maudon may also have been responsible, since it happened before he knew what you were to me. Maybe he was simply trying to finish what he started with the werewolf."

"But he was at the ball with Silvea when I was attacked."

"He could have acted through someone else, just as he did with Silvea's transformation. He has his methods. And the signs point even more strongly to the Black Court than to an enthralled werewolf this time. Your attacker used a dread blade and vanished without a trace. *Mistwalked*, I believe," she says meaningfully.

There are only a few who can shadowstep outside of the Black Court. Even fewer can mistwalk. I shudder.

"I hoped Silvea's arrival meant Maudon didn't know who you were. But he saw me come to your defense when she first confronted you. I think he understood after that."

So *that* was why Claudia raced up the stairs at the ball, after Silvea. "You were worried about me," I say faintly. "Protecting me. All this time, I've thought . . ."

"I've *kept* protecting you from the both of them," she insists. "I refused to have Silvea in Blades to keep her away from you, and arranged for a novices' competition in the Arena in an attempt, I admit, to raise your estimation in the eyes of my House, in case you ever needed their protection. Not that you humored my efforts. I still thought I was being subtle, but by then Maudon understood what Silvea *wasn't*. And yet he'd already turned her for me, giving himself and the Red Court an inconvenient burden." She sighs, sitting up straighter against the wall. "Which is why, I believe, Silvea ended up dead."

"Maudon did it?" I whisper.

"I imagine so. I was trailing you and Marai at Spring Nox, so I didn't witness it." I remember seeing a creature—a lynx—under a seat in my novice box when I challenged Kashire. "But I assume he arranged her death to send a message to me. The same message he has sent by doting on you. Silvea wasn't what *you* are to me, Fin, and he knows it."

Marai looks gutted. Her maker only seems to have eyes for me. Not to mention she's my *mother*. I'm happy to change the subject. "But there's something else going on here."

Claudia glances down at her bloodstained arm. "Apparently so."

Kashire holds up an elegant hand. "This pesky business with Fin and Maudon aside, my Blue Court novice was killed at Winter Sol. A Red Court apprentice at Spring Nox. And now Pavella at Summer Sol." He ticks them off on his long fingers. "The undying season matches the House each one belongs to. Do you recognize anything in this pattern?"

Jaen bites his lip, as if debating what more to say. "And the victims are subsequently more mature in age."

Claudia blinks. "I hadn't noticed. I was scouting tonight because I was concerned about Fin and Marai, as usual." At the mention of her name, Marai looks up hopefully. "I thought Maudon might try to send yet another message by killing my novice. He has no reason to kill Pavella that I know of, but he's already enthralled one werewolf. He could have enthralled the others tonight." She looks directly at me. "What do you think it all means?"

I glance at Jaen.

"You have my permission to tell her and only her," Jaen says, and some invisible bond within me relaxes.

"We think someone is trying to raise the Founders with these sacrifices," I say.

Claudia's red eyes fly wide.

"It's a long story," Jaen adds. "Best not to get into details. But you're sure Maudon could be involved?"

She nods, eyes narrowing. "Gavron isn't with you, either."

"No," I say. I'm suddenly breathless. "This couldn't be him."

Everyone shares an uneasy look.

"I hate to say it, but the Black Court is obviously involved now, Fin." I don't like how gentle Kashire's tone is. He's never gentle. "I don't want to believe it of him, either, but his connection to his House raises my suspicions."

"He never believed the worst of *you* when all evidence seemed to point to you," I snap.

"Because he knew it wasn't me. Yet . . . I don't know with regard to him now." Kashire rests his chin on his fist, looking disturbed. "It's all a tangle. Maudon's obsession with Claudia and you, the Black Court's clear involvement in something bigger . . . But Gavron *might* yet be separate from all of this. Or even the majority of the Black Court. It could be just a few, going against their House."

"So what are we going to do?" Marai asks. "We can't trust anyone else with this information! Even sharing our concerns with Revar is dangerous at this point."

Jaen grimaces, but before he can speak, Claudia says, "It's none of our concern."

Both Marai and I turn on her. "*What?*"

Claudia drags herself upright, using the wall for support. "At least, if the other courts want the Founders to rise, it's not *my* concern," she clarifies, though it doesn't clear up much. "I only care about the here and now."

"How can you say that?" I demand. "Don't you know what that could mean? What upheaval it could cause both the vampire and human worlds?"

"It's the downside of the Red Court, I suppose, to not care about much outside of the given moment—even if the upside is that we're likely not involved in all this." She shrugs off the threat just like that.

"*I* care," Marai declares, standing.

"You are not of the Red Court yet, my dear," Claudia says. "Think carefully about where you want to align yourself." Her words seem to wind Marai as much as a blow to the stomach, but Claudia only adds, "I need to have a word alone with Fin before I go."

"Yes, all this talk is wearying," Kashire says. "It's about time to depart before we're implicated in Pavella's murder. Coming, Jaen?" He grins suggestively. "Marai, you can watch and learn."

He's likely trying to give Marai a graceful exit, but his jab doesn't even earn a responding salvo from her. Jaen puts his arm around her shoulders and begins to guide her away. She leaves with them reluctantly, casting worried glances back at me and Claudia.

The door out of the furnace room opens without much trouble, and thankfully the hallway on the other side is completely dark and silent. They close the door behind them.

"Let's move," Claudia says, "out of the same concern Kashire had. Shall we go to your bedchamber? I suggest we shadowstep most of the way, to avoid anyone following us. That is, if you'll *allow* me to now." She eyes me with a mixture of irritation and approval.

I grimace at her, chagrined, almost like an errant child would.

<hr />

Once we're safe in my room, thick curtains secured over the window, the door shut and barred, I don't know what to say.

Claudia peers around at my things for a moment, poking at items here and there on my washstand and dresser, as if trying to find me somewhere in here. Or perhaps she's just curious, like a cat.

"A fine bed," she says, nodding at the curtained monstrosity. "I approve."

"Gavron's idea," I mumble.

She spins on me abruptly then, introductions apparently finished. "I *do* intend to cast aside Marai. I only took her on as a novice because you were friends, to keep a closer eye on you. I couldn't take you then because of Maudon. Now that he knows who you are, you're better off closer to me."

"But—but that's cruel!" I sputter. "Marai respects you—loves you! Not like that," I add quickly. "Though I was worried for a time. Now I'm especially glad she's not infatuated with my *mother*."

"I told you, I'm not your mother, not anymore. And I'm fond of her as well." She meets my eyes. "But it's *you* I want to make my apprentice."

I'm dumbfounded yet again. "But . . . *why*? You just said you weren't my—"

"Maudon means to take you from me, but we can still be bound to each other by a stronger tie. As your maker, I can be something like your mother again. Our bond will be more powerful than it ever was."

I shake my head. "There's nothing more powerful than that. I don't care what they say—what *you* say. You'll always be my mother. I won't forget."

"I didn't forget, either." She sighs, looks away. "But, oh, Fin, it's not the same . . . after."

It's like she's reaching for something that's not there anymore. A phantom limb.

I bite back tears. "Then it will never be like that for you again. My becoming a member of the Red Court, even your apprentice, won't make things how they were. That changed when you lost your human life."

She knows I speak the truth. I can see it in her distant expression.

"Take Marai as your apprentice," I urge, choking down a fiercely painful lump. "She's more than worthy. And she adores you . . . like a daughter would."

I mean it, though it takes something from me to say.

But if I can give that to Marai, after everything my friend has done for me, then it's worth it. Besides, I have unfinished business with the Black Court. I can't just walk away, or hide behind Claudia, if it means the Founders could rise.

Claudia nods, accepting my decision just like that, still not looking at me. "I can't call you my child, even to please you. That information is still too dangerous in the wrong hands."

My throat is almost too tight to speak. "I know."

"Except maybe one last time." She leans in, kisses my forehead. "Be well, my child. Be strong. Strive to be happy. And most importantly"—she grips the hair at the nape of my neck and stares at me intently—"*kill* anyone who stands in your way."

Not exactly motherly advice, but I nod just the same.

She's not quite done, though she releases me and steps away. "Maudon is probably waiting on my next move. I suppose he'll have to keep waiting, and then make a decision as to what he wants to do with you. I'll still watch over you for a time. But I have to be discreet, and I can't do it for long if you won't join me. I don't want to get involved in whatever this is."

It's not everything, but it's something. "Thank you," I whisper.

"You're welcome." It sounds like goodbye, even though she doesn't say it.

When she turns to go, part of me wants to stop her. Reach for her desperately like in my nightmares, to keep her from being taken from me again.

Except she's not the mother in my dreams. Not the loving human parent, mouthing my old name. She's not even the cruel, bloody vampire.

She's a vampire, to be sure. And she can be cruel and filled with bloodlust. But she's also much more than that, like so many vampires. Capable and determined. Fierce and protective. Powerful and brave. She sees me for who I am, and I see her.

She's someone else now—something sharp and blazing. I'm proud of what she's become, what she's made of herself from the wreckage of her old human life. She's thriving on her own, without me, and I don't want to hold her back.

It's time to let her go, even if it breaks my heart to do it.

I have my own path to walk. It's enough that she's given me hope that I can be proud of *myself*, someday, for forging my own way— even as a vampire.

She opens the door, but she doesn't simply turn her back to me. She melts, becoming the red-eyed lynx.

And then she darts away. Gone.

I close the door behind her, unable to contain the sob that rises in me. It's both grief and a release, as I slide down against the door and put my head in my hands.

I found my mother, even though she's not the mother I once knew. And even though it feels like I lost her yet again.

I'll remember her. *Both* of her faces.

25

The rest of summer fades as quickly as the dying rays of sun beneath the horizon.

After the Summit, almost all I can do is pour myself into my lessons until I have nothing left, as if bleeding out my last drops of blood.

My future, I've decided, is to become a vampire, although hardly anyone knows for sure which court I want to choose. As far as most know, Gavron has abandoned me. I've been left to pick another House.

Deciding which one is a problem I'll be lucky to have.

I haven't seen Gavron since Maudon brought me to the Black Gates before Summer Sol, but he has to face me soon. His attendance is required. It almost makes me look forward to tomorrow night. *Almost.*

Whether I like it or not, the time is upon us. It's the day before the Becoming. Tomorrow night, we'll be made into vampires. Or else . . .

Fear threatens to eviscerate me. Tomorrow night, *I* have to face my worst nightmare. But I hope it's worth it. And not just to see Gavron. I have a plan.

Once I explain what I want to do to Kashire and Jaen and get their grudging approval, I sneak into Marai's room before dawn, the day before summer season ends.

The undying cycle. I hope it's undying, anyway, for me.

Slipping into her bed is like a tiny homecoming of sorts. I wonder if this is what having a sister feels like. And yet, this will be the last time she makes a tent for me under these covers. By dawn, she'll move out of Courtsheart proper to the grand, outer hall belonging to the Red Court.

It's why I've come—for old times' sake. For comfort. But also something else. I've hardly had time to talk to her since the Summit. To truly *apologize*.

I hug her tight. "Marai, I'm so sorry."

"I know," she says, and I can hear her smile in the dark.

I assumed she would know what I meant, but I still feel the need to explain. "You were right about Claudia. None of it was her fault. It was all Maudon."

"I know," she repeats. "And it should be obvious by now that I forgive you."

"Thank you." I let out a deep breath. "If Maudon offers me his mark of approval—and I think he will—I'm going to choose the Black Court tomorrow night."

Marai jerks in my arms, not expecting *that*. "But he's dangerous! He's likely involved with the plan to raise the Founders!"

"The better for me to spy on him," I say, ignoring the fear churning in my stomach. "And that way, Claudia won't feel torn between you and any half-dead loyalty to me. She'll be entirely free to choose the apprentice who deserves it the most."

This is my opportunity to pursue my own path. It's the chance I never had in my village. My goals have changed since then, but they're bigger now. Far more important than killing nameless, faceless monsters. I'm going to stop something truly monstrous from happening with the Founders' rise.

But only *if* I can become a vampire of the Black Court.

"Do you know for sure what's going to happen to you tomorrow night?" Marai murmurs. We both know *she'll* be fine. She's done well under every House's tutelage but Black. "Will you earn three marks of approval to pass?"

"I don't know. I've lost Gold and Silver for certain." I wasn't meant for the shiny Houses, obviously. "I've likely gained Blue and Red. But Black?" I shrug, trying to sound casual. "I don't know."

"Do you think Maudon will keep his word?"

"I *think* so. Yet it's Gavron who has to turn me." And I don't know if he will. He won't even show his face around me. But I don't speak the doubt aloud, so as not to bring it to life.

"Are you afraid?" Marai whispers.

"Yes," I finally admit. My voice is a choked thing.

Marai buries her face in my shoulder, holding me.

We fall asleep like that, wrapped around each other.

No matter what happens, at least I still have my best friend. Despite the mistakes I've made, it's *one* thing I've done right.

———✦———

"Fall is when some forms die, and others are preserved," Revar intones in the grand hall of Courtsheart. Their voice echoes through the marble pillars and arching balconies up to the painted ceiling above. I can see it so clearly now, when it was all so shadowed and mysterious before. "Welcome to the first night of autumn, to the Choosing of Houses, and to your Becoming. Tonight, as befits the season, some of you will die—and thus be preserved. Forever."

The Council of Vampires is arrayed off to the side this time; only a single representative from each court stands on a dais before us— the instructors who've taught us the past few seasons. Since they trained us firsthand, it's their honor to convey their House's favor. Or disfavor. Appropriately, for the occasion, they're all wearing the colors of their courts.

Gavron would be wearing black anyway, appearing like a handsome shadow wherever he goes. He looks the same as the day I met him, and yet so much has changed. His hair is pulled tight, daggers strapping him. His eyes are fathomless. He's so beautiful and distant, it hurts to see him.

Likewise, Revar appears as serene and dignified as they always have in their long silver robes. "For those of you who gain the approval of their chosen House, this will mark the end of your human lives. But it's only the beginning of a new life, the true start of your undying seasons. You will become one of us . . . and the rest will become our servants."

Revar regards us novices, arrayed in our finest. All of us are harder, sharper, and brighter than when we first got here. And yet, all of us are terrified. Marai clutches my hand like she did at our Beginning. The strength of her grip now would have shattered my bones then.

Revar starts with the Blue Court novices first. We watch as they step forward. A few are approved. One is dragged away screaming, to become a thrall.

They move on to the Red Court just like that, as if the ruination of someone's life was only a matter of ceremony. Maybe it was, for them. My knees start to shake.

"Gabriella, come forward."

It goes smoothly for her. She has enough marks of approval and chooses the Red Court. No surprises. Her head is high as her future maker guides her away. Which means the next one to be called will be—

"Marai, come forward."

With a shuddering breath, Marai releases my hand.

She needn't have worried. It's just like we thought. Full marks of approval from all but the Black Court. Claudia takes her arm, leading her away. Claudia doesn't even look back at me.

But Marai does, giving me a hopeful smile.

Revar carries on with the Gold and then the Silver Court novices. Yuhan weeps as the stand-in for Pavella from the Gold Court tells him he earned their approval to join their House if he so chooses, which of course he does.

Finally, I'm the only one left at our Becoming. Almost like I was at our Beginning, save for Lief. He didn't make it this far. And the very court I want to join might be responsible for his murder.

"Fin, come forward." Revar smiles tranquilly. "Let us see what you will become."

The Blue Court speaks first, as always. Kashire steps forward to say, "Fin has earned the approval of the House of Winter Night. While she found her inner animal last of all, albeit a lovely one—I just *love* snow leopards—she found her mask first in the class, even though she hid it from me, the ungrateful wretch. But we all make mistakes, and she always manages to impress me." He grins. "Even when I want to kill her."

Coming from Kashire, those words flatter me.

Havere comes forward next. He's been speaking for both himself and Claudia since she left with Marai. "Fin has earned the approval of the House of Spring Dawn. She was exceptional in Blades, according to Claudia, and surprisingly adept at Seduction."

Exceptional at Blades. That's all my once-mother has to say on the occasion that might mark the end of my human life.

I'm cringing inside before Pavella's haughty stand-in even steps forward. "Fin has *not* earned the approval of the House of Summer Day. Pavella found her abysmal in every regard. She's not fit to join the Gold Court, nor do we believe her fit to join any other."

"That's not your decision," Revar remarks.

"We just want it to be known, for the record," she says, bowing her head and stepping back.

Yuhan smirks at me.

I swallow nervously as Jaen steps forward. I know I didn't gain the Silver Court's favor, but this is still going to hurt, coming from her.

Jaen, of course, makes it as kindly as possible. "Fin has unfortunately not gained the approval of the House of Autumn Twilight," she says. "She was an adequate student of Vampire History and quite adept at Vampire Anatomy and Physiology. Where she failed was in the subject of Healing, which is critical to our House's mission of preservation."

My stomach churns. This is it. The end. *My* end, one way or another.

"Normally, that would only be sufficient for you to enter the service ranks of Courtsheart," Revar says to me, sounding unconcerned. "But you have been studying under another House, have you not?"

Everyone turns to Gavron, the dark shadow up on the dais. He looks sick—probably because he's going to have to tell them he refused to keep teaching me a while ago.

Before he can open his mouth, Maudon surfaces from the shadows behind him, putting a hand on his shoulder. "Yes, she has. I've undertaken her training in Gavron's stead, and not found her lacking. She's fit to join our House. But it is up to you, Gavron," he adds, turning to him, "to grant her our favor, as you would be her maker."

My throat tightens as if Gavron's hands are wrapped around it. If he still hasn't forgiven me, then I really am doomed.

At first he looks utterly shocked by Maudon's admission, and—I hope?—relieved. But then his dark eyes narrow down at me.

"You'll join us, if I give you my approval?" he asks, sounding wary. "You won't take our favor and join another House?"

You won't betray me yet again? his words seem to say.

Maudon wears a small smile. It's the choice that is no choice—all he would have wanted for Claudia, I now know. But she forged her own path, and so he's getting his revenge by taking that choice from her human child.

At least, he's *seeming* to take it from me. Good thing this is exactly what I want.

I clear my throat and turn to the Council. "I swear before all present that it is my wish to join the Black Court with Gavron as my maker," I declare, not a waver in my voice.

Gavron's eyes widen a fraction.

I hold my breath.

"I need a word, first, Fin. In *private*," Gavron emphasizes.

"That would be highly irregular——" Revar begins.

Maudon frowns slightly.

"Please?" Gavron asks. But he's not looking at the Silver Court vampire or Maudon. He's looking at me, and he doesn't exactly wait for a response, only steps off the dais. My legs feel wobbly as I start after him, glancing nervously at the waiting crowd. All eyes are on us as I follow him between a few marble pillars until we get deeper into the shadows. There's a door in an alcove, and he eventually leads me into a small room.

"I can't stand having an audience," he mutters, closing the door behind us.

"Me, either." I glance around, nervous. "Why didn't we just shadowstep?"

"I figured taking you this far without giving my decision was already enough violation of ceremonial decorum."

"So . . . why *not* give them your decision?" I ask, a little breathlessly.

"Fin, I——" He stops, looks away, a strand of his dark hair falling in a line across the plane of his cheek. He's so beautiful. "I need——I need to——" he stammers.

I know what he needs. What kind of reassurance.

It's exactly what I want, too.

I throw my arms around his neck and press my mouth to his as if his lips are air and I'm drowning. I kiss him fervently. Unabashedly.

For a second, he freezes. But then his strong arms come around me, lifting me off my feet. He returns my kiss just as fiercely, even while I wrap my legs around his waist and he slams my back up against a stone wall. Our hands are everywhere, pulling, seizing, seeking. His muscles are taut under my fingertips, and I dig my nails in. He groans into my mouth. There, I feel the sweet sting of teeth and taste his blood, mine, mixing on our frantic tongues, inflaming our hunger. It's still not enough. I need more of him after all this time. I need him even closer.

When I tear the laces of his shirt in my haste to undo them, his fingers close around mine, stopping me. He eases away from the wall, letting my legs slip down around his thighs. His lips linger on my mouth, but he manages to withdraw, biting my bottom lip as he does, sucking gently. When I strain toward him, he leans his forehead against mine and shakes his head with a regretful sigh.

"You wanted this before," I gasp. *Wanted me*. "Why wait?"

"Remember the part about ceremonial decorum?" It sounds as if *he's* having a hard time remembering. "If we don't stop now, you'll miss the rest of your Becoming." He licks the blood off his lip. Swallows. "I'm already taking enough from you."

My life. Right. I suppose we have more important things to focus on at the moment.

When he sets me back on unsteady feet, I'm more than a little breathless. "I didn't know if you would let me kiss you at all. I'm sorry, Gavron, for hurting you. I never meant to, and I've missed you so much. I want this, with you. I want *more*."

"Well," he murmurs, bending his mouth to my neck. "That certainly makes it easier."

The movement of his lips against my throat makes my eyes flutter and my heart race in both fear and need. "Makes *what* easier?" I say, half teasing.

"Draining you nearly to death. It's what must happen. It would be much worse if you were resistant."

A thrill of alarm goes through me, which I quickly silence. I suppose I fought him at my Beginning, but we've come so far from that. This is my Becoming. I won't resist this time.

Even if it's frightening, this is exactly what I want. He should know that.

"Why would I——?" But then his teeth sink into my neck, and I lose the thread of my question. As he takes more and more blood from me than ever before, I unspool deliciously. My limbs feel loose, like they're coming apart. I come undone.

I can't stand up on my own when he's finished. I can barely hold my eyes open. He supports me in his arms, gazing down at me with that insatiable hunger. That bottomless need for me. I didn't know if he would ever look at me like that again.

"That might be the last time I get to do that," he murmurs dreamily. "I'm going to miss it."

"Because you can't drink my blood when I'm a vampire or else I'll gain control of you?" I slur, laughing drunkenly. "Doesn't sound so bad to *me*."

He only half smiles, and then hefts me in his arms, threading his fingers through my hair. He tilts his head almost coyly, exposing the strong curve of his neck. My blood stains his lips a red so deep it's almost black. "Your turn. From the throat this time. You need to drink a lot."

I can smell his blood already, through his skin. But I don't immediately bite him. "Aren't you supposed to give the Council your decision first?"

"Kissing you made me irresistibly hungry. Now *you're* starving nigh to death. Go on. They can wait a little longer. This may be your final time, too."

My mouth is watering, but I also can't bear the thought that this is *it*—the last of him I might taste. "How will I know when to quit?" I ask nervously, my lips brushing his throat.

"Afraid of hurting me?" He scoffs lightly. "Don't be. I'll stop you. Even after you drink your fill, I'll still be much stronger than you."

I trust him, and I can't help myself anymore. My teeth sink into him as if it's the most natural thing in the world.

Somehow, his blood is more delicious than I remember. I don't try to withhold this time, crushing my lips against him. I let myself go just as much as when he was drinking from me. Except now, I'm not unspooling. I'm *respooling* myself with the black ribbon of his blood, threading it through my flesh and bones. Soon, it will become me. His strength, now mine.

I'll become a vampire.

But first, he has to kill me.

When he gently shrugs me away from his neck, I'm suddenly scared. It doesn't help that I no longer feel so wonderfully intoxicated. I'm alert now, jumpy, with so much of his blood. Colors are too bright. Even the sound of my heart beating is too loud. My stomach feels strange. I should be sated on his blood, but all I feel is a cold emptiness. So much hunger still.

Maybe I'll feel it forever.

"Are you ready?" Gavron asks, tucking my hair behind my ears.

"*Is* this it? When you"—I force myself to say it—"kill me?"

He smiles that half smile again, shaking his head. "I told you, I had something to tell you first. I *tried* to tell you, but then you started kissing me, and I only wanted to kiss you back. One thing led to another."

My own smile is tentative. Something about his expression is beginning to bother me. When he drags his fingers down my neck, my spinning mind finally recognizes the pattern of motion from Seduction.

Gavron is literally trying to seduce me. *Lull* me.

"What is it?" I ask, alarmed. "What do you need to tell me?"

He leans forward. The words are a whisper in my ear, skimming so lightly that it takes me a moment to realize the weight of what he's saying: "I killed Lief. And Silvea. And Pavella. I even tried to kill you at Winter Sol, when you found Lief's body. I was the one who cut your throat."

I jerk away from him, staring in horror. "What?" I back away from him so quickly I nearly trip over my own feet. "Why?"

"I had to." He suddenly grimaces, his throat bobbing like he might throw up. He sounds like he's in pain. Ragged. "Fin, I'm sorry. I told you to stay away from me and my House. I *tried*. But you didn't listen. You never listen."

Part of me can't believe what he's saying. But part of me can—the part that's terrified.

Then I remember how he looked at Winter Sol after he found me in the hallway with my throat slit: disheveled, in a rush. Kashire hadn't even known where he'd been. I also remember him giving me my fillet knife back, the night of Spring Nox. Which meant he'd seen Silvea recently—and perhaps done more to her. Pavella's killer could have been anyone—anyone who could both shadowstep and mistwalk. He can do both.

Gavron manages to get himself under control, looking at me levelly. "What do you know about these murders? Their purpose?"

I open my mouth. Close it. I can't say anything about it, not after being impelled. *Thank the Founders*, I think ironically. *No, thank Jaen.*

I get the sense that Gavron is trying to impel me himself. Maybe he won't know if I lie, or if I speak around the truth.

"I don't know anything!" I insist. "I thought it was Kashire murdering foundlings. Obviously, I was wrong." I back myself into the corner of the small room, my chest heaving. "What are you going to do now?"

He looks relieved, though his words are anything but relieving. "I'm going to say you confessed in private to the murders—Lief's, Silvea's, and Pavella's. There's sufficient evidence already in place to lay the blame at your feet. You've long wanted to kill vampires anyway."

"If you know that much, then you should know I don't anymore!" I shake my head. "Why didn't you say anything?"

"At the time I admired your determination. I knew you weren't strong enough to act on it, and I hoped you would change your mind. Now, your secret serves my purposes. Killing vampires without sanction is a crime, one that will prevent you from ever gaining the Black Court's mark of approval. I'm sorry, Fin. I can't kill you now, because I can't let you turn and tell the truth as a vampire."

"But you're the one who just told me what you've done! You didn't have to!"

"I need to keep you away from me."

"Then why do all *this*?" I shout incredulously, gesturing down at myself. "I'm nearly a vampire already! Why replace my blood with yours if you don't want to make me one of you?"

"To protect you a while longer. My undiluted blood within you should keep you unmolested for some time before its potency fades. Seasons, perhaps."

"Why would I be—?"

"Because vampires generally like to feed on thralls," he interrupts. And then I realize.

It's not just that I won't become a vampire. I won't be put to death, either, not while I can rise again as one of them. I won't even rot in the dungeon, because that would be a waste of labor.

I'm going to become a thrall.

"*No!*" I scream. I try to shadowstep, but he jerks those dark edges out of my hands. I try to dash past him, but he catches my shoulders. Forces me to look into his eyes.

I sink into them as if into a black pool.

"You are under my control," he says, his voice ringing through me, "and these are my orders: You are to tell no one that you didn't kill those three, or that I did. You are not to leave Courtsheart. You are neither allowed to use a mask to change your face, nor to shapeshift. You are forbidden to shadowstep. You are not permitted to hurt another vampire, or to willingly allow a vampire to hurt you. You are

304

not allowed to harm yourself or take your own life. You are to defend yourself at all costs if anyone tries to kill you. You are to do as you are told by other vampires, so long as it doesn't contradict my orders." He blinks, as if remembering something important. "And you are not permitted to drink human *or* vampire blood."

Darkness starts to fall over my eyes, like curtains in front of a window. Distantly, I hear my own strangled, despairing laugh. "Why do you care about *that*?"

"Another's blood will push mine out faster. If my blood stays within you, a vampire won't want to risk my wrath or my influence by feeding on you. The effect should be lasting. This is for your own benefit, even if you won't believe me. The hunger will be . . . extreme. But it will ward off the hunger of others."

A pit opens up inside me. I feel like I'm falling into it, sinking into terrible depths within the confines of my own body. Fear claws at me, but I can't do anything against it.

"Why do you care?" I whisper. He doesn't answer. A weight tugs at my mind, my body, dragging my eyes closed. "Why are you doing this to me?"

He sounds miserable. "You gave me no other choice. Good night, Fin."

I drift away in his arms. Just like at the Beginning, I think deliriously.

———

When I next wake up, I'm in the servants' quarters. Surrounded by thralls with faintly glowing eyes and placid smiles. I wonder if my eyes look like theirs.

I'm certainly not smiling.

Not yet, a terrified voice says inside me. *Perhaps only because Gavron didn't command it.*

Immediately, I try to hurt myself, digging my nails into my own wrist. I can't do more than poke at my skin. My fingers simply won't obey.

Unlike the other thralls, I seem to have more awareness. More horror. Gavron's enthrallment isn't so all-encompassing, apparently, to keep me from *knowing* I'm a thrall.

That would have been a mercy.

It's then I begin to scream.

V

FALL

26

The first few days are the worst, even if my screams are quickly silenced on command.

For the supposed crime of killing vampires, I'm sent to "the other kitchen," as Kashire once dubbed it. I can't be drunk from, not with Gavron's blood entirely replacing my own, but the smell of free-flowing blood is a wicked torment. It's like being invited to a feast when you're starving and yet forbidden to partake.

And, of course, Yuhan finds me there. He believes I killed Pavella. I confessed as much, after all. He plagues me whenever he can spare the time.

Lounging on a bench in one of the curtained alcoves, he holds up the crystal glass of blood, which he's just filled from the wrist of another thrall. "Want a drink? Tell the truth now." He makes the last part a command.

"Yes," I can't help but say pleasantly.

He knows I do, and how much I hunger. This is a game we've already played. Insofar as he or anyone else understands, the reason I've been forbidden to drink blood is that starvation is part of the punishment handed down by Gavron. No one knows the true reason—that feeding would dilute his blood within me, making my own more palatable in a shorter span of time.

"Tell me how badly you want it. Beg for it."

I do. Deep inside, shame eats away at me almost as much as my hunger.

After letting me go on at length, Yuhan says indulgently, "Fine, you've convinced me." He offers me the glass. "Come, take it."

He knows I can't drink, but I still have to obey. When I reach out, he lets the goblet slip through his fingers. It shatters on the stone floor. The smell of blood was already strong before. Now it explodes around me, making me dizzy with hunger.

Yuhan's golden eyes gleam with malice. "How clumsy of me. Fetch me another goblet." He gestures at a low table lined with them.

"Yes, my lord," I say, because I can't say anything else. I return quickly with a goblet, but he holds up a hand to stop me.

"Crawl to me," he says. "And keep smiling."

I'm always smiling now. Those were the first instructions I received: Stop screaming. Keep calm. Smile.

I have no other choice but to crawl through the shattered glass and spilled blood. I'm not allowed to harm myself, and I must flee or defend myself if someone else tries to—and *they* would have to face Gavron's wrath—but the glass isn't trying to hurt me, and neither is Yuhan, at least not directly, and so I have to obey. The shards cut my knees through my servant's skirts and the palm of the hand not holding the glass. I bleed black, even if the cuts heal over almost immediately. Despite the sting and my burning humiliation, I keep smiling.

Yuhan frowns down at me on my knees. As if my torment isn't enough for him.

"You can't hurt yourself, but you *can* hurt others, yes? The activity you found so distasteful in Healing?" He smirks. "Rise."

He takes the goblet I offer and, shockingly, replaces it with my old fillet knife. He must have pillaged it from my old room after I was made a thrall. My hand clenches repeatedly around the hilt.

I would give anything to stab him with it.

Yuhan gestures at the thrall from which he's been feeding. "Refresh my drink, will you, Fin?" His golden eyes hold mine with molten hatred. "Cut her slowly, across the length of her, from one hand to the other." He turns his irresistible words on the other thrall. "Feel *everything*. But don't scream. We wouldn't want the noise. Keep smiling."

She smiles, even if, deep behind the glowing sheen over her eyes, I see panic surface.

I want to scream as I move inexorably for her, readying my fillet knife as if she were just another fish. Of course, I can only smile along with her.

Right before the tip of my blade touches the soft flesh on the inside of her wrist, a blurring hand snatches the knife from my grip. Another strike sends Yuhan's head snapping backward.

Marai is suddenly standing between us. She bares her teeth at Yuhan, fangs gleaming underneath her brilliant red eyes. She wasn't a small person before, but now she dominates. Her curves draw the eye like flame, her presence sucking all the air from the room.

"Torment Fin again, and I'll torture you for eternity," she snarls.

Yuhan wipes the golden blood from his nose and rubs it between thumb and forefinger. He's already stopped bleeding. "She's just a human. Pavella was worth far more. Do you think your memory of your friend will be stronger than mine?"

"My arm definitely will be. I'm still far better with a blade than you. And while your enthrallment tricks won't work on me, my steel will work on you, at least for a moment." She smirks at the blood on his fingers. "How quickly you heal will only force me to get more creative."

Yuhan sputters. "You wouldn't dare——"

"I have and I shall. Care to try me?" When he doesn't answer,

Marai seizes my arm, hauling me away from him and the other thrall. She drags me into the hallway.

She's so much faster now. I stumble to keep up with her, but it takes her the length of the hallway to realize it. She jerks to a stop, wincing.

"I'm sorry, Fin, I move quickly when I'm angry." She sags against the wall, but even that's too fast to look human. "I'm sorry it took me this long to find you. No one has been forthcoming about your whereabouts, and they've been keeping me busy—"

"Whatever pleases you—" I begin.

"Don't say that! And stop smiling." She grits her teeth. "I command you. Show me how you truly feel."

My smile slips like thawing ice from a cliffside. When it falls, I nearly fall with it, my face crumpling.

Her red eyes bleed with pity. "Oh, Fin. How are you?"

"Hungry," I rasp.

"What can I do? I can try to feed you my blood but—"

"You can't," I say shortly. "I'll fight you. Gavron forbade it."

"What can I do?" she repeats desperately.

"Nothing. Just leave me." It's hard to bear her looking at me like this—not because I don't want her support, but because she can't always be here for me. If I start to lean on her, I won't be able to stand on my own anymore. I'll crumble all the sooner.

"I don't believe you killed them. Don't tell me that you did," she adds, forestalling me. "I'll never believe it. But no one listens to me."

"Claudia?" I hate to ask.

Marai glances at me guiltily. "She doesn't say much about you, but I know she's furious with how things turned out, as am I." She growls, throwing herself into motion, pacing in front of me in a blur. "I won't let this rest. As soon as I know what to do, I'll do it." She seizes my arm. "In the meantime, I'm getting you out of here. I'll get you somewhere safer. Less torturous. I don't care who I have to enthrall or stab to keep it that way."

She drags me off down the hall, leaving me little room to argue, even if I could.

The following weeks, bleeding into months, are significantly better, thanks to Marai. But it's not hard to improve upon hell, and I'm still in it.

At least horses make decent companions. They don't talk in absentminded pleasantries or smile vaguely beneath their vacantly glowing gaze. Their big, soft eyes often have that eerie light behind them, but they just stand, eat, snort, and swish their tails. I want to scream less in their company than I do in that of human thralls. Certainly less than in the company of vengeful vampires.

The crisp fall air swirls around me as I brush Gray Mist—I don't actually know if that's her name, but it's what I call her—a stunning mare belonging to a recently arrived Silver Court vampire. More vampires are arriving every night for Autumn Nox and what they call the Symposium, a gathering of the brightest minds belonging to the House of Autumn Twilight. I mostly only see their mounts.

Soon, it will be time for this year's Beginning. I wonder if they'll give my room to a new arrival.

I'm deep in the stables, where I sleep alone during the day in a dark loft, buried under hay, rather than the servants' quarters. Now, beneath the strong odors of horse and dung, I can scent oncoming snow gusting through a shutter that's open to a sliver of outside darkness. My senses are still sharp. Too sharp for me to feel numb to anything but the increasing cold.

Autumn is waning. Winter will be here soon enough. The undying cycle repeating. I hope not forever, for me.

I clutch my stomach as a particularly bad pain gnaws at me. My hunger feels like it will eat me from the inside out. I'm not sure how much longer I can go on like this. Food helps, but not for long. There's only one thing I truly want. It's also why I prefer the company of horses to humans. I don't particularly want to bite *their* necks.

Good thing, I think, patting Gray Mist's withers as I brush her mane. Because I would in a heartbeat if I thought it would help. But animal blood doesn't offer much relief. I've tried it.

I take a long pull of the bottle that's never far from my side. Gavron didn't forbid me from drinking *wine*, after all, and it not only helps dull the pain of my hunger but everything else. It numbs me where enthrallment can't. Except it's still not enough.

At least Marai commanded me to stop smiling if I didn't want to. I haven't smiled since.

If my ceaseless hunger doesn't kill me, I hope a vampire will. Gavron's blood will eventually grow stale within me, losing that potency so off-putting to another vampire and allowing my still-human blood to rise to the fore. Tempting someone to drink, hopefully beyond the point of no return. That will be a mercy. But it hasn't happened yet. And it might not for a long while.

Gavron said it might take *seasons* with how far gone I am.

Marai is the only one who's tried to help me, and she's just about given up. Claudia hasn't visited at all. I suppose she offered me a chance that I refused, and now I'm on my own, in her eyes. Maybe even *safe*, according to her strange vampire logic. I haven't seen Gavron or Kashire, either, not that I expected the latter.

I keep hoping Gavron will visit, despite what he did to me. Because something about all of this isn't quite lining up, like a torn painting. I need to see him again to try to make out the fuller picture. Sometimes I feel like I sense him, watching me, but when I turn there's no one there. I feel that way now, but I refuse to look. I lean against Gray Mist for a moment and close my swimming eyes.

313

"Good evening!" a cheery voice exclaims behind me.

I jump so high I could leap onto Gray Mist's back. I spin to find Kashire standing behind me, grinning. All I can do is stare. He's wearing deep gray silk with accents of blue—the scarf at his throat, the jewels on his fingernails, and of course his eyes. He's dressed subtly, for him, and yet he's the most beautiful sight I've seen in weeks—*months*—aside from Marai.

"I command you to speak freely." He flicks me on the forehead, making me wince. "Come now, are you still in there, little thrall? At least you haven't asked how you can serve me yet."

"Eat dung and die," I say. "And don't call me a thrall."

His grin widens, revealing his brilliant fangs. "That's more like the Fin I know!" He snatches the wine bottle from my hand and downs it in a single drag. When he's through, he smacks his lips, tossing the bottle aside. "You weren't supposed to continue your lessons in Revelry without me."

"Yes, I'm really reveling in all of *this*." I sag against Gray Mist's side. "What do you want, Kashire?"

"Is it so strange to want to visit my one-time favorite student?"

"Yes," I say. "You haven't come before now."

"Neither has Gavron, and I'm quite positive he's madly in love with you."

I nearly fall over. Even now, the thought of Gavron loving me is enough to make my knees weak. *Bloody bastard.* I should hate him. Part of me does.

But another part of me knows there's something else going on here.

"Gavron was lying to me," I say as soon as I can find my tongue. It's clumsy in my wine-drenched mouth. "When he did this to me. I don't think he wanted to."

I can only speak the words because I don't mean when he accused me of murder. He was lying about that, too, but I'm not allowed to talk about that. Kashire's command to speak freely still only allows me to do so within Gavron's rules.

Kashire looks me over, his bright gaze lingering where bits of hay poke through my hair. "Pretty convincing lie."

I straighten, self-consciously brushing at my clothing. "No, I mean he used blatant moves from Seduction. He's always called those tricks 'lying.'" It's hard to speak around the enthrallment, but I try my best. "He never wanted to hurt me. I think he's been trying to protect me by staying away from me, and he's trying to protect me still."

"That doesn't mean he was lying. He just as easily could have been doing a painful duty." Kashire nods at me again. "Some protection, anyway—enthrallment and starvation. But I guess that's all a murderer of vampires like you deserves, eh?"

He looks at me expectantly, as if waiting for me to defend myself. Except I can't.

"Yes, I'm well aware of my situation," I say bitterly. "He told me he had to do this to me, that he didn't have a choice, and that he was sorry. Maybe he was only referring to his duty. But he *also* told me he tried to kill me at Winter Sol."

That was one thing Gavron never forbade me to admit. I smile in grim satisfaction when I'm able to.

Kashire's eyes pop. "That was him?" But in an instant, he squints at me and taps his chin. "And yet, if you're somehow responsible for all the rest, then that would mean you'd already killed Lief at that point. It would have been his duty to end you then, as well."

I open my mouth, but nothing comes out.

Kashire folds his arms. "You can't say, as I guessed. Frankly, I have a very hard time believing you're the killer. Funny, I know, after all that you've accused me of." It's such a colossal relief to hear that tears flood my eyes. "But I *also* have a hard time believing you wouldn't happily see Gavron on the pointy end of a stake to the heart."

I *should* want that. And yet there was also that note of Gavron's that I didn't quite understand, after Winter Sol. *I'm sorry*—words written with such force they tore through the parchment.

"He apologized after Winter Sol. Like he did before doing *this*." I glance down at myself, hoping that Kashire understands I mean more than the enthrallment.

He shrugs. "Given that he apparently slit your throat, an apology might have been warranted. Some might see it as falling far short, especially after he framed you for murder." Before I can try to nod, he rolls his eyes. "Framed you for the petty, jealous type of murder, not even the insidious ritualistic type it truly is. It's all rather pedestrian. So why do you seem bent on defending him, even in your pathetically limited fashion?"

I throw my hand at him in frustration. "You were the one who just said he loved me! And he told me himself that I gave him a reason to care that he desperately needed. Something of his own. If he truly wanted to kill me at Winter Sol, why did he feed me his blood— twice—to save me after? He gave me a dread blade, too. I think partially to defend against *him*." I spin away, pacing alongside Gray Mist and kicking up hay with the force of it. "And after he stabbed you to save me at Spring Nox, he was horrified. He said, 'Not again!' I think he was remembering attacking *me*. He kept telling me to stay away from him. And he didn't forbid me from mentioning his attempt on my life, even though he did forbid—" I choke, unable to continue until I swallow the words that want to come out. "You know. And then he gave me so much of his blood that I couldn't be fed upon or easily killed. All I've had is time to think about what he's done to me, Kashire, and it doesn't make sense that he's doing it happily. I think there's something wrong with him, and he was trying to tell me."

"I agree," Kashire says, and I turn to face him, hope trying to rise in my chest like a drowning thing. "There *is* something wrong. Jaen is missing."

I blink at the abrupt change in topic. "What?"

316

Kashire stares at me levelly. "You need to help me. You know which season this is—which court's sacrifice is next."

Of course. Autumn Nox is tomorrow night.

"Despite what everyone would have me believe," Kashire continues, "yourself and Gavron included, I don't think you're behind the murders. Frankly, I think Gavron is, and you would tell me if you could."

All I can say is, "Why come to me with Jaen's disappearance? Why not tell Revar?"

"They could be in on it."

"Why not get Claudia and Marai to help you?"

"Claudia doesn't care about Jaen, and Marai won't go against her maker, especially not as a new apprentice. But *you* care about Jaen."

I flap my arms, drawing a soft knicker from Gray Mist. "What can I do, like this? And why should I care, even if I do? Jaen didn't try to save me from this fate."

Kashire's icy gaze is pitiless. "We did talk about it: Jaen, Claudia, and I. Making you a vampire anyway and setting you free. But no one could agree on who would be your maker. Claudia would have wanted to, but she already has an apprentice and thought it too dangerous for you to be out on your own, anyway, as a newborn vampire without the protection of a House. Here, at least, as a powerful thrall, we could look out for you. That was her motherly logic, anyway."

So she *did* figure I was safer here. "Very motherly," I growl. "Like I'm a pet."

"Jaen agreed it was too dangerous for you to make you a lone vampire, and also refused to become your maker on the grounds that you never earned the Silver Court's favor. Stubborn stickler." Kashire eyes his nails. "But now that Jaen is missing and can't complain, I need capable help, and there's yet one who doesn't have an apprentice."

"You?" I shake my head before he can say anything. "I want to join the Black Court!"

He glares down at me. "You of all people should know that doesn't matter."

I back into Gray Mist's steady flank. "That's where I belong."

"Anywhere could be where you belong, you dolt—other than a *stable*. You really think blood matters, when you're half-dead?"

"Vampires say blood doesn't matter"—which sounds rather ironic when I stop to think about it—"but Maudon says—"

"Maudon isn't here! Do you know who is?" He waves exaggeratedly at himself. "Where is your not-mother? *Not* here right now!" He goggles at me and then down at himself, as if seeing the obvious on my behalf.

"The Blue Court will never accept me," I insist stubbornly.

"You earned their mark of approval," Kashire fires right back.

"But I didn't earn Gold, Silver, or Black."

He scoffs. "Silvea didn't either. The Red Court still took her in . . . grudgingly."

"And look where that got her. I *need* a House—" I say almost desperately. I'm still craving that image of family that Maudon painted for me.

Maybe I am being a fool. The Black Court has utterly forsaken me. They made me a thrall, my worst nightmare.

Kashire must read something in my mind of what I'm thinking, because he says, "Houses are merely a recobbling of this idea of family that vampires purport to hate. Even *I* see that, and I love my House. But they're not my entire world when I have eternity at my disposal. Do you know what the Blue Court loves? Chaos." He holds out his arms, the gems on his nails winking. "And I am beautiful chaos. Why do you think I risk loving Jaen or Gavron, from different Houses? Why do you think I bother with liabilities like you and Marai, when you could hurt those I love?"

I open my mouth to protest the designation of *liability*, but he speaks over me. "*Because*, as you should know by now, family is what you carve out with your teeth." He grins, showing his fangs again.

I burst into delirious giggles, pushing off from Gray Mist to stand on my own shaky legs. "Kashire, you hate me."

"You know who hates one another?" He raises his eyebrows. "Family!"

As quickly as laughter has come, I'm suddenly exhausted. "So why are you here? To replace all my blood with your own?"

"Founders, no." Kashire drops his hands to his hips and sniffs in disgust. "I don't *actually* want you as an apprentice. You do like to assume things about me and carry on like a fool."

I gape at him. "Then what was all that about chaos and family and breaking the rules?"

"I still stand by much of that. But, me, your maker? Not a chance."

I want to tear out my hair. "Who, then?"

"Gavron." I freeze at the name. "I came to this conclusion on my own," he continues casually. "It's the simplest. He wants you as his apprentice, if I can ever get him to think straight. I know it. You want to join the Black Court. And so, you see, I'm not here to *make* you. You're already mostly there. I'm merely here to kill you."

"What?" Fear spikes within me. I glance to the window, the nearest exit. I can't help trying to escape, even if I would prefer death to life as a thrall. Gavron told me resist. To run.

But I know I'll never be fast enough.

"Your inability to drink from other sources of blood means his remains as undiluted within you as it needs to be. That, and he has particularly potent blood—you reek of it. You're like a walking wineskin filled with his essence. If I kill you now, *poof*"—Kashire snaps his fingers—"you'll be a Black Court vampire! You get what you want, and he gets what I want him to want. I forced him to take you on as a novice. Now as an apprentice. I told you, I love poetry."

My entire body tenses. "I'm enthralled to defend myself if—"

"Darling." Kashire laughs, teeth flashing. "How amusing that you still think you're a match for me. I feel like I owe you one, anyway."

I stumble away from him, fetching up against the stable wall. Splinters poke at my shoulders. "You do not! I stabbed you only because you stabbed me first! I even apologized for it! And then you threw me in the pit with wolves and bears and *rats*—"

He taps his chin. "Okay, maybe we are even."

But then he lashes out, faster than a striking snake.

My neck breaks. It makes a *crack* like a large stick snapping in two. Except the horrible sound comes from inside me and echoes down the length of my body, which goes utterly limp. I slide down the wall, slumping on my side.

"And now we're *not* even," he says, looking down at me with those cold blue eyes. "Now you owe *me* for this immeasurable gift, and I require your help." As the light fades from my vision, I hear his words, dancing away from my drifting consciousness. "Gavron was right. Death suits you. See you on the other side, love."

27

I open my eyes.

I'm lying on a white-cloaked table in Jaen's study. Flat on the table next to me is an enthralled human. I must be about to get carved up for demonstration purposes, along with him. But, unlike him, I'll probably be aware of everything that is happening to me. I'm cold, but I can feel so much, down to my fingernails and the tips of my toes.

I fly off the table, springing harder than I mean to. I hit the ceiling with bone-breaking force. Except, I don't break any bones. I simply bounce off in a shower of stone flakes and smash back into the table, shattering the wood beneath me.

Marai peers down at me as I blink up through the wreckage. "That's one way to wake up."

"Marai?" I croak. "What's happening?"

"Shh." She crouches down, putting a calming hand on my shoulder. "Take a moment. You've been out since last night. It took a while for you to finally go."

Go . . . where?

She's wearing wine-colored breeches and a loose white blouse bound by a brown leather corset. Clothes meant for action. My gaze darts all around, trying to sense danger. Everything is moving too quickly, until I realize it's simply my eyes flicking from one thing to the next while my brain struggles to follow. I feel the splinters of the table stabbing my back, the silk of my clothes against my cold skin.

Silk. I haven't worn that for a while. It feels better than a caress.

"It's Autumn Nox. What do you remember last?" Marai asks gently.

Her eyes are redder than they've ever looked to me before, even after she was made into a vampire. Redder than human blood.

The thought makes my stomach growl. And then I can smell him. The human thrall. Suddenly, it's all I can focus on.

I'm atop him in the blink of an eye. I even shadowstep. My teeth sink into his neck as if into a soft piece of fruit. Rich warmth fills my mouth. It's not as good as Gavron's blood, but it's damned close, starving as I am.

And then it hits me—I can drink human blood. I can shadowstep. Which means I'm not enthralled. Because I *can't* be, anymore, as a—

A firm hand hauls me away from my meal. I hiss in anger, spitting blood and thrashing. But someone grips me by the back of the neck like I'm a child throwing a tantrum.

"You realize," Kashire says behind me, even as I struggle against him, "for all your painting us as monsters, we don't *have* to kill? You can control your instinct, feed, and heal whatever human you 'borrowed' from? You can even entrance them to feel good and impel them to forget the experience if you so choose. Or you can kill, but only feed on the worst of the lot. You can read their minds to know, of course. I don't usually bother, but I thought you might." He sniffs down at the man as I look back and forth between Kashire and the bleeding neck. "This one wasn't particularly pleasant. He's actually a broker of thralls. Finds desperate people with debts and so forth, promises to pay them off, and then sells them into vampire servitude for a tidy profit. Some poor children he's simply kidnapped, and some of the debts are created by he himself. With your distaste for enthrallment, I chose him specially as your first, in case you felt like killing him. But it should be a *conscious* choice."

Ever the teacher. But it's also a kindness. I truly appreciate Kashire choosing someone who wouldn't necessarily be missed. Someone *I*, in particular, would hate. I lunge away from him as soon as he lets me go, and I drain the man dry.

I can't help it; I'm so hungry. He could have been a savior of orphans and it might not have stopped me. His blood is warm nectar in my mouth, and it feels like it's filling every part of me, not just my stomach.

When I pull away from the corpse, red blood coats my chin. I dash it away on a black silk sleeve. I'm wearing my old Black Court training garb. But now all I can see is Kashire.

"*You*," I snarl. "You *killed* me."

"You're welcome!" Kashire says. "And before you do something so foolish as challenge me and find out what I can *still* do to you, you might want to take a look at yourself." He gestures at a large mirror in the corner.

I move faster than I mean to, and nearly fetch up against the mirror before I catch myself on my toes. My movements in the silver glass are unnatural, jerky.

My eyes are black as pitch, not a streak of white left in them. My skin is paler than before, luminous and flawless, my hair thick and the color of sun-ripened wheat. But even before my eyes, my face flickers back and forth between this once-human one and the one I discovered in Masks. It comes as naturally as breathing—my hair silvering, lengthening on one side and shrinking to nothing on the other, my features sharpening and softening in turn. I feel my snow-leopard claws at my fingertips, ready to burst forth with less than a thought. The power I have now . . .

What's best, there's no faint glow in the blackness of my eyes. No enthrallment that can hold me any longer.

I feel a tickle in the back of my mind, like I've forgotten something without knowing what. But I don't have time to dwell on it.

"Welcome to your true undying seasons," Kashire says, oddly serious. His intonation reminds me of Revar's, and not in mockery.

Before I can respond, I'm hit by what feels like a battering ram of a hug. Marai squeezes me hard enough to crush a human rib cage.

"Fin," she gasps. "You're here, finally. I've missed you so much."

Here. As I return Marai's hug with equal force, I can't help but recall Maudon's words about the promised land: *I don't believe that promise is a place. It is a state of being . . . This is the promised land. Right here.*

Marai feels more like a sister than ever before. Which makes me wonder . . .

I catch the ruby-red gaze of someone else in the mirror. Someone I never expected to see. She was there at my birth, and yet, I didn't think she'd want to be here at my *rebirth.* She's watched me awaken as a newborn vampire with a total lack of expression. But I understand now. As a human, I would have seemed fragile and pitiable and *different*—a blind kitten born to a world it can't see or comprehend or withstand.

Before I can move, Claudia's hands are on my shoulders. She plants a kiss on my forehead like a declaration of war.

"Without being your maker, I didn't know if I would see in you what I hoped," she says, sounding breathless, "but I do see it."

I'm not sure what I see in her. It's not lesser, exactly. It's different. And yet it's *recognition*, all the same.

We're the same species now, after all.

"I thought you didn't want to get involved in all of this?" I ask, my throat tight.

A frown flickers across her face. "*You* involved me—rather, your becoming a Black Court vampire after failing to gain their mark of approval has."

"*Kashire* involved you," I say, spinning to glare at him. He glows like a brilliant flame in my new sight, but it's not enough to keep me from snapping, "You ensured more than just my help, I see? Claudia wasn't interested before."

He only grins at me.

"Maybe Maudon will try to intervene with the Black Court on your behalf," Claudia says. "But I don't trust him." She pauses. "Your own court will most likely try to kill you once they find out. I don't care what they're plotting for the Founders, but I would prevent your death at their hands if I could."

"How will the Black Court find out about me?" I ask, feeling a chill.

"*One* of them already knows," Kashire says, folding his arms and leaning back against the table holding the dead man, as casual as can be. "Gavron would have sensed you the moment you changed. He's your maker. The question is: Will he come to you first or confess the truth of your new status immediately to his House?"

"A fun puzzle for you, I'm sure." My eyes narrow farther. "Let me guess: You're hoping he comes to me first. You know how he feels about me. So you not only turned me into a more capable helper, one with allies, but also *bait*. And once you have Gavron, you can use him to try to figure out where Jaen is."

He shrugs. "Can you fault my plan?"

I pause. "It's not terrible, actually."

"I came up with it under pressure. We're out of time, after all." He nods at me. "You inspired it with your original scheme to enter the Black Court as a spy. This is the messier version."

Messier, indeed. Especially for me. And arguably Jaen. The thought of someone else snags at my whirring attention.

I stare at Kashire. "You don't care if Gavron gets hurt."

"And *you* do?" Kashire throws back his head and sighs. "I was worried about this."

"He's my maker! And he loves me."

"That shouldn't matter to you," Claudia says. "Have I taught you nothing?"

"And I might love him," I continue pointedly, "if I didn't hate him so much."

"So at least you're not a *complete* fool," Kashire says.

"I don't think he wants to be doing this," I insist. "He murdered all the others." I can finally say it. It's like releasing a heavy burden. "He's the one the Black Court is using to perform the sacrifices. But I don't think he wanted to. He *had* to."

I still feel like I'm forgetting something important.

"Because he's a duty-bound *arse*——" Kashire begins.

"It's more than that," I interrupt. "I can just feel it." I can still see the pain, the desperation, in his eyes, and hear the helplessness in his voice when he said, *I had to.*

Forgotten memory tickles at me again, but this time I catch a glimpse: Gavron's pale face in the gloom of the stable. His hand reaching up to cup my cheek. Holding me still while he raises his black-bleeding wrist to my lips.

He *did* come to see me. He even fed me, perhaps to ease my hunger, perhaps to reinforce the protection of his blood. He just enthralled me to forget, because he must have been doing it in secret. Not even Kashire knew.

I still can't see the bigger picture or remember more than that. Even if my new status as a vampire frees me from enthrallment, memories lost while human must not fully return.

But now I feel something else that might help fill in the gaps. Some deeper bond to Gavron. I can feel *him* at the edge of my mind.

"You can *feel* whatever you want," Kashire sneers. "Don't let it get in the way of saving Jaen."

"How are you so sure I'm going to be much help anyway?" I throw up my hands and nearly fling myself over. My body is so strong now; I'm still regaining my balance. "I don't know how the connection works with your maker once you turn. Can he still command me to obey him?"

"No," Claudia says. "Nothing so strong as that. Unless he forces his blood on you, you should be able to resist him."

Marai glances at Claudia with unmistakable fondness. "You *want* to listen, but you don't have to."

"So!" Kashire says, clapping his hands. "What you will do is draw Gavron out by waiting in a more secluded spot, seemingly alone for the taking——or for the kissing or the murdering, whatever he wants to do with you. Meanwhile, the rest of us will be waiting nearby to pounce."

"Kashire," I say, leveling a flat look at him. "He can shadowstep. He can mistwalk. All you'll be pouncing on are your own two feet. Or talons. Or paws. Whichever."

"Not after you give him this." He whips a vial out of his breast pocket and flips it in his hands. Through the flicker of glass, I spot a gleam of silver.

My eyes narrow. "What is it?"

"Something that Jaen gave me before he vanished. We were preparing for a moment we might have to subdue Gavron without killing him." He holds the vial up to my eye. "It's made with Silver Court blood, among other things. As you know, ingesting another vampire's blood leaves you under its power, which in *this* case has been alchemically fixed to make whoever drinks it fall asleep."

"So I just hand it to him in a goblet mixed with a little bloodwine as if he won't suspect a thing?" I ask dubiously.

"That's how some have managed it, but I share your skepticism that Gavron would be in such a trusting mindset. He knows we're onto him. That's why he enthralled you and has nigh disappeared. And if he's set on capturing or killing you, having it in your mouth in preparation for a kiss will be equally ineffective. Fortunately, since neither of those tactics would have worked for *me*, either, Jaen also left me this."

He slides what looks like a tiny silver dagger out of his other breast pocket. Except, when he flicks it with a blue-jeweled fingertip, it sounds hollow.

"You fit the vial into the hilt here," he says, demonstrating. "When you stab, the contents will be forced into the wound. So try not to miss. It should knock Gavron out long enough to get him to a place that can hold him. Reinforced chains will do. With this little brew, even after he wakes up, he won't be able to focus enough to shapeshift or shadowstep, let alone mist himself. Claudia already tested it out, while you were taking your little death nap."

She grimaces. "It was unpleasant."

I eye them all. "What then?"

"We'll get him to talk. If there's any love left in him for us, he'll tell us what's happening and where."

I snort. "So I'm both the bait *and* the trap. Did you save anything for yourself to do?"

Kashire purses his lips in thought. "Maybe I can carry Gavron after he's unconscious? No, you can shadowstep with him more effectively than I can carry him, so that's on you, too." I open my mouth, but he raises a finger, his voice sharper than steel. "What I will do is question him until he tells me where Jaen is, *whatever* that might entail. I know you don't have the stomach for that, my dear. I do."

I'm not afraid of Kashire anymore, exactly, but there's something in me that recognizes another predator. My already cold skin prickles in warning. "If he hasn't had a choice in any of this, I don't want you to hurt him."

"How has he not had a choice? Duty is a choice. Loyalty is a choice. *Killing* is a choice. Always."

I glance at the dead man on the table. *Caring* is also a choice now. But maybe love isn't. And I might love Gavron.

I gnaw on my lip, nearly breaking the skin. "Okay."

"*Okay*, you agree with me, or *okay*, you'll help me?" Kashire's smile hardens as he raises the vial. "Because I'm not beyond pouring half of this down *your* throat and leaving you lying about as unwilling bait."

"Okay, *I'll help you!*" I scowl at him. "Don't prove yourself to be more of an arse than he's being."

Kashire actually looks away. He's worried. No, he's *fraying* at the edges with worry over Jaen. He's truly in love with the Silver Court vampire.

Love might not be a choice for any of us.

I turn away for a moment, and then I feel a hand on my arm. I didn't hear her approach, not even with my new sense of hearing.

"Fin?" Marai says.

I spin on her so quickly that she starts in readiness. We're both creatures of such speed and violence now.

Violence, if you choose it, I think.

Fittingly, she passes me my fillet knife. She must have saved it after rescuing me from Yuhan. I buckle it onto one of my belts gratefully.

"It's no dread blade, but it's something," she says, "and I know it matters to you."

"Thank you. You don't have to be a part of this," I say in a rush. "I've dragged you into enough ridiculous schemes."

She cocks her head like a predatory bird, so much the falcon, the vampire, already. "I want to."

"Because she's going?" I nod at Claudia, who's wandering off into her own corner of the study as if trying not to listen. I lower my voice as much as possible. "You're not upset that she's now involved in this . . . because of me?"

"No!" Marai says, taking a step back. "Have you not noticed that *I've* been involved this whole time? I wanted Claudia to get involved so I could stay that way. Jaen aside, the Founders shouldn't be raised. It wouldn't be good for the human world if they were. I still care about that. Although I care about other things less now." Her red gaze flickers away and then back to me.

"I know you were sometimes jealous of me," I say, softer.

"Fin." She giggles, putting a hand to her mouth. "Your skull can be terribly thick for someone so scrawny. I was jealous of Gavron." I blink at her. When I still don't respond, she says, exasperated, "I liked *you*."

"Oh." My eyes widen. "Oh! I thought you wanted Jaen!"

"I told you, I'm fully capable of lusting after more than one person." She smirks. "But I was so shy then as a human. I know I seemed loud, but when it came to things like that, I wasn't used to being free with my feelings. I don't care anymore. So"—she takes a deep breath—"I *think* I feel that way for Jaen, more and more every passing night. But you, I admired from the beginning. Silvea almost revealed what I felt for you in Mind Reading. That's why I hit her. And that's why I went along with your absurdly dangerous plan to hunt Kashire, even though I should have been too smart to go near it. I was like one of those besotted fools in a romance novel." She shrugs. "I'm not sure I feel that way for you anymore. But knowing what I know, I still think we should stop the ritual to raise the Founders. And not only because I want to save Jaen."

I stare at Marai, seeing her in an entirely new light. "I was so convinced I was unlovable after Silvea turned against me," I say, "—*before* she turned against me, even—that it didn't occur to me, with you. I was even convinced Gavron only felt this way about me because he had to—"

"Which way does he feel," Marai interrupts, "in betraying you and turning you into a thrall?" She shows a startling length of teeth. "Fin, that bastard is not good for you."

I sigh. "You're convinced that he's doing all of this because he wants to?"

"His actions speak loud enough!" she hisses—*loud enough* for me to raise my finger to my lips. We both look at each other, and we start chuckling silently.

Even as vampires, we're the same in some ways.

"Fin, whatever happens, you're my friend," she adds, seizing my wrist. She smiles, glancing at Claudia. "You're as good as family."

<hr/>

I'm back in our clearing, but it's as if I've never been here before. I'm seeing it with new eyes. The leaves fall in a rain of frail bones from the skeletal trees, whispering and rattling their demise, trunks tall and crooked against the night sky, their roots holding within them what was lost. Light snow covers the ground in a blanket of white embroidered with silver. The stars are out tonight, and for a moment all I can do is stare at the glittering expanse overhead, so intricate in its light and deep in its darkness that it's like nothing I've ever seen, even if I've seen it a thousand times.

There's a risk, coming here to this secluded spot. But Maudon won't know I've been changed into a vampire unless Gavron has told him, and if Gavron has, then . . . I don't stand much of a chance, anyway.

I never thought I would be seeing the world as a vampire . . . and that it would look so beautiful. I thought it would look monstrous, reflected in my own eyes. But it's stunning. I don't make a noise, and yet my body is singing. I'm not sure how long I stand there, my arms spread at my sides, feet planted in the snow. Now that the nights have grown longer, I could stand here for hours.

Except tonight is Autumn Nox. A sense of urgency rises in me, upsetting my new sense of timelessness. It reminds me of those moments past, which already feel strangely distant even though they occurred right here not that long ago. I remember chasing Gavron through thawing spring snow and mud, feeling desperate . . . and then waiting for him for so long in the warm summer air, feeling equally desperate, with only crickets chirruping around me. I remember that one night, turning to find someone behind me—Maudon, offering me a home.

I don't need to turn now to become aware of a new arrival.

This time, it's not Maudon.

I would know him anywhere, at any distance. He's my home now, his blood mine, even if he's been many different things to me.

My enemy.

My teacher.

My heart's desire.

My betrayer.

Now more than ever, my maker.

I can smell him on the light breeze that rustles the falling leaves. He smells of night and darkness and mist and stone . . . and blood, both his and whatever human's he most recently fed upon. I inhale a long breath through my nose, savoring his scent.

I turn to face him.

Gavron stands at the edge of the clearing, shrouded in shadow. Yet I can see him clear as the night sky. Impossibly, he's more beautiful than I ever remembered him. He's dressed in black silk and leather, his usual belts and daggers strapped in place. His hair is pulled tightly back, exposing the shaved sides of his head. One strand escapes to fall across his sharp cheekbones like a blade of shadow. The mere sight of him cuts me, but I don't let it show.

"Gavron," I say calmly.

"Fin," he says. "I need you to come with me."

"To the Black Court?" I ask, unconcerned. I start toward him. My steps are smooth and measured, utterly silent over the crust of snow. As if he were prey I was sneaking up on, even though he's looking right at me.

He nods. "They need to know what you are now."

"And what am I? To them? To you?"

"You're—" His throat bobs. "You're mine. My apprentice. Or you would be, if I didn't have to end this as quickly as possible."

"Do you have to?" All the while I'm stalking closer to him.

"I do." There's that pain in his voice that was only barely audible before. Now I can hear it as if he's screaming.

I step right up to him, tipping my head back to study his face. "Why did you do it? Why did you kill them—Lief, Silvea, Pavella— and leave their bodies for others to find? Why make me a thrall when all I wanted was to be with you, like I am now?"

I reach out a finger to brush the back of his hand, like he once brushed my leg during the opera. A question, waiting for an answer.

He freezes. He doesn't seem able to respond.

"You told me I filled a void inside you," I murmur softly, "a need for something *yours*—someone to care for. Because *you're* not your own, are you? You haven't been for a long time. You've only been made to hurt or kill on command, when you didn't want to. Right?"

His voice is choked. "I had to," he repeats.

I can see it in his eyes. Recognize it now with my sharper sight, like I couldn't before. Not what a vampire sees in another vampire, which I see, too, now.

It's what a thrall would see in another thrall.

I don't know how it's possible. It shouldn't be. That's all I've ever been told: Vampires can't be enthralled. But that's what he is. Now I can read it in the tearing force behind his apology note. Hear it in his longing words. Feel it in the shiver under my skin, in the ache in my bones. I can sense him, imprisoned.

Kashire will torture him needlessly, and Gavron won't be able to tell him anything even if he wants to. It doesn't matter that Gavron forced me to undergo my own kind of torture, kept me from telling the truth; I'm not going to do the same to him. Because he had— *has*—no choice.

I do.

He's taut, quivering. With me so close he must want to seize me. Or shove me away. The two forces must be at war within him.

"You came to see me in the stables, in secret. I remember glimpses. I know you're trying to help me, even as you hurt me. And I know why you can't help yourself."

I lean in, as if I'm going to stab him or kiss him. Gavron braces himself, ready for it. Ready to fight me.

"You're enthralled," I whisper.

His black eyes widen in shock.

Standing on my tiptoes, I take his moment of surprise to kiss him. His lips part with a gasp, and my tongue slides into his mouth. I slip him a few drops of my blood. I bit my tongue only a split second before, so he wouldn't have time to smell it.

His eyes pop even wider at the taste—just a taste, but it's enough to make him groan. I'm sure he's under orders not to drink my blood to not fall under its influence, so I don't kiss him for long. But it's still long enough, I hope, for him to listen to me.

"Run," I whisper, pulling away just enough. "The others are here to capture you. Shadowstep away. Go to Jaen."

His eyes dart frantically, settling on me one last time. There's wariness, anger, and somehow *relief* there. And then he vanishes. But not faster than my hand flashes out—not with Jaen's delicate dagger. Rather, I part the closing gap behind Gavron just enough to reach for one of the two dread blades from his belt. I'm fast enough to snatch it. And to attach something else.

A thread, of sorts. And then Gavron is gone.

Kashire's enraged cry cuts across the clearing: "*Fin!*"

Then he's upon me, his hand clamped around my throat. He raises me off the ground.

"I am going to tear your deceitful corpse limb from limb," he snarls, his fangs elongating in his mouth. I feel the claws of his night terror start to pierce my skin. "You never meant to trap him, did you?"

I don't bother squirming. I don't even try to shadowstep—yet.

"I—can—explain," I wheeze.

"Kashire," Claudia says warningly, Marai standing ready at her side. "Let her go."

Kashire snarls in disgust and drops me, stalking away. "Well?" he asks, his voice deceptively soft. "Explain."

I rub my neck reflexively—the wounds have already healed. I still have to clear my throat to speak; Kashire half crushed my windpipe. I gesture at where Gavron vanished.

"We can follow him," I say, ignoring Kashire's dubious eyebrow. "And he'll take us straight to Jaen."

28

Maudon showed me how," I say. Kashire, Claudia, and Marai stand in a semicircle in the clearing, all looking at me with some degree of suspicion. And then I explain.

I learned it from Maudon as we were shadowfighting for endless hours in the summer night—what I already suspected could be done. Gavron once admitted that mistwalking was nearly impossible to track . . . meaning that shadowstepping *could* be tracked. With a fine blade of shadow, you can peel away a thread from the edges cut in space, attach it to whoever passes through, and let it unravel, leaving a trail behind. You can use it in the heat of a battle, or over longer distances. In that case, the thread is faint, stretched across impossible gaps. Only one who is trained to follow can do so.

You can even shadowstep along it, as if tracing a rope through a dark tunnel, and appear exactly where the person who first traveled that path did, even if you've never seen the destination before. But only if you're fast and skilled enough.

I am. Claudia can do it, too.

"So you won't have to torture Gavron—which I *know* you won't enjoy," I spit at Kashire. "And we can get to Jaen all the sooner. Time is short, like you said."

Kashire gives me a grudging nod.

Claudia frowns. "I don't see how jumping into what is likely a nest of Black Court vampires intent upon a ritualistic sacrifice is going to keep you safe *from* the Black Court."

"If we can save Jaen and Gavron—"

"Excuse me, why does Gavron need saving?" Kashire interrupts.

I groan. "Just trust me."

"*No.*"

"I've trusted you!"

"And I kicked you into a pit of wolves and snapped your neck."

I grimace, already knowing how this is going to go. "Gavron is enthralled."

All three give me blank stares.

"Fin," Marai says slowly, as if I've hit my head. "Vampires can't be enthralled."

I fold my arms stubbornly. "I know that's what they say. But I can see it in him. I can *feel* it in him, and you should believe that I can recognize it."

Kashire does the worst thing he could ever do: He gives me a pitying look. "I think you might still be affected by your experiences as a human as well as your feelings for Gavron. I know what the latter can do to you, trust me. But you're seeing what isn't there." His expression hardens. "Don't botch Jaen's rescue by focusing on the person who doesn't need rescuing."

"Maybe we *should* focus on him if he's our enemy, just in a different way," Marai says, and Claudia nods.

"Enemy or not," I say, "if we get Gavron out of there, we can convince him to clear my name and give me the Black Court's mark of approval."

"Didn't you just have him in your grasp?" Claudia says, back to disapproving.

Despite being a murderous vampire, she can be so mothering at times.

"But not Jaen. And I know you don't care for Jaen, but Kashire, Marai, and I do, and this gets us to both the quickest. I can still stab Gavron with this, wherever we end up." I flip the thin silver dagger in my hand.

"It still could be a trap," Claudia insists.

"Whoever is behind this—likely Maudon—won't have many others behind them," Kashire says. "Our Blue Court spies would have heard about it. Even so, you can still back out, Claudia. Go back to indifference."

She scowls at him in response.

I don't know if he actually thinks my plan is solid, or if he's just anxious to get to Jaen. Whichever the case, I'm grateful for his support. "Let's go then, before my thread fades. Claudia, you know how to shadowstep and follow it."

She nods. "I'll take Marai."

Kashire and I look at each other.

He grimaces. "At Summer Sol, you said you weren't strong enough to take me along with you."

"I am now," I say, and then add for purely his benefit, "I think."

"I'm putting my life in *your* hands?"

"Like you said, you're the one who's killed *me*."

"Is that reassurance or a threat?"

"Another mystery to solve." I march over to him and wrap one arm around his waist, feeling for the thread left in Gavron's wake with my other hand. I hold it out for Claudia until I can feel her sense it, too.

"Well, hello, dear," Kashire says, batting his eyelashes down at me and nudging me with his hip.

"Kashire, please don't act strange."

"I am strange. But, trust me, you're not my type."

"You just mocked me for trusting you," I say, before I realize what I'm implying. And then it's very strange, indeed. "Shut up," I say, and then I seize the thread I attached to Gavron and I shadowstep.

———— ·⚬· ————

"Oh," Kashire says cheerfully. "I guess Fin was wrong."

Not *him*, of course, only me.

When Claudia and Marai appear next to us, Marai gasps. The bare stretch of floor we arrive on is surrounded by ten snarling were-wolves.

We're in a cavernous, black stone room, with stairs—benches—dropping down to a wide, sunken dais and a disturbing contraption atop it. It looks like the stocks you'd find in a village, except it's made of iron, and black spikes encircle the collar with an ominous lever and crank attached. Maudon and Gavron are here, too, along with the enthralled werewolves, and so is Jaen. She's kneeling at the base of the contraption. Standing next to her is a man with long blond hair wearing a black velvet cape—the man I saw in the Black Court's most prestigious box at Spring Nox's Salon. Otherwise I've seen him not at all.

Maudon might be the Black Court's commander, but he reports to *him*. I feel it in my veins. This man is *old*. Terribly old, now that I'm able to see him closer and with vampire eyes.

"Run," Claudia gasps.

"Stay," the man says. "We hoped you might come. Don't move, any of you."

And we don't. We can't. Because he told us not to, and I feel his will seize me in an unshakable grip. It's far stronger than Jaen's impel-ling or Gavron's enthrallment. Not even Kashire twitches a muscle.

No wonder Gavron had a hard time resisting his own enthrall-ment, unable to even signal that he was forced to act as a puppet. The control is absolute. Perhaps the others will believe me about him now, though that's the least of my worries.

My eyes dart around. I've never seen this room before. It's like the torture-chamber version of the pit. Based on the color and dampness of the stone, I would bet we're somewhere deep inside the Black Gates. Maybe their dungeon.

The contraption is obviously for bleeding out vampires. Diffi-cult to do, Kashire said, without constantly reopening the wound, because the vampire keeps healing, but Jaen said the Black Court had the tool. These spikes, and the crank, obviously keep the pressure on, so to speak. This must be where Gavron killed the others—aside from Lief, perhaps—before leaving the bodies elsewhere, for some reason. Perhaps so it would be harder to trace them to the Black Gates? Perhaps as a grim message meant for each court?

We have to get out of here. I want to scream, but I can't.

Kashire's blue eyes flicker to me, somehow reassuring.

The only truly reassuring thing is that while we have more company than expected, they're mostly enthralled werewolves. As for our vampire opponents, it's still only Maudon and Gavron and admittedly the most ancient vampire I've ever seen—one who can enthrall other vampires. But I saw far more members of the Black Court at Spring Nox, and the Black Gates are the very seat of the Nameless House. This place is full of Black Court vampires even if they're not often seen.

They aren't *all* behind this plot to raise the Founders. Far from it. At least I hope.

"I suppose you can talk while we wait." The ancient vampire nods at us, and suddenly my jaw, lips, and tongue are free to move.

"Gavron!" I shout. "Stop this!"

"I can't," Gavron says, his voice anguished.

The ancient, velvet-cloaked vampire raises a hand. "No more from Gavron. He's had his time," he says. Gavron's mouth clamps shut, but he still looks at me in desperation. "My name is Beltharius."

"I know," Kashire and Claudia say simultaneously.

"I was rather speaking to the newborns. While the rest of you've no doubt heard my name in passing at frivolous balls and the like, I bet only Fin among you—and Gavron, of course—can sense how old I am, because they share my blood. I made Gavron, and he in turn made Fin."

Gavron can't say anything, so I say to the others, "He's very old."

"How precise," Jaen says from where she's kneeling. At least she's not so impelled or enthralled that she can't be sarcastic.

"He makes Revar feel young," I add.

"Oh," Jaen says with mild surprise. "That is unfortunate."

"Jaen!" Marai cries. "Are you all right?"

"Aside from having been impelled not to move by the strongest vampire I've ever encountered, yes." She clears her throat. "I imagine I'm about to be sacrificed, so I'll take this moment to tell you—"

"*No*," Kashire snarls. "We are not declaring affection or bidding our farewells." His shoulder jerks the slightest bit. He's trying to fight his invisible bonds but having as much luck as I am.

Beltharius chuckles. "No one is going anywhere." I can't tell if the words are comforting or threatening. "But, please," he continues, "do declare your affections. Gavron has told me what he feels for Fin and such things warm this old heart to hear."

No one says anything, because we're all staring at him in incredulity. He's holding us in what looks like a torture chamber, and he wants us to do *what*?

"Or refrain, suit yourselves." He flicks his head at the werewolves. "Ionante, Nezante, guard Jaen. I think the time has almost come. Maudon, it's your chance to have a word, if you'd like. Our guest should be here shortly."

Two of the werewolves shift, blur—and become two tall vampire women with pale skin and tight braids of red hair, adjusting the belts on their Black Court garb. They look similar enough to be twins.

I gape. Even Kashire's jaw drops.

Claudia glances around at the other beasts. "These aren't enthralled werewolves. They're all Black Court vampires. Another one of their secrets, I suppose."

"A skill we only learn as mature vampires," Maudon says, stalking closer to Claudia. "Just as we wield dread blades that can kill vampires, so too can we shift into the creatures with the same ability. Someday, you could learn, too, Claudia. If you join us." He nods at me. "You, as well, Fin. You have my welcome. Both to the Black Gates and the Black Court."

That means the other eight werewolves around us are all mature vampires.

We're dead.

"Shouldn't that be an advanced Blue Court skill?" Marai asks, drawing Maudon's attention from me. "Shapeshifting is their realm."

I shoot her a silencing glance, but she's not looking at me. I dragged her into this mess, and I need to get her out of it. And Claudia and Jaen and Gavron. But the numbers are well stacked against us. Never mind that we still can't move.

"The Black Court belongs to no realm," Maudon says. "And is yet part of all. Nowhere and everywhere."

Claudia responds to her apprentice, not him. "Shadowfighting could have severed roots in the Red Court, no?" Her lips twist. "Who knows what else they're hiding."

"The Nameless House," Jaen muses. "No one knows how they lost their name."

"This is why the Blue Court likes to *remember*," Kashire says grimly. "We don't only like to celebrate who and what we are. We remember the terrible things, too. If you erase a legacy, especially one of blood and fire, you, yourself, forget. You forget the knife in the darkness. That's why it's good to remember—so you can catch the blade that comes for you. Perhaps the other courts will take the lesson from us next time, that forgetting the past is foolish."

"You expect there to be any courts but one after this," Beltharius says.

My blood grows colder. "Why would raising the Founders leave only one court?"

He merely smiles.

"What are you doing?" I whisper.

"Why, enjoying this display of affection. Of family." He waves between Maudon, Claudia, and me. His black eyes grow distant. "In the end, they're all that matter."

Claudia sneers in disgust.

Coming from the oldest vampire I've ever encountered, his words sound distinctly *un*vampiric. But Maudon is watching him avidly, his eyes flashing to Claudia.

Maudon did tell me that in the Black Court, the idea of family is still a lauded one. Maybe, for them, it's important above all else. Maybe there's a reason that lies deep in a forgotten past.

"Family." Claudia smiles humorlessly at Maudon. "*You* were the werewolf that attacked Fin in the woods."

"Ah," Beltharius says, "that would be my fault. He was acting on my orders to clear up Gavron's little . . . *preoccupation*. Gavron was never supposed to take on a novice, you see. But after that—after *you* fought off Maudon, my dear Claudia—Maudon insisted Fin was important to him, as well."

"Because that's when you knew what she was to me," Claudia says to Maudon. "Not after Winter Sol, like I suspected." Her red gaze cuts to Beltharius. "Why did Gavron almost kill Fin at Winter Sol, then, if you were respecting your loyal commander's wishes to preserve her life?"

"A simple accident," Beltharius says regretfully. He sounds so oddly *sincere*. Grandfatherly. "She interrupted Gavron's task, and he had orders to eliminate anyone who did so. He needed to send the message that none of the Houses were safe, that a reckoning was coming. That's why I had him leave the bodies exposed rather than hidden."

"But why are you forcing Gavron to do all this?" I ask desperately.

"Many reasons. His lineage, most importantly. And his other connections turned out to be more convenient than anticipated. No one truly suspected him of killing his dear friend's novice, after all, or his own novice's childhood companion, or his fellow instructor here at Courtsheart. He's also one of the best assassins the Black Court has ever turned out, despite his young age. Especially when I'm in control of him."

"Yes, yes, we all know how *fabulous* Gavron is," Kashire says, rolling his eyes. "Though it does tarnish his dutiful-to-a-fault image a bit to discover he's been enthralled. Wait, Gav, is *that* why you broke my heart—you had no choice but to? Never mind, don't answer." He grins, knowing full well Gavron can't. Kashire turns his gaze on Maudon and says coyly, "But *you're* not enthralled. What do you get out of this?"

"I don't need anything. I'm devoted to my House." Maudon nods at Beltharius. "And yet our Founder is generous."

Jaen looks sharply at Beltharius at that, as do Kashire and Claudia. "Founder?" Marai gasps.

Maudon ignores their reactions. "He's granted me the right to a family." His dark eyes find mine. "I was meant to be your maker, Fin, and Gavron merely the lure to the Black Court. At your Becoming, he was only supposed to deny you his approval and briefly enthrall you, so he could learn what you knew of our plans. Instead, he gave you too much of his blood for me to drink from you and turn you myself. He accused you of the murders to keep you as a thrall. Clever fool. He wanted this, in the end. To be your maker, to ward other vampires off you. I would have come for you earlier, brought you *here* to turn you, but it wasn't permitted."

"It would have disturbed the boy too much," Beltharius grouses mildly. "He needs to be calm and unresistant until the ritual is complete. Fin has been enough of a distraction already, worse whenever I've tried to remove her. So I let him keep her for a time, figuring indulging him was the better course. It makes no difference in the end. Besides, their secret trysts in the stables were quite touching."

For him, maybe. I wasn't allowed to remember. Instead, I suffered as an unwitting thrall for months—like a strange pet for *Gavron*. But perhaps it kept me safe from Maudon.

"Quite unfortunate, as well," Maudon says as if agreeing with me, glancing at Beltharius with the barest hint of frustration, "since it gave someone the chance to kill Fin."

Kashire winks at me, though Maudon doesn't see before turning back to me.

"I hoped if I became your maker you could convince your mother to join us. Now I'll have to resort to other methods," Maudon continues.

So Gavron was the lure for me, and I was supposed to be the lure for *her*.

"She's not exactly my mother anymore," I say.

"And I didn't kill one husband just to gain another," Claudia snarls. "Leave Fin to me. Promise me your court will grant her their approval. And in return, I promise that Fin, Marai, and I will leave here without trouble. You can even impel us not to speak of your plans."

"*What?*" Marai demands, the same time I say, "We will not!"

Claudia hisses at us both to be silent. "This is not my fight, and it shouldn't be yours, either." She turns back to Maudon, gritting her formidable teeth. "*Please.*"

"This doesn't have to be a fight," Maudon says. He holds out his hand. "Not if you join me. We can still be a family."

"How romantic, to offer such a thing here of all places." She scoffs, glancing at me. "This is where the Black Court oversees the painful process of switching courts, and those who undergo it aren't always willing. It's difficult to argue with *that*—a bloodletter." She nods at the contraption and says to Maudon, "I suppose you want to stick my neck in there, so you can turn me into another Black Court devotee. Yours, in particular. What you've always wanted."

"You don't have to see it that way."

By which he means *yes*, of course.

"I change my mind," Claudia says, her snarl turning into a genuine smile, her red eyes gleaming. "This *is* my fight."

"Oh dear." Beltharius sighs. "I hoped you would all get along better than this."

"If you wanted genuine displays of affection, might I advise against the mental bonds next time?" Jaen says dryly. "Can we get on with bleeding *me* out before anyone else?"

"*No!*" Kashire and Marai cry.

"All of you misunderstand," Beltharius says, holding out his black-gloved palms as if in peace. "I don't want to kill Jaen."

Jaen smiles a cold little smile, her silver eyes colder. "Then why am I here, if not for an untimely death?"

"You didn't tell anyone about your suspicions regarding the Founders?" Beltharius clasps his hands behind his back. "You wouldn't want to let the other courts know of such a ritual because of what they might do. Only you know, and the rest of you here, of course. And Revar. They'll know." He smiles wistfully. "What *strength* they have to offer me!"

"Revar is a part of this?" Kashire growls.

Jaen has frozen.

"Not in the way you think," Beltharius replies, "though I did send them a special message about our gathering here. They should be arriving any moment now. And, like you, Revar no doubt hasn't trusted anyone else with any knowledge of our actions. Which means no one else is coming to help you." He raises a hand. "Don't worry. I don't want to kill *any* of you here, not even for what you know. Everyone will soon realize our long-held secrets. Consider yourselves blessed to be the first."

Jaen's silver eyes are wide. "You want Revar. I thought because you took me, and because I'm older than Pavella was——"

"You're still *so* young, dear Jaen. Still a young blood, if barely. I would hate to see you squander your potential. No, for my purposes, I needed someone much older."

"You're *using* me to get to Revar," Jaen snarls, rage twisting her features like I've never seen.

"They are your maker. They'll not be able to resist coming to your aid. Ah, and I do believe our guest has arrived."

"*Revar!*" Jaen screams. "Don't!"

Suddenly, Revar is in our midst. They can shadowstep. Of course they would have studied it—they've spent their endless life studying *everything*. Their long white hair and silver robes hang utterly still about them as they take in the scene.

"'Don't'? I don't see why not," Revar says, as calm as ever. "I've come for Jaen."

The Silver Court vampire is surrounded, but they don't look terribly concerned when they raise a pale finger and *point* to one of the werewolves.

The werewolf comes apart.

Fur and skin peel away first, muscles fan out like wings, entrails splay on the ground. All in the blink of an eye. And the deconstruction continues, everything splitting into finer and finer segments until the werewolf is a mass of pink, black, and white threads branching through the air as if strung on a loom. And then it collapses into a stringy pile with a wet *splat*.

All I can do is stare, as do the others.

Then the werewolves snarl and lunge.

Revar walks forward, flicking out their finger, stopping every single beast in its tracks by blowing it into fleshy ribbons and slivers of bone.

"Stop," Beltharius says.

Revar pauses in midstep—they're barefoot—shudders, and then carries on, speaking as they do. "You're aware of how those in the

Black Court can piece themselves apart and then reassemble their bodies in order to move about unseen? Dematerializing and rematerializing? Well, the very oldest in the Silver Court can take *other* things apart to understand how they work. Including vampires."

As Revar passes by, the werewolves continue to unravel in place.

"Seize Jaen," Beltharius commands.

The redheaded, twinlike vampires reach for her, but Revar flicks a hand at them. They *both* blast apart simultaneously, splatting into heaps of gooey flesh and black blood on the floor.

Maudon lunges for Jaen—but he stops dead, black eyes wide. And then he collapses, a piece at a time. Practically dribbling, like a melting candle. It's not quite as explosive as the others, but just as effective. Claudia and I both gasp.

But he's not down for long. The bits of Maudon quiver, and then he's once again upright. He cracks his neck as if realigning it.

I suppose it makes sense that a Black Court vampire who can *dematerialize* and *rematerialize* would know how to reassemble himself.

It takes the other two twinlike vampires longer to literally pull themselves together, but they do, bits slithering wetly across the stone to join the others.

None of the other werewolves manage. They must not have been as strong or as skillful as these three. I've never seen anyone shadowstep or mistwalk while in animal form—maybe one can't hold on to oneself quite as well, like that. Maybe the animal mind sets one *too* free.

Note to self, I think.

Revar arrives at the foot of the dais. "Release Jaen."

Beltharius is breathing hard. His body shivers like Revar's did—almost as if Revar is trying to use their power on *him*. But he doesn't collapse into pieces.

"Look at me," Beltharius growls through his teeth.

Revar has been looking at Jaen. But, at the command, those silver eyes begin to shift toward the ancient vampire.

"Don't do it, Revar," Jaen says. "You're the one he wants—leave me!"
But Revar can't seem to resist.

"You're stronger than I ever expected," Beltharius pants. "Good. Your blood will be especially potent."

"Ah," Revar breathes out a sigh as they finally meet his eyes. "I suspected as much. We've traced the roots of most of your carefully guarded skills to the other Houses. Your werewolf form to the House of Winter Night, your shadowfighting to the House of Spring Dawn, and both your dematerializing and your ritualistically sustained states of hibernation to my own House of Autumn Twilight, since we specialize in both deconstructing *and* preserving."

Revar starts up the steps to the dais. When they reach the top, I expect them to point at Beltharius and rip him to shreds. Instead, they turn and walk slowly over to the bloodletter.

When they kneel before it, Jaen cries out in dismay.

I can only stare in horror. Beltharius's control can reach even Revar. We're most assuredly dead.

"We didn't yet know which of your court's skills linked you to the House of Summer Day," Revar carries on in an academic tone, even as they carefully insert their head into the spiked ring, their long white hair swinging forward. The inner part of the contraption beneath their neck sinks into a sort of funnel that empties into a large silver pitcher.

Revar looks levelly up at Beltharius. "You can enthrall vampires."

Beltharius nods in concession. "Only myself and one other of my House can."

"Will you do the honors?" Revar glances at the crank. "It would be so unseemly for you to make me do it myself."

"I would never want that," Beltharius says. He steps over to the lever and cranks it without further hesitation. "The honor is indeed mine."

Jaen screams as the spikes pierce Revar's neck. I can't watch, so

I focus on Kashire, who's closest to me. He doesn't look away from Revar, perhaps out of respect, but his eyes are as cold as the depths of winter.

Perhaps he wants to *remember*.

"You have it backward, though," the Black Court vampire says as silver blood begins to flow and fill the jug. "The other Houses' roots lie in *our* soil, that of the Nameless House. Their skills come from us. Parceled out in lesser form to grow into these newer offshoots."

"I see. Just as black is all colors in one," Revar rasps, their voice broken but somehow unperturbed. Their tone is intrigued, if anything, as if some piece of a puzzle just clicked. "Of course. I can guess the other among you with the ability to enthrall vampires now."

Who? I wonder. But Beltharius doesn't give us the answer. He only says, "Then you know why I've kept my abilities a secret for longer than you've been walking this earth."

"Must have been challenging, not to openly indulge in such power until now." Revar's voice is getting fainter. I risk a glance. The skin of their pale hands is sinking in on itself, tendons standing out.

Jaen is sobbing. I wasn't sure vampires could cry. Her tears shine silvery on her face.

"It will be worth it," Beltharius says. "I had to wait for the right moment. The right portents. The right vessel."

I think he must mean Revar until they say, "Not yourself? Ah, but of course." They manage to twitch their chin at Gavron, who's staring fixedly ahead at nothing. "Gavron is the vessel. Why sacrifice yourself, after all, when you have another who can do it for you?"

"What?" I cry. "A vessel for *what*?"

No one answers me.

Jaen stares at Revar, almost pleading. "It should be me in your place."

"Nonsense," Revar gasps. "It's not very Silver Court of me to say, but let the old give way for the new." Fading eyes flicker to Beltharius. "And preferably not for something even older."

And then Revar's head falls slack. The room grows deathly silent.

Beltharius waits for the last drops of silver blood to drip into the pitcher. Revar's body resembles a long-desiccated corpse. "Farewell, my dear friend," he says, laying a hand on that white hair, eliciting a snarl from Jaen. "Since I know how long it will take you to truly go, let me ease your passing. Regretfully——"

He twists off Revar's head. Before the white-haired bundle can finish bouncing along the dark stone floor, both it and the sagging body turn to pale dust at a flick of Beltharius's fingers.

I can hardly believe my eyes. From the beginning, Revar struck me as an immortal among immortals. Wise. Unchanging. Invincible. And somehow still curious enough to leave their books and experiments behind to come find a human like me to bring into their world.

And now they're gone. If Beltharius's command weren't still holding me up, I would fall to my knees with the weight of it.

Jaen doesn't scream or cry. It's as if her tears had never been. She stares at Beltharius with the brightest hatred I've ever seen.

He holds out a placating hand to her. "Please understand, I didn't want to harm any of our kind. I want to make us *better*. I've only sacrificed those who wouldn't be missed, or were absolutely necessary sacrifices. The boy, Lief, was hardly a loss. Silvea was a mistake to begin with." He glances at Maudon without specifying *whose*. "And Pavella was actually the least useful for her own House's purposes. The Gold Court is all about diplomacy, and yet she had a rather repellent disposition, did she not?"

"And Revar?" Jaen asks, her voice cold. "They won't be missed? One of the greatest scholars and keenest minds of all time?"

Beltharius actually sounds regretful. "This is where necessity enters into it. There aren't many older Silver Court vampires in residence. They prefer their own libraries and institutions once they've read every book in Courtsheart. The truly old ones don't even bother to come to their own Symposium. Despite their years, Revar was dedicated to the training of novices and apprentices . . . and of course their own pupils. Which not only left Revar *here* where I needed them, but gave them a weakness. Namely, you." He raises a finger. "And we'll spare you, if you can be faithful to your species. You can live to fill the space your maker has left behind, serve your kind in the same way Revar did."

Jaen laughs, and it has a frightening edge. "Just because our motto isn't more garish like *Revel and Remember* doesn't mean it's *Forgive and Forget*. In fact, I believe anecdotal evidence has shown the philosophy of *Protect and Preserve* to lead to powerful manifestations of reprisal."

Even Beltharius blinks.

"I'm going to fucking *kill* you," Jaen clarifies. "And I won't rest until I do."

"Ah, I see," says Beltharius. "Though you don't look to be in much of a position to deliver on your threat." He scans the group. "What about the rest of you?"

"I'll be satisfied with Maudon's death," Claudia says.

"I won't," Marai spits. "I'll be satisfied if the Founders stay where they are."

"Likewise," I say, my eyes darting to the still-frozen shadow at Beltharius's side. Gavron.

And I'm going to save you, I say silently, but as loud as I can in my head, as if I can reach him.

"I'm just here because it's where the party is," Kashire says, but he's looking at Beltharius with the same cold, bright hatred as Jaen.

"Alas, then." Beltharius sighs. "I may not see your precious faces again if you insist on such youthful intransigence. I assume you know what to do, Maudon. I must conserve my strength, so they'll be free to challenge you in a moment. Subdue whom you wish, if you can, but otherwise clean up this mess of yours." He glances meaningfully at me and Claudia, and then he turns to the two vampire twins. "Stay with him. Come, Gavron."

And then he dissipates into mist, taking the silver pitcher of blood with him. With my new eyes, I can still pick out the bits of silver. Perhaps Revar's essence. The sparkling mist vanishes into a deep groove in the floor—a crevice.

I trace the line of it and realize it's depicting some sort of shape on the dais, spiraling out from the hideous contraption of the bloodletter.

Gavron gives me one long, excruciating look and then mistwalks after him. I can see more of Gavron than I did Beltharius—perhaps I can feel him, as my maker—as he sinks into the same crevice.

Going below. I can almost follow the path.

Maudon's old words flicker back to me. *The very roots of the Black Court are buried deep in this soil, too . . . Courtsheart was built on the bones of the oldest Black Court fortress . . . a tomb.*

The Founders' tomb is under the Black Gates. We aren't only positioned at the entrance to Courtsheart, but to something else. A buried past.

And one must be able to mistwalk to get in. A skill only taught after joining the Black Court.

I've felt myself at that precipice before, of letting myself go so completely that I might drift forever and ever, off into oblivion or eternity. But I've never made the full leap.

Maudon regards all of us as our fingers start to twitch. As if we're stirring from a slumber.

Kashire rolls his shoulders and grins, showing fangs. "Shall we dance?"

29

"Don't harm Claudia—yet," Maudon says ominously to the twinlike vampires.

Before I can fully move he's upon me, hauling me up the dais steps with a dread blade at my throat. I try to shadowstep, but he slaps the shadows away from me as if I were a child. When I try to shift into my animal form, I gasp—because he stops me there, too. It feels like he's slammed a hatch down upon the creature trying to spring out of me.

I didn't know he could do that. Obviously, he didn't show me everything he could do.

He never really trusted me. Or cared about me. I was just a tool to get to *her*.

Claudia follows quickly after us, crouched and ready, blades out at her sides. They're not dread blades. No one has them but the Black Court vampires—though I have the one I stole from Gavron. Out of the corner of my eye, I see Kashire's night terror form explode into the cavernous room, and the two other Black Court vampires leap into action—one for Jaen and one for Marai.

It's too easy for the first to shadowstep behind Jaen, drawing a dread blade as she does.

But Jaen splashes something into her face in the same moment. The other vampire staggers away, screeching and clutching her cheek. When her blistering hand comes away, it reveals half her face left in ruin. Ear melted off, eye socket empty.

Acid. Gavron mentioned that the Silver Court likes acid.

"Thought I was the weakest link, did you?" Jaen sneers.

"My turn," Kashire snarls through elongated teeth. He slams into the injured vampire in a flurry of wings and claws.

I can't quite see how Marai is faring, but against a Black Court vampire, she'll need help, fast.

"She's fine, Fin. *Focus*," Claudia snaps, drawing my eyes back to her.

I'm not sure how I can focus on anything but our imminent, permanent deaths, with Maudon's dread blade at my throat.

He keeps backing up the stairs, leading us to the bloodletter. "Put your head inside, or I'll slit her throat right here," he tells Claudia, and I know he means it.

She knows it, too. She lowers her daggers. Not that they could have done much, anyway.

Still, I shout, "No!"

She wasn't supposed to care about me anymore. Not like this.

I hiss when the edge of the dread blade presses deeper into my neck, parting the first layer of skin with a whisper-light kiss—followed by a line of fire.

But then I see Claudia, my one-time mother, kneel in front of the bloodletter. Fearless. My entire body grows still. Cold.

This is what I was born for. This is what *she* gave me, even before she was a vampire. A gift or a curse, I'm not sure.

I'm a blade.

My hand finds the hilt hidden among my knife belts.

Claudia meets my eyes, shakes her head just once in the barest twitch. "You win, Maudon," she says. "I'll do this for you. I'll become yours, but you have to spare Fin—not just for me, for *us*. We can be a family. Let her go now."

My heart ices over as she leans forward and fits her head into the spiked ring, her long dark curls framing her face as she looks up at

Maudon with red, red eyes. Eyes that won't be red for much longer, if he has his way.

Maudon takes a shaky breath and puts one hand on the lever. "You mean it?"

This is all he's ever wanted: to turn her into a Black Court vampire with his blood, forcing her to belong to him. He only has to drain her first.

"Yes," she says tremulously.

Founders, I think. Claudia knows the art of Seduction as well as any Red Court vampire. What did Havere say? *It will take but a glance.*

What did she and Gavron call it?

Lying.

She adds, blinking away red-tinged tears, "Only when you release her."

Maudon does, shoving me off the dais with such force that I fly right into the Black Court vampire fighting Marai. At the same time, he cranks down on the lever. The spikes drive home.

I shadowstep away just as Marai slams a dagger into the redhead's gut, exactly where I'd been. Too bad it wasn't a dread blade. I appear behind our opponent to draw *that* across her throat. But then she's gone. I try to follow her, but the shadows are snatched away from me when I try to make the cut. I turn to snarl at Maudon. *His* doing.

He's watching me from the top of the dais, Claudia bleeding out next to him. Her red blood runs in rivulets around the spikes, draining into the funnel. There's nothing to catch the flood. It only dribbles onto the floor in a widening sea of scarlet. Still, she shakes her head at me, her expression pained.

With a cry of rage I explode into my animal form and fling myself at the Black Court vampire. Maudon again tries to block my transformation, but he can't. He's distracted by Claudia. His obsession.

She's buying me time. She doesn't want me to tip my hand before the right moment.

I rake deep gouges down the Black Court vampire's back with all four claw-hooked paws, making her scream. My sudden attack as a snow leopard startles the vampire enough that Marai ducks in to score several more hits, nimbly dodging when the vampire shadowsteps away from me to appear behind her. Spinning, Marai stabs her again.

Marai fights with a singular focus I've never seen in her before. Still, she's without a dread blade. The most she could hope to do is slowly bleed her opponent to death. I shift back to human form to draw that weapon again, concealing it in my palm. But Marai shakes her head, glancing at Maudon and Claudia. She's right. Once Maudon knows I have a dread blade, all his attention will turn on me. I switch it out with my fillet knife and dive back into the fight.

The Black Court vampire is good, but I've been sparring against Maudon while Marai has been with Claudia, who has obviously trained her against shadowfighting. Before that, Marai and I fought with and for each other more times than I could count in Blades.

Together, Marai and I are better.

It's an advantage we apparently have that Kashire and Jaen don't seem to possess over their opponent. We have our twin pinned against the wall, smeared in dark blood even if no wounds are visible, when I hear Kashire cry out.

I spin to find him on the ground, his wings slashed to shreds. There are multiple bloody patches all over the other twin looming above him. Some are from obvious rents from Kashire's claws, as I can tell by the shredded clothing, but others are small, isolated. I see a strange blade in Jaen's hand. Jaen has obviously been ducking in to jab her with it whenever possible. It's somewhat similar to the one I also carry—the one I almost forgot I still had.

Maybe Kashire's attacks have merely been a distraction, allowing Jaen to get in close. *Masking* her movements.

And yet, the blade doesn't seem to have worked. Their opponent's wounds have healed over, Jaen is flagging, bleeding silver all over her body, and Kashire is down, having taken the brunt of the assault.

Right when the vampire is about to drive a dread blade into Kashire's heart, Jaen staggers back heavily. She's near ready to collapse, but she can still lift her hand and snap her fingers.

Little *pops* answer her. The Black Court vampire's eyes widen. And then she explodes—not like how Revar did it, piecemeal. But with blasts of fire and light and sound that throw a head one way and arms another. I have no idea what Jaen or the Silver Court has cooked up there, but it's more than effective.

Claudia, hanging limply and nearly bled out, takes advantage of the moment to spring to life, lifting her head and previously dangling hand—now clutching a dagger from her sleeve, just like I am. She hamstrings Maudon so severely that she cuts halfway through the back of his leg. The wound will heal, but it's enough to drop him to one knee next to her as he slips in her blood.

"You traitorous bitch," he says through clenched teeth.

"Maudon!" I cry.

He glares at me, pain lighting his dark eyes.

I hurl the dagger that he's already pivoting to block—a move we practiced over and over again on those warm summer nights. He doesn't even deign to shadowstep, let alone mist, because he knows he can catch it.

But I don't throw it at him.

Claudia catches it.

And she slams my dread blade into Maudon's chest.

Maudon gapes at me, and then down at the dagger buried in his heart. Black blood pours around the wound. Claudia twists it viciously, driving it deeper until they both collapse, him to the ground and her sagging against the bloodletter. His blood mixes with hers in a black-and-red spiral on the ground.

Marai rushes to her maker as Claudia falls utterly limp. I don't let myself look at her. She wouldn't want me to be distracted.

I shadowstep over to Maudon, crouching down next to him as he tries to reach for the dread blade, as weak as I've ever seen him. I take the hilt in my hand—and stab him again. And again.

"You're the bitch," I say. I keep stabbing until his shining black eyes grow dull and clouded over with white. I don't know where this anger has come from, these tears.

Maybe they're for my father, too. Maudon, like him, promised me something—family, belonging—but it was poisoned.

I wipe my eyes. My hand comes away grayish.

"Founders, Fin," Kashire breathes, staring at me. He's back in human form and absolutely drenched in blue and black blood, but he's standing. "I never thought I'd say this, but . . . I *really* like you."

"Jaen, help!" Marai cries, easing Claudia's unmoving body to the ground. Her curls drag in her own blood.

Jaen limps around, industriously stacking the already flaming body parts of the Black Court vampire into a lit brazier. She's doing it one-handed. In her other, she has one of the dread blades from the fallen twin.

I spin to find the remaining twin leaning against the wall, even more bloodied from where Marai stabbed her approximately fifty times while I was otherwise occupied. Dread blade or no, Marai is a deadly force.

I leave the blade in Maudon's heart—I won't be satisfied that he's dead until he's dust—and I stand. "What about this one? She can mist herself."

"Trust me," the redheaded vampire says, "I don't want to follow you below." She's even sheathed her own dread blades. Her eyes flicker to the lit brazier. "If anything, I would rather join my sister."

"I see," Jaen says, suddenly at her throat, leaning in close to hiss in her ear. I barely saw the Silver Court vampire move. "Then you get to live. You get to suffer her loss. As I get to suffer Revar's."

The Black Court vampire's eyes drift away, as if dead already.

"Jaen, please!" Marai cries.

Jaen follows the sound of her voice, over to Claudia.

"Fine, you can live," I say. It doesn't matter to me, one way or the other, and I wouldn't want to cross Jaen, anyway. "I just need one more thing from you."

"What?" the vampire asks, defeated.

I wrench both of her dread blades out of her sheaths and stalk away, back toward the dais.

"If she moves, kill her," I say over my shoulder.

"With pleasure," Kashire purrs, holding his own dread blade to her throat.

I stare down at the gouges in the dais's stone, pooled now with red and black blood. It marks out a strange symbol like a rune, but one I don't know.

That's where I need to go.

"Burn Maudon," I say.

Marai nods grimly, already moving to do so. Jaen is bent over Claudia.

"Don't relax your guard for him," Marai says, shooting me a look.

I know whom she means. But Gavron has been living a nightmare, same as I was. It doesn't matter that he put me there. He didn't have much choice, and he was even trying to help me in small ways. Besides, he's been in such a terrible place for far longer than I've ever been.

"Marai, after you burn Maudon, guard the prisoner, please. Kashire, turn into a bat or a bird or whatever, and get out of here. Alert the other courts."

"Why?" he demands. "I thought we wanted to avoid that."

"In case I fail," I say, and then I shrug. "I think they all might want to be ready for what's coming."

"What's coming?" He barks a laugh. "Aside from the Founders?"

"Something bigger than them," I say, and his blue eyes widen. "Something absolutely huge. I can feel it. Like the sun never rising again."

"Wouldn't that be nice," Kashire says, but it doesn't have his usual cheer behind it.

"No," I say. "It wouldn't. We need balance, or we all fall."

I close my eyes. I grope for that precipice in my mind, as if edging forward with my toes. The cliff with the endless drop, unless I can fly back up.

I step off the cliff. It's just like shadowstepping, except I keep going. And going and going. Breaking myself into pieces. Shattering as I fall.

I turn myself into mist.

30

·──·•∾⌒∾•·──·

I come apart and apart and apart until I don't really know who or
even what I am. But I know where I need to go. I feel it like one
sees a signal fire in the distance.

I sink through cracks in the stone like a maze, into confusing,
endless darkness, but I can feel the light guiding me.

And suddenly I'm floating in a room even bigger than the previous one, a massive cave. The floor is as polished as dark glass, and
there are four evenly spaced alcoves branching off from the central
chamber. There's no raised dais in the middle of it all, but a wide
square basin, like a cistern for catching rainwater. Except we're deep
underground, and the basin seems designed to catch only one thing.

At one end of the basin, there's another bloodletter. While the
one up above was for changing courts, here, it's for something
else entirely. Built for only one purpose and hidden from the eyes of
the vampire world.

I float above as mist, unseen, taking it all in. This is the tomb.

In each alcove, there's a sarcophagus made of what looks like
glass. Atop each one, there's a bowl set above where the occupant's
mouth would be, as if that's where to pour whoever is inside a
drink.

Where to pour each sacrifice's blood to complete the ritual.

Each bowl is damp. One is dark, vaguely brownish—Lief's blood,
I gather, in the alcove decorated with faded blue tapestries. In the
alcove hung with scarlet turned pale pink, a bowl is bright red

with Silvea's blood. The bowl in the gilded alcove is golden hued with Pavella's. And the last bowl is so silver it's like liquefied metal has been poured inside—Revar's blood, far brighter than the filigree and tapestries now gray with age.

Black spikes like those of the bloodletter have been jammed through each crystalline sarcophagus—more than long enough to spear a body through. And so many of them that they make a pincushion of each one. The spikes must be the same material as dread blades, I realize. So the inhabitants can't move or heal after they've been raised by their sacrificial offering.

The glass is cracked so I can't see what or who's inside. But I can guess, if I had a mind to.

The occupants of these sarcophagi—they've been raised to *die*. The Founders were never meant to rule again.

Their blood runs in rivulets, following channels carved into the stone. Each channel enters one corner of the square basin in the central room, dropping down in strange, spiraling patterns to a dark hole in the very center. Unlike the offerings in the bowls, *this* blood is so bright it nearly glows. Brilliant blue, red, and gold. Even the silver is brighter than Revar's, seeming to shine with an inner light.

The blood of the vampire gods. The oldest among immortals. *They* are the true sacrifice. But for what?

The Founders aren't meant to rule again . . . but perhaps someone else is.

And theirs isn't the only blood being spilled in the room. I drift toward the light that has been guiding me, and I find it's fading. Gavron is bleeding—dying. He's at the edge of the basin, his neck pierced through in the iron ring of the bloodletter. A hammered bronze dish beneath him is filled with his black blood.

There's a stone channel underneath the bloodletter, as if waiting for the dish to be tipped in offering. It, too, runs to the hole in the center of the basin, forming a crowning fifth branch that will soon be as black as the others are blue, red, gold, and silver. Gavron's skin is sunken, his tendons standing out.

I need . . . someone needs . . . to save him. To stop this. But I can't seem to gather my thoughts. They're as scattered as my body.

Gavron's eyes flicker in my direction, which is no direction at all. Their inky darkness is glazed. Cloudy. He gives his head one solitary jerk.

Just like Claudia and Marai. *Not yet.*

A shadow shifts, and I realize Beltharius is crouched at the center of the basin, staring down into the hole where the blood drips.

He turns to Gavron. "Nearly empty? We need to have almost none of you left, so you can hold what's mine. What's *hers.*"

He strolls over to Gavron, black velvet cape swirling. "It's an honor, to be where you are, taking up this mantle of power. Such a strong vessel." He puts a kindly hand on Gavron's head.

For a moment, fear flickers through me like lightning across a storm cloud. I remember those same hands tearing off Revar's head when the Silver Court vampire was pinned exactly like this.

Again, Gavron twitches in my direction, feebly, but I sense it. *Wait.*

Beltharius must think Gavron is shaking him off, because he pulls his hand away. "Do you not want to be made into the Founder of your House? I admit, I don't like the term much myself." He glances down at the bright rivers of blood around him. "*They* called themselves that, after . . . after what they did to her. Their mother. The atrocity they committed against her throne. Her own children bound her by draining her blood to nothing, and then they sealed themselves in here so she could never rise again. They ensured that they themselves were thought of as the beginning. The foundation. But they built their empire on her bones. They had the nerve to call their mother's House—the only true House—*nameless.*"

He crouches in front of Gavron, staring into the small pool of black blood. The bronze dish is nearly full.

"The Nameless House." Beltharius scoffs. "They wanted *her* name forgotten."

He abruptly lifts Gavron's head to meet his eyes. Gavron lets out a horrible rasping groan. His lips—that once-beautiful bow of his mouth—are pulled back in a corpselike grimace from his teeth. It must pain him horribly to be moved like that, with the spikes through his neck, but grandfatherly Beltharius doesn't seem to care.

"You should know your House's history," Beltharius says to him chidingly, "even if your time as its Founder won't be long. There was never supposed to *be* a Founder, or Founders—anything other than our queen. *I* was never supposed to be. But when her four children combined forces and came to break her crown, they murdered every vampire of mature blood in her realm. Thousands were slaughtered. The best and oldest that vampire kind had to offer—gone. They left only the youngest alive, to be molded in their own broken design. Those like myself."

His face suddenly twists into something far less grandfatherly. Something ancient and inhuman. He wrenches Gavron's head closer. "Her children didn't know how to destroy her, only bind her, so they *sundered* her tower. They made us *forget* her name. They made us *serve* the other Houses they created from the wreckage as a balancing force, in penance for her once-great power. They *buried* our history along with her."

So the Black Court didn't put a stop to the Founders and hide the secret, like Jaen suspected. The Founders put a stop to the Black Court—their mother—and tried to erase the past.

Beltharius sighs, his features relaxing. He loosens his hold on Gavron and gazes off as if seeing something long ago. "But they didn't manage to overpower her before she summoned me. I was one of her lowliest servants—she didn't even allow thralls to serve her, only her own kind. *I* never expected her to make me her equal in power. She . . . fed me her blood. Bound me." He says it reverently, as if he

365

can still hardly believe it. "She did it to save her legacy. After, she sent me back to the servants' quarters as if nothing had happened. Her children never discovered that I harbored her powerful blood and abilities. Her promise."

He stands. "Nor did they ever imagine I would be here now, to resurrect her and take our revenge against them." He turns in a slow circle, looking into each of the alcoves. He raises his hand before him, and then makes a fist.

Same as Revar's gesture—the one to take things apart.

The ancient bodies in the impaled sarcophagi simply burst. Clouds of gray ash rise out of each alcove and begin to dissipate in the air. Now they're dust. Never to return to themselves.

The four Founders, gone. Just like that. Truly dead, even for the already dead.

Beltharius turns back to Gavron. "Now that's finished, it's time to make you the final Founder."

Beltharius cranks the spikes back from Gavron's neck, leaving him hanging awkwardly in the bloodletter, little more than skin and bones. Beltharius bites his own wrist and holds it to Gavron's mouth.

Gavron's eyes fly wide. They're still cloudy, but they almost immediately begin to darken, such is the power in that old blood. Drinking a vampire's blood might lend you their strength, but in the end—unless you drink it all, to the last drop—they'll own you.

And Beltharius *already* owns him, with his ability to enthrall vampires.

He wrenches Gavron's head up again, forcing him to meet his eyes. "You will not move, only drink. Once you have drunk until my veins offer no more, you will crank the lever and put the spikes back into your neck." He frowns. "I would give you the same honor as I did Revar and do it for you, but I might be too weak from blood loss."

Even where I am—nowhere and everywhere—I hear the power in Beltharius's command. Total enthrallment.

"This might help me." Beltharius pulls a silver chalice out of his cape and scoops up a small amount of Gavron's blood. The rest, he splatters across the stones in a wide arc when he kicks the bronze dish aside. None of it makes it into the channel.

So much blood, wasted. Because that's not the blood the sacrifice demands. Gavron's blood was never meant to drain into the basin. The ritual requires the final Founder's blood along with the rest, and he's not the final Founder. Not yet.

That must be the deeper ritual, beyond raising the Founders. It required the appropriate victim from the appropriate House at the appropriate time to wake those in the glass sarcophagi. And in turn, this . . . Nameless Queen . . . needs *their* sacrifice—her children's—to rise again, since they stole her blood and bound her using their own lives.

But Beltharius's blood is necessary, too. Because it's hers. She gave some of it to him for safekeeping over the ages. And now, his sacrifice is the final key.

Or, at least, Gavron's sacrifice will be. Because Beltharius is going to make Gavron the final Founder, in his stead. The *vessel* for her blood to be returned to her, so Beltharius himself can live to see her.

Beltharius sets the cup aside on the stone floor. "I don't need much. All my strength must go to her. So I'll take only this blood from you, to survive a little longer. And you will take all of mine . . . and die." He crouches in front of Gavron and bites his own wrist again. "Drink," he says. "And bite, as soon as you are strong enough to do so, and keep biting until there's nothing left."

His command leaves little room for dissent.

Gavron begins to drink. And drink. Soon, his reconstituted hands haul himself farther upright, gripping the bloodletter with powerful fingers. But he doesn't shove himself away from it. He sinks his teeth back into Beltharius's wrist and keeps drinking, his head still thrust through the ring.

The spikes remain withdrawn. For now.

Beltharius, for his part, seems entirely at peace, kneeling there. "Perhaps it should be me in your place, since she's given me so much. But I must see her again—my queen. If she requires my death, I will give it in an instant. But I want her to see a familiar face after being bound in darkness for so long. To wake to the devotion of her most loyal servant. I hope she lets me drink of her font once more . . . so I can truly belong to her . . ."

He slumps sideways, leaning up against the bloodletter as Gavron shoves into it. Gavron seizes his arm now, dragging it closer, biting harder. Drinking deeper.

Beltharius begins to look distinctly hollow as he tells him, almost irritably, "You have a love, too, I know. I gave you what time with her I could, but you were bred for this purpose. Not to create, but to be destroyed. You were never supposed to take a novice or make an apprentice. Never supposed to love her. Foolish boy. You were only meant to love your queen. But even Fin's weak human blood influenced my sway over you." He sighs, but it's feeble. "I won't begrudge her that, if she lives. Our queen will need strength in her new realm. And I spoke truly when I said your love warms this old heart. It's reminiscent of my own."

Gavron glares as he keeps devouring Beltharius's wrist. His eyes are dark, so dark, gleaming with vigor. *Power.* But it's still Beltharius's strength, Beltharius's blood. Gavron keeps predatory eyes locked on him. Wide, furious. In the darkness of his mind, he's screaming at him.

I know, because I can hear Gavron now, even as mist. Such ancient, powerful blood has amplified his mind.

Beltharius sags back against the stone floor, little more than a skeleton. One bony hand grasps for the goblet of Gavron's weaker blood. His other hand has been gnawed nearly off, still in Gavron's clutches. Beltharius brings the goblet to his lips.

When his dry stump of a wrist finally falls from Gavron's mouth, Beltharius just manages to tip the goblet back into his mouth, pouring in a trickle of blood and spilling half down his chin.

He gives a great gasp, sitting more upright and dragging himself away from Gavron. He looks ghastly, but he's somehow still moving.

Gavron looks more than alive. I feel a pull toward him like never before. He's radiantly beautiful, glowing like the full moon against the darkness of my strange, diffuse senses. He could rip the bloodletter apart with his bare hands. He could destroy Beltharius with a flick of his finger. He could mist out of here without a moment's thought or worry.

But, despite his power, Gavron's not in control.

Instead, his hand lifts to the lever and starts to crank it. He doesn't make a sound even as the spikes pierce his neck. He keeps turning the crank until those vicious points extend all the way, pinning him brutally in the center of the ring. And then he bleeds.

Gavron is a vessel, indeed. No more than a goblet for Beltharius to use and cast away, to transfer his blood without requiring his own sacrifice. And now it's time for the vessel to empty into the Nameless Queen's waiting maw.

It's time for Gavron to die.

Gavron's entire body is taut and shaking with suppressed strength. Helpless rage. That rich, potent blood, straight from the ancient vampire, drains out from Gavron's neck as if from a faucet.

It pours into the channel, flowing toward the mouth of the Nameless Queen.

I need to . . . do something . . . I need to be somewhere.

But I think I might be lost.

I'm drifting away. Disappearing. I've stayed as mist for too long.

Fin. Come back. Gavron's voice, floating to me in the silence of the room, where there's only the sound of blood pattering on stone and Beltharius shuffling dustily over to the center of the basin.

Gavron's voice pulls me, but I still don't know what *back* means. *Back where?*

Back to yourself. Remember, I know you. I made a map to you. Follow it now. Visions flicker in my mind, of a young person with a sharp cut of wheat-colored hair, flashing black eyes, and an excessive number of daggers. *I love you, Fin. I need you. Everyone does.*

The words stick inside me. An anchor point.

There's an echo of a different voice, from the past. Revar's: *As thin as parchment, nigh translucent . . . Deceptively simple.*

My own voice, now: *Fin. Parchment thin. Invisible. Nothing.*

And then Gavron, speaking now what he said to me back then: *So quiet and so still, moving as if you are nothing until you strike . . . you incredible creature.*

And then, suddenly, I'm both Fin *and* mist.

Fin. I'm Fin. It doesn't matter that I'm barely here anymore. I'm doing what I do best. What I came here to do—to sneak up on this insufferable bastard, Beltharius.

As Gavron gives a shuddering gasp, the ancient vampire turns to him, raising arms of leathery skin and frail bone, mistaking the noise for protestation, perhaps.

"Be strong. Give the final drop of your Founder's blood until you are no more. The House of the Forgotten Name shall be reborn. Your life will nourish her, and once more her reign will fall upon the earth like the darkest night." He breathes a sigh. "And I will see my queen again."

"Are you sure you don't belong to the Red Court?" I ask, behind him. "Because that sounds like romantic drivel to me."

Before Beltharius can turn, I stab Jaen's thin dagger into his sinewy neck. Silver Court blood and potent alchemy squirt into what's left of his flesh.

"That's for Revar, courtesy of Jaen," I hiss.

Beltharius collapses. He's not dead, only unconscious, but I don't have time to try to finish him. I tear off his velvet cloak as he falls, shadowstepping just in time to stuff it in the canal and block the flow of blood. It's the first thing I can think to do. And for a moment, it works, soaking up the blood and damming it.

But there's *so* much blood.

"Gavron, make it stop!" I cry, wadding more material into the stone crevice. "Turn the lever back!"

Of course, he doesn't listen, enthralled as he is. He only looks at me with dark eyes, his hair hanging messily in his face. Bleeding.

I scramble around, shadowstepping, snatching up the silver goblet and the emptied bronze dish. I dive for the channel and use the goblet to madly scoop up the potent blood, splashing it into the bowl. After I manage to drain the reservoir built up behind the velvet cloak, I reinforce my dam with more material and shadowstep my way back to Gavron. I need to stop the flow at the source. I put the dish directly under him, catching the fall of blood. Which is getting more sluggish now.

His eyes are losing their luster.

You will not move, only drink, Beltharius told him.

He can drink, then. I need to give him my blood. It will have sway over him, just like Beltharius's. But even if I gain some measure of control, I'm not sure Gavron won't still be enthralled by a vampire far more powerful than I am.

I need equal power.

I look down at the dish. Technically, the blood came from Gavron, even if the potency comes from someone far older. Beltharius might still try to enthrall me—if he weren't on the ground. Maybe giving up all his blood made him lose the power to enthrall vampires. For now, at least, I hope I'm shielded from his influence.

I dip the goblet in the dish. Gavron's hazy eyes widen. I raise the cup to him.

"To your health," I say. That silly human phrase.

And then I start drinking. I drink and drink—almost everything that was meant for the Nameless Queen. Her legacy. I gulp it down, refilling my goblet over and over and over again between ecstatic sighs of pleasure. This is more decadent, more rapturous, than anything I experienced in Revelry or anywhere else. I feel like I might burst with it.

And yet I'm unbreakable. So I keep glutting myself while Gavron watches.

Until he begins to die.

I smile dreamily at him, lost in a euphoric haze of memories and delicious, body-thrumming power. I feel strong enough to tear down walls. To destroy the world.

I slit my wrist, like he's done for me so many times—feeding me. It's my turn. I use my dread blade so the cut won't heal. I hold the wound to Gavron's mouth.

I don't retract the spikes of the bloodletter. I keep him bleeding into the dish, even as I keep drinking out of it with the goblet. I have to be sure that Beltharius's power over him is diluted. That *I've* gained a stronger hold over Gavron by feeding him my blood, even as Gavron gains an equal hold on me.

"I'm sorry," I say, as some of the intoxicating power fades, letting me think a little more clearly. "I need to make sure. I need to balance you."

Gavron gulps from my wrist. He needs it to survive, because he's still bleeding out. But that's probably not why he does it. Beltharius told him to drink. And so he keeps drinking. And I keep refilling my goblet and tossing it back.

An endless, circular flow—his blood to me, my blood to him.

When Gavron's hand shifts on the lever, trying to crank the spikes back, it gives me the proof I need that Beltharius's grip on him has weakened. I leap to help him, unwinding it with furious speed. I nearly pitch myself halfway across the room with the force, but Gavron catches my shoulders as he pulls himself free of the bloodletter.

We stare at each other. His eyes are gleaming. *He's* practically shining, like the gods of the stories. Devastatingly beautiful.

I have no idea what I look like. I might not be as powerful as I was before I gave half of his blood back to him, but I'm still shaking with it. I'm his equal in strength now. My skin fizzes like sparks, even though my flesh is ice cold.

Gavron smells like the night, and I want to fly with him.

I hope that's all I want to do—all that *he* wants to do, with our newfound strength. I don't know what hold Beltharius might still have over him. I, at least, have no urge to sacrifice him, or myself, to some Nameless Queen.

He once needed someone to care for, since he had no choice but to hurt and kill. He needed someone belonging to him, since he didn't belong to himself. I became that, for him.

Now, will he want me alongside him, as his equal? Someone to love and respect, as I do him?

Can we belong to each other?

"How do you feel?" I ask absurdly.

Gavron takes my wrist, where I'm still trickling blood from the dread blade's cut. Surprisingly, it's already starting to close. Not even dread blades seem to be permanent on me now. He lifts my hand to his mouth, running his tongue along the wound. Healing it completely. Once he's done, he kisses the inside of my wrist.

"My paramant," he says softly. The wounds in his throat are already healed. "You're more than I could ever have hoped." He cups my face and kisses me gently on the lips.

He pauses, as if waiting for an answer.

"Paramant?" is all I manage to whisper.

"Yes—my other half. Mutually blood bound to each other." Gavron glances at Beltharius, where he lies in a heap above the tomb of his beloved. "That's what they were, and yet he was only her servant in the end."

The ancient vampire stirs.

Both of us fly into action at once, shadowstepping the distance. Gavron still has his dread blade, unsheathing it as he flashes above Beltharius.

"Stop," Beltharius croaks at us.

Gavron *stops*, freezing in place. Same as me.

The ancient vampire is little more than a skeleton. "I'm not so weak as that, after these thousands of years."

He can still enthrall vampires, and we're filled with his blood. *All* his blood . . . which means it's not his anymore.

Besides, there are two of us, and *my* blood is in us both, as well, young as it is. Maybe that makes the difference.

Gavron's hand begins to inch down.

"Heed my commands—" Beltharius insists.

"Blood and piss, shut *up*," I hiss.

Surprisingly, Beltharius's mouth clamps closed. I ram my own dread blade into his throat a second later. Gavron's blade slams into his skull just after mine.

Horrifically, Beltharius's mouth still moves, rasping voicelessly, teeth clacking. I remember Jaen's warning about what a head injury without death might do to a vampire, especially a powerful one.

"Hold him," I say.

Unquestioning, Gavron grips Beltharius's shoulders. I seize his skull between both hands. It's the first thing I think to do.

I rip his head clean off.

Unlike Revar, he doesn't turn to dust. Perhaps that was Beltharius's work, too, but I don't know how to do that. There are many things I still need to learn.

"Should we burn it?" I ask, hefting the head by the hair and holding it as far away from me as possible. The eyes are rolled back in their sockets, but the jaw is still twitching.

"Yes, but not here," Gavron says. "Not yet. They need to see." He glances upward.

The other vampires, I realize. Or else they'll never have proof of what happened down here. They'll never be sure I was innocent of the murders, or that Gavron wasn't in control when he committed them. They need to know it was Beltharius, and that we stopped him.

Gavron turns to me. "How did you do it?" he breathes, staring at me in awe. "I could feel you all around us. How did you stay misted for that long? You've never done it before. You should have been lost."

"You helped," I admit. "But I've spent a long time trying to disappear. To make myself invisible. I'm good at it, and I know the way back to myself now. I don't need anyone else's map." I smile at him. "And I know what I want."

"What do you want?"

To kill vampires. That's what I always thought, to get revenge for my mother.

But my mother is a vampire. I'm one. My truest friend is, as well, never mind Gavron, my maker—my *paramant*, whatever that strange word entails. I wouldn't even want to see Kashire dead, whatever we are to each other. Friends?

Vampires are strange and complicated, just like humans. Good and bad and often somewhere in between. But we *are* more powerful than humans, and that's dangerous.

No, I don't want to kill vampires. I glance down at the head in my hand. Other than this one, perhaps.

I want to do something *more*.

It's time for more than survival, or even revenge.

"I want to change us," I say.

31

———— ·✦✦✦· ————

Gavron and I emerge as mist from the tomb to find Jaen, Claudia, Marai, and Kashire receiving healing attention in the small courtyard across the bridge from Courtsheart. Kashire listened to my request, miraculously, and notified the other courts of the extreme danger brewing within these walls.

Which seem to be why there's a blockade on the bridge, keeping us and the gathering forces of the Nameless House away from the castle proper. More Black Court vampires than I've ever seen, more than I ever knew were here, are appearing seemingly from nowhere. They face the entire Council of Twelve—eleven, rather, with Revar's usual place conspicuously empty—standing in a semicircle on the bridge.

A tall, powerful-looking vampire with ebony skin and a shaved head, the new representative of the Silver Court, steps forward to address us. "We would like to speak to the new seats of the Nameless House," she declares, her voice echoing across both courtyards.

The Nameless House. I don't think I'll ever know its true name now. I don't know that I want to know.

Like my old name, it's dead. Time for something new.

Kashire nudges my shoulder. "I think that means you and Gavron. You're the new seats."

I stare at Gavron in shock. He glances at the assembling members of the Black Court, turning out in such numbers and in such plain sight probably for the first time since the fall of the Nameless House. They've kept themselves hidden, scattered, since then. Not anymore. And none of them argue with Kashire as they stare back at us, taking our measure.

Apparently they don't find it lacking.

"Age is what's respected among us," Gavron murmurs to me. "We're young, but we now have the oldest blood here. Beltharius's blood."

And her *blood*, I think. He's no doubt thinking the same thing, but he doesn't say it aloud.

I shiver. "Fine. Let's go." I'm still carrying Beltharius's head. It's in a sack now, but I won't let it out of my sight. "You're coming with us, though," I say to Kashire, Jaen, Claudia, and Marai. It's not a question at first—and then it's almost a relief to remember I have no authority over them, at least. "Please?"

They all nod, and I'm unspeakably grateful.

Together, we step out onto the bridge as the horizon begins to glow around us. I barely resist seizing Marai's hand. It's not the time to look weak.

The Council faces us with a shocking number of vampires filling the massive courtyard at their backs. The towers of the four other halls rise around us like dark claws. All the Houses seem to have assembled their representative forces here at Courtsheart against the Black Gates—against *my* House, I remind myself.

Just like what happened in the old days, I think wryly. But Gavron and I aren't going to be anything like the Nameless Queen.

I brace myself, taking a deep breath. And then the six of us explain what happened to the best of our abilities. After Gavron and I finish telling the last part only we witnessed in the tomb, I open the sack and send Beltharius's head tumbling at the Council's feet. A couple of them grimace in distaste. One even jumps back.

The Silver Court representative asks the most pressing question before anyone else speaks. "Did this abominable power to enthrall vampires survive Beltharius?"

"No," both Gavron and I say quickly. He follows up more slowly with, "It seems that diluting his blood even the smallest amount has left us with normal skill level for a vampire in this instance." He smiles disarmingly. "But we're much more capable elsewhere."

Her eyes narrow, but she doesn't say anything else.

The Red Court representative is the first to step forward after their Council members confer among themselves. "The House of Spring Dawn is willing to forgive the Black Court for Silvea's death. And we're proud of our own Claudia and Marai for the role they've both played in keeping this . . . Nameless Queen . . . from rising. You have our thanks."

"Your thanks?" a Gold Court vampire hisses. He nods at the head still lying—and twitching—on the bridge. "This traitor just turned your Founder and the rest of ours to dust, and yet somehow leaves these two to rise from the ashes?" He gestures derisively at me and Gavron.

I can hardly blame him. The weight of what I've become now still staggers me, even if Beltharius didn't exactly hand over his mantle of power willingly. I seized it from him and the Nameless Queen.

"As for Pavella," the Gold Court vampire continues, "she was beloved."

"*Beloved* is a stretch," Kashire says, yawning. His shirt is still a mess, but he manages to look nonchalant. "Even ole Bel here said that's why he chose her—she'd be the least missed. So stop politicking."

"You speak to us of politicking while this young blood and his apprentice suddenly ascend to take control of the Black Court?"

Gavron's tone is dangerously soft when he speaks. "My blood is no longer young, and she's not my apprentice anymore. She's my paramant and my equal in power. Watch yourself."

The Gold Court vampire shoots me a look that is somehow both disbelieving and deadly.

The other Gold Court Council members don't appear pleased. But they step back without saying anything more, clearly waiting to see how things play out with the other courts.

The Silver Court representative steps forward once again, her broad shoulders squared. "Revar was more than beloved. They were irreplaceable. The Black Court must pay beyond Beltharius." She turns to the rest of the Council. "We vote they be dissolved."

"What?" Marai cries. Claudia shushes her.

Jaen glances at us, her silver eyes calculating. Kashire puts a hand on her shoulder and starts whispering in her ear.

"You, who are all about preservation?" Gavron says darkly. "You would destroy us?"

"We are also about protection," the Silver Court vampire says. "Your House is too dangerous to exist anymore. The Founders were too merciful."

The Gold Court begins to buzz. Kashire moves to mutter in Gavron's ear.

"Didn't we prove that we can fix our mistakes?" I demand. "That we can change?"

"I'm afraid we cannot trust you. Ever again."

"What if we give you the Nameless Queen?" Gavron cuts in, his powerful voice slicing through the hum of talk. "We will let you unearth her tomb where she lies and move it to a hidden location of your choice. For you to protect and preserve."

Even the Silver Court vampire looks taken by the thought.

"Or to destroy her, if you can manage it," he adds. "Though the Founders couldn't."

"Before you do that," another voice cuts in, "we, too, have our own recommendations to put forth." The Blue Court representative steps forward on the bridge, just as the sky begins to grow a little *too* bright.

Gavron gives Kashire an apologetic glance. "Lief's death, while unfortunate, is hardly grounds to——"

"We want an alliance."

Many in the crowd now, especially among Gold and Silver, gasp. The buzz of conversation rises to a low roar.

"Your House, joined with ours," the Blue Court vampire continues, raising his voice over the clamor, "will be nameless no more! It's where you belong. Where you've always belonged. And the Silver Court can't object, since you will no longer be the Black Court, but an entirely new House." His voice drops until it's only for Gavron and me. "Think on it. Give us your answer at Winter Sol." He turns to the Silver Court representatives. "Can you at least stay your strangely destructive impulses until then?"

No one would ever have accused the Silver Court of being *impulsive*, but these are strange times. The old gods are dead, ancient queens are trying to rise, and new Founders are walking around right under their noses.

I'm now a Founder, I think in disbelief.

Jaen confers with the Council members of her House and returns to me and Gavron a moment later, keeping her voice low. "We don't want a war. If you hand over the Nameless Queen, my court will stand down. With one final request."

"Which is?" Gavron asks.

"I get to light that thing on fire," Jaen says with a nod at Belthari-us's head. "Right now. I'll leave the ashes in the courtyard to turn to dust with the dawn."

"Great, perfect, yes. And then can we bloody get inside?" Kashire says, rubbing his arms with a mock shiver and eyeing the sky warily.

Gavron smiles grimly and gestures in invitation.

Jaen is good for her word.

* * *

Claudia is entirely sick of all the so-called *politicking* and drags Marai back to their sanctuary in the Red Court's Spring Hall. The remaining four of us take refuge in, of all places, Maudon's massive war room in the Black Gates. *Our war room now*, I think—Gavron's and mine. And Kashire's and Jaen's, if they want. It has thick walls to hold out the sun, and far too many intriguing documents and maps on the sprawling table.

In the chaos, no one among the Black Court has seemed to notice we're in here yet. Or else they don't know how to approach their new Founders. With the old head of their House literally beheaded and their commander dismembered and burned, I imagine the chain of authority is smashed to pieces. I'm not sure what we should rebuild yet, Gavron and I.

"If the Blue Court had better central leadership," Jaen muses, "they would be a force like no other."

"That's why the seats of my House approached yours with an alliance," Kashire says, flipping through a stack of letters. "We wouldn't be able to stomach one with the likes of the Gold Court, but the Black Court—"

"I still can't believe it," Gavron says, throwing up his hands. "You *hate* us. I mean, not you, Kashire, but even so you're always going on about how stuffy and boring we are."

Kashire meets his eyes over a desk. "Because that's what *I* thought. But the seats of my House—their dislike was a mask. We're adept at putting those on, if you recall. We're also adept at remembering. They would never so readily propose a union between our courts if they weren't already planning it. They *remembered* your House.

381

Knew its history, at least a slice of what Beltharius intended. And they kept it from the other courts, made a pact with him to join your legacy instead of proudly maintaining our own." His face stills. "And for that, I'll never forgive them. They longed for the old ways so much, they stabbed the very heart of our House in order to claim a past that wasn't ours—was *against* ours."

"Then why would they still want to join the Black Court, now that Beltharius is gone and the Nameless Queen will be in the Silver Court's hands?" I ask.

"They want the skills that you have. And yours is the oldest claim to a vampire throne that exists," he says, his look taking in both me and Gavron. "They want to rule. They want war."

We all look at each other uneasily, even Jaen.

I've never considered what war might look like among immortals.

It would probably shake the earth.

Eventually, Kashire and Jaen wander off to find somewhere to sleep, while Gavron and I sit next to each other at the table. The carved chairs have plush velvet cushions—black, of course—but they're no replacement for lying down.

And yet, neither Gavron nor I is exhausted, despite what we've been through. I'm not hungry, either, for the first time in a long while, or sore. I feel invincible.

That doesn't stop my body from slipping into a more horizontal position. Somehow, my feet find their way into Gavron's lap, and he pulls off my boots. My transformation into an incredibly powerful vampire doesn't change the fact that his thumb digging into my arch feels divine.

"Are you sure it's not too dangerous to let the Silver Court have her?" I ask for what feels like the hundredth time. "You realize all the Nameless Queen needs is the blood of one of us."

Gavron arches an eyebrow. It's such a familiar look that I melt farther into my chair. I didn't know if I'd ever see it again. "Let them try," he says.

"It would be easy enough," I say, growing somber again. "All they would need is a bloodletter and maybe one of Jaen's sleeping tonics."

"Not with what we can do." When I wave him away, he says, "Fin—"

"I don't want to hear it."

"You have to face it. I saw what you did. You told Beltharius to be silent. And he *fell silent*." He hesitates. "Fin, we both have the power to enthrall vampires now. It's a burden we have to bear."

My face screws up. So I *can* still cry.

He's sliding out from under my legs and next to me before I can blink, his hands on my shoulders. "It's not so different from the power you had before. You could enthrall humans, but you chose not to."

"It *is* different." I bite my lip. "I intentionally didn't learn how to enthrall humans, and I would never use such a weapon against them, anyway, because they can't really hurt us." I meet his eyes. "But against vampires who can? I might. And that's what terrifies me."

"I understand why you hate it." He bends closer to me, touching his forehead to mine. "More than you could possibly know."

I meet his agonized gaze. "I know. Gavron, I forgive you. That wasn't you."

He straightens and turns away from me. When he turns back to me, his face is clear. "No one else knows what the Nameless Queen still requires to wake. Revar is dead." I flinch, but Gavron carries on ruthlessly. "And Jaen never knew the scope of the ritual. We don't know how to destroy this queen, and we can't just leave her there for someone else to take. This is the perfect solution. The Silver Court won't challenge us now, and they'll be the Nameless Queen's keeper. They want to protect vampire kind more than any other House."

"And to perhaps preserve things they shouldn't," I mutter. "What if they can't—or won't—destroy her?"

"I don't know." Gavron runs a hand through his hair. "I had to offer them something or it would have been war for certain. Silver and Gold, the most cunning strategists and sharpest minds, would have allied against us, and we would have to accept the Blue Court's offer. Turning over the Nameless Queen was actually Kashire's idea. Even *he* doesn't want us to ally with his House."

I shrug low in my chair. "We would have the best fighters, especially if we could convince the Red Court to join us."

"I think the Red Court would let us all annihilate ourselves and simply go live among humanity."

"Without the might of the other Houses . . . humans might rise up against them," I say slowly.

Gavron sighs and leans heavily against the table. "And that could be the end of us."

"Would that be so bad?" I whisper.

He frowns at me. I pick at one of my long canines with a thumbnail, deep in thought. "I thought you didn't want to kill vampires anymore," he says.

"I don't." I drop my hand and sit up to take both of his in mine. "But I don't think vampires should rule the world and subjugate humanity, either."

"That's how it's always been."

I click my tongue and grin. "Then try to think better."

Winter Sol is as beautiful as I remember it, if not quite as frightening.

I'm a vampire now, after all. A *frighteningly* powerful one, at that.

There seem to be no bounds to what I can do, what I can be. Gavron and I have shadowstepped so quickly through the night sky that we end up as mist under the stars. We've raced through the forests as snow leopard and wolf, flickering through the trees. I've sat at the edge of cliffs that should be impossible to climb. I've jumped off them and landed on my own two feet.

Now, we stand at a new precipice. This one is in the grandest ballroom of Courtsheart. The Blue Court seems to have dressed to impress us, because the theme this year is the deepest night. Everything is black and lush to the touch. Black velvet curtains cover even the constellations of stars set into the walls.

Meanwhile, I have as many sharp edges as ever. I wear all belts this time. They strap my arms and chest, wrap down around my hips. From there they only twine down one leg. Not pants. Not a dress. Simply me, with daggers attached.

Gavron, finding me in the crowd, smiles lopsidedly. "You're perfect."

It's what Maudon once said to me, but coming from Gavron, it means so much more.

It wrings a smile from me. He's rather devastating, himself, with his kohl-lined eyes and black shirt and leather vest—the perfectly smooth complement to myself.

"Are you ready for this?"

He takes a deep breath—something endearingly human, reminding me how young he truly is. "As I'll ever be."

When we deliver our answer before the assembled Blue Court seats, his tone doesn't waver.

"We respectfully decline your offer to unite our Houses. *But*," he says louder over the murmur that arises, "neither will we play our former role. We won't be the keepers of peace or deliverers of justice on behalf of vampires. That's your own business within your own courts. If there are disagreements among Houses, we can solve it in the Council."

"Are you stepping away entirely, then?" one of the Blue Court Council members says, disdain dripping from her tone. "Dissolving?"

"No, quite the opposite. We would like to be more present, less in the shadows. We would like a seat on the Council." Gavron glances down at me. "Fin and I."

"Oh?" Her icy blond eyebrow climbs. "And what exactly are you representing if not peace, balance, and justice?"

"Those things, still," I say. "Just not among vampires. On behalf of humanity."

Absolute silence falls in the grand room.

"They share our world," I continue. "We have abused them viciously. Treated them no better than livestock."

"What do you propose to do with them, instead?" another Blue Court seat asks with a laugh. "They would put us all to the torch if they could."

"Build a world we can both share in peace," I say. "Work with them to achieve balance. And we will defend them. Against you, if necessary."

"Is that a threat?"

I shake my head. "It doesn't have to be. Revar named Courtsheart the greatest endeavor in vampire history, the crossroads between the mortal and immortal worlds . . . built for the protection of *all*. I think it can become that."

———◦✦❦✦◦———

Later, I find Gavron for a dance.

Kashire is dancing with Jaen, the two of them cutting beautiful shapes across the ballroom in blue and silver silk. They, of course, didn't bend to the pressure to wear black. I spot Marai watching them for a moment until she drags a highly reluctant Claudia out onto the dance floor.

I've never seen my mo—Claudia dance before. For a minute, I just watch the two of them, something swelling in my chest.

All of them are my family. Not how the Black Court envisioned family, with blood mattering above all else. Just . . . mine. And I'm theirs.

Family is what you carve out with your teeth.

I seize Gavron perhaps a little too fiercely, enough to make his eyes pop. "What are you—?"

I interrupt him with a kiss. We keep kissing, even when he starts spinning me in a dance.

When I finally pull away, he looks more peaceful—*happier*—than I've ever seen him. He leans his forehead against mine.

"I doubted your plan at first," he admits softly. "But we're *new*, Fin. Despite our old blood, we're young. We can both remember where we came from . . . and we can change things."

"We'll meet resistance," I warn him. "We'll make so many enemies. But—"

"That just means we have work to do," he says, and sighs. "At least I have you at my side."

"No one should have this much power alone," I whisper. I drop my head onto his shoulder and simply breathe the scent of him for a moment. "But it's a balance. Just like the Black Court has been for an age, except more so. And you and I will balance each other."

We can be a force weighing in humanity's favor. Even though we have the most monstrous abilities of all, we can be different.

I don't want to lose myself to the callousness of immortality. It would be as easy as going to sleep. Caring is now a choice I have to make, over and over again.

"Balance each other, indeed." He grins at me. "Now that you're my paramant, do you know what that means?"

"No one has undue influence over the other?" I laugh shakily. "Most importantly, neither one of us can enthrall the other?"

"It means we can drink each other's blood freely."

I freeze, interrupting our dance. We've been so busy, I didn't think—I haven't needed it. I'm so strong I hardly even need *human* blood to sustain me.

But now, I feel a deeper desire for the release that Gavron's teeth bring me than I ever have. A craving in my very core. Consuming me as I want to consume him.

He leans in, his breath skimming across my neck. I run my tongue along his throat and close my eyes at the sweetness I can already taste through his skin.

I know what I want.

The thought throbs through me like a heartbeat: I want to live my life as I never have. I want to devour. And I want to feel a love that threatens to devour me. And then I want to do it all again.

And maybe, while I do, I can build something new. Something better.

I am a monster. I think we all are—humans, vampires.

It's what I do as a monster that makes me who I am.

ACKNOWLEDGMENTS

Like many writers, I've wanted to write a vampire book ever since I was a kid sneakily reading *Interview with the Vampire* in my room late at night. And yet, also like many writers, I missed the vampire boat, which came and sank as a trend before my writing career started, and I thought I might never have the chance. A decade later, during the depths of this miserable (ongoing) pandemic, while isolated by sickness and loss, I figured, "I'm going to write what makes me happy because why the hell not? Life is short!" What apparently makes me happiest while surrounded by the all-too-real horror of death is the romantic horror of the *un*dead. (Makes sense, in a way, to counter such traumatic exposure to mortality with escapist fantasies of immortality.) I had no clue if anyone else would want to read this, but as it turns out—fittingly—vampires never truly die, and right now they're once again rising from the grave. Timing aside, I'm also incredibly fortunate in my professional partnerships, which have given me the means to share my vampires with the world—and perhaps even with odd-duck kids like myself who want to see themselves in all stories, including those involving fangs, blood drinking, and unbeating hearts.

In celebration of unlocking a serious lifetime achievement, I must first thank the dauntless Hannah Bowman for not laughing at me when I pitched the idea to her (though not even she anticipated selling a young adult vampire book anytime soon, rock star agent that she is) and for finding it the perfect home. Equal thanks to Rachel Diebel, my wonderful editor, for taking in my story and helping it grow into something sharper and more romantic (but without coffins!!). Thanks to Jean Feiwel, publisher extraordinaire, for building the house around it, so to speak. And to Rich Deas, for your fabulous design skills (seriously, you're my favorite cover designer ever, how lucky am I?), and Ilana Worrell, production editor, for shepherding the book of my dreams out into the world.

Many thanks to the folks already out there waiting with open arms—Hannah Whitten, Andrew Joseph White, Allison Saft, and Laura Pohl, for your kind words; Dahlia Adler, Patrice Caldwell, Julie Daily, Richard Kadrey, Christina Orlando, Rachel Strolle, Rosiee Thor, and Kiersten White, for your enthusiasm and support. You make the world a less scary place.

I have so much admiration for talented artists Therese Andreasen, for the intricate banner designs and mind-blowing character portrait, and Winter of Her Discontent, for painting stunningly ethereal portraits of all my main characters at this point. Your lines inspire mine.

As always, much love to my "first responders," Lukas Strickland, Deanna Birdsall, Michael Miller, Margaret Adsit, Terran Williams, and Pamela Strickland. You guys always see the gory innards before I sew my stories up into their final monster shapes, and I appreciate your strong stomachs and unflinching gaze. Thanks also to more family and friends: Daniel Huff, Dan Strickland, Dunedin Strickland, Taelyr Pfeiffer, Auberin Strickland, Brittany and Jessanna Ramirez, Robert Birdsall, Laia Jiménez i Danés, Alli Harvey, Wes Hoskins, Gintė Skersytė, Chloe Fraser, Andreu Falgueras, Marta Bautista, Andrew Howe, Alyssa Coll, Jenny Cooper, Max Amiach, Ismael Maurice, Sara Savant-Moton, and last but not least my D&D group—Austin Bachman, Casey Cooley, and Nicoll Pallotta (suck it, Strahd!)—for helping me keep it together these past couple of years and still being there whenever I haven't. You're literal lifesavers. Love you all.